Helen Grant

DEMONS OF GHENT

CORGI BOOKS

THE DEMONS OF GHENT
A CORGI BOOK 978 0 552 566766

Published in Great Britain by Corgi Books,
an imprint of Random House Children's Publishers UK
A Random House Group Company

This edition published 2014

1 3 5 7 9 10 8 6 4 2

The Random House Group Limited supports the Forest Stewardship
Council® (FSC®), the leading international forest-certification organisation.
Our books carrying the FSC label are printed on FSC®-certified paper.
FSC is the only forest-certification scheme supported by the leading
environmental organisations, including Greenpeace. Our paper procurement
policy can be found at www.randomhouse.co.uk/environment.

MIX
Paper from
responsible sources
FSC   FSC® C016897
www.fsc.org

Set in Minion by Falcon Oast Graphic Art Ltd.

Corgi Books are published by Random House Children's Publishers UK,
61–63 Uxbridge Road, London W5 5SA

www.randomhousechildrens.co.uk
www.totallyrandombooks.co.uk
www.randomhouse.co.uk

Addresses for companies within The Random House Group Limited
can be found at: www.randomhouse.co.uk/offices.htm

THE RANDOM HOUSE GROUP Limited Reg. No. 954009

A CIP catalogue record for this book is available from the British Library.

Printed and bound in Great Britain by
CPI Group (UK) Ltd, Croydon, CR0 4YY

Helen
Grant

DEMONS
OF
GHENT

Also by Helen Grant:

Silent Saturday

*For Robert L. Grant and in memory
of Edith Grant*

1

The old city centre of Ghent famously has three medieval towers: the belfry of the cathedral, Sint-Baafs, that of the Sint-Niklaaskerk, and the Belfort, which stands between the other two. The church towers are generally closed, but it is possible to ascend the ninety-one-metre Belfort and gaze out from the arches of the stone arcade that runs below the clock faces. The arches are unglazed, so it can be glacially cold up there, and the wind skimming through the arcade gives it an uncomfortably insecure feeling, but if you can stand that, the views of the old city are stunning.

The Belfort is open for most of the day, but it closes to visitors at six p.m.

It is difficult to get into the building after that, but not impossible – not if you know the timetable of the ancient city, the ebb and flow of the human tide. Not if you have a key.

The man in question had a box of them – far too many to carry them all with him – accumulated over long years of working in menial jobs for the Ghent city council – the *Stadsbestuur* – and for businesses around the city. He had worked for a long time as a stonemason, then as a roofer, and as the decades took their toll he had worked as a maintenance man and cleaner. All this work was less than the life he had once known, but he accepted it, and became invisible. Nobody looks too closely at the hulking and dusty workman as he slouches past, or stumps up the stairs to the roof carrying the tools of his trade.

Laying hands on the keys was not difficult; it merely required patience. Sometimes he was able to make duplicates himself. Sometimes he went to one of the various locksmiths dotted about the city and had a copy made; he had a story ready, about doing a favour for a workmate who had lost his own key, but he never had to use it. Sometimes he went to the foreman, touching his cap and apologizing roughly for having lost his key, and thus got a second one, although he could only ever do that once in each new position. He also stole them.

The manager who went for a break leaving a bunch of keys lying out or hanging from the lock of the door generally wouldn't notice that one was missing until very much later. He might assume he had lost it himself; certainly he was unlikely to know exactly when it had disappeared. That manager might bluster and complain and look askance at everyone else, but when nothing came of it, no overnight break-in or thieving, the incident would be forgotten.

Eventually he had enough keys to gain access to almost any block in the old part of Ghent. Once inside a single building it was easy enough to make his way to the roof, and from there he could move freely until he came to one of those great canyons that represented a street far below.

The oldest keys in the box were larger, more roughly made

than the new ones. Some of them opened doors to the most ancient buildings in the city; some opened nothing at all any more. They lay crowded lengthways in the box, stark as bodies in a plague pit. When he handled them, as he liked to do, gloatingly, they were as cold as corpse-flesh, warming only temporarily from the touch of his hands; they clinked together like a hoard of coins running through a miser's fingers.

There was only one place in the old city for which he had tried repeatedly, and in vain, to obtain keys, and that was the cathedral of Sint-Baaf. The cathedral had the tallest of the three towers, measuring about ninety-five metres in height, and for that reason alone a set of keys would have been a prize worth having. But there was more to it than that: the old church was a reliquary, a treasure box. He would have given much to have thirty minutes alone inside it. He would have given his life.

Sint-Baafs was closed to him, though. Instead he decided to ascend the second-highest tower, the Belfort.

He waited until after nightfall. The three towers were illuminated throughout the night, so there was no cover to be found in the darkness. After the shops closed and all the day-time workers went home, however, there were fewer people on the streets, and once the bars and restaurants were closed too there was hardly anyone to see him as he passed.

The last trams were running so he waited until one had just passed and he was confident that there would be no more until the early morning. He looked to left and right; he was alone in the street. He climbed the steps, drawing the keys from his pocket, and a minute later he was inside the building, closing the door behind him.

He ascended the spiral stone staircase with dogged patience, toiling upwards like an insect crawling up a wall. He passed through the room that housed previous incarnations of the gilded dragon that topped the tower's spire. The very oldest was little more than a metal framework now, like a carcass that has rotted down to the bones. Further up the tower was the great bell Roland, whose voice had warned the city of approaching danger in centuries past. He passed that too, and Roland was strangely silent.

He stepped out into the arcade. The wind was cold on his face, and that was *right* because it was like the unnatural breath that chills and withers – the breath of pestilence, exhaled onto the sleeping city. It plucked at the collar of his coat with icy fingers.

Here he would keep watch. The old tower was a place he favoured for his night-time vigils. It commanded a view not only of the square and the streets below, but also the rooftops of Ghent, with their peaks and towers and plains.

He watched for them, the denizens of the rooftops, dark forms who moved between the chimney stacks with stealthy confidence. They were shaped like human beings, but that was not what they were. They were there to stop him. They were his enemies.

He had come to see his arduous task as something almost holy. Yes; it was possible for the bringing of death to be a holy thing – hadn't the Lord God Himself sent the Angel of Death amongst the Egyptians? Out there in the city, sleeping perhaps, or keeping a midnight vigil like himself, were those who were marked out for death; those who had warded it off for far too long. He would find each one of them, no matter how much time it took, and wreak God's will upon them. The things that clambered over the rooftops, snarling and chittering, would not hinder him in his task. Whenever he encountered one of them he would cast it down from the rooftops to destruction. They could be killed, he knew that; he had exterminated some of them already. If necessary, he would cleanse the upper reaches of the city of their foul presence entirely.

He searched for them now, looking out through the nearest arch of the arcade, his gaze sweeping the skyline and then swooping down to the square far below, the Sint-Baafsplein. He expected to see them here; the cathedral was the epicentre. The demons would be unable to resist it; they would be drawn to it, as he was himself. They felt the power of the ancient building and the talisman within it. It drew them to it, like the drag of a strange tide.

Once, he had seen one of the marked ones down there in the square before the cathedral; perhaps it drew them to itself too. He had been struggling in the grip of two hefty officials; otherwise he might have followed her there and then, and ended her life in some quiet street or on the doorstep of her own home. The men had been dragging him away from the cathedral door, and he had come almost face to face with her. He knew her instantly. Unconsciously, she had struck a pose he recognized, her right arm bent, the hand raised, her left arm hanging at her side. Her fair hair hung down over her shoulders. She was even wearing something familiar – a short dress of some dark stuff, leaving her shoulders and knees bare.

The sight had angered him; it was as though she had done

it deliberately, taunting him by her presence when he was unable to act. He had begun to struggle even more violently, and in the ensuing mêlée he had lost sight of the girl. Afterwards, she had gone. No matter. He had seen her once; he would see her again, and he would finish her.

He gazed down now, trying to pick out the spot where he had seen her, and that was how he came to pick up the flicker of movement far below. Someone was crossing the square, keeping close to the façade of the old cathedral.

Instantly his interest was piqued, flaring up like a gas jet firing. Unconsciously he tensed, watching the progress of the tiny figure as it passed the great doors of the cathedral, apparently making for the south side of the square.

But no; the figure went unerringly to the narrow door set into the south tower – a door that was always locked: hadn't he tried it himself, a hundred times? A moment or two of fumbling about the door, and it was *open*.

Even before the figure had vanished into the darkness beyond the door, he turned and strode swiftly from the arcade, back into the Belfort. The descent of the spiral stone staircases seemed to take for ever, each turn of the stairs a penance. He would like to have spread great wings and sliced across the empty space between the Belfort and the cathedral like a scimitar sweeping through the air. The beating of his heart was like the striking of a hammer on the rim of a bell; it resonated through his body, filling him with savage joy.

Fear my coming, he thought. *I am Death.*

2

Ninety-five metres is a long way to fall.

It might not be the full ninety-five metres, Luc reminded himself. *It depends how high you can climb. If you got to the top level but you couldn't climb one of those conical things at each corner of the tower, well, you could take off at least five metres.* He considered. *You'd still be dead, though.*

He was standing at the corner of Biezekapelstraat, keeping close to the wall, doing his best to vanish into the shadows. He hadn't done anything wrong yet, but there was no point in drawing attention to himself.

Luc was watching the area in front of the cathedral, the Sint-Baafsplein. It was very late, and there were few people about, but you never knew. It didn't help that the cathedral itself was illuminated, drenching the square with golden light. The trams had stopped running a little while ago, but there was always the risk of someone reeling home from the local bar on foot. It would take only one nosy person to wreck his evening's activities.

Luc felt in his pocket, as he had done perhaps a dozen times that evening. The keys were still there, the metal cool under his fingers.

I still can't believe I got them, he thought. *The keys to the bell tower. I've done the impossible.*

They weren't the *actual* keys, of course. Those were locked away somewhere inside the ancient building, where only the cathedral guides and the clergy could lay hands on them. The keys in Luc's pocket were copies.

It was a mystery to Luc why they never opened the bell tower – well, hardly ever, anyway. One measly week in the summer, when the festival was on. The rest of the time the tower was kept locked. Most people probably didn't even notice the narrow wooden door, studded with black iron nails, at the south corner of the façade. Why would you, when no one ever went in and out of it?

A couple of months ago, though, there'd been a problem. Something had fallen from the cathedral's lofty heights onto the stones of the Sint-Baafsplein. Just something small – a tile, or a splinter of stone. It hadn't hit anyone when it fell, no harm done, but the incident had alarmed someone enough that a surveyor had been called in, and then workmen had come.

Luc had seen them all come and go from the other side of the square, where he had been sitting on the stones in the summer sunshine, sipping a can of Coke and masquerading as a tourist. He hadn't bothered trying anything when the surveyor was there; the man had been accompanied at all times by a stern-looking clerical type, and anyway, he'd looked as miserable as sin. Not exactly approachable. The workmen, though – that had been another matter. Luc had perked up the moment he saw them unlocking the door to the tower. They didn't look as unfriendly as the surveyor; they looked like Luc's sort of people – informal, a bit scruffy, not too up themselves. Even so, he might have hesitated to try anything, except for one thing. He knew one of them.

Wout, he thought, remembering. *Good old Wout. Good old stupid Wout.* They'd been in Vocational School together. Luc had recognized those blunt features, that shock of pale hair, immediately. Neither of them was ever going to be a brain surgeon, Luc knew that, but Wout ... Luc had grimaced, hoping that the works foreman, whoever he was, wasn't going to give Wout anything too taxing to do. *Like holding a hammer, for example. Not with people walking about underneath.*

However, the unfortunate foreman's responsibility was Luc's opportunity. He had got to his feet, unfolding his long limbs gracefully, lobbed the Coke can into a bin and ambled slowly towards the cathedral.

When he got to the doorway the other workmen had disappeared inside. There was only Wout standing there, looking slightly baffled as usual. Luc had gone right up to him, resisting the temptation to snap his fingers in Wout's face and say, *Wake up.*

'Wout,' he'd said, and Wout had looked at him. Luc could swear that in the two full seconds it had taken Wout to respond, he could see the thought processes, the dawning recognition, spreading across those ponderous features like a puddle spreading out around a badly trained puppy.

Luc had kept a friendly grin fixed on his face while Wout greeted him back. He kept the conversation going with ease; it was like playing table tennis with a very small child, he thought. He waited until Wout glanced away, digesting some nugget of information, and then he looked past Wout, at the door. The keys were there, one of them inserted into the lock, the others hanging from the ring. Luc had felt a thrill of excitement so acute that it was exhilarating. He hadn't let it show in his face. There was still one thing standing between him and those keys, between curling his fingers around them, drawing them out of the lock and running off to the very first key-cutter he could find. Just one thing.

'Wout . . .' he had begun.

Five minutes later he'd been sprinting down the street, the keys clutched in his fist and his wallet twenty euros lighter. He'd been surprised that Wout had the nous to ask for money. Evidently he'd learned something from his apprenticeship after all. He'd made Luc promise not to drop him in it, either; if the foreman came down before Luc was back, Wout was going to say he didn't know him – he was just a thief who'd snatched the keys when Wout's back was turned.

The foreman didn't come down, though, thought Luc, staring at the great illuminated bulk of the cathedral jutting into the night sky. *Nobody knows I've got these keys except Wout, and he's probably forgotten his own surname by now.*

He was beginning to feel really jittery. His heart was thudding, and his skin was hypersensitive, pleasurably so, as though he were tangled in satin sheets, the smooth folds slithering across his naked flesh. He measured the distance from the spot where he stood to the narrow door at the south corner of the cathedral façade. How long would it take to run across to that spot, how long to slide the key into the lock and fumble the door open? He hadn't seen anyone cross the square for at least twenty minutes now; perhaps no one would cross it again before sun-up.

Now or never, Luc, he thought. *Now or never.*

He wasn't a great philosopher. Rationalizing things wasn't his strong suit. Either you did something or you didn't; thinking too hard about it complicated things.

Before he knew it, Luc was running across the stones, aiming for the bell-tower door. He tried to tread lightly, but his footsteps and the sound of his own breathing were the only things he could hear. Nobody shouted, *Hey, you!* There were no answering footsteps, no one came running to intercept him.

He reached the door and slid the key into the lock. It was a little stiff; the mechanism was antiquated. He struggled with it for a moment, all the time expecting to hear a shout behind him, or feel a hand coming down on his shoulder. Then the door was swinging open, and he was inside, closing the door behind him, shutting out the yellow light from the square.

Darkness closed in on Luc. The interior of the tower was horribly cold, even at this clement time of year; the warmth of the sun was never going to penetrate the thickness of those stone walls. He might have been in the black depths of a well sunken into frozen ground.

Verdomme, he thought, fumbling for the little torch he had slipped into his inside pocket. He was having to bite back panic, and that was not cool, that was most certainly uncool. He dragged out the torch and thumbed the little rubber button. The light it produced was feeble, but it was a hundred times better than being in the dark. He swept the torch in an upward arc, picking out the stone steps by its faint light, noting the way each one was a kind of wedge shape, with plenty of room for ascending feet at the side by the outer wall, but narrowing to a point where it met the central pillar.

You wouldn't want to meet someone on these stairs, thought Luc, and the idea gave him another of those frissons, the ones he had decided were not cool. *Stop freaking yourself out*, he told himself. *There's nobody in here except you, unless you count spiders.*

He began very slowly to ascend the stone staircase. There were over four hundred steps – someone had told him that . . . or was it five hundred? If you went up to the very top and then turned straight round and came back down, that was somewhere between eight hundred and a thousand steps. *Worth it*, Luc reminded himself. *Wait till the others hear about this. They'll be begging to borrow the keys. Nobody's ever* done *Sint-Baafs.*

The stone stairs went up the flank of the building. Then there was a door and then a metal walkway leading across to the central tower. Luc went across it, conscious of the ringing of his footsteps on the metal. He stopped for a moment and listened, but aside from his own breathing there was perfect silence.

What are you expecting to hear? You think the bishop him- self kips in the tower, just in case anyone breaks in? Or maybe the legendary Demons of Ghent are creeping up the stairs after you . . .

He hurried along the remainder of the walkway. A few moments to catch his breath, and then he was labouring his way up more of those stone stairs. Perhaps halfway up he began to think that it wasn't so amazing after all, being the first one to get inside the bell tower of Sint-Baafs. He was perspiring in spite of the chilly atmosphere. His chest felt tight and his heart seemed to be trying to climb up into his throat. He was treading heavily, scuffing his feet on the stone steps.

The sound echoed curiously.

It really sounds like there's half a dozen of us climbing these stairs, thought Luc. He stopped and leaned his shoulder against the wall, resting, letting his heart rate and breathing slow to a more comfortable pace. Experimentally, he held his breath for a moment. Silence.

Luc sighed, and resumed his painful slog up the stairs, past a stone room looking out over the city, following the dim circle of light from the torch. On and on the stairs went, until Luc began to think that he had been wrong about the number: it wasn't four hundred and something, or even five hundred; it was at least a thousand.

It's like climbing Mount Everest. If I get to the top without having a heart attack I ought to plant a flag up there or something, he thought, and he would have laughed if he'd had enough breath to do it. He was still grinning when he completed another turn of the stairs and opened a door onto the freezing night air.

Luc found himself in a stone octagon, with eight elegant carved arches. Four of them looked out onto the four turrets that crowned the cathedral tower; the other four looked straight out onto the city of Ghent. None of them were glazed. At street level the air was still; up here there was a cold breeze. Luc felt the wind pushing back the hair from his face, dizzying him with its frigid breath. He ducked underneath the safety bar and stepped between the pillars of one of the arches, the one that looked out over the Sint-Baafsplein. Although there was a stone wall between him and the drop, and although he had been up dozens of high buildings, and thought he'd shed his fear of heights long ago, still he felt a sickening lurch in the pit of his stomach, as though he were perched in the crow's nest of a great ship that had suddenly plunged down into a great trough between the waves.

It's so verdomd *high.*

Luc could see the Belfort on the other side of the square, and even though he had seen it hundreds of times before, possibly thousands, it looked subtly different. He was seeing the top section straight on, he realized, instead of looking up at it from below and getting a crick in his neck. He had a clear view of the dragon spitted on the very top of the spire. Empty space yawned sickeningly between him and the gilded creature, as though they were on either side of an immense canyon. He put his hands against the stone parapet, reassuring himself of its solid bulk between him and the drop.

OK, he thought after a minute or two. *Time to do the last section and get to the very top before I freak myself out.*

He turned, so that he was facing back into the octagon, and as he did so he had a sickening shock that instantly sent adrenalin blazing through him like an emergency flare. There was someone there.

'Fuck,' said Luc, taking an involuntary step back. The shock was so severe that for several seconds he actually thought he would faint. His legs were weak underneath him; it was like a nightmare – one of those in which you need to run, you *have* to run to save yourself, and yet your limbs won't do what you want them to do – and anyway, where would he run to? *I'm on the top of a fucking bell tower*, thought Luc. *There is nowhere to run.*

He stared at the figure, half hidden in shadow, and the white was showing all around Luc's grey eyes, and all the time his mind was running around like a rat in a trap, testing the possibilities. *I didn't see him when I came up here – is it possible he was here already? Did he follow me up here? But the square was deserted. Why doesn't he move? So silent – so still – like a statue.*

And then he had it; he understood what he was seeing. A statue – yes, it had to be a statue. A grotesque thing, for certain, with that long heavy face and the almost lipless mouth and the myriad tiny wrinkles that gave the skin the appearance of aged linen, all the visible features uniformly sallow in the light of the cathedral illuminations. The eye sockets were sunk in shadow, the hollows under the cheek-bones were dark smudges.

Too ugly for a saint, thought Luc. *Why would anyone carve something that ugly?*

His panicked heart was slowing a little, but still it gave him the creeps, that silent figure. He didn't fancy brushing past it to get to the stairs.

I didn't have to brush past it on the way out here, he thought, and almost before the thought was fully formed he realized that he was wrong; that no, it wasn't a statue after all, because the withered lips moved and it *spoke*.

'You will not stop me. Go back to your master and tell him so.'

What the—?

There was no more time then for Luc; no time to think, no

time even to scream. The figure lunged at him, ducking under the safety bar, but Luc still had no idea what was happening to him – not until he felt his legs being seized in an iron grip. He was forced back onto the stone parapet. Up went his feet, down went his head over the wall, and for one appalling second he saw the whole of the Belfort tower *upside down*. Terror exploded inside him like a supernova. The keys he had so carefully copied slid out of his pocket and vanished into the chasm. The next instant the grip on his legs was released and Luc dropped into nothingness.

The floodlit Gothic façade of Sint-Baafs flashed past him, faster than an express train, a blurred streak of golden stone. Luc did not scream once as he accelerated towards the stones below. There was no time to form a coherent thought, to understand what had happened. Simply one long inner howl: *No no no no no—*

Luc hit the ground with explosive force, splattering the stones with scarlet.

3

I am Death.

He had cast the thing that looked like a man down from the bell tower to its destruction. He did not stop to gaze down from the heights at what he had done. Time was short. Even at this hour someone might pass by. Interruption now meant failure.

The climb almost to the top of the tower had tired him; if he had not been used to making such ascents on his nightly excursions it might have exhausted his strength altogether. Going down again was easier, but still, by the time he reached ground level pain was burning with savage brilliance in his hips and knees. His kneecaps could have been fastened on with iron rivets, heated red hot; every step was fiery torture. He endured it as a martyr would, his unbending will carrying him on.

I must complete it.

When he emerged from the narrow doorway at the south side of the cathedral he was almost delirious with exertion and agony. The golden light that flooded the great Gothic façade and the square below was indistinguishable from the pain, which was so huge it seemed to fill the world, pulsing and throbbing to the beat of his heart.

The dead thing lay on the cobbles, with the scarlet radiating out from it like gleaming wings. It looked less like a man now.

He approached it slowly, thrusting his hands into his pockets for the things he needed. He glanced around once, but the square was silent and empty. His luck had held.

Bare skin – that was what he was looking for. He had to lean right over the body; with the disordered clothes and the Rorschach spattering of red it was hard to pick out the patch of bluish-white that he needed.

There – a few square centimetres of unmarred flesh at the side of the throat. And now iron: an ancient nail, gouged from an oak door; let it drop so that it falls onto that pale skin, nestling into the side of the neck like a tumour. And salt, sprinkled carefully so that it powders the exposed flesh.

He whispered some words too, but he believed in the salt and the iron more than he believed in the words. There was power in them, power to rout his enemies.

When he had finished he thought of the keys. The man-shaped thing that lay dead before him – had it had keys to the cathedral? From the arcade high on the Belfort tower he had only been able to see that the door had been opened – not how. He thought that something had fallen from the clothing of the thing before he had released it to plummet onto the cobbles, but he could not be sure that the something was a bunch of keys.

He spent a few precious minutes scanning the red-stained cobblestones, but found nothing. He dismissed regret. There was no *Open sesame* to let him into the cathedral, no short cut. He must complete every painful step of his great task, like a pilgrim toiling mile by laborious mile through mountainous terrain.

It was not safe to stay here any longer, as the blood cooled and dried around the body. He turned his back on it, and walked away across the south side of the square until the shadows swallowed him.

Luc lay on the cobbles for a long time, surrounded by the ragged red stain that was the map of his own destruction. Even after the police came, they didn't move him immediately. It was obvious that he was dead, and how; the police officers had only to look at the narrow door in the south side of the cathedral, still standing open, and then up at the Gothic façade that towered above them.

A light wind had picked up; it passed over the still body like a smoothing hand, brushing away much of the sprinkled salt. It lacked the strength to move the iron nail, which still stood out like a dark mole against the white skin at the throat. The iron nail told the police very little, though. Supposing you have a young man who has apparently gone to the trouble of breaking into an ancient building, with the aim of climbing to the top of a ninety-five-metre-tall tower and flinging himself to his own destruction . . . well, you might expect to find a nail or a splinter of wood or some chips of stone with the body, either from damage when he climbed over the parapet far above, or from having hit something on the way down.

The police did find one thing that Luc's killer had missed.

When the body was finally lifted with useless care onto a waiting stretcher, the keys to the cathedral were found underneath it. They had hit the cobblestones instants before Luc had, and he had slammed into them so hard that even through the fabric of his jacket they left an imprint on his flesh, like a brand.

4

Veerle De Keyser sat cross-legged on one of the metal benches in the Sint-Baafsplein, sipping from a can of iced green tea and looking at the cathedral. She watched people going in and out of the main door. Most of them were tourists carrying rolled umbrellas and cameras; perhaps a few were local people going in to pray.

Trying for a quick fix from God, Veerle thought.

She wondered whether she should go inside too. She didn't want to pray, but it might be warmer than sitting out here. It was a sunny autumn morning, but it had rained in the night and the air was cool. If she sat on the bench too long she would probably stiffen up. She sighed. There were bits of her that seemed to ache all the time, even though the casts were off and everything had in theory healed. *Good as new,* she thought. Only she wasn't, not really.

She fished in her pocket, looking for the little foil blister pack with the painkillers in. Nothing too heavy – not morphine or anything – just the same stuff you took if you had a fever or a thumping headache. Or you'd fallen off a castle while someone was trying to shoot you with a crossbow.

She pressed one of the tablets out of the pack, put it into her mouth and washed it down with a mouthful of the iced tea.

I wonder if they've missed me yet, she thought. She hoped they hadn't. It was a new ruse, going into school for registration and vanishing afterwards. *It might work. If none of the others tell on me.* It was the only option, anyway, if she couldn't face school and wanted some time to herself. Since he'd found out she was cutting school, Geert De Keyser had taken to walking her there himself in the morning, and waiting until she had gone inside. Every morning they'd leave the flat on Bijlokevest together, Veerle with her school bag slung over her shoulder, Geert carrying his battered leather briefcase. Anneke, Geert's girlfriend, would see them off, her hands over her pregnancy bump. She always kissed Geert, never Veerle, but that was OK with Veerle. Anneke was growing so enormous that she made Veerle nervous, as though a single touch would set her off like a mine.

Geert never said very much on the way. He probably disliked having to walk his daughter there as much as she disliked him doing it.

Or maybe he's just not a morning person, thought Veerle. There was a whole mountain of stuff she didn't know about her father.

Geert would walk right up to the school with her, and then he'd stand on the pavement and watch her go in. He'd tried to come in with her once, but Veerle had put her foot down.

No knowing what he'll do now, though, if he finds out I've bunked off again, she thought.

Last time he'd been furious; even his habitual stolidness had been disturbed. Veerle remembered him saying several times that she was *supposed* to be at school. That had struck her as somehow ludicrous.

I'm not supposed to be in that *school*, she thought. *I'm not even supposed to be in Ghent. I'm not from here. It's not my home.*

Home, though; where was that? The house she had grown up in, the house on Kerkstraat in her home village, was shut up, the roller blinds lowered, a TE KOOP sign fixed to the front wall. Three boxfuls of Veerle's stuff had been retrieved from the house, but she hadn't even been through it all. She'd emptied the first two boxes, but when she'd opened the third there had been a soft toy on top of the other stuff, a big floppy rabbit with large gauche stitches running across the seams. Veerle had taken one look and closed the box again. She'd hated that rabbit for years, and now she couldn't bear to throw it away any more than she could bear to look at it.

Thinking about the house in Kerkstraat made her think of Kris Verstraeten. Everything had started with him. He'd been the one who suggested they go up the tower of the Sint-Pauluskerk in the village when she was only seven and he was nine. She'd been up the tower when all hell had broken loose in the village, and her mother, Claudine, had panicked, not knowing where she was. Claudine might have turned out the way she did anyway, people sometimes did, but Veerle didn't think so. That day, the panic, had triggered something, she thought. Then, when Kris had reappeared in her life, no wonder Claudine had reacted the way she did.

Thinking about her mother made Veerle feel the way she always did, as though a weight had settled on her chest; a feeling that managed to be heavy and empty at the same time. It was no use wishing Claudine were here – no use wishing that ever again.

Kris, she thought, yearning for a familiar face, a voice.

Veerle slid her hand into her jacket pocket and pulled out her phone. It wasn't the same one she'd had before. That had been shattered, alongside several of her bones, when she hit the ground at the bottom of the castle tower. This phone wasn't quite as good, because Geert didn't want to spend the money. It didn't have the same number as the old one either, and Veerle was wondering about that – whether it was possible that Kris had made some mistake, had been trying to call her old number.

He's called you on this one before, she reminded herself. She touched the screen and checked the display. No missed calls, no messages. *Maybe he's done something stupid, like accidentally deleting the new number and keeping the old one.* She slid the phone back into her pocket. *So why doesn't he answer when you call him?*

Veerle shifted position. The bench was becoming un-comfortable. Sure enough, she was stiffening up.

What the hell – I'll go and look at the cathedral. I might as well. Nothing else to do.

She got to her feet, reached under the bench for her bag, and set off across the square.

Halfway across the Sint-Baafsplein she had to break her stride when a skateboarder shot across her path, a blur of

24

sun-bleached hair and green shirt, the tails flapping. Veerle ignored him. She had the cathedral door in her sights. A moment later he did it again, but this time he cut it too close and they almost collided.

'Hey,' said Veerle indignantly, though she suspected she was wasting her time.

'Sorry,' he said cheerfully.

She put her head down and walked on, but suddenly he was in front of her, the board under his arm, walking backwards and doing his best to catch her eye.

'You're the girl from the wall,' he said. When she didn't immediately respond he went on, 'The climbing wall. Sundays. You're definitely that girl.'

Veerle looked at him. *I don't need this*, she thought. She said, 'So what?'

He tried a grin, blue eyes looking at her appealingly through untidy strands of blond hair. 'You're good.'

'I'm crap,' said Veerle shortly.

'No, you're not.'

Veerle stopped, fighting the desire to roll her eyes. 'If you were there on Sunday, you saw me fall off. *Three times*.'

'Well, before that. You were good.'

No, I wasn't, thought Veerle. *I was rubbish. You didn't see me before I fell off the castle tower and smashed myself up. I went higher, I didn't worry about peeling off and landing on the arm I broke. I was fit, because I hadn't spent weeks in plaster, doing nothing. Back then, I wouldn't have fallen off an easy climb* three *times*.

Her thoughts must have showed in her face because he said, 'Hey. You really were. Good, I mean.'

Veerle shrugged. 'Well . . . thanks.'

'Bram.'

'Thanks . . . Bram.'

He was still standing in front of her, not showing any signs of moving away.

'I have to go,' said Veerle, hitching up the bag that was slung over her shoulder.

'Where? I might be going your way.'

'The cathedral.'

'Hmm. The cathedral.'

There was a hint of something in his voice – humour or scepticism – that almost prompted Veerle to add something, to justify herself. *I'm doing a school project about it.* She caught herself just in time. It would only lead to more questions.

Instead she said, 'Really. I have to go.'

She brushed past him and headed for the cathedral doorway, but as she strode across the grey stones she was aware that he was keeping pace with her.

'Are you going to be at the wall again on Sunday?' Bram was saying.

'I don't know. Maybe.' It was the truth; Veerle wasn't even sure herself. She knew she wouldn't build up her strength again without practice, but it was too depressing seeing how much ground she had lost.

'What did you say your name was?'

'I didn't,' said Veerle.

She reached the great Gothic doorway of Sint-Baafs and went inside via the right-hand door without looking back. Bram couldn't follow her inside, even if he wanted to, not with that board under his arm.

Inside the cathedral it was cool and airy, voices and foot-steps echoing off the ancient stonework and the black-and-white floor tiles. Veerle was dwarfed by the immensity of the interior, the great fluted columns disappearing up to the ceiling vaults high above her.

I suppose I was rude to him, she said to herself. *He was probably trying to be nice.* She let out a sigh. *Same as school,* she thought. The people who asked questions were probably just trying to be friendly. If she didn't keep brushing them off, they'd probably get on OK. It was just . . .

Veerle had tried to imagine telling people why she was in Ghent, why she had changed schools in the critical final year. Why she was living with her father and her soon-to-be-stepmother instead of her mother. She foresaw where the questions would lead. *They'll ask me about her, about Mum, and everyone will look really sympathetic, but all the same, they'll have to ask, what happened? And maybe someone will ask, was I with her, and I'll have to say no. And if they ask me where I was, I don't know what I'll say, because if I tell them the truth they'll think I'm mad or lying . . . and if they believe me they'll keep on asking more and more questions. Anyway, I don't really know what the truth is myself.*

Veerle was moving now, wandering further into the interior of the cathedral without really thinking about where she was going. Her gaze drifted over carved stone and murky oil paintings and coloured glass without her really taking them in.

What did I see? she asked herself for the thousandth time. In her imagination she went back to that moment, that terrible moment months before, when she had gazed down

27

from the gallery on the first floor of a dilapidated castle and seen a killer standing there below her, like some brutal idol surrounded by the rising incense of petrol fumes. She had looked down, and suddenly the years had rolled back like a tide and she had *recognized* him. Joren Sterckx, the child killer. The child *hunter*.

She had known him because she had seen him before, the day he had slain a child in her own village. The seven-year-old Veerle and her friend Kris had gazed down from the bell tower of the church and seen him striding across a piece of open ground with his victim in his arms and the front of his shirt dyed red with blood. It had been Silent Saturday, the day no church bells ring in Flanders, but the air had rung with her own screams.

She had buried that memory, buried it deep, but when she had seen him again in the castle she had known him instantly. It had been terrifying, that moment of recognition. Terrifying – and utterly impossible.

Joren Sterckx is dead. He died in prison, long ago.

Even now, she couldn't understand what she had seen, how it could be possible. There had been hundreds of questions afterwards, of course, and she'd known perfectly well what everyone had been thinking: that she'd been mistaken, seeing things, or maybe she'd concussed herself in the fall and wasn't thinking straight. Then someone had told them about Silent Saturday – it must have been Geert, because it couldn't have been Claudine – and after that it had been tacitly accepted that she had imagined it, seeing Joren Sterckx.

But I didn't imagine the deaths.

Vlinder, the girl found frozen into an icy lake. Horzel,

buried in a shallow grave miles from home. And Hommel. Hommel was the worst of all because Veerle and Kris had known her personally – and because she had never been found. She had been spirited away, leaving no trace – no way to know how she had died, or where, or when. Her killer, whoever or whatever he was, had perished in the flames when the castle went up; Veerle had heard him die. So he was never going to tell anyone what he had done with Hommel. And not knowing was terrible. When Veerle remembered what had happened to the others, she shuddered for Hommel; imagination filled the void in ways too horrible to contemplate.

Veerle stopped in front of a large block of stone. It was some kind of modern sculpture; not the sort of thing you normally saw in a Gothic church – it wasn't figurative at all; in fact she had no idea what it was supposed to be.

She thought, *Whoever he was, he can't hurt anyone now. He died in the fire.*

He's gone for good.

Still she didn't feel entirely easy, thinking about it. *I know Joren Sterckx died long before, but I saw him.* She shivered, glancing around her. *Is it impossible?* She looked up the aisle towards the ambulatory and saw an elderly nun standing there, her stout figure swathed in black. *She probably doesn't think so,* thought Veerle. *Her whole faith is based on the idea that a dead man came back to life.*

None of this was making her feel any better; in fact she was making herself feel worse. She tore her gaze away from the nun.

I should go somewhere else. Down to the canal or something.

She turned to leave, and *Verdomme*, there was Mevrouw Taelemans from the school.

What's she doing here?

No time to debate it. Veerle looked for a way out. As far as she could see, there was no way of reaching the exit without crossing the teacher's line of vision. She thought quickly, and then she reached into her jeans pocket and dragged out a fistful of change. Close to where she stood there was a booth selling tickets for the Ghent altarpiece. She stepped up to it and hurriedly put four euros on the little counter, three of them in one-euro pieces and the rest in change. She resisted the temptation to turn round while the man in the booth took the money and handed over the ticket. Then she slipped past him, into the enclosed space beyond, out of sight of Mevrouw Taelemans.

5

That was stupid, Veerle said to herself almost before she had done it. *Four euros. That's half the cost of a session at the wall. And for what? To look at a painting.*

All the same, as hiding places went, it was a pretty good one. Hot on Veerle's heels came a party of foreign tourists, well-dressed and voluble; she thought they were Italian. Unless Mevrouw Taelemans came right inside the little room and pushed her way to the front, there was no way she could see Veerle, not through the jostling mass of people with their smart jackets and elegantly dressed hair.

There was a young man offering headphones and an audio guide, but Veerle shook her head. She went to the left-hand side of the room and stood with her back to the wall. Her shoulder was beginning to ache with the weight of her school bag, so she put it down on the floor at her feet.

She looked at the painting for a while. Impressive. She could hear the tourists murmuring, '*Magnifico . . . stupendo.*' It wasn't just the massive scale of it (it had to be twice as tall as she was), nor the photographic quality of the painting. It was the sheer opulence of it: the gilding, the jewels, the brilliant colours. There was a central figure, whom Veerle assumed was supposed to represent God, dressed in crimson draperies studded with pearls and wearing a crown encrusted with gemstones. On his right was a bearded male figure clad in emerald green, holding a book upon his knees. Veerle had no idea who he might be, but she recognized the female figure on the left immediately: the Virgin Mary, dressed all in blue. On the outer panels flanking these figures were angels in finely embroidered robes, playing instruments and singing, and, at the very extremities, two naked human figures, one male and one female.

Adam and Eve, thought Veerle.

Underneath these virtually life-sized figures was another row of panels depicting a landscape crowded with people, gazing towards the central point where a lamb, representing Jesus, stood upon a scarlet altar, surrounded by kneeling angels. If you looked closely you could see that there was some kind of cup standing on the altar in front of the Lamb. Veerle thought it was the sort you called a chalice. There was a thin jet of blood arcing out of the Lamb's breast into the cup, which was nearly full of the crimson liquid.

Veerle had absolutely no interest in religious paintings, and yet she could see why people made such a big thing of this one; why they were so fascinated by it. She picked up her bag again, pushed away from the wall and edged a little closer to the reinforced glass protecting the painting. *All those hundreds of figures*, she thought. *Was there a real-life model for every single one of them? And why is that one on the right, the one in the red cloak, so much taller than everyone else?* It was odd too that when you first saw it you thought that everyone was looking into the middle, at the Lamb on the scarlet altar, but when you studied it more closely you could see that some of them weren't looking there at all, they were looking away. Some of them were looking at each other, and now she saw that one of them, a dour-looking bishop in a gold mitre, was staring directly out of the painting, challenging the viewer with his eyes.

Maybe you're not supposed to notice that, Veerle thought. *Maybe you're supposed to be too busy looking at the Lamb too.*

She thought the landscape in which the Lamb stood was intriguing as well. Beyond the dark masses of trees there were buildings in the distance, spires, perhaps whole towns.

Real places? she wondered. *Maybe one of them is Ghent.*

On the whole, Veerle thought that she was *impressed* by the altarpiece but she wasn't sure she actually *liked* it. There was something unnatural about it. It wasn't just the creepiness of the man staring out at you from the middle of the crowd, it was the whole scene, the way everyone was arranged so stiffly, almost geometrically, around the bleeding Lamb. All those tiny figures, so meticulously painted, so realistic in every detail and yet so static.

Like insects in amber, she thought. *Beautifully preserved but frozen for ever.*

And such a bizarre thing to be staring at for all eternity too: an animal with its heart's blood pouring out of its chest in a neat little arc.

Veerle decided that she had seen enough. The painting gave her the creeps, and she had been in here for at least ten minutes now, long enough for Mevrouw Taelemans to have moved on. It was a little claustrophobic too in this enclosed space, with so many people. She began to push her way towards the door.

There were more people coming in, and at first she found it difficult to make much headway. There was a couple standing directly in front of her, the man in a smart charcoal-grey coat, too warm for this mild autumn day, and the woman in a shiny black padded jacket, streaked blonde hair curling over her collar. They hadn't turned towards the painting; they had their backs to it because they were trying to look at something in a guide book, so they didn't realize that Veerle was trying to get past.

She tried saying, 'Excuse me,' but either they were too engrossed or they didn't understand her, because they didn't move an inch. Frustrated, Veerle dodged to the side to go round them, and found herself face to face with someone else. Their faces were literally centimetres apart.

It was a girl, perhaps a couple of years older than Veerle, with very light, very sleek blonde hair pulled back from her face, accentuating her fine-boned, angular features. Her eyes were large and a very clear grey-blue colour, and as Veerle stared into them she saw them widen, saw recognition flooding into the girl's expression just as it came crashing into her own consciousness.

For a second Veerle was so astounded that no words came at all; she was conscious of a pressure in her chest and realized she had been holding her breath. She let it all out in a gasp.

'*Hommel*,' she said.

6

Hommel. Veerle's mind was failing to grasp what her eyes were telling her; she felt as though her entire world had tilted and she was sliding screaming into nothingness, grasping uselessly at reality as it streaked past her in a blur. *Hommel. How can Hommel be here? She's dead. She can't be here – she can't—*

For a couple of seconds they gaped at each other, Veerle's hazel eyes staring into Hommel's blue-grey ones. Veerle read shock in those eyes, then panic. Hommel turned on her heel and lunged for the doorway, pushing blindly at the people pressing into the little chamber. Veerle heard mingled exclamations of '*Pas op!*' and '*Attention!*' and '*Hey!*' as Hommel forced her way towards the exit.

Stop, thought Veerle. *I have to know . . .*

But she saw that Hommel was not going to stop; she was going to vanish again unless Veerle caught her. Galvanized into action, she launched herself into the gap that Hommel's flight had created in the packed bodies. Now people were getting really irritated, and someone gave her an ill-tempered shove as she went past. Veerle staggered, righted herself, and stumbled out of the exit in time to see Hommel take off at top speed, sprinting across the black-and-white-tiled floor of the cathedral, heading for the door. Veerle saw heads turning as Hommel raced past, her sleek blonde ponytail flipping from side to side as she dodged past stationary groups of tourists.

I can't let her go. The inertia of shock had cleared and now Veerle wanted to catch Hommel very badly. She wanted to ask her a thousand questions.

'Hommel!' she shouted, and realized her mistake as all those heads turned away from Hommel, turned to look at *her*. Hommel didn't even break stride. She was making a bee-line for the exit. Veerle gave chase, threading her arms into the straps of her rucksack as she went. She made it halfway to the door before someone appeared in front of her, arms out-spread to block her way: an older man, with close-cropped grey hair and a grim expression, and a plastic security badge pinned to the front of his jacket.

'No running in the cathedral,' he was saying angrily.

Veerle feinted to the left and then lunged to the right, pass-ing within five centimetres of the man's outstretched fingertips.

'Sorry,' she shouted over her shoulder as she ran for the door.

Then she was out in the square and the sunshine was blinding after the dimmer interior of the cathedral. She paused for a moment, scanning Sint-Baafsplein for a glimpse of Hommel.

There she is.

Veerle saw the other girl running at full tilt down the tramlines that ran along the side of the square, towards the Belfort tower. It was the movement that caught her eye; Hommel was dressed all in black, with no flash of colour to make her stand out. No time to think about why Hommel was running away from her, no time to guess where she might be heading.

If I lose sight of her, I'll never find her in a city this size.

She threw herself into the chase, tearing down the street after the other girl, her feet slapping on the stones, her bag thumping unpleasantly on her back.

Hommel was passing the steps at the foot of the Belfort tower, with their ornate black railings, and here came a tram, rattling up the street behind them, the bell sounding a metallic bleat of warning. Hommel cut over onto the other track, and Veerle followed her. Up ahead she saw the great church of Sint-Niklaas, with its grey-tiled turrets and geometrically precise tower, and then the tram was rattling past her, blocking the view.

Hommel dodged left, into Magelein, narrowly avoiding a stand of brightly coloured postcards on the corner.

If I'd been the other side of the tram I'd have lost her, Veerle realized grimly. She did her best to speed up, but the school bag was slowing her down, and she could already feel how out of condition she was.

Magelein was pedestrianized and it was crowded, even this early in the day. It didn't help that an already narrow street was choked with restaurant boards and racks of merchandise. Both Hommel and Veerle had to drop their pace a bit, but it became harder for Veerle to keep sight of her quarry because they were both having to dodge their way round obstacles.

A mother pushed a buggy straight out in front of Veerle,

who almost fell over it. She stumbled, catching the woman's eyes; she saw outrage there but she didn't stop to apologize.

Look where you're going, she thought, but she didn't stop to say that, either. Her gaze flickered back to the street ahead and for several seconds she couldn't pick out Hommel at all, couldn't see her anywhere. There were half a dozen other people in black or dark-coloured jackets. Veerle set off again, but she was slower than before, confused, her gaze scanning the street ahead.

Then she saw her: at the intersection of Magelein and Bennesteeg. Hommel had made the mistake of pausing to look back, to check whether Veerle was still following her, and Veerle had a glimpse of the pale oval of her face before she ducked to the right, into the side street.

When Veerle rounded the corner herself Hommel was still visible, perhaps thirty metres ahead. Bennesteeg was quieter than Magelein. It was narrow and shady, with one or two silvery puddles from the previous night's rain; running along it was like sprinting down a damp and lonely canyon. With no one to dodge round, Hommel had increased the distance between them. Veerle raced after her, the slap of her shoes on the stones echoing off the walls.

I can't lose her, I can't.

Veerle tried to step up the pace but she was tiring, she could tell. Another intersection was coming up, and this time Hommel turned left without hesitation.

Veerle followed, her breath rasping in her throat. As she came to the corner she glanced right, orienting herself, and saw the great bulk of the Sint-Niklaaskerk at the end of the street.

She's leading me around in circles.

No time to think about that, though. She turned her back on Sint-Niklaas and pelted down the street after Hommel, who was already at the next junction. They were running along tramlines again, between glass-fronted shops.

With a sinking feeling Veerle saw Hommel turn right. She couldn't remember the name of the street Hommel had taken, but she knew it was lined with shops. If Hommel managed to get inside one of them before she, Veerle, had rounded the corner, that would be the end of the chase.

Veerle felt sick with exertion and her school bag was a lead weight on her back. She stumbled round the corner after Hommel, and there she was: she hadn't gone into one of the shops after all; she was still racing down the road as though the demons of hell were on her heels. The pavements were peopled with slow-moving strollers – tourists and window-shoppers – so Hommel simply ran down the side of the road.

I know this street, thought Veerle. *She's heading for the bridge.*

She could see the bridge now in fact: the two central struts of grey-blue metal and the perforated crossbar were distinctive, forming a gigantic letter H. It spanned the smooth green waters of the canal that ran north–south through the old part of the city.

Veerle ran on towards the bridge, her chest tight and her heart thumping. She looked at the fleeing figure and she was pretty sure that Hommel had widened the gap again.

I'm not going to catch her, she thought.

When Hommel ran onto the bridge, Veerle was perhaps forty metres behind her. She had her gaze fixed on the other girl, watching to see which way she would go when she reached the other side of the canal: left along the road that edged the canal or straight ahead down the shady Zwartezustersstraat with its decorative façades and elegant balconies. Veerle was so busy watching Hommel that she didn't see the bicycle until it was too late. There was a rank of them parked on the pavement, and this one had fallen over. Half of the back wheel was lying in the road. Veerle ran straight into it.

As the pavement came up to meet her she thought, *My arm . . .*

Instinctively she held up the arm she had broken, but came down on her shoulder instead with a thump that forced the breath out of her.

For a moment she lay in the road, aware of the bulk of her school bag digging painfully into her shoulders. Then she rolled onto her stomach, head up, eyes desperately scanning the bridge.

If I can just see which way she goes—

'Are you all right?' said someone close by.

It was no use. Hommel had vanished.

'Yes, thanks,' said Veerle unconvincingly.

She got to her feet a little gingerly, brushing herself down. She was aware of the concerned passer-by hovering at her elbow but she didn't look round. She couldn't help staring at the bridge, as though by some miracle Hommel might change her mind and come back into view; as though she might say, *That wasn't fair, you falling over, so I'll wait for a minute and then we can start again.*

Veerle walked down to the bridge, walked right over it in

fact, scanning the waterfront on the opposite side, but she couldn't see anyone who looked like Hommel.

I could walk back to Bijlokevest from here, she realized. She didn't call it *home*. She gazed south down the canal, the smooth façades of the riverside buildings reflected upside down in its green water. *Where has Hommel gone?* she wondered. *Maybe she was just running anywhere, just trying to throw me off the track. But then wouldn't she have ducked into one of the shops back there? Why keep running on the open streets, unless she was aiming for something specific? But what, and where?* She chewed her lip, considering. *What if she's staying somewhere on this side of the city? She might be in the next street to Bijlokevest and I didn't even know it.*

There were bigger questions than those to consider, though. Veerle went over to the railings at the side of the canal, swinging her school bag off her shoulders. She dumped it on the ground and leaned on the metal railings, gazing into the glossy water as though it might provide some answers.

When she'd started running after Hommel she'd had no thought in her head other than to catch the other girl before she vanished again. Then she'd been absorbed in the chase, in the aching of her limbs and the tightness in her chest and the urgent need to keep up with someone who had a head start and who really, really wanted to get away from her. Now other questions were crowding into her head.

Hommel isn't dead. That was the first thing, and that was the big one, that was the one that she was still struggling to get over. *Well*, thought Veerle, *we never had any proof that she was dead. We just assumed that whatever happened to Vlinder and Egbert and the rest of them happened to her too. Maybe she did just run away, to get away from that* klootzak *of a step-father of hers.*

Which brought her to the next thing.

Why did she run away from me?

Veerle thought about that for a while, turning the question over and over in her mind, but she couldn't make any sense of it.

It was her, she thought. *There wasn't any mistake about that. She recognized me too. So why did that put her in such a panic?*

There was no way of answering that question without speaking to Hommel herself, and Hommel had vanished into the streets beyond the waterfront.

There was one other thing. *I have to tell Kris.* She drew out her phone, but she didn't call immediately. She held the phone in her hands, looking down at the tiny screen.

I haven't spoken to him for a week. I can never get through, and he never calls me back.

Whatever that meant, it wasn't likely to be good.

He'll have to call me back if I tell him this, she thought. But was she ready to hear what he had to say?

She was very much afraid she knew what that would be. They had spoken every day in the weeks and months since Veerle left hospital and moved in with Geert and Anneke, in spite of her father trying heavy-handedly to put a stop to it. *Every day – until a week ago.*

The first few times she had tried and failed to reach him, Veerle had shrugged it off. *Busy. Working. Hung over.* Now she had an ominous feeling inside her, a hard, dry, brittle feeling, as though some soft essential part of her had been mummified. She thought of Kris hearing his mobile phone ringing and looking at the display, seeing her name come up and pressing the OFF button. She thought of how he might describe what he was doing: *moving on*, the same way as people called dying *passing away* or *falling asleep*. She could feel the snapping of the last thread that bound her to her old life in the village south-east of Brussels, the life with her mother, Claudine, and her old school, and the places and people she had grown up with.

I knew him when I was seven, she thought. If it all ended now it would be like scribbling *The End* across an unfinished story. It would be like taking that book she had loved so much when she was a kid, the one about explorers, and hurling it into the canal, watching it sink inexorably into the opaque green water, condemning it to pulp.

In the end, though, she *had* to call. Someone was alive, after all, someone whom they had both thought dead. Someone Kris had been close to. He had a right to know.

She was not sure whether it was a disappointment or a relief when Kris's phone went straight to voicemail again.

7

Veerle walked back to Sint-Baafsplein. It wasn't even lunch time; she couldn't go back to the flat in Bijlokevest, and she had no intention of going back to school. What she thought of as *the tourist part of town* was as good a place as any to hang out; it was always packed with people, and most of them were foreign visitors who had no idea who she was and wouldn't have cared anyway. All the same, she kept a wary eye out for Mevrouw Taelemans. When she found herself back at the corner of Sint-Baafsplein and Magelein she scanned the square before launching herself out into the open.

The bench Veerle had occupied before was taken now, so she went and sat on the steps outside one of the pavement cafés on the north side of the square. She liked to watch the groups of tourists going in and out of the cathedral. The way they moved together in a group, separate but somehow synchronized, and sometimes even *dressed* the same, reminded her of shoals of fish. She could imagine attaching herself to one of those shoals and simply darting away when they did, moving on to wherever they were going. *It's not like I belong here, any more than they do,* she thought. She shaded her eyes with her hands and watched a group of them milling around the cathedral door like coralfish clustering around a reef. *Germans*, she guessed. Every single one of them was dressed in a matching red shell suit.

'So you can run as well as climb,' said a voice very close to her.

Veerle looked up and saw a green shirt, a shock of blond hair.

Bram.

She didn't reply, didn't give him any encouragement at all, but that didn't stop him settling himself comfortably on the steps next to her, the skateboard still tucked under his arm, his suntanned knees protruding from his shorts.

'So what was that, a race?' he went on.

Veerle opened her mouth to tell him to mind his own business, that she was really quite happy sitting here all on her own, thanks, when a thought occurred to her. She turned and looked at him, and was only mildly irritated to see a gratified smile spread across his face.

'Did you see the other girl, the one I was following?' she asked.

'Sure.' He shook strands of sun-bleached hair out of his eyes. 'Couldn't miss her. She nearly knocked me over.'

'Did you get a good look at her?'

'I guess.' He shrugged. 'What, did she steal your wallet or something?'

'No . . .' Veerle hesitated. 'It's kind of difficult to explain. I know her and I really need to talk to her, but . . .'

Bram laughed, showing even white teeth. 'She doesn't want to talk to you, right?'

'I guess not,' said Veerle. 'Look, are you here a lot – the cathedral square, I mean?'

'Quite a lot.'

'Well, have you seen her before? That girl.'

'Yeah, I've seen her. She's here pretty often, lunch times.'

Veerle stared at him and she could feel excitement sparkling in the pit of her stomach. 'You're sure? That it's her, I mean?'

'Yeah. Hard to miss. Good-looking but snotty.'

'Snotty?' *She hasn't changed, then.*

'Doesn't speak to anyone. Marnix tried to chat her up once and she cut him dead.'

'Marnix?'

'He's someone I know.'

'Is Marnix here today?'

'Nope. He's probably working.'

Veerle rubbed her face with her hands, thinking. 'Look,' she said, 'I really do need to talk to her. This guy Marnix – he actually spoke to her, then?'

'He tried. I think it was all one way.'

'But she didn't actually run away, like she did from me?'

'I guess not.'

'So it was really me she was trying to get away from.' Veerle let out a long sigh. 'I suppose I could sit here every day and wait for her to come back, but if she wants to avoid me that much she probably won't.'

'Probably not,' agreed Bram amiably.

'Shit.'

'Look,' said Bram, 'if it's such a big deal, I could talk to Marnix when I see him. Ask him if she said anything that would help. It's a long shot, but . . .' He shrugged.

'Better than nothing,' finished Veerle. 'Thanks,' she said,

and meant it. She felt her conscience pricking her; she'd been short with him earlier and now he was helping her. She gave Bram a tentative smile.

'Her name is Els. Els Lievens. I guess it's too much to hope that he got her number, but if he can tell me anything – anything at all . . . Like if he's seen her anywhere else but here in the Sint-Baafsplein.'

'What if he asks me why?'

Veerle let out a long breath. 'I was afraid you were going to ask me that.'

Bram didn't say anything and she realized he was waiting for her to go on.

'Look, it's difficult.' She glanced away from him, towards the ornate façade of the Belfort tower.

What can I tell him? We didn't even tell the police the half of it.

Eventually she said, 'I used to live in a village in Vlaams-Brabant. I knew her when I lived there. She's not really a friend, more of . . . a friend of a friend. All of a sudden she just disappeared, and nobody knew where she'd gone. We thought maybe something had happened to her. You know, something bad. There are people who'd still like to know where she is,' added Veerle. She looked at Bram. 'At least, to just know she's OK.'

Bram had his head on one side. 'It sounds like she doesn't want to be found,' he commented.

'She doesn't get on with her family,' said Veerle reluctantly. She felt uncomfortable talking about Hommel's private life.

'OK,' said Bram. 'And what if Marnix wants to know who's asking?'

'You can say Veerle.'

'Veerle?'

'Veerle De Keyser.'

'And how do I get hold of Mevrouw Veerle De Keyser to tell her what I've found out?' Bram was looking at her slyly.

'I'll come back here,' said Veerle.

'When? I'll need a few days. I don't see Marnix every day. He works, I study. Archaeology.'

'Friday?' said Veerle. Then she thought, *Not Friday. If Geert finds out I've bunked off school again today he'll probably step up the security – start sitting next to me in lessons or something. Then I won't be able to get away to meet anyone on Friday.* 'No – Saturday,' she said. 'How about Saturday morning?'

Bram grinned at her. 'It's a date,' he said.

8

Veerle lay on her back on the bed in the small second bedroom of Geert and Anneke's flat and listened to the raised
voices coming through the wall from the room next door. It
was only nine-thirty in the evening but Veerle was pretending
to be asleep. Instead she lay looking at the stripe of yellow
light from the streetlamp outside her window bisecting the
narrow rectangle of ceiling. There were shutters but Veerle
never put them down, though Anneke nagged her to. The
room was very much smaller than her room in the house on
Kerkstraat had been, and with the window blanked out it was
almost claustrophobic. A car passed by in the street outside,
and brighter light swept across the ceiling.

'What am I supposed to do?' Geert was shouting.

Veerle could hear every word quite clearly through the
wall.

'Nobody wants to buy that old place. She hadn't done a
single piece of work on it for years. We can't rent it out like
that, either. Not without investing a packet in renovating, and
we don't have the money, you know that.'

'Well, how are we supposed to manage when the baby
comes?' That was Anneke.

'We've been over this. The baby will have to share with us for the time being.'

'When he's tiny. But what about later? He needs a room of his own.'

'Anneke, what do you expect me to do?'

'We had *plans*, Geert.'

'Keep your voice down. I *know* we had plans, Anneke.'

'I wanted to decorate that room for the baby – decorate it properly. Not just shove the cot in a corner of our room.'

'Look, it's not for ever. It won't be long—' Perhaps Geert De Keyser realized that he had been speaking at the top of his voice, because suddenly his voice dropped to a murmur and Veerle couldn't make out the words any more. All the same, she could guess the gist of them. *It won't be long before Veerle leaves. We just have to wait until she's eighteen, until she's finished the last year of school. Just a little longer, and then she'll be gone.*

It hurt, knowing that they were thinking like that, that they were just waiting until she was off their hands; it gave her a tight silvery feeling in the throat, as though tears were about to come, even though her eyes were dry. *The trouble is*, she thought, *I can't blame them. I don't want to be here, either, and we all know it.* Veerle could see no solution to the problem, though, any more than Geert and Anneke could. No solution other than to get through her final year at school, pass her qualifying exams and move out.

Veerle's gaze roamed restlessly around the darkened room with its bare walls and dull furnishings. There was still that third box in the corner, the one with the rabbit, waiting to be unpacked. Somewhere she had posters and a couple of framed pictures, and she hadn't put those up, either. She couldn't summon up the energy to personalize the room. It wasn't home.

She thought, *I can see why they go nuts when I bunk off school. They're afraid I'm going to fail the year and have to stay and do it again.*

She rolled onto her side.

If I keep missing stuff I am *going to fail the year.*

Admitting it to herself gave her a sick feeling in the pit of her stomach.

But ... but ... I'm not supposed to be here, this is not supposed to be my life, thought Veerle. As long as she could hang onto that, a tiny part of her was still safe; her old life wasn't entirely gone. Cutting school didn't feel like a deliberate act of rebellion, an attempt to flout her father's wishes; it felt like a bid for survival.

The school didn't see it that way, of course. When they called Geert to apprise him of Veerle's truancy they had said all the right things about sympathy and patience and time, but they weren't going to bear with her for ever. She wasn't going to get her ASO diploma on sympathy alone.

And when I fail ... ?

She wondered whether it was possible that Geert and Anneke would actually ask her to leave. Once she was past eighteen no one could make her stay at school and re-take the year. Already she felt like the cuckoo in the nest, the oversized intruder, eating up time and resources that were not hers by right.

Where would I go? she wondered.

She heard Geert's voice rise in the next room again, though

she only caught the words '. . . not enough money . . .' before he caught himself shouting and lowered it once more.

It was useless trying to sleep. The room felt like a cell. Veerle got off the bed and padded over to the window, taking care not to make a sound. She pulled aside the curtain and gazed up at the night sky.

It was not like being at home in her own village. There were streetlamps there, of course there were, but you could still see the stars on a clear night, thousands of them. In the city there were more lights, there were late-night cafés and shops and floodlit buildings and bridges, and well-lit main roads. You had to look for the stars through a haze of yellow artificial light. You could see the moon, though, and Veerle liked to look for that. She liked to think that the same moon that floated over the spires and corbie steps of Ghent was also shining down upon her home village. It was the one thing she could see from here that you could also have seen if you were standing in front of the house on Kerkstraat, with the bulk of the Sint-Pauluskerk rising into the night sky.

She opened the window, taking care not to rattle the latch, and the cool of the September evening leached into the room.

Air, thought Veerle gratefully. She rested her elbows on the windowsill and gazed down at the street. The flat was on the first floor; you could watch the comings and goings below without anyone being able to stare in. She watched a man of perhaps fifty walk by with a small dog on a lead. Further up the street someone was trying to get a car into a parking space. She could see lights in some of the windows opposite, the ones that didn't have their shutters down. *City people*, she thought. *Living in their little boxes, like battery hens.* Then she thought, *I wonder where Hommel is. Is she in one of those little boxes too?* She let her gaze wander up and down the street. *She could be on this street somewhere, or the next one. She's out there somewhere.*

Veerle leaned a little further, resting on the windowsill. Her room just had an ordinary window, but the room next door, the one in which her father and his girlfriend were conducting their heated debate, had a balcony. Geert and Anneke weren't enjoying the cool night air, though; they had put the roller shutters down. *What a waste*, thought Veerle. She measured the distance between her own window and the balcony. It was too far to step across, or even jump safely, but there was a metal drainpipe halfway between the two, and she thought that if you were able to step onto the bracket holding the pipe to the wall, and if it held your weight, it might be possible to get across. *Not that I'd do it*, she thought. She didn't fancy sitting on the balcony listening to Geert and Anneke arguing about her. She didn't move away from the window, though. She kept looking at that drainpipe; at the brackets screwed into the bricks. *You could go across to the other balcony, all right*, she thought. *And you could also get down to the ground.*

She was terribly tempted to try it.

9

You know, Veerle told herself, *there's really no point in doing this. Where are you going to go when you get down into the street?*

She was standing, fully dressed now, on the windowsill of her bedroom window. The frame was not that tall, so her hands gripping the top of it were at hip height and her nose was a centimetre from the brick wall. The next move was going to be the tricky one: she had to step with her left foot onto the bracket fixing the drainpipe to the wall, and then transfer her weight onto that foot. The building was fairly old and the pipe was a heavy-duty metal one, not a modern plastic one, so she was hoping it would take her weight.

Veerle was very conscious of the empty air behind her; she could feel a cool breeze on the skin of her face and neck.

At least there are no railings down there, she told herself. *If you fall off you'll just be smashed, you won't be skewered.*

She grinned in spite of herself, in spite of the strain on her fingers and the ache in the shoulder that had hit the pavement earlier. She felt better than she had all day. All week, in fact. The strain on her body, the urgent need to maintain her balance, the hard wood of the windowframe, the rasp of the brickwork when her skin touched it and the soft caress of the breeze – all of it was real, a problem to be solved with strength and concentration and nerve. Best of all, it demanded her whole attention, and crowded out all those other problems that she *couldn't* solve.

She kept her weight on her right foot and reached out with the left, letting the toe of her Converse trainer find the metal bracket. Her left hand crept like a spider across the rough surface of the brickwork, found the drainpipe and grasped it. It felt rock solid. All the same, she had a moment of apprehension before she shifted her weight across. The bracket held.

Veerle clutched the pipe with both hands and began to climb down. The brackets were too far apart for her to rely on those so she had to brace her toes against the bricks. With so much of her weight on her arms, the strain on her shoulders was immense, a savage ache. If she didn't get down quickly her shrieking muscles would give way. She went down hand over hand, as swiftly as she could, and when she was nearly at the bottom she let go of the pipe and dropped the last metre, her feet landing on the pavement with a slap.

She glanced about her, wary of nosy neighbours, but the ground-floor shutters were all down and there were no lights on in the building opposite. Veerle put her head back and looked up at her window.

I left the shutters open, and *the window. Anneke will go mad if she sees that.* Still, she didn't think anyone would be climbing up there in a hurry. It had been difficult enough getting down.

What now? Veerle wondered. She could walk into the heart

of the old city in perhaps twenty minutes, she supposed, but there was not much point, with no one to meet. *I could climb back up, but that would be lame, and anyway, my shoulders need a rest. I feel like my arms have been pulled out of their sockets.* She decided to walk down to the Coupure canal, along and back. She had a vague idea that if she saw a call box she could try phoning Kris from that; if he was avoiding her she'd have a better chance of reaching him from a number he didn't recognize. She didn't hold out much hope, though; she couldn't remember seeing a single call box since she'd arrived in Ghent. All the same, it was a plan.

It didn't take long to reach the waterfront: perhaps five minutes. Veerle only had to walk up Bijlokevest a little way and then take a dogleg down a couple of smaller streets. The last of these passed between two tall buildings so that little of the canal could be seen until you emerged from between them.

The Coupure was beautiful after dark, she saw. The façades of the buildings lining the banks were gilded by the yellow light of the streetlamps and the dark water glittered, the lights reflected in it as golden columns.

Its beauty was a pain, a hard little knot in the centre of Veerle's chest.

Beautiful, but not home.

She wanted to be able to hate Ghent whole-heartedly. Instead she found herself thinking how magical it looked, and then she felt guilty – guilty and resentful. It made her feel the way she had felt when Bram had smiled at her and said, *It's a date*: as though she were being dragged unwillingly into something, as though she had said yes without meaning to.

Veerle looked at the canal, at the golden flecks of light

dancing on the black water. The thought of Bram made her uneasy. *I wish I hadn't agreed to meet him again*, she thought, biting her lip. *But I have to find Hommel, and I don't know where else to start.*

It would be easier if he wasn't so . . . She grimaced.

Attractive wasn't the word she was looking for; she was with Kris – at least she *hoped* she still was. But when you looked at it objectively, with that sun-bleached hair and those very blue eyes – well, if Kris were here, if he had seen her talking to Bram, he might have jumped to the wrong conclusion. *A lot of people would think Bram was attractive*, Veerle conceded to herself.

She began to walk along the path at the side of the canal, intending to turn up one of the side streets further down and circle back to the flat. The question of whether it was going to be easy or even possible to climb back up to her bedroom window was becoming more pressing. There was an ominous dull ache in her shoulder.

I could ring the bell, she thought. *And say I let myself out without them hearing. But if Anneke works out what I did she'll try to stop me doing it again. She'll lock the window at night or something.*

Her glance flickered over the dancing lights on the black water of the canal.

OK, there's no reason to go out that way.

She grinned to herself.

You never know when it might come in useful, though.

She was considering this and walking rather briskly along the path when something shattered under the sole of her Converse trainer with a brittle crunch.

Veerle stopped. Whatever she had trodden on was substantial enough to arouse her curiosity. She looked down, and by the sallow light of the streetlamp she saw that it was a plastic case, the sort people used for glasses. It had split right along its length, and she could see one of the earpieces sticking out.

Veerle bent to pick it up, thinking that if the owner were ever to come this way again, looking for it, it would be better to leave it at the side of the path where nobody else would finish the job she had started and flatten it completely. As she did so she caught a flicker of movement out of the corner of her eye. She turned to look and felt a cold jolt of shock. Someone was standing there, not two metres away, in the shadow of the nearest tree.

'Shit.' Her first impulse was to drop the glasses case and move away as quickly as she could. She hesitated, though.

The person under the tree wasn't the bogeyman – it wasn't even a man in fact, she saw. It was a woman of perhaps sixty, grey-haired, soberly dressed in a dark suit and court shoes. She was leaning against the tree – that was why Veerle hadn't seen her as she came along the path: she had been concealed by the trunk.

Not just leaning – almost hanging onto it, Veerle thought.

She heard the woman gasp and wondered whether she was ill. All the same, she stayed where she was, on the path. If you met someone after dark in a quiet place it was wise to be cautious. *Especially*, thought Veerle, *if you have climbed out of your bedroom window and nobody knows where you are.*

'Mevrouw?' she said. 'Are you all right?'

She heard another gasp, and then the woman said something indistinct. Veerle caught virtually nothing of it, just a single word that might have been *fright*.

Did I make her jump? she wondered. *It's not like I sneaked up on her or anything.*

She glanced down at the ground, and now she saw that the glasses case was not the only thing that had been dropped there. The grass and the edge of the path were strewn with items: a tub of butter, a little tin of pâté, a packet of coffee filters and, incongruously, a couple of loose onions.

'Dropped my bag,' said the woman breathlessly.

This was so self-evidently true that Veerle shrugged off caution. She picked up the onions, which were lurking in a tuft of grass by the edge of the path like a pair of unexploded bombs, and then the tin of pâté.

'Thank you,' said the woman. She was still holding onto tree.

Veerle found her bag, which was on its side on the grass. She didn't like to repack it so she piled the items carefully next to it, placing the glasses case on top.

'I'm not drunk,' said the woman suddenly.

Veerle glanced at her sharply. The idea hadn't crossed her mind until that moment. There had been nothing to suggest it, no astringent whiff of alcohol.

She heard the woman laugh; the sound was tremulous and unconvincing.

'I saw them,' she said, nodding, and instinctively Veerle turned to look behind herself at the dark waters of the canal with the lights reflected in them and the illuminated buildings beyond. She could see nothing untoward.

'I saw them,' repeated the woman. She put a hand to her breast. 'It gave me such a start.'

Perhaps she is *drunk*, thought Veerle uneasily.

'Whom did you see?' she said aloud.

'On the rooftops,' said the woman. She laughed again, nervously. 'You hear the stories but you never think you'll see them yourself – it's crazy, impossible . . .' She put a hand to her face, and Veerle saw that it was trembling. 'You must think I'm quite insane.'

Veerle's gaze flickered back to the buildings on the other side of the canal.

On the rooftops? There's nobody up there.

She picked up the tub of butter and added it to the little pile next to the bag. Then she took a step back, back onto the path. 'I should go,' she said.

'Did you see them?' asked the woman suddenly. 'The demons?'

Demons?! Now Veerle really began to think that she should put some space between herself and this woman. *Did she really say demons?*

'No,' she said aloud. 'I didn't see anything.'

She saw the woman let go of the tree and she took another step back.

'You're not from Ghent,' said the woman.

'No,' said Veerle. The feeling of unease was growing at an exponential rate, like a time-lapse film of a plant hurtling from seed to bud to flower, unfurling into some monstrous bloom. 'I really have to go,' she said, and she walked away as decisively and rapidly as she dared, hurrying but not quite running.

She's nuts, Veerle thought, and as she walked away she was listening for the sound of footsteps on the path behind her, the sound that would say that she hadn't shaken the woman off, she was going to follow Veerle and grab her sleeve, start raving on about demons on the rooftops. No sound came, and when she judged that she had put enough space between them, that the woman must be at least twenty metres behind her, Veerle risked turning round to look.

The woman was standing motionless in the middle of the path. In her rather formal clothes she could have been a statue, if she hadn't had that rather incongruous bag of groceries dangling from her left hand. She wasn't looking at Veerle; she was gazing across the canal at the row of apartment houses opposite. Veerle followed her gaze. It was impossible not to, really; there was such an air of fixed concentration about that still figure that you had to look and see what she was staring at . . .

A minute later Veerle was hurrying down the street, looking for the turning that would take her back to Bijlokevest and the flat, and the difficult climb back up to her bedroom window. She listened to the slap of her feet on the pavement and her breath shuddering in and out, and as she went she asked herself: *Who or what was that moving along the rooftops?*

10

The following morning Anneke made waffles for breakfast. When Veerle got up and dressed she could smell the sweet aroma on the air, warm and enticing.

She knows I heard them arguing about me last night, she thought.

Normally she had to fend for herself. Anneke was heavily pregnant, after all; if anyone was being waited on it ought to be *her*, as Geert was fond of reminding Veerle if she left her T-shirt on the bathroom floor or her mug on the coffee table in the living room.

The waffles were the nearest Anneke was likely to come to a peace offering. Veerle wasn't all that fond of them; she preferred the Liège kind, which were thicker and sticky and crusted with sugar. She didn't tell Anneke that, though, and she ate three of the waffles with as convincing a show of relish as she could manage, the fork scraping at the plate.

When she'd cleaned her teeth and fetched her school bag, Geert was at the door, waiting to walk her to school again. Anneke came to the door too, to see them off, as she always did. She looked wan. Veerle thought that she probably couldn't wait for her and Geert to leave so that she could put her feet up.

'Thanks for the breakfast,' said Veerle, hoisting her school bag onto her shoulder. She watched Anneke lean in to kiss her father.

When they had reached the street Geert said, 'It isn't easy for Anneke. She's very tired.'

He didn't say *what* wasn't easy for Anneke. Veerle waited for a moment, wondering whether her father was trying to open a discussion, whether he would follow it up with *Did you hear anything last night?* or *Anneke doesn't always mean everything she says, you know.*

Geert said nothing more, however. They walked on in silence. That was fine by Veerle. She was thinking about the night before, about the encounter with the woman at the Coupure.

Did I imagine it? she wondered. *Whatever it was I thought I saw on the rooftops?* She couldn't decide. It had been weird, hearing that ordinary-looking middle-aged woman say, *Did you see them? The demons?*

It made Veerle's skin prickle, just remembering the conversation. She thought, *Who goes around looking for demons in a city after dark?*

And then there was the way the woman had still been standing there when Veerle looked back, just standing and staring fixedly at the buildings on the other side of the canal. It was . . . creepy.

She tried to rationalize it away, that feeling of wrongness. *Supposing there* was *somebody up there – what's the big deal? Maybe you can get up there from the top floor of those flats.*

Maybe it was just someone getting a bit of air and admiring the view.

That was certainly possible.

It was weird, though, Veerle thought. *The way she said, You're not from Ghent. Like she thought I wouldn't understand whatever it was, because I'm not from here.*

It was puzzling. Unsettling, even. The woman was probably crazy – had to be, when you thought about it – but still Veerle couldn't dismiss the incident as easily as that.

She wondered whom she could ask about it. Not Geert: she couldn't ask him without revealing that she had been wandering along the bank of the Coupure when he and Anneke thought she was asleep in the next room, somehow magically snoring her way through their argument.

Bram? She stifled that idea sternly.

Geert stopped on the pavement outside the school. There was something about the decisive way in which he came to a halt that told Veerle he was going to wait outside again until he was sure that she had gone in.

Verdomme, does he have to? she thought.

She said goodbye and went inside. There were still a few minutes before lessons began, so she waited, and then went back to check whether he had gone.

Geert was still there, standing impassively on the pavement, his battered leather briefcase in his hand. As Veerle watched, he shot his hand out of his sleeve and checked his wristwatch. He was obviously planning to wait until the bell rang.

Why? she thought. *Is he so desperate to make sure I get through the year and leave?*

She looked at her father, at his heavy, sleepy-looking features, his shock of light brown hair touched with grey. It was hard to tell what Geert was thinking or feeling; he wasn't a demonstrative person. All the same, Veerle thought he looked weary. He probably didn't want to stand there outside the school any more than she wanted him to. He probably wanted to get to his office, make himself a cup of strong coffee and collapse into a chair. Still he stood there, the last of the students pushing past him in their haste to get into school before the bell rang.

He's my dad, thought Veerle. Perhaps it was as simple as that. *Maybe that's what dads do.*

It was unknown territory as far as she was concerned. Her parents had split up when she was only eight or nine and she'd rarely seen her father. Until this summer, when the thing had happened that she didn't want to think about, it had just been her and her mother, Claudine. Claudine could be strong, but in the way of the ivy that clings to an ancient wall, insinuating its roots between the crumbling bricks, adhering so closely that to tear it down would bring chunks of brick and mortar down too. Claudine's influence crept up on you through closed doors and pursed lips and infectious worries that nibbled at the edges of your consciousness. Geert, on the other hand, had a way of attacking problems that Veerle found jaw-droppingly direct.

He wants me to stay in school, so he stands outside and makes sure I do.

Veerle chewed her lip. The bell was going to go at any minute, and there was no way of getting out of school without passing Geert.

65

Well, he's won. For now, anyway.

She turned her back on the door and began to walk down the corridor, towards the first lesson of the day. The thought didn't exactly fill her with joy, but she felt less rancour towards Geert for his vigil than she might have done.

After all, she thought, if *I were him, it's what I would have done.*

11

As soon as Veerle entered the classroom, she could see that something was wrong. The English teacher, Meneer Ackermans, wasn't there, that was the first thing, and the bell was already ringing. Half the class weren't sitting at their desks, either. They were clustered in little groups and there was no merry buzz of voices, no friendly shoving or clapping on the shoulder going on. Everyone looked sombre. Even the boys who habitually sat at the back, their long legs sprawled out in front of them, had a grim self-conscious look on their faces, as though they had been caught out in some unseemly display of emotion. Veerle looked around and saw reddened eyes, puffy faces streaked with mascara. Two girls were openly weeping.

Veerle stood in the doorway with a cold feeling of dread in the pit of her stomach. *What's happened?* she wondered, but she wasn't sure she wanted to know. It meant something bad for someone, that was clear; the sort of bad that meant knocks on the door in the middle of the night or phone calls from the hospital and people saying *Oh my God, I'm so sorry*, just like—

Her mind swerved round the thought like a figure skater

sweeping round a patch of rotten ice. She might simply have turned and left the classroom again, but for the knowledge that Geert was still standing outside the school. There was nowhere to go.

Veerle swung her bag off her shoulder and made for a seat at the back. It wasn't possible to ignore what was going on, though; you'd have to be blind and deaf or made of marble. She knew one of the girls standing there talking in low tense voices; they'd been paired for a science project.

'Anne?' she said, and the girl turned to look at her, blue eyes rimmed with pink under her fall of light hair. 'What's the matter? What's happened?'

'Haven't you heard?'

Veerle shook her head.

'It's Daan De Moor.'

'Daan De Moor?' The name didn't mean anything to Veerle.

'From the parallel class. You don't know him?'

Veerle shook her head. 'What's the matter with him?'

'He's *dead*.' The girl's mouth stretched into a rictus of grief. The girl next to her, a dark-haired girl whose name Veerle couldn't remember, put an arm round her. She looked at Veerle with such naked anger in her eyes that Veerle was taken aback.

'Killed,' she said. 'He was killed.'

It's not me she's angry with, Veerle realized.

'They're saying it was suicide,' the girl went on. 'But he wouldn't do that. Daan wouldn't do that.'

Anne was crying now, big racking sobs. The dark-haired girl wasn't looking at Veerle any more; she was rubbing Anne's shoulders, whispering something to her.

'That's terrible,' Veerle managed to say.

'It was murder,' insisted the dark-haired girl.

'You don't know that, Merel,' said one of the boys.

'He wouldn't have jumped,' the girl said angrily.

'Jumped?' said Veerle.

'They found him on Belfortstraat,' the boy told her. 'He'd jumped from the top of one of the buildings.'

'I heard it was the *Belfort*,' said another boy, sitting on the far side of the first.

'Belfort*straat*. Look, it can't have been the tower. They've upped the security on all those places since the other one, the guy who jumped off Sint-Baafs. No way could you get into the Belfort at night.'

'The other one?' said Veerle incredulously.

'Yeah. Some guy threw himself off the cathedral tower a few months ago. Freaky.' The boy shook his head. 'He went to all the trouble of getting duplicate keys. The tower's normally only open for maybe one week a year, in the summer. They didn't open it at all this time, because of this guy. He got these keys and just let himself in one night, went all the way up to the top and jumped off. It's – I don't know, maybe a hundred metres high, that tower.' He looked at Veerle, his head on one side. 'You didn't hear about it?'

'I wasn't here then,' said Veerle. *And I had other stuff on my mind.* She didn't say that. Unconsciously she rubbed her left forearm. The cast had itched so badly.

'Well, it was bad. We had a lecture from the directeur – you know, about talking to someone if you're thinking of killing yourself. I guess there'll be another one now.'

'Stop saying Daan killed himself,' said the girl called Merel.

The boy shrugged. 'Just saying what I heard.'

'Maybe he didn't,' said another girl who was leaning against the back wall, standing a little apart from the others. She had a round, pallid face, her big grey eyes outlined heavily with kohl, her red hair pulled into two bunches so that you could see the light brown roots. She looked like a grubby version of a Manga character; she even had the knee socks under her short skirt. 'Maybe it wasn't murder, either. Well, not normal murder. Maybe it was *them*.'

'Oh, shut up, Suki,' said the boy disgustedly.

'Don't tell me to shut up.'

'It's crap. Demons on the rooftops. Crap.'

Demons? Veerle stared at the boy, open-mouthed. For a moment she wondered whether she had misheard. It was too unlikely, hearing two different people talking about demons on the rooftops within twenty-four hours.

It flashed through her mind that perhaps this was some kind of ongoing local joke, something to tease outsiders with, but instinctively she knew it wasn't that; the older woman's face had been too shocked, and Suki's was too avid. They believed it, both of them: that there were demons lurking on the rooftops of Ghent.

She didn't believe it herself – of *course* she didn't – but still she felt a slithering chill in the pit of her stomach.

Demons on the rooftop. The whole idea *was* crap, but she'd have found it easier to shrug off if she hadn't seen something up there herself, indistinct in the darkness but definitely there.

'Merel said Daan wouldn't top himself,' Suki was saying, as though this constituted proof of something.

'So what?' returned the boy, sticking his jaw out

aggressively. 'You're sick, Suki. If he didn't jump, either it was an accident or someone pushed him, but it wasn't a demon.'

'What about the salt?'

'Salt? What salt?' The boy looked at Suki incredulously.

'There was salt around the body.' Suki's gaze flickered up and down the boy, daring him to contradict her. 'My uncle's a policeman and he said so.'

'So what?'

'So salt's what you use to ward off demons. Maybe Daan knew it was dangerous up there, so he went prepared.'

'*Verdomme*, Suki, you should hear yourself. Why would he go up there if he thought it was dangerous?'

'Maybe he wanted to confront them.' Suki folded her arms.

'Jesus.' The boy was shaking his head in disbelief. 'You know your problem, Suki? You watch too much *verdomde* Buffy.'

'I'm not the one saying that Daan didn't kill himself.' Suki's gaze slid resentfully towards Merel. 'If he didn't go up on the roof to jump off, why *did* he go up there, then? He must have had some reason.'

'Have some respect, Suki,' Merel cut in angrily. She still had her arm round Anne. Now she was glaring at Suki as though the girl had made a deliberate attack on her friend. 'Daan's dead and you're still talking that rubbish.'

'It's not rubbish,' said Suki resentfully. 'I've seen them.'

For a moment no one said anything. They all gaped at her. Then Merel broke the silence.

'That is such *crap*, Suki. You haven't seen demons, except maybe in your dreams. It's just another of your sad little bids for attention.'

'Fuck you, Merel,' snapped Suki. She pushed away from the wall and stalked to the front of the classroom, where she slumped into a chair with her back to the rest of them.

'Whoa,' said someone.

Demons. Veerle was still having trouble getting past that idea. She had a feeling it was just going to annoy Merel and Anne if she pursued the topic, but she had to ask.

'What's this thing about demons?'

Merel simply gave an exasperated sigh and turned back to her friend. For a moment Veerle thought her question was going to go unanswered.

Then the boy sitting nearest to her, the one who had told her Daan had died on Belfortstraat, said, 'It's just this rumour going round. Like a – you know, whatever it's called, an urban legend.'

'An urban legend?'

He shrugged. 'Supposedly the rooftops of Ghent are haunted by demons.'

Veerle had worked that out for herself. She waited, but it seemed that nothing more was forthcoming.

'Why the rooftops?' she said.

'You're really interested?' He raised his eyebrows.

He's probably wondering if I'm like Suki, thought Veerle. 'It's kind of unusual,' she said, trying to sound as non-committal as possible.

'OK . . . well, I don't know the whole story. It's kind of old – you know, the stuff your grandma tells you. Years and years ago, I mean *hundreds* of years ago, there was this rich guy who lived in Ghent and he's supposed to have summoned these demons up to protect him and his family, so nobody could kill them. I think that was it. Anyway, I guess they were easier to call up than to get rid of, because supposedly they're still here, up on the rooftops, watching the city every night.'

'That's creepy,' said Veerle, imagining the stepped façades of the guild houses on the Graslei or the turreted roof of the old Post Office as a nest of grim and angular things like gigantic bats, chittering shrilly, jostling for position with the scuffling of curved claws upon stone, taking to the air with the rustle of leathery wings.

'I guess.' The lack of enthusiasm in his voice was palpable.

Veerle didn't like to ask any more, and anyway, here was Meneer Ackermans in the doorway of the classroom, his expression grave. Evidently the anticipated lecture was on its way. Veerle gave the boy a rueful smile and went to sit down.

At the end of the first lesson she went down to the front door, her bag over her shoulder, and looked out. To her amazement, Geert De Keyser was still standing there on the pavement opposite, watching the school door with a stolid expression. Veerle stepped back, wondering whether he had glimpsed her peeping out. There was nothing for it: she turned her back on the door and went to her second lesson. She didn't try to leave again that day until the final bell rang.

12

No two dreams were ever the same, and they were all terrible. Veerle never dreamed about Joren Sterckx himself, that was the odd thing. He stalked across her waking mind often enough, but he was curiously absent from her dreams. Once she dreamed that she was inside an enormous house, but it was no house that she had ever visited, no house that could possibly exist, because instead of proper rooms and corridors it consisted of a seemingly endless series of tiny chambers, each just big enough for her to crouch in, connected by even smaller passages, all panelled in worn and shiny oak. She would squeeze her way along the passages, struggling from room to room, twisting her limbs in the confined spaces, hoping to find a way out, afraid that the passages would instead narrow to the point where she could neither turn round nor go on. She woke up panting and perspiring, sick with horror.

This time it was voices. She was in the house in Kerkstraat, the one she had grown up in, the one now emptied and up for sale. Veerle herself did not seem to have any physical form; she drifted like tendrils of fog in the heart of the house, absorbing the sights and sounds. The house was not empty, she observed; the old furniture and ornaments were still in place. Most of the internal doors were open but the door to the living room was closed, and it was through this door that she could hear the voices. One of them was her mother's; she recognized it at once, the fearful, irritable tone. The other voice was male. *Kris.* They were arguing.

The cloud that was Veerle drifted closer to the door, and now she could hear actual words, ragged fragments of the argument.

'No, no, no,' Claudine was saying, over and over again, like an audio clip on eternal replay, and Kris was speaking over her.

'It's not possible,' he said forcefully. 'It's not *possible*.'

'No, no, no.'

'It's not possible.'

'No, no, no.'

Open the door, Veerle wanted to scream, but in her formless state she was unable to make a sound. She wanted desperately to see her mother, to see Kris, but the door remained stubbornly closed. *Open the door!*

The voices fell silent, and for a moment she thought they had actually heard her. Then they began again, but this time the litany had changed.

'You have to choose.'

'It's him or me.'

'You have to choose.'

With horror Veerle realized that they were no longer arguing with each other; now they were addressing her directly.

'It's him or me,' insisted her mother's voice.

I can't choose!

'You *have* to choose.' That was Kris.

Veerle awoke to morning light slanting in between the curtains. Her throat felt tight, as though a cold hand encircled it; her mouth was full of saliva. She rolled onto her side and gazed at the window, letting time and place coalesce around her. For one long moment she thought that bright strip of sunlight was the door opening at last on the two people she longed to see. But the voices were fading. The sun went behind a cloud, and suddenly the blaze of light was simply a dingy-looking windowpane.

I'm not at home, I'm in Ghent. I don't know where Kris is, and Mum . . .

She grimaced, squeezing her eyes shut, but then she opened them again. Even the dull impersonal interior of the bedroom was preferable to the images that lurked behind her eyelids.

It's Saturday, she thought, and sat up.

Geert and Anneke had already left the flat. Anneke wanted to buy baby clothes, and Geert had gone along to carry the bags and buy cups of coffee when Anneke got tired. Veerle ate breakfast standing by the kitchen window: a glass of juice and a pastry from a box she found in the fridge. She looked out of the window at Bijlokevest without really seeing it and thought, *Please God let Bram have found something out.* It was a slim hope, really. Ghent wasn't like the village; it had nearly a quarter of a million inhabitants. The chance of finding one person by asking around was tiny, especially if that person didn't want to be found. *Probably more realistic to let it go*, Veerle thought. *So I've seen her. I know she's alive. Maybe that's enough.*

Only it wasn't.

If I don't find her, I don't have any proof I saw her at all.

She remembered the expressions on the faces of the police officers when she told them she had seen Joren Sterckx. They had pitied her, the ones who didn't think she was making it up to draw attention to herself. If Kris looked at her like that she didn't think she could bear it. Then there was the question of Mevrouw Coppens, Hommel's mother. *Do I tell her I've seen Hommel? She'll probably go straight off and tell Jappe, Hommel's pig of a stepfather, and if he's the reason she left in the first place, maybe that isn't such a great idea. Maybe I should talk to Hommel herself before I go telling anyone.*

Veerle finished the pastry, still gazing out of the window. Then she fetched a jacket from her room and let herself out of the flat.

It was a dry clear morning, quite warm even though it was late September. Veerle considered the tram, and then decided to walk to Sint-Baafsplein, following the Coupure and then the canal that led north to the bridge where she had last seen Hommel.

You never know, she thought.

She reached the bridge without seeing anyone she knew, however. The skyline viewed from the path along the Coupure looked ordinary and undramatic this morning too.

No demons.

Veerle wondered whether it was possible that she had seen nothing more than flickering shadows thrown as something passed in front of the light cast by the streetlamps – a fluttering bird, perhaps. She stared up at the parapets, but nothing moved there now.

After she had crossed the bridge it was a five-minute walk to the square in front of the cathedral, reversing the route along which she had chased Hommel a few days before.

Most of the shops and cafés were open by now, but here and there someone was putting out a menu board or wheeling a rack of cards onto the pavement. Veerle walked quickly, threading her way through the early strollers with her head up. There was a tight little knot of excitement in her stomach.

Don't build your hopes up, she chastised herself. *Bram might not have found out anything at all. What are the chances of this Marnix guy actually knowing something?*

All the same, she couldn't stop herself hoping. When she emerged from Magelein and turned along the tramlines towards the cathedral her heart was thudding. Unconsciously she had picked up the pace, wanting to be at the rendezvous as quickly as possible, and her breath was coming fast now, shuddering through her nostrils. As she passed the foot of the Belfort tower she glanced up. At these close quarters its towering bulk was dizzying to contemplate. It seemed to loom over her, and the motion of the banner that hung outside the great arched doorway, billowing in the breeze, threw her momentarily off balance. She stumbled and looked down at the cobblestones under her feet, steadying herself.

That guy, Daan De Moor – he can't have jumped off there, Veerle thought. The idea was appalling. She could not imagine wanting to be rid of life so badly that you would launch yourself from such a height to sure detonation on the stones below.

The Belfort tower was behind her now and she slowed to a halt, scanning the square for a glimpse of green – Bram's shirt

– amongst the figures who crossed and re-crossed the stones: tourists, locals with shopping bags, workmen.

'Hi,' said a voice next to her, so close that she jumped.

Bram was almost at her elbow. He had on a red shirt over a white T-shirt, not the green one she had been looking for.

Stupid, said Veerle to herself. *He's not going to wear the exact same things every day.*

Otherwise he looked exactly the same as he had the other day: irrepressibly friendly and a little too engaging for comfort, with those wide blue eyes and carelessly tousled blond hair. He looked relaxed and open, and so guileless that it made Veerle suspicious. It occurred to her again that she would not have liked Kris to witness her tête-à-tête with Bram.

'Hi,' she said, trying to inject a brisk and business-like tone into the monosyllable.

'You came,' said Bram. 'I wondered if you'd turn up or not.'

'Yes,' said Veerle. She couldn't very well say, *Of course I did; I'm dying to know if you've found anything out,* so she left it at that.

'You want to get a Coke or something?'

'OK.' Veerle thought she would die of impatience, but she bit it back.

They walked across the square to a little cafeteria. Veerle dug into her jeans pocket for change, but Bram had already fished two Cokes out of the cooler and was paying for them at the counter.

He really is acting like we're on a date, thought Veerle. She chewed her lip.

They went over to a table by the window, looking out onto

the square. As Veerle slid into her seat it was all she could do not to blurt out, *Have you found her?* She watched Bram unhurriedly pulling back the tab on his can of Coke, and she wanted to lunge across the table at him, grab a handful of the red shirt in her fist and shout, *What did Marnix say?* at him. She made herself sit still.

She said, 'Thanks for the Coke,' and then forced herself to wait another moment or two before saying, 'So did you see Marnix?'

'Yeah.' Bram looked at her, his head on one side.

'And?' Veerle was almost choking in her impatience to know.

'I saw him on Wednesday. If you'd given me your number I could have called you.'

'But what did he say?'

'He knew whom I meant right away.' Bram grinned. 'She must have pissed him off pretty badly, whatever she said to him. He's still kind of annoyed about it.'

With a sinking feeling, Veerle said, 'So I guess he didn't get her number, then?'

Bram shook his head. 'Nope.'

That's it, then, thought Veerle. *A dead end.*

'But,' added Bram, 'he has seen her again.'

'Where? Is he sure it was her?'

'You really want to find her, don't you? Yeah, he's sure it was her. She made a big impression on him, I guess. He says he's seen her in a shop, here in the centre. He thinks she was working in there.'

'A shop? What kind of shop?'

'Music. CDs. Vinyl too. It's got some name like . . . I don't know, Muziek City or something. It's only open half the time. Not doing well, I guess, and not surprising really, if all the staff are as rude as your friend is.'

'You know the shop?'

'Sure. It's on . . .' He thought for a moment. 'I can't remember the name of the street. I can take you there, though. Hey,' he added. 'Sit down. At least finish your Coke first.'

Reluctantly Veerle sat down again. She looked at her Coke but didn't touch it. Nervous energy was thrumming through her in waves, like electricity down a wire. She felt as though it might come crackling out of her fingertips at any moment, like blue lightning.

'There's one thing,' added Bram. 'Marnix says her name's not Els Lievens. He heard the guy in the shop calling her Hannah.'

'Hannah?'

Maybe it isn't her. Veerle had a moment of sickening disappointment, and then she thought, *It doesn't mean anything. If she's somehow hiding here, she's not going to use her real name.*

It was no use. She couldn't bear to sit there any longer.

'Bram? I'm sorry, but can we go? I really have to know if it's her.'

She was conscious of the gaze of those blue eyes on her, studying her.

'All right,' said Bram. He pushed away his Coke and got to his feet. 'Look,' he added, 'I'd kind of like to know what this is about, if it really *is* your friend in the music shop.'

'OK,' said Veerle, in a fever to be away. She would have promised him anything, just to get to the shop and see for herself. In her imagination she was already phoning Kris, or if he still wasn't answering she was emailing him with just enough information to make sure he called back.

They left the shop and walked back to Magelein. Veerle was not surprised when Bram led her down Bennesteeg; it was the route Hommel had taken when she was pursuing her. They didn't go as far as the bridge, though. Instead, they took a dogleg down a series of small streets, stopping just short of the canal; when they came to a halt Veerle had a glimpse of its glossy green water between two buildings.

'There,' said Bram, pointing.

Veerle didn't remember ever seeing the shop before, although admittedly she didn't know every street in the city centre. She didn't think she had been down this one. The building was an old one, a once-elegant nineteenth-century creation of red brick with black wrought-iron balconies, four storeys high. At some point an evil-looking shop front had been grafted onto the ground floor. It had been painted matt black like the backstage of a theatre, and indeed it had something of the tawdry impermanent look of stage flats. The name of the shop, MUZIEK CITY, was executed in large pink-and-orange letters in a style that could have been trying to suggest anything from Art Deco to Glam Rock. There was no window display to speak of; behind a couple of faded posters Veerle could see the backs of CD and record racks.

It would be no use trying to see if Hommel was inside from out here, that was very plain. The interior of the shop behind the display racks was as dim and obscure as a cave.

'You're in luck. It's open,' said Bram.

Veerle looked at the door and saw that he was right: it was

half open, not so much inviting as reluctantly allowing customers inside.

'Thanks, Bram,' she said, firmly enough to let him know that she could handle this alone.

He didn't take the hint. As she crossed the street to the music shop, he was at her elbow; the red shirt was a blaze of colour at the edge of her vision.

'Can't you stay out here?' she growled at him out of the corner of her mouth. She didn't wait for his reply, but as she entered the shop she was aware that he had remained outside.

After the autumn sunshine, the interior of the shop was almost dark. Veerle stood just inside the door, letting her eyes adjust to the dim light. Whoever owned the shop appeared to have equipped it entirely with forty-watt bulbs, perhaps working on the assumption that the scruffy décor, like that of a run-down nightclub, was best not exposed to too much light. Music was playing somewhere, but it was so muffled that Veerle could make out nothing except an insistent beat. There was a very faint smell of burning on the air, something sweetish and spicy.

Veerle looked around and saw racks of CDs and vinyl records in dog-eared sleeves. To the right was a wall painted in the same dusty black as the shop front, but with a long strip of mirror at head height. The mirror had probably been intended to create the appearance of greater space inside the shop, but now its blotched and smeared surface merely gave Veerle the impression that she was peering into an adjoining chamber even murkier than the one in which she stood.

To the left was a cash desk, the front of it papered with faded concert posters. It was unattended.

There's no one here, she thought, nonplussed, and then she caught a flicker of movement from the gloom at the very back of the shop, a white hand flitting across the rack of CDs.

Hommel, she thought.

It had to be her. The girl had her back to her, apparently intent on rearranging some of the stock, but with that slim build and sleek pale hair it had to be Hommel, or else her twin. It had not escaped Veerle, either, that the girl had not bothered to turn round to greet her customer, although she must have heard Veerle come in.

Typical, she thought. Still, so much the better; it gave her the opportunity to approach Hommel unawares. She began to move stealthily towards the back of the shop.

Veerle was perhaps three metres from Hommel when the other girl turned to meet her. There was an expression of ironic enquiry on her face, as though she were expecting whoever was approaching her to ask some question of staggering stupidity. It dropped from her features in an instant, replaced with a look of blank horror.

'Hommel . . .' began Veerle, but Hommel wasn't listening. She was frantically looking about her for a way out, and she made as if to lunge past Veerle, heading for the door. Then she checked herself, her eyes wide and panicked. Veerle glanced behind her and saw Bram in the doorway, blocking it. She looked back at Hommel, but Hommel had already turned and was wrenching open a door at the rear of the shop. Veerle hadn't even seen it before; it was painted the same matt black as everything else and blended into the wall almost perfectly. Hommel had dived through the door and slammed it shut behind her before Veerle had had time to react.

Veerle heard fumbling on the other side of the door as Hommel tried to secure it, and flung herself against it. After a couple of seconds of resistance it burst open and she staggered into a narrow hallway. Daylight streamed down from above, showing faded striped wallpaper and worn floorboards. Hommel was already at the other end of the hallway, racing up a flight of wooden stairs painted white so long ago that they had turned a dirty shade of cream.

By the time Veerle started up the stairs, Hommel had turned a corner at the top. Veerle heard her footsteps pounding along the upstairs landing. A second later a door slammed.

Veerle stopped taking the stairs two at a time and stood still, listening. She could hear her own breathing sawing painfully, and the sound of a car passing outside. Inside the building there was nothing. She began to climb the staircase again, running her hand along the banister. It had been painted over many times without the existing coats being removed, and the surface had a strange waxy feel to it.

The upstairs landing was just as shabby as the hallway below. The daylight that streamed through the front and rear windows simply exposed the grimy wallpaper and the chipped and yellowing paintwork. The floors above the shop appeared to be derelict.

Hommel can't hide up here for ever, thought Veerle.

She began to walk along the landing. There were two other storeys above this one, but she didn't think Hommel had gone any higher. Almost at the end of the landing there was a door, and that door was tightly closed. Veerle thought Hommel was inside.

She went up to the door and tried the handle. It was the same as the banister rail; it had been painted over so many times that it was encased in a thick glossy shell. It was difficult to get a good purchase, but after trying to turn it several times, she knew that the door was locked.

Leaning close to the wooden panels, she said, 'Hommel?'

Silence.

If she thinks I'm just going to give up and go away, she's wrong.

'Hommel?'

Veerle banged on the door with the flat of her hand. Then she listened.

At first there was nothing, and then she heard it: the creak of a board. Someone was on the other side of the door, no doubt listening as carefully as she was.

'Hommel,' she said again in a loud voice, 'open the door.'

Still nothing.

Veerle looked at the blank and implacable face of the closed door and felt the hot anger uncoiling inside her, a serpent waiting to strike.

You owe me an explanation, damn it. You owe Kris one. You can't just shut the door in my face and think if you wait long enough I'll go away.

She let loose a volley of blows on the door, hammering it with her fist. 'Hommel! I'm not going away!'

Veerle paused from her hammering and blew strands of dark hair away from her face. She threw back her head and shouted, 'We thought you were *dead*, Hommel.'

If there was anyone else in the building, the owner of the shop for example, they couldn't help hearing her now; she was yelling at the top of her voice. Veerle found that she didn't care. She was determined to know the truth.

'Kris and I risked our necks for you,' she shouted at the door. 'Did you know that?' She took a deep shuddering breath. 'We could have walked away but we didn't. Because it was personal. Because Kris knew you.' She thumped the door again with all her strength, a savage blow that sent pain streaking up her arm to the shoulder. 'We could have *died*. So the least you can do is open the door and talk to me, you – ungrateful – bitch.'

She cradled her hand, rubbing the offended fingers. Her breath was coming in short gasps, as though she had been running at full tilt. She glared at the door as if she could will it to open, but even so she was taken by surprise when she heard the sound of a key being turned in the lock.

The door swung inwards and there was someone standing there, and in the split second before she realized that it wasn't Hommel she had glimpsed the room beyond: comfortless as a squat, with clothes scattered on the bare boards and a mattress on the floor. Then she was staring at him – not Hommel at all, with her cold angular face and severe blonde hair, but a tall young man with untidy dark hair and aquiline features, clad in jeans and a white tank, his feet bare on the floorboards.

It was Kris Verstraeten.

13

Veerle saw it at once. Not all of it: there were parts of the puzzle missing, things that didn't occur to her until later. But enough. She saw the mattress on the floor, the sheets rumpled as though someone had only just got out of bed. She saw Kris's bare feet, his bare arms, and in her mind's eye he was struggling into his jeans while on the other side of the door she thumped and shouted. She looked past him and saw Hommel standing by the curtainless window with her arms wrapped around her slender body, staring defensively through strands of pale blonde hair.

He knew, she thought. *He knew she was here, here and alive. That's why he wasn't taking my calls. He was with her.*

Something was crumbling inside her, painfully.

He knew.

Already that knowledge was running like a shock wave through her memories, overturning everything in its path, going further and further back.

– He knew a week ago; that's when he stopped taking my calls.

– Maybe he tracked her down after we met Fred and Fred told us she was still alive because she sent him the keys back.

– Maybe he's known all along, and this was his way of keeping it going with both of us at once.

'Veerle,' said Kris, and now he was telling her something in a regretful voice; he was saying *sorry* – and that confirmed it for Veerle because he wouldn't be saying sorry if he hadn't done anything wrong. Behind him Hommel had turned her back and was staring out of the window, still hugging herself, waiting for the conversation to be over, for Kris to get rid of Veerle.

Veerle stared wordlessly at Kris, at the face she knew almost as well as the one she saw in the mirror every morning: the bold dark eyes, the fall of dark hair on his forehead, the wide mouth that always seemed to have a hint of an ironic smile hovering about the corners of it, though now he was deadly serious. She looked at him, and it was like looking into the eye of a storm, because on all sides the tempests of anger and jealousy and betrayal were raging, but through it all she knew that she still wanted him, and that hurt more than anything else.

She took a step back, and Kris reached out, trying to take her arm.

Veerle found her tongue. 'Don't touch me!'

'Veerle—'

'Just don't!' She was almost screaming.

'Veerle, is everything OK?' said someone behind her. She turned, and there was Bram at the head of the stairs, as incriminatingly good-looking as usual but without his habitual amiable expression. Now he looked grim and, from the way he was squaring his shoulders, ready to fight. He saw Kris standing in the doorway with his hand reaching for Veerle's arm and his chin came up.

'No,' Veerle blurted out. It was impossible to explain. She was choking on emotions so hot and toxic that they felt radioactive. She stumbled towards Bram, her eyes stinging hotly and her throat suffocatingly tight, as though she were fighting her way through a cloud of poison gas.

When she got to the top of the stairs she glanced back at Kris, and he was still standing in the doorway, motionless. He was staring at her and Bram, and his expression was unreadable.

Veerle made a sound in her throat, halfway between a groan and a sob, and then she plunged down the staircase, not caring whether Bram followed her or not. At the bottom she looked around and ran for the door leading into the dark tunnel that was the shop.

After the sunlit hallway the interior was a gloomy pit and Veerle did not realize that there was anyone in it. She ran the length of the shop between two long racks of CDs, and it was only when she heard someone shout, 'Oi!' that her head turned and she saw him standing in the next aisle: a heavyset man in an overstuffed black T-shirt and jeans, a tuft of beard in the centre of his vast jowls like an oasis in the middle of a fleshy desert. Veerle ignored him and went for the door. As she burst out into the street she heard him bellow, 'Hannah!'

She pelted down the street and dodged round the corner. Then she had to stop to catch her breath, leaning against the stone wall.

A moment later Bram appeared, also breathless.

'The owner, I guess,' he said, coming over to her. '*Klootzak.*'

'Is he following us?' asked Veerle between gasps.

Bram shook his head. 'No. Too unfit, probably.'

Veerle turned to the wall, resting her head on her arms. She didn't want to look at Bram. She didn't want to look at *anything*. She was still trying to blot out from her memory the sight of Kris standing barefoot in the doorway of that room, with the unmade makeshift bed behind him and Hommel standing by the window with her arms around herself. It was too much to take in; it was like trying to swallow down something so big that it would choke you.

Concentrate on the feel of the stones under your hands, the weight of your head on your arms. Don't think.

She felt Bram touch her shoulder.

'Veerle?'

'I'm ...?' She was going to say, *I'm OK*, but it wasn't true. She ground her forehead into her arms as though she could burrow right through the wall and get away.

'Don't you think you'd better tell me what's going on?'

14

She almost told him to go to hell. Why should she tell him anything, after all? She felt so bitter against every member of the male gender at that moment that she could cheerfully have given up their company for ever and gone to live like a nun in a *begijnhof*. Anyway, who *was* Bram? Just some uni student who hung about the Sint-Baafsplein and for all she knew chatted up a different girl every single day.

In the end, though, she didn't tell him where to go. She had to talk to *someone*; the feelings raging inside her were like the noxious contents of a boil, waiting to burst. And who else was there? She couldn't talk to Geert, that was for sure. He hadn't approved of Kris in the first place. Now he'd probably say, *I told you so*. Veerle wasn't remotely close to Anneke. She had her friends back home, her classmates from the high school, like Lisa, but she'd never told them the whole story. She'd never told *anyone* the whole story. She couldn't imagine explaining it all to Lisa down the phone now.

Bram didn't say anything trite. He didn't say anything at all. He just waited.

Eventually Veerle turned a set and dull-eyed face to him. 'OK,' she said.

They went back to the cafeteria near the cathedral. Veerle didn't wait to see what Bram was ordering, and she didn't ask him for anything in particular. She felt curiously hollow but she wasn't sure she wanted to eat or drink anything at all. She went and slid into a seat near the back, away from the other customers, who mostly wanted a view over Sint-Baafsplein.

When Bram came over, carrying a tray in one hand and sliding his change back into his pocket with the other, she was sitting with her elbows on the plastic table-top and her head in her hands. Veerle looked up and saw that he had brought her a glass mug of hot chocolate with cream on it. She started to say that she wasn't hungry or thirsty, but then she looked at the hot chocolate and decided that she was, after all.

'So,' said Bram when he had sat down opposite her, 'it *was* her. Els Lievens.'

'Yes.'

'And the guy?'

'His name is Kris.'

'You know him, then.'

'Yes,' said Veerle in a low voice. She looked down at the glob of cream slowly melting into the chocolate. For a while she watched it dissolving. Then she began to talk.

She told Bram about Silent Saturday, the day before Easter the year she turned seven. How she and Kris had climbed the tower of the Sint-Pauluskerk in the village where she had grown up. They had climbed it to see whether the bell really had flown away to Rome to collect Easter eggs, as the grown-ups always claimed it did. It hadn't, and they had decided to make the most of their disappointing expedition by looking out of the windows, over the village. Gazing down from the tower, they had seen something terrible.

'You've heard of Joren Sterckx, the child murderer?' asked Veerle.

Bram nodded, as she had expected he would: the case was notorious.

'It was *him* you saw?'

Veerle nodded. 'Kris remembers it, but I can't. Well, I didn't think I could . . .'

She picked up the thread again, telling Bram how she had met Kris again years later, the night she had gone to explore a light in the derelict castle, a light that should not have been there. She tried to play the whole thing down, the way she had jumped off the bus on impulse and walked through the castle grounds alone in the wintry dark. At the time it had felt like an adventure; now it seemed terrible, like dancing on a grave. All the same, she was aware of a subtle change in Bram's body language. He shifted in his seat as though impatient, as though her actions that night had spoken to him in some way. He didn't interrupt her, though.

She paused for a moment before she told him what Kris had been doing in the deserted castle. It was very tempting to gloss over the existence of the Koekoeken, as they had done with the police. An online community swapping details of empty properties, and how to get into them: the police would have been *very* interested in that. It was impossible to approach the subject without dropping the other members of the group in it.

Supposedly the web forum that had connected them had been long since erased, but Veerle knew quite well that once something was out there in cyberspace it was pretty much impossible to delete it altogether. It was a lot safer for every-one to think that she and Kris were a couple of bored thrill-seekers who'd had the evil luck to cross paths with a dangerous lunatic looking for someone to use as target practice.

Lying – or at least, lying by implication, by neglecting to tell the police everything – still weighed on Veerle's conscience. *Still,* she told herself, *the guy is dead, whoever he was – Joren Sterckx or his twin. They found the body. He's not going to shoot anyone else where he's gone.*

She looked at Bram, trying to decide what to tell him, try-ing to work out how far she trusted him. It was hard to see how she could explain about Hommel without explaining the rest of it. Hommel had been the fourth person to vanish, at least the fourth that they knew about; the others had been Vlinder – the girl in the lake – her real name Valérie Renard, a software engineer called Egbert Visser and Clare, the daughter of an expat family. It was that pattern, the con-nection with the Koekoeken, either through membership or through the houses, that had made them fear the worst when Hommel disappeared. Otherwise, well – if your boyfriend's ex suddenly went off, you'd probably be pleased, Veerle thought. You wouldn't move heaven and earth to track them down.

What's Bram going to do with the information anyway? she reasoned to herself. *I can make him promise not to tell anyone, and if he does, who's going to believe it? They'll probably think it's another of these urban legends, like demons lurking on the rooftops of Ghent, throwing people to their deaths. Without names and dates and places it might just be that, a made-up story.*

She took a deep breath, looked Bram in the eye, and told him everything.

'So this girl, Els, or whatever you call her, Hommel – you thought she was dead too, right up until you saw her in Sint-Baafs?' asked Bram. He had been leaning forward across the table towards her, straining to take in every word of the story, but now he sat back with a big sigh. 'Shit,' he said.

'Even her mother didn't know where she was,' Veerle pointed out.

'And the guy at the shop, Kris?'

Veerle avoided his gaze. 'I don't know. I'm not sure when I last spoke to him' – that was a lie; she could have named the day and hour – 'but up until then I could have sworn he didn't know.' She dug her fingers into her dark hair, raking back the strands. 'Maybe he's known for ages,' she said, trying and failing to keep the bitter note out of her voice.

'And you and he were—'

'Not any more, it seems,' cut in Veerle. 'I guess that's why Hommel ran away. She knew if I found out I'd want to kill the pair of them.' Involuntarily she clenched her fists. 'I can't believe it,' she said. 'It was her disappearance that made it personal. When the group shut down, the whole thing would have ended, if there *was* anything going on. We still weren't sure then. But Kris *knew* her. He didn't want to discount the possibility that someone had done something to her and got away with it. So we used ourselves as bait, for God's sake, to get him to show himself.' Impulsively she pushed back her sleeve and showed Bram the scar on her left arm. 'You remember at the wall, how I fell off three times? That's why. I broke my arm and a whole lot of other stuff climbing down the castle wall, trying to get away from that guy.' She pulled the sleeve down again with angry energy. 'I'm still not as strong as I was before.'

'Keep practising. It'll come back.'

'Maybe.' She scowled.

Bram sat in silence for a little while. Then he said, 'The killer – who did the police think it was?'

'They don't know. The body was really badly burned. He'd doused the whole place in petrol.' Veerle shrugged. 'They didn't think it was Joren Sterckx, though.'

'And you? What do you think?'

'Well, it can't be him, if he died in prison.' She sighed. 'But I saw him from the gallery in the castle, before the fire started. I had a really good look at him, and I was so sure it was him. It was like . . . I don't know, like the years just rolled back or something, and all of a sudden I remembered. I recognized him.' Veerle shook her head. 'When they found out I'd been in the village the day he killed that boy, they just assumed it was because of that. Either I was sort of scarred by seeing him, or I was just making it up.'

'And he's definitely dead?'

'The police said he was.'

'Could it have been someone that looked like him?'

Veerle looked Bram in the eye, and her expression was grim. 'There's no one who looks like Joren Sterckx, believe me.'

A shark, she thought. *That's what he reminded me of. A great blunt-headed, dead-eyed killing machine. A sledge-hammer of muscle and bone.* She shuddered.

Aloud, she said, 'I hurt myself pretty badly when I fell off the castle wall. I had concussion as well. So maybe I did get things mixed up in my head.'

'But you don't think so,' said Bram.

'No,' said Veerle finally. 'I don't think so. But I can't explain it. I saw a dead man.'

'Well,' said Bram, 'whoever you saw, he's definitely dead now, if they found the body.'

'Yes,' said Veerle. She didn't tell him that she sometimes lay awake at night in the little second bedroom at Geert's flat, the perspiration cooling on her skin, listening for a stealthy tread in the hallway or a rattle at the door or – God forbid – a dark shape at the window, however impossible it was. *If I saw a dead man walking, then anything is possible.* She found it hard not to think of Joren as something more than human, something malevolent and implacable.

'He's dead,' she said.

'So,' said Bram after a moment, 'that's why you moved to Ghent? To get away from where it happened?'

Silence stretched out between them.

'No,' said Veerle eventually. 'It wasn't that.'

When she didn't elaborate Bram said, 'Look, you don't have to tell me.'

'I know,' said Veerle. She looked at him and then she looked down at her hands. 'I'd like to, though.' She sighed. 'My mum died.'

'Shit, I'm sorry.' Bram sounded stricken.

He probably wishes he hadn't asked, thought Veerle. All the same, she really *did* want to tell him now. She wanted to get it off her chest; she wanted to put it all into words and see if it seemed any better than the way she remembered it.

'It happened when I was in hospital,' she said. 'I was pretty much out of it for a day or two, and when I woke up my dad and his girlfriend were there, and Mum wasn't. I kind of knew something was wrong. She was such a worrier, and she hated my dad too. There was no way she wouldn't have been there, and no way she would have wanted *him* there, either.' She shook her head. 'I didn't want to know what had happened at first. I thought maybe . . .' She drew in breath, shuddering. 'I thought she had killed herself.'

'But she . . . ?'

'No, she didn't.' Veerle sighed. 'It was an accident. A stupid, stupid accident.' She glanced at Bram. 'The thing is, she worried about just about everything. When I was a kid, every time I got sick she thought it was meningitis or pneumonia. She used to go round the house every night switching off every single thing at the wall in case it started a fire. And it wasn't just stuff like that, stuff that could happen, even if it was a bit unlikely. She worried about completely crazy things too, like a block of ice falling from an aeroplane. She spent her whole life worrying about something like that happening, and then she had this accident, and it was one thing she just hadn't thought about at all.' Veerle took a deep breath. 'She was out on the street – I guess she was probably waiting to cross the road or something – and a lorry got too close to the kerb.'

'She got run over?'

Veerle shook her head. 'Not even that. The wing mirror hit her on the side of the head. She had a massive bleed into the brain and she just . . . died.'

'God, Veerle, I'm sorry.'

Veerle wasn't listening. She said, 'You know, when I heard what had happened, it was almost a relief in a way. Is that awful? I was so afraid she'd done it herself.' She rubbed her fingers across the plastic surface of the table, drawing invisible hieroglyphs. 'I was afraid she'd done it because of me.'

Bram was silent; she wondered whether she had shocked him. *Too late to go back now.*

'I've thought about it a lot,' she told him. 'And now I don't feel relieved any more. Mum knew what had happened. I mean, she didn't know all of it, but she knew I was in hospital. I think maybe she didn't look out like she normally would have done. She was always so careful. I think she was upset and she didn't look out.'

'You don't know that,' said Bram.

'No,' said Veerle, and she looked him in the eye. 'I don't.'

15

At a little past one a.m. the man who was Death left his hiding place and took to the streets of Ghent.

The night favoured a mission like his. He felt his purpose unfurl around him like great black wings. Pain bit deeply into his limbs, a searing agony, as though his body were red-hot iron, forged in a glowing furnace, prodded by grinning demons. It would fade as he moved through the chilling dark, he knew; the liquefied white heat that ran through his veins would cool and he would solidify into something almost human. His purpose urged him on, deadly and implacable, like a dark soul driving the ravaged body.

He slowly descended the flights of stairs from his eyrie. The building was deserted, as it always was when the shop below was closed. The shop sold expensive gifts – hand-made soaps and scented candles and dainty useless ornaments in cream and silver. It smelled of lavender and roses and cocoa. The staff never ventured above the ground floor: they had no reason to brave the creaky stairs and dusty rooms of the upper storeys. There was never any interest in renting them, either. Who wanted an expensive flat that had to be accessed through a shop? He was able to hide up there undisturbed, baleful as a wasp's nest under the eaves.

He let himself out through the fire escape at the back. It was good to feel the cool night breeze on his face, to feel air and space all around him. He always kept the roller shutters down on the top floor: opening and closing them might have attracted attention, and they needed to be closed at night to prevent anyone seeing light within. Coming outside was like leaving a dark and stifling cave.

He limped down the steps, the pain flaring and smouldering, burrowing redly into his joints. The stiffness, the creaking articulation of his limbs, the hotness: he felt like a brass automaton, exuding scalding steam with every heavy step. Down he went, down, and out into the street.

The city was not dark, not in the way of the countryside and villages. There were always streetlamps; there were always lights left burning uselessly in the windows of shops. The trams would stop running for the night very soon, but here was one of the very last rattling its way down the street, brightly lit and empty. Many of the ancient landmarks of Ghent were floodlit all through the night, the lights coming on at dusk and only fading with the dawn. The great bell tower of Sint-Baafs cathedral was a splendid golden monolith against the night sky.

Death walked the cobbled streets, and as he strode onwards, stepping out with greater and greater ease and confidence, he felt his strength growing. The pain that glowed like red-hot coals in his limbs gradually cooled and almost, *almost* died. His footsteps ate up the ground; behind him the silent streets folded up like origami and vanished. There was nothing in the world except him and his goal, and the space between them was dwindling like the last grains of sand running through an hour glass. Time was indeed running out for his target.

Let it be tonight, he said to himself. *Let it be now.*

From time to time he glanced up at the old buildings as he passed, searching with glittering eyes for signs of movement on the rooftops and parapets, daring them to show themselves, daring them to try and stop him.

Demons. Let them take human form; he knew what they were. And in human form they were vulnerable; a knife would kill them, or a fall from the roof to the cobbles below. Iron and salt would prevent them from returning.

He passed down Sint-Michielshelling, crossing the canal by the Sint-Michielsbrug. It was a less direct route than crossing it at Hoornstraat. He would have to double back upon himself, rounding the massive bulk of the Sint-Michielsplein, the great grey stone church with its stump of a tower. The bridge was well-lit, but it had the great advantage that it was wide. He need not pass within close range of any other person, should there still be anyone wandering the streets at this late hour, anyone who might gaze too long at his seamed face and blazing eyes, and remember them later.

It gave him some small satisfaction too to pass within the shadow of the Sint-Michielskerk. On the bridge was an iron statue of the saint himself, the Angel of Death, preparing to slay a dragon that writhed under his armoured feet. It looked like a dragon, with its scaly tail and leathery wings, but he knew what it really was: a demon.

He glanced up at it as he passed, and he could *feel* the blow that was about to descend upon the struggling creature; he could feel the weight of the sword in his hand and the rush of air as his arm descended in a great arc, slicing with deadly force. *Death*, he thought; *the person who made that statue understood what a glorious thing it is*. He would have liked to pour it out upon the sleeping city like a floodgate bursting, let it rage through the ancient streets in torrents.

He did not let himself be distracted from the task in hand, however. Death is not only strong and implacable, he is wily. How else could he be sure of taking each one of his victims, no matter where they hid, no matter what subterfuge they attempted, whether it took five years or a hundred and five?

He had rounded the church now and was moving down Onderbergen towards his goal, silent and ominous, like the drifting smoke of a burning.

He passed ornamental trees and close-clipped hedges, and then the façades of buildings, brick and stucco, their big windows dark. None of it interested him; he was looking for something specific.

This was not his first attempt and he knew that it might come to nothing, as the others had. He knew that, and yet he felt a growing conviction that this was the time, at last; he could feel it *preparing* to happen, like an increase in atmospheric pressure building up to thunder.

And he was meticulous; he would search Onderbergen from end to end and then he would visit every one of the surrounding streets. If it was to be found, he would find it.

And he did. There it was: a sleek black Audi, polished to such a high shine that it gleamed like a bubble. As if its outward appearance were not ostentatious enough, the parking was deliberately careless: much of Onderbergen was punctuated with bollards designed to prevent anyone leaving their vehicle on the street, but the owner of the Audi had simply pulled up onto the pavement on the corner of an intersection where there was no bollard, and left it there. There was less risk of being booked by the police if you left your car there at, say, 11.30 p.m., and removed it again at 4.30 a.m., of course. Or if the police recognized your car and tactfully ignored it.

These considerations were of no consequence. The important thing was that the driver of the car was here, and not at his well-protected villa with its subterranean car park and state-of-the-art security system. Here he was almost as vulnerable as he would have been on the open street. There were many ways in which Death might gain access to him.

The front door of the apartment block was an old-fashioned wooden one, with a slot for letters in the middle rather than a box attached to the wall outside or embedded in it. It was a small slot, perhaps thirty centimetres long and four high, but it was enough. There only needed to be one small breach in the building's defences, like a tear in a hazmat suit.

The hallway inside had some kind of matting on the floor, and there was a little wooden console supporting a large and elegant display of dried flowers, subtly coloured, beautifully arranged and tinder dry. These things were no secret; anyone who passed the block regularly would be bound to see the door open now and again as someone carried something in or out – a delivery, or shopping, or a suitcase.

The man who was Death stood before the door and gazed up at the parapet of the building, far above. There was no movement up there, no deceptively human form crouched there, watching with inhuman eyes. Now was the right time; the demons had scattered, defeated.

There was no need for ritual. The man he had come to kill had escaped Death too long, but he was as mortal as any other man. Iron and salt were not required to seal him in his grave. A blade would have been enough. Fire would be enough.

He had fire with him, corked in a bottle. He drew out the cork and put the neck of the bottle to the letter slot cut into the door, as tenderly as a priest putting a chalice of sacramental wine to a parishioner's lips. The liquid passed easily into the house through the slot, with a sound like the falling of rain or blood. His nostrils flared at its evil perfume.

With great care he lit the match and let it fall inside the letter slot. The petrol went up with a great sigh that lit up the window above the door like a pumpkin lantern. The matting was swift to kindle, and then the dried flowers went up, orange and yellow like the spread tail of a phoenix. Flames leaped at the staircase, adoring the wooden banisters, curling lovingly around them. Already it would be almost impossible for anyone to escape that way, even if they awoke before the smoke took them.

He watched for as long as he dared, the lines in his face deeply graven by the glare of the fire. There were four floors in the burning building; as the smoke and flames moved up them, he could be more and more sure of success.

The man he had come for was dead, or as good as.

For the certain deaths of other people in the block he felt no remorse. He had brought them a blessing, not a misfortune: an end to the suffering of existence.

And God shall wipe away all tears from their eyes . . . neither shall there be any more pain.

He looked at the flames and felt only joy.

Very soon now the orange glare and the sound of cracking glass would alert the neighbours. The building was beginning to look like one of the quaint little ceramic houses that tourist shops sold, with a space for a tea-light inside so that it could be lit from within. Flames flickered and danced behind glass that could not hold for very much longer before it blew out, and the building inhaled, drawing in more and more oxygen to feed the fire.

It was *glorious*, thought Death, and then he turned and vanished into the night.

16

Veerle slept badly, hovering just under the surface of sleep as though she were drifting through dark murky water. She woke several times, retaining nothing but fragments of unpleasant dreams – dreams of fleeing or stifling or scream-ing. Once she thought she heard sirens some distance away, perhaps in the north or east, faint and urgent. The sound still chilled her, reminding her of darkness and smoke and break-ing glass, and the long drop that had broken her like a teacup dropped onto quarry tiles. She stretched out her limbs in the dark, reassuring herself of their integrity.

The sirens had fallen silent and she wondered whether she had dreamed them, but in the morning she discovered that Anneke had heard them too. Geert had heard nothing; he had slept like the bear he resembled, deep in hibernation.

Over breakfast Veerle checked her phone for messages. One from *Bram De Wulf*. Nothing from Kris. She sighed, and then wished she hadn't; Geert glanced up from his coffee and pastry and gave her an enquiring look.

I know what he's thinking. He's thinking it's Kris and now he's considering telling me not to see Kris. Again.

She flashed Geert a quick tight smile, hoping to put him

off, and was relieved when he went back to his pastry. She looked down at the phone again, at the message from Bram waiting to be opened, and for a moment she almost wished she hadn't given him her number. It had been hard to refuse, after she'd spent an hour pouring her heart out to him. All the same, seeing his name there on the screen just underlined the absence of any message from Kris.

She touched the screen to open the message.

Wall tonight, 6 p.m.?

Six p.m. That was still eight hours away, but somehow she'd thought she would have more time to think.

Do I want to see Bram? she wondered, and it was a question she couldn't answer. Veerle wasn't even sure what she would have answered if the question had been *Do I want to see Kris?* What she actually wanted was impossible; she wanted yesterday not to have happened, or for Hommel to have been alone in the shabby flat above the music shop. When it came down to it, you could go a lot further back than that. She wished she had not had to move to Ghent at all, she wished that Claudine, her mother, difficult though she could be, were still alive, she wished she and Kris were still having fun exploring the unbelievably fabulous houses of absent rich ex-pats. One thing she did know: she didn't want to see Kris if he had Hommel hanging off his arm. She didn't want to hear his excuses, and she didn't want to see Hommel's face, the expression as cool and bland as milk but hiding the inevitable smugness of victory.

None of this was helping. *Do I go tonight or not?* she thought. Her finger hovered over the tiny screen.

There seemed to be 101 reasons to go, and as many not to

go, the chief one being that Bram might take her acceptance the wrong way. He might think she wanted to start something, whereas actually she wanted a lot of time to digest the fact that something else had ended. *Maybe I need to tell him that*, she thought.

The thing was, she *did* like Bram. He was friendly and kind, and (she reflected ruefully) a very good listener. It was just that starting something with him or anyone else right now didn't feel possible; it was like being offered a glass of wine when you were desperately thirsty and dying for a drink of cold water. There was nothing wrong with the wine, but it was the water you longed for.

Do I mean never? she wondered, but she couldn't even answer that question.

She thought that she had decided to text Bram and tell him she wasn't coming, and half a minute later she thought that she would text him and say she *would* come.

For the hundredth time since she had moved in with Geert and Anneke she wished that there was someone she could confide in, someone who didn't have an angle of their own on the situation. She imagined talking it over with Lisa, the friend she had left behind in the old place.

Go, Lisa would say. Veerle could almost hear her saying it, in her mind. *You can always tell him you're not ready to start anything new. And anyway, it's not like you're being unfaithful to Kris. He's just dumped you, Veerle.*

Veerle texted Bram back and said, *OK, 6 p.m.* No kisses, no smiley face, no initial. Then she slid the phone into her jeans pocket and finished her breakfast.

* * *

Later she took the tram part of the way to the climbing wall, and walked the rest. Although it was a Sunday evening, the tram was relatively full. Two women in their late fifties or early sixties were standing behind Veerle and she heard one of them say, 'The whole street was taped off.'

'They still don't know exactly who was in there,' said the other one in a tone of grim satisfaction.

Veerle had to ring the bell, and that meant leaning between the two women to press the button. They fell silent, regarding her with faint disapproval, and said nothing more until she had got off the tram.

When she got to the climbing wall she went straight to the desk, deliberately not scanning the place for a glimpse of Bram. She couldn't imagine giving him a dizzy little wave. She paid, and just as she was putting her bank card back into her wallet, there he was at her elbow, looking as disconcertingly good-looking as usual in a blue T-shirt that matched his eyes and a pair of loose-fit climbing trousers.

'Hi,' he said.

Instantly Veerle thought, *This was a mistake; I shouldn't have come.*

But there was nothing for it. She *had* come; she might as well get on with it.

She gave Bram a tight smile. 'Hi.'

After she'd changed her shoes she followed him through the bar into the climbing area. There were three halls, with a mixture of levels, including a bouldering area and an intimidating competition face. Normally Veerle was on her own, so she mostly stuck to bouldering unless she could find another lone climber prepared to belay her on one of the higher climbs in exchange for her doing the same for them. Having Bram to climb with was a definite advantage; she could tackle anything she liked, even the twelve-metre climb to the very top of the highest section.

After a while she forgot to feel self-conscious about being there with him. The climbing itself, the solution of a vertical problem, drew her in and absorbed her totally. For once the arm that had been broken wasn't bothering her. Nothing hurt. She felt as though the tracery of tiny aches and pains that so often covered her body like a roadmap had dropped away like the shed skin of a snake. She felt *good*.

Veerle shifted her weight from side to side, weaving her way up the wall. She didn't have to tell Bram when to take in the slack rope or when to let it out a little. He just watched her from below and did the right thing without being asked. In spite of the exertion of climbing it was relaxing in a way, putting herself in someone else's hands. If she fell, she knew absolutely that he would hold her up.

She didn't fall, however. Some of the power that had seemed to burst out of her when she fell from the castle tower had flowed back in. When her rock shoes touched the thick crash mat again she was grinning from ear to ear.

After that she belayed Bram while he climbed, and then they spent some time in the bouldering area.

Just before seven o'clock they took a break and went to the bar for cold drinks.

'That was *great*,' said Veerle as they sat down.

'You were good,' Bram told her sincerely.

They chatted for a while – about Bram's course (his family was from Ghent but he had digs of his own), about the routes they had just done. Veerle couldn't help enthusing: it was so *good* to feel like this, as though she had suddenly surfaced from the depths of a black and stinking lake to feel sunlight and air on her upturned face. She had got out of the habit of being happy, it seemed, and now she remembered the feeling. The shock of yesterday's discovery had been terrible, and yet something of the kind had been hanging over her for more than a week, ever since Kris stopped taking her calls. To get away from that feeling of lowering misery for a while was such a blessed relief, and anyway she couldn't help it; she felt like the shoot of a plant that has lain buried in the cold black earth all through winter, blindly growing upwards, seeking the light.

After a while she realized that Bram wasn't saying much. She was chattering on but his replies were slower in coming. He looked at her thoughtfully, as though he were summing her up.

Veerle stopped talking. 'What?' she said.

'You want to climb some more, or are you finished for tonight?' asked Bram.

'I'm not tired,' said Veerle. 'Well, not very.'

For a few moments Bram didn't say anything at all. He seemed to be considering. 'You've climbed outdoors, right?'

'Kind of,' said Veerle. 'Not cliffs or anything. I've done a fancy villa and the front of an apartment in Brussels.' She grimaced ruefully. 'And a castle, only I messed that one up a bit.'

Bram leaned towards her across the little table. 'It's going to be dark soon. The sun's going down. You want to go and do something now, before it gets too dark?'

Veerle looked at him. 'How do you mean, do something?'

'Outdoors. Want to climb a few cliffs?'

Veerle put her head on one side. 'Cliffs?'

'Yep.'

'In the middle of Ghent?'

'Uh-huh.' Bram was looking at her through those unruly strands of sun-bleached hair, and although he was grinning there was something serious in his expression.

This is some sort of big deal to him, thought Veerle. She was puzzled: she couldn't think what he meant. Cliffs? Ghent was as flat as a chessboard.

'Okaaay,' she said cautiously.

'Have you finished that?' asked Bram, nodding at her drink. 'Then let's go. Now is the best time.'

A couple of minutes later they were out on the street and Veerle was having to trot to keep up with Bram. He wasn't giving anything away and she couldn't think of a way to frame a question to make him explain.

The evening was cool without actually being cold, and dry. The sun was very low, giving the sky a lurid tint.

Veerle thought they had been walking for about ten minutes when she saw a landmark she recognized: the great bulk of the moated Gravensteen castle, over eight hundred years old, with two flags flying from the turrets, the yellow and black lion of Flanders and the black and white lion of Ghent.

This was not, apparently, their goal; Bram continued past the fortified gate, now closed to visitors for the night, and led Veerle into the network of streets that lay beyond it. Here there were fewer tourist shops and grocery stores and tobacconists. Instead there were very old houses, exquisitely kept, some with window boxes or trailing ivy, and occasional wine bars or restaurants with snug dark interiors.

Bram turned a corner into a side street and stopped. 'Here,' he said.

Veerle stared at him, and then she looked around, glancing up the silent street to see whether anyone else was about, and then up at the nearby buildings.

Does he mean what I think he means?

'We have to be quick – on the first bit, anyway,' said Bram. 'I'll go first, you follow.'

He shot a quick glance to either side, satisfying himself that they were alone. Then he turned to the wall and began to climb.

The location was well chosen. Many of the buildings along this street had three or four storeys and were faced with stucco, presenting a smooth and intimidatingly high front. This one had only two storeys topped with corbie steps so that the façade tapered almost to a point. It was very old, with rough stone lintels to the windows and various pieces of ironwork, both ornamental and supportive. Even better, there was a glass-sided lamp attached to the bricks by a very sturdy metal support. It could have been designed for climbing.

Bram was up it in double-quick time, and then he was crouching on the roof behind the corbie steps, beckoning for Veerle to follow.

Veerle stood for a moment looking up at him, silhouetted against the evening sky. Half-formed thoughts were whirling about her brain like a flock of birds wheeling through the sky. She was conscious of the pulse beating fast at her throat.

Most of all she was conscious of the *itch* to do it, to climb up after Bram.

She glanced around; still no one in sight. Up she went, ascending without too much difficulty, although she could feel a little strain in her muscles now. *Out of practice climbing buildings*, she thought. She would not have tired so soon – before.

She climbed over the corbie steps at the top and crouched next to Bram on the sloping roof, breathing rapidly. Bram raised a finger to his lips, indicating that they should remain silent.

A moment or two later, Veerle heard voices and footsteps in the street below.

Verdomme, she thought. *Did they see me?*

She telegraphed the question to Bram, but he shook his head. When the footsteps had died away he rose from his crouch and indicated that they should go on. Neither of them spoke. Veerle had a thousand questions she was dying to ask Bram, but she made herself keep silent; this close to the edge of the façade there was a risk of being heard by people below. Instead she looked about her.

The house they had climbed was the smallest in the street; on either side the buildings overtopped it. One of them was impossible to scale, being high and sheer and virtually featureless, but on the other side there was a narrow flat area less than a metre wide and an actual metal ladder bolted to the wall, leading up to the roof of the neighbouring house – a fire escape perhaps, or an access ladder for working on the tiles. Bram went up it swiftly and silently, and Veerle followed.

At the top they stepped onto a flat roof covered with sheets of dull grey metal. The new landscape revealed at this level was surprising. Although some of the roofs were sloping, particularly those facing the street, a startling number of them were flat, although of slightly different heights, so that the whole effect was something like an enormous set of child's building blocks, stacked up unevenly together. Veerle measured them with her eyes and quickly saw the potential. With a little effort you could go half the length of the street along the rooftops, perhaps further. Now her heart was really racing; she couldn't wait to do it. She stepped forward and Bram grasped her arm.

'Hold on,' he said in a low voice. He pointed at an adjoining section of roof, a flat area some metres square. It was shining darkly with collected rainwater. 'Don't go on that one,' he told her. 'I don't trust it. If you have to cross it, use the stone bit at the edge.'

'OK,' said Veerle. She looked at the wet black surface. 'Why don't you lead, then? Or are we stopping here?'

'I thought we'd go sightseeing,' said Bram.

'Sightseeing?'

'Yeah.' He tilted his head to indicate the direction they should take. 'Coming?'

Veerle followed him across the grey metal rooftop. They trod carefully; the roof seemed to be perfectly sound but it was inadvisable to blunder across it with thunderous footsteps.

'They might ignore noises if they thought it was cats or birds,' said Bram, meaning the people in the houses below, 'but not if they think it's elephants.'

Veerle stifled a snort of laughter.

They clambered over a small parapet and onto the next roof. Here there were a couple of skylights that they had to skirt round. Veerle could see why Bram had chosen this time of day; the light was fading, giving them a little cover, but it was not so dark that you couldn't see what you were doing. Those glass skylights were as treacherous as rotten well-covers; step on them in the dark and you could be in for a long drop and a painful landing. She could feel her body quickening, as though some internal metronome had been set to a higher speed; the old exhilaration was back, the joy of doing something that she shouldn't be doing in a place where she shouldn't be, of seeing and experiencing things that most people never dreamed of. The cool air on her face and neck, the glorious pink and orange of the evening sky, the murmur of distant traffic, voices, footsteps from the streets below, like waves breaking against the foot of the brick island on which they stood: all of it seemed intense and real in a way that the rest of life *never* was.

Bram was climbing a wall perhaps a metre and a half high, forming one side of a brick-built block with a grimy window on its other visible face. With the glowing coral tints of the sky behind him, Veerle saw him as a dark silhouette, tall and broad-shouldered, and for a moment she forgot that he wasn't Kris.

She felt a rush of emotion so intense that it was like gazing into the sun – hot, white, blinding. The next second it had shrivelled into cinders.

It's not Kris.

The cold bleak disappointment was as acute as the joy of recognition had been.

Of course it's not Kris. How could it be Kris? He's with her.

Veerle had to compose her features, try to look cheerful as she clambered up onto the brick block next to Bram; she couldn't bear the idea of fending off his questions if he noticed that something was wrong.

But Bram was unexpectedly preoccupied. He was squatting on the rough grey surface, one hand outstretched to touch it, his expression thoughtful. Veerle followed his gaze and saw that there was a narrow gutter running along the side of the block. The nearside edge of it was clogged with a white rime. Bram put his forefinger gingerly into it; it came away coated with white powder. He muttered something under his breath, then dusted his fingers against his trouser leg.

'What's that?' asked Veerle.

'I'm not sure without tasting it,' said Bram, 'but I think it's salt.' He glanced around, still rubbing his hand absent-mindedly against his leg.

'Salt?' repeated Veerle. She had a vague recollection of someone saying something about salt; something that had surprised her. But she couldn't remember exactly, and she couldn't work up much curiosity about it; she was still too full of the leaden misery of missing Kris. Still, she was grateful that Bram's attention was focused elsewhere, that he wasn't looking at her face and seeing the woe written there.

'Yeah.' Bram was still looking down at the gutter. 'It's weird. I've seen it before, only not here. A line of it, like this, only on a roof on another block.'

'Maybe it's . . .' Veerle thought about it. 'Maybe it's to keep insects off, or something.'

'Off what? There's nothing growing up here.'

For a moment they both considered in silence. Then Bram shrugged dismissively. 'Well, who knows?' He sat down, sprawling comfortably on the flat roof. 'I didn't come up here to look at a pile of salt, anyway.'

Veerle sat down too, but she was careful not to sit too close to him. She still felt a kind of cold ache inside her, as though she had suffered some kind of shock. The thought of pressing herself close to him, of his putting an arm round her, was impossible. Instead she settled herself cross-legged on the roof, leaving space between them so that someone else could have sat there, had there been anyone else up there but themselves.

'Look,' said Bram, pointing. 'That was what I wanted you to see.' Outlined against the lurid sunset was the uncompromising bulk of the Gravensteen castle, rugged and massive as a mountain peak, the castellated walls like rows of teeth fixed into the belly of the sky.

'It looks like a mountain,' said Veerle. Even with that dragging feeling of sadness gnawing at her, she couldn't help being a little impressed.

'Yeah.'

'That was what you meant when you talked about cliffs,' said Veerle. 'Cliffs and mountains made out of metal and bricks and glass.'

Bram looked at her, and in the fading light she saw the flash of white teeth as he grinned. 'The mountain ranges of Ghent,' he said.

17

Bram kept looking at her; he didn't turn back to the sunset and the great dark hulk of the Gravensteen. Half his face was gilded by the setting sun, the rest in darkness. Veerle felt as though she should be remembering something half forgotten. The way Bram was looking at her was making her self-conscious; she felt a warmth in her face and tried to find something to say to fill the speaking silence.

'This is amazing,' she said eventually, and actually she meant it; the sunset behind the castle was impressive.

'Yeah.'

'How did you get into this?'

'Friends. But it's not like your Koekoeken in Brussels. It's not organized. It's just something some people do.' Bram shrugged easily. 'Sometimes Marnix does, and there are other people I know. We see each other at the wall or wherever, and sometimes we pass on information. That's about it.'

'So places like this are your cliffs?'

'Yeah, but you know, it's not just about climbing up, doing difficult routes or whatever. It's about being in a different place.' He pointed back over his shoulder with a thumb. 'That house we climbed up – we call it *de ladder* because it's so easy to do. Once you're up here, it's' – he thought about it – 'just different. You get a new perspective on everything. It's the last unspoiled part of Ghent. One place the Brits and the Dutch don't get to go. Sometimes in summer I lie on the roof of some building and look down over the edge, and you can see them all swarming around like ants, everyone going *click, click, click* with their digital cameras. Up here, it's peaceful. Sometimes I spend the whole night up here.'

'The *whole night*?'

Bram nodded. 'I have a bivvy bag. Easier to move than a tent, and not so obvious. But there are people who pitch tents up here, on the higher roofs where nobody's overlooking them.'

'That's amazing,' said Veerle. She glanced around. 'Do you ever spend the night here, on this block?'

'Not here,' he said. 'I come here to look at that.' He nodded towards the Gravensteen. 'I'd like to do that one day. I don't mean go round it during the day with all the foreign tourists. Anyone can do that. I mean at night. I'd like to go up to the top of the battlements and see the whole city lit up, and the three towers floodlit. If it was a good night I'd sleep out up there.'

'That would be unbelievable.'

Bram shot her a glance. 'If I did it, you could come too. It means all night, though.'

'All night?' said Veerle cautiously.

'Has to be,' Bram told her. 'You can't just nip in and out of there. They knew what they were doing, back in the twelfth century. That place is impossible to break in or out of. We'd have to be in there when they locked up.'

'I don't know,' said Veerle. 'I'd have to find some excuse for being out all night, and that could be really difficult.'

'Your dad?'

'Yes,' said Veerle. She hesitated. There was something on her mind, something she wanted to ask. 'Bram,' she said slowly, 'when you're up here on the rooftops, have you ever seen . . .' She paused, thinking, *This is going to sound crazy. I can't say, Have you ever seen anything that might be* demons *up here, Bram?*

Bram was looking at her, waiting for her to go on.

'. . . anything strange?' she finished, self-consciously.

'Like what?'

'There are these stories going around,' said Veerle. 'About things being seen on the rooftops.'

'Demons,' supplied Bram. He said it so matter-of-factly that for a moment Veerle was thrown. He put his head back, gazing at the sky. 'Yes, I've heard those stories.' Then he looked at her. 'Where did you hear them? It's usually the really old people, the ones who've always lived in Ghent, who go on about that stuff.'

'There's this girl in my class. She's called Suki. She's been telling people she's actually seen the demons on the rooftops, and they think she's completely insane, or else trying to get a rise out of everyone.'

'Well,' said Bram casually, 'she probably has seen someone up here.'

Veerle stared at him. '*You . . . ?*'

'Well, not just me.' Bram was grinning now. 'The others too. And I'm not saying some of them aren't a bit strange.'

'That's not what I meant,' said Veerle, laughing.

'I know. They're just people, though. But it's kind of useful, that thing about the demons on the rooftops, because if anyone sees anything, people react the way you said they did to Suki. They just think the person has a screw loose. Marnix, he actually got some of those plastic demon horns, the ones you get for fancy dress, and wore them a few times when he was up here.' Bram laughed. 'Probably gave a few people a heart attack.'

'So this whole story about the demons – did one of you start it?'

'Oh no,' said Bram, shaking his head. 'There have been rumours going round about it for . . .' He thought. 'Over five hundred years.'

'*Five hundred years?*'

'Like I said, we didn't start it. It's just . . . convenient.'

'So who did?' asked Veerle.

'You sure you want to hear this? It's kind of a long story.'

Veerle put her head on one side. 'Yes.'

'And it's just a local legend. It's not written down anywhere, and it's definitely not in any of the guide books. It's not the kind of thing the Ghent tourist board is promoting. It's just some old story that's been around for ever.' Bram nodded at the street behind Veerle. 'Most of the people down there don't know it, and definitely not the ones whose grandparents weren't Ghent born and bred.'

'Mysterious,' remarked Veerle. She was wondering whether Bram was setting her up, preparing to spin her a line.

'OK, well, you know the painting in Sint-Baafs? *The Adoration of the Mystic Lamb?*'

'Ye-e-s . . .'

'People say it's a Van Eyck.'

'Jan Van Eyck, right?' said Veerle, plucking a scrap of remembered detail from her visit to the altarpiece in its glazed room in the cathedral.

'Not *just* Jan Van Eyck,' said Bram. 'The painting was started by his brother, Hubert Van Eyck. It was Jan Van Eyck who finished it.'

Veerle looked at him, then shrugged. 'So?'

'The point is *why* it was Jan who finished it. Hubert was the elder brother and the court painter. He was the one who was commissioned to create the altarpiece, not Jan. Some people say that Hubert was the greater painter. Only maybe,' said Bram, 'he was too good. And that was when the rumours started. People said that what Hubert was doing wasn't right.'

'Because he was too good?' Veerle raised her eyebrows. 'How could that be a problem?'

'Because of who was helping him. Supposedly.'

'Let me guess. The devil?'

Bram nodded.

'That doesn't make sense,' said Veerle. 'He was doing the painting for the *church*.'

'He was doing it for his patron,' said Bram. 'Not the church itself. Look, you've seen the altarpiece, right? Did you go round the back?'

Veerle shook her head.

'Well, if you ever do, there are portraits of the guy who commissioned the painting, and his wife. He was called Joos Vijdt and his wife was Lysbette Borluut. They were rich but they never had any kids. By the time Hubert started painting them, Lysbette was too old anyway. So the altarpiece was their way of making sure they were remembered.'

'I guess it worked, then,' commented Veerle. 'But I still don't see where the devil comes in. Anyway, whoever paid for it, it was still supposed to go in the cathedral.'

'I told you it was a long story,' said Bram. The light was fading fast now and Veerle could not see his face very clearly, but she could hear the grin in his voice.

'OK, go on,' she said.

'Hubert's painting has some kind of power in it, if you believe the story. And not a *good* power. Did you know that every single figure that appears in the painting had a real-life model? Not just Joos Vijdt and his wife. There are a hundred and seventy people in that painting, and every single one was a portrait of a real person, back in fourteen hundred and whatever.'

'So this strange power – it was like voodoo or something?' said Veerle. 'Anyone he painted, something bad happened to them?'

'The exact opposite,' Bram told her. 'Anyone he painted . . . didn't die.'

'So he painted them and nothing happened to them? I don't see—'

'No, I mean they *didn't die*. Ever.'

Veerle stared at him.

'Well, they didn't get *old* and die,' Bram qualified. 'They could still die by violence. And they could still die if something happened to the painting. I guess that's why Joos Vijdt commissioned it as a gift to the cathedral. It would be safe in there, or so he thought. A hundred years later rioters got into Sint-Baafs and tried to destroy it, only he had no way of foreseeing that would happen. Anyway the church staff hid it, so maybe old Joos was right to trust it to them.'

'This is a completely *weird* story,' said Veerle.

'That's not all of it. Halfway through completing the painting, Hubert died and his brother Jan had to step in and finish it. That's what it says in the guide books, anyway, and on Wikipedia: that Jan took it over when Hubert died. Keeping it in the family or something. But actually Jan was going to take over long before his brother's death. A year before he died, Hubert had a visit from the town magistrates. Maybe there were already too many rumours going around about that painting, and about what Hubert was trying to do with it, and they were trying to put a stop to it. Supposedly they went to see him to commission a painting of Saint Anthony, but Hubert never painted it.'

'So that was just an excuse?'

'An excuse . . . or a warning. Saint Anthony – he's nearly always painted being tempted by the devil.'

'How do you know all this?' asked Veerle.

Bram shrugged. 'Grandparents, Ghent born and bred. My grandfather didn't have much time for any of this stuff, but my grandmother was into it in a big way. She was really superstitious.'

'It's incredible. So what happened when Hubert died?'

'They buried him in the cathedral.'

'Even though he'd been doing black magic?'

'Well, that's the point. They buried most of him in front of the altar, but they cut off his arm and put it in an iron casket over the main door. It was his *right* arm, the one he painted with.'

Veerle shivered, suddenly conscious of the cooling night air. 'That's nasty.'

Bram moved a little closer, leaning towards her in the dark. 'You know, *The Adoration of the Mystic Lamb* is the only surviving painting by Hubert. There are loads by Jan, even though Hubert was the older one and the court painter. My grandmother reckoned they destroyed them all when they found out what Hubert was doing.'

'They must have realized there wasn't really any magic, though,' said Veerle, 'when Joos Vijdt and the other people in the picture started dying.'

'That's just it. According to the legend, they didn't.'

'Oh, come on.'

'I'm not saying *I* believe it. That's the story. Joos Vijdt and his wife Lysbette and all the rest of them just carried on living, not getting sick, not getting any older.'

'That's insane. If that were true, there'd be a hundred and seventy people walking around Ghent right at this moment, looking just the same as everyone else, except they'd be over five hundred years old.'

'Assuming none of them got killed in a war or died in an accident. In five centuries some of them would be bound to have been killed.'

'You're talking like it's *true*,' said Veerle.

'I'm just saying.'

'And I still don't see where the demons on the rooftops come in. Are they trying to kill off these people, or what?'

'No, they're preventing them from dying.'

'*Preventing* them? Why?'

'It's their punishment. They didn't want to die, so now they can't. They have to keep roaming the streets of Ghent. As long as even one of them is left alive, the souls of the other ones can't rest. So the demons are there to make sure they never do get to rest.'

'Not guardian angels . . . guardian demons.'

'Fallen angels.'

Veerle hugged her knees, resting her chin on them. For a few moments she was silent, then she said, 'Suki must have got the wrong end of the stick.'

'Well, yeah, obviously,' said Bram.

'No, I don't just mean because she believes in them – the demons.' Veerle glanced at Bram. 'Look, there was a guy at my school, Daan De Moor – I didn't know him but he was in my year. He fell off a building somewhere near the Belfort tower – or maybe he jumped.'

She saw Bram wince. She went on, 'The school seem to think he jumped. They've been giving us lectures about talking to someone if . . . you know.' Veerle sighed. 'Suki was winding everyone else up by saying that it was the demons who did it, that they pushed him. But that wouldn't make sense at all – if they were supposed to be *preventing* people from dying.'

It came back to her then – the mention of salt, where and when it had been. Suki had mentioned it, saying perhaps Daan had gone to the rooftops prepared, armed with salt to keep the demons off. That didn't make sense either, though, not if the demons were there to *prevent* people coming to harm.

'Only *some* people,' Bram was saying. 'The people in the painting. It's just an old story, anyway.'

'I know,' said Veerle, 'but doesn't it creep you out just a little bit? I mean, when you're up here on your own?'

There was a pause as Bram thought about that. Veerle had expected him to come straight back with, *No, not at all,* but after a brief silence he said, 'Not really. I've never seen anything.' He put the merest emphasis on the word *I've.* Veerle thought he would say something more, but he didn't.

The light had almost gone. Bram was simply a silhouette against the darkening sky.

Veerle pulled her jacket closer around her body. She felt chilled. The surface she was sitting on was suddenly numbingly cold. Even the great bulk of the Gravensteen castle no longer looked grand and romantic now that it had lost its halo of flaming sunset. It looked like what it was: a twelfth-century fortress with a torture chamber at its heart.

No need to make up stories about demons, she thought. There were enough human ones; she, more than anyone, had cause to know that. Unconsciously she rubbed the scar on her forearm.

'I should get home,' she said. She slid off the block they were sitting on. As Bram jumped down beside her she said, 'That was an amazing story. It's like the plot of a film or something. I didn't expect to end up discussing guardian demons.'

'Me neither,' said Bram.

There was something in the way he said it, some very slight emphasis, so slight as to be almost unnoticeable, that warned Veerle what was coming, but it was too late to step away.

Bram slid his arms around her and then he was looking at her, his face very close to hers, and *that* was the moment when she should have pushed him away, but didn't. The feeling of his arms around her, the warmth of his embrace, were so unexpectedly comforting. He smelled faintly of citrus and pepper, clean and masculine.

It was simply too easy to let him go on holding her. She hadn't actually seen Kris in person for weeks before yesterday's débâcle. Geert never really hugged her, except in an awkward, arm's-length sort of way; they had been apart too long. Anneke certainly never did. Veerle hadn't realized how much she had missed the simple human warmth of being held. She felt *safe*, and that was strange because safety wasn't something she normally craved, not after years of being told to *be careful* all the time. She'd learned to wear her independence like a suit of armour, never revealing all of herself to anyone. Concealing her activities from her mother. Keeping her relationship with Kris and everything that went with it from Lisa and her other school friends. And Kris – she'd agonized for ages before telling him about her problems with her mother, wanting to keep the part of her life that was with him separate from all of that.

But Bram – she'd told him everything, hadn't held any of it back, even the things that could have incriminated her if he were the sort to tell tales. And here he was, with his arms around her, holding her tight, and for once it was such a relief to lean on someone else that she just closed her eyes and let him hold her.

It was now so dark that she wondered dimly how they would manage to climb down the front of the house again, but mainly she was glad of the darkness because they could not clearly see each other's faces when he began to kiss her. She felt his lips touch the side of her face, close to the jaw line, and then his hand pushed her hair back and he was kissing her in earnest, first on the soft skin close to her ear and then on the mouth.

Somewhere at the very back of her mind an alarm bell was ringing, but it was distant and useless, like the beeping of a fire alarm drowned out by the roar of a conflagration and the bursting of windows. Bram's arms around her were comforting, that was true, but he was undeniably attractive as well; he even *smelled* good, and he was incredibly good at kissing. *Embarrassingly* good at it, in fact. Veerle was tingling all over, as though her entire body were blushing at the effect he was having on her.

It was not until she found herself pressed back against the wall and there was a more insistent tone to Bram's kissing that she came to her senses. When they came up for air she placed the flat of her hand on his chest and held him away from her.

'Bram . . .' she began.

When he tried to kiss her again she almost weakened, but then she made herself push away from him, gently disentangling herself from his embrace.

'Veerle . . .'

'Bram, it's too fast.' There was a riposte to that – they both knew it: *Kris has dumped you for someone else. Forget him.*

Reaction was setting in; guilt was seeping in at the edges of Veerle's consciousness.

If he says it I'll never forgive him, she thought.

He didn't, though. What was passing through his mind at that moment, it was hard to say. It was so dark now that she couldn't see his expression and she supposed, thankfully, that he couldn't see hers, couldn't see what an effect he had had on her.

'OK,' he said at last. Veerle felt him touch her face in the dark, his fingers warm against her skin as he brushed the hair back from her brow.

There was a long silence between them, silence that could have been filled by one or the other of them saying *Sorry*, or Bram saying *When . . . ?* or Veerle saying *I don't know when.* Instead, neither of them spoke, preferring not to conjure up the spectre of the word *Never.*

At last Veerle said, 'I have to get back.'

They crossed the rooftops, moving carefully in the dark. Once or twice, when she was waiting for Bram to go ahead, Veerle paused to look around, scanning the rooftops for any sign of life, feeling foolish even as she did so. Everything was silent and still.

Veerle had been wondering whether it would even be possible to climb back down the house Bram called *de ladder* now that it was so dark. Bram didn't seem concerned, however, and in fact when she peered down from the safety of the corbie steps at the top she realized that the climb was well lit, thanks to the lamp on the wall.

Footsteps sounded on the cobbled street below, and voices floated up: a couple of women, chatting animatedly. Veerle ducked back, out of view. She was very aware of Bram at her side, although he was little more than a dim silhouette in the gloom. She was beginning to feel very anxious to get down to street level and make her way back to Bijlokevest. It was not that she wanted to get away from Bram, exactly. She just had to be alone for a while, to think.

The last time I did any exploring like this it was with Kris, she thought, remembering the time she had clambered through the bathroom window of a big Art Deco villa after a hair-rising climb up the stuccoed walls. The bathroom had been decorated with a dizzying pattern of black and white tiles and she had sat on the floor, feeling slightly light-headed and full of relief, before getting up and going downstairs to let Kris in. They had eaten pizza from the freezer at an enormous dinner table designed for many more than two.

The thought of Kris was like an actual physical ache under her breastbone. Veerle looked down at the cobbles below, gilded now by the soft yellow glow of the streetlamps, and she felt Bram touch the side of her neck, very lightly. She knew that if she responded, if she turned towards him, he would kiss her again.

You can think about this for ever and there won't be any answer, she thought.

The women had turned the corner at the end of the street and disappeared. Bram glanced swiftly left and right, ascertained that the coast was clear and swung himself over the corbie steps onto the façade of the house. He climbed down swiftly and efficiently, looking up several times to make sure that Veerle was following.

When they were both standing on the cobbles Bram said, 'I'll walk you home.'

'No,' said Veerle instantly, and then, realizing she had spoken abruptly, 'My dad will just ask millions of questions.'

Bram shrugged. 'Nearly home, then.'

There was no arguing with that. They set off side by side down the lamplit street, and when Bram took her hand Veerle didn't try to pull it away. By the time they came out of the maze of backstreets into the square in front of the Gravensteen the floodlights had come on, turning the ancient stones gold.

Even at this time of year, when the summer holidays had long gone, there were still tourists in the city, strolling about or sitting outside the bars and cafés. As Veerle and Bram passed across the square she heard snatches of different languages – German and what might have been Spanish. Nobody took any particular notice of her and Bram. They were just another couple enjoying a clear dry evening in the old part of the city.

It made Veerle feel strange, as though there were some disconnection between her inner self and the girl who was strolling along Rekelingestraat hand in hand with the blond-haired boy, as nonchalantly as though she had always lived here, as though it were her city. The outer Veerle did live here now, of course; she had a life in Ghent – a school, a place to live; even, apparently, a boyfriend. So why did she feel as though her real self were somehow inhabiting an avatar?

Bram was true to his word: he walked her nearly all the way home, but left her at the corner of Bijlokevest, where there was no danger of Geert or Anneke seeing him unless they were actually hanging off the front balcony wielding a telescope.

'I'll phone,' said Bram when they parted.

135

Veerle thought perhaps he would try to kiss her again, but when he leaned towards her, all he did was brush his lips lightly against her cheek. Then he was gone, and she was alone. Veerle looked after him for a moment, and then she turned and walked back to the flat.

18

On Monday morning the sky was grey and there was a coolness in the air that suggested rain to come. As Veerle walked to school, Geert pacing along beside her, she came to a decision. When they got to the street where the school stood she said, 'You don't need to stay.'

Geert stood still in the middle of the pavement, his battered briefcase clasped in his large hands, and looked at her carefully.

'Really,' said Veerle.

'All right,' said Geert. He continued to study her for a moment, his lips pursed, and then he said, 'See you later,' and turned to go.

'Bye,' said Veerle to his retreating back. Then she went into the school.

At the first break she went down to the front door and looked out. The street was empty. Geert had taken her at her word, and really gone. If she wanted to leave school herself, skip the rest of the day, there was nothing stopping her.

She didn't, though.

When she got back to the flat on Bijlokevest that afternoon, Anneke was waiting for her. Anneke was mostly there when she got home, but quite often she would be taking a nap on the bed she shared with Geert, pillows supporting her on all sides like ship wedges, or else sitting on the couch in the little living room, with her feet up on a padded stool. Today, however, she was on her feet, and when she heard Veerle's key in the lock she came out of the kitchen into the hallway, moving ponderously with a hand under her belly. It always made Veerle nervous when she walked around like that: it looked as though Anneke was about to give birth at any moment. Being alone with her was about as relaxing as spending the night of a full moon alone with a suspected lycanthrope.

Worse, Anneke did not look happy. There was a peevish expression on her face; her eyebrows had drawn together so that there were little vertical creases between them, and the gaze of her grey eyes was distinctly hostile. With her free hand, the one not supporting her belly, she was holding onto the doorframe, as if to say, *Look, you made me get to my feet and I can barely stand.*

Which, thought Veerle, was probably true, but she had no idea what she had done.

'Someone called here for you,' said Anneke.

'Oh?' said Veerle. She could not think of anything else to say until she knew the reason for Anneke's indignant expression. *Bram*, she thought.

But it was not Bram.

'He said his name was Verstraeten.'

Kris.

Veerle felt a cold lurch in her stomach, as though she had trodden on rotten ice and gone right through; as though she were falling. The shock was followed by a swift and entirely irrational stab of guilt: *He knows I was with Bram.*

But that was impossible, and anyway, how could he dare to object?

Anneke saw Veerle react. 'It's that boy who got you into all that trouble, isn't it?'

'Anneke,' said Veerle as levelly as she could, 'you know his name. It's Kris Verstraeten.'

'Geert doesn't want you seeing him.'

Veerle found that she was completely unable to tell Anneke the truth, which was that she wasn't seeing Kris any more. Apparently. Not since Saturday, when she had found him with Hommel. It would probably have ended what was shaping up to be a bad-tempered argument, but she simply couldn't make herself do it.

'I know,' she said, looking Anneke evenly in the eye.

'Well, what is he doing, coming to the flat, then?' demanded Anneke. She was pale – she always looked tired these days – but there were spots of colour in her cheeks now.

'I don't know,' said Veerle truthfully. 'I didn't ask him to.'

'So he came all the way from wherever he lives, in Vlaams-Brabant, for no reason?'

Veerle took her school bag off her shoulder and dropped it on the floor. Suddenly she felt very weary. Automatically she rubbed her left forearm, although she was not conscious of any pain.

'Anneke . . .' She really didn't want to argue. 'I don't know why he came, and I really didn't invite him.'

'Then what was he doing here?'

'What did *he* say?'

'He wanted to talk to you.' Anneke scowled. 'He was very persistent. Veerle, even if you don't intend to respect your father's wishes, you could have a little consideration for me. He was quite threatening.'

I don't believe that, thought Veerle. Then she thought, *I don't know what to believe. I don't think he'd threaten Anneke, but then I didn't think he'd go behind my back, either.*

It would have been too easy to take out her frustration on Anneke. Instead, she simply said, 'Sorry,' and picked up her school bag.

'Sorry? Well, *I'm* sorry too,' snapped Anneke in a significant tone.

Sorry I'm here, thought Veerle.

They stared at each other, Veerle's hazel eyes meeting Anneke's grey ones. Veerle saw something dull and ugly – regret? – guilt? – seeping like a grubby stain into the older woman's expression. She had not meant to speak so hastily, Veerle was pretty sure of that, but the knowledge was as much use as thinking that someone had not really intended to turn round suddenly with a breadknife in their hand when it was sticking out of your midriff.

There was no point in fighting. Geert would be angry if she did; he would say that she should make allowances for Anneke's condition, and he was probably right. Veerle said, 'I think I'll go to my room,' and Anneke stood back to let her pass.

My room, thought Veerle bitterly when she had closed the door and was standing there between the bare walls that should have been decorated with bunnies and ducks and elephants. She put her bag down on the floor and went and sat on the bed.

Kris, she thought. *I wonder why he came. What was he going to say?*

That scene flashed through her head again: Kris standing in the doorway, Hommel behind him in the shabby room.

There is nothing he can say. Perhaps that was why he came during the day, when he must know perfectly well that she was at school. Just to make it look as though he was sorry, without having to face her.

And me? Could I face him?

She remembered Bram kissing her on the rooftop the night before, how his kiss had begun gently and become gradually more insistent; how she had responded in spite of herself – who wouldn't, considering how very, very good at it he was? – and how she had had to push him away when her head had given her susceptible heart a dressing down.

Perhaps, she concluded, it was better if she and Kris didn't have to face each other.

19

At midnight Veerle awoke to the sound of her mobile phone ringing. It took her a little while to realize what had woken her, and when she did, it was already too late; after six rings the phone had diverted to voicemail.

Veerle lay in bed looking at the slender wedge of light created by the streetlamp outside her window shining through the gap in the curtains. She felt groggy and disoriented, and when she shifted in bed, trying to make herself more comfortable so that she could sink back into sleep, she could feel the evening's exertions in her joints and muscles.

Out of practice, she thought.

She was almost asleep again when she heard a beep from the mobile, the signal that a text message had come in.

Someone wants to get in touch with me really badly. There were very few possibilities, given that her father and Anneke were asleep a couple of doors down from her own room, she'd seen Bram a few hours ago, and as for Kris . . .

Finally curiosity got the better of her and she leaned out of bed to switch on the light. Her jacket was lying on the floor by the bed. She grabbed it with one hand, pulled it to her and lay on her back feeling in the pockets for the phone.

1 message from Kris Verstraeten.

Veerle lay there looking at the little screen.

Is he deliberately trying to miss me?

First the visit during the day, when she was clearly going to be at school, and now a call in the middle of the night, when she was probably going to be fast asleep.

She was still trying to decide whether to open the message when the phone began to ring again. Veerle started, and nearly dropped it. She didn't have to look at the screen to see who was calling.

Kris Verstraeten.

It briefly flitted through her mind that she could touch the red symbol to end the call, and then switch the phone off to stop him calling her again.

No, she decided. *Let's call his bluff. I want to know what he has to say.*

She touched the screen to accept the call and put the phone to her ear without saying anything, gazing sternly at the ceiling.

'Veerle?'

That one word, her name, nearly undid her. His voice was so familiar, and when he spoke her name something inside her seemed to *jump*, as it always did when she saw him. The things she had said to him in her head over the last day and a half, the angry, indignant words, drained out of her in an instant.

When she didn't reply Kris said, 'Veerle? Are you alone?'

'Yes,' she managed to say at last. Her mouth was dry.

'I'm outside.'

It took Veerle a moment to digest that, and when she did she sat up in bed, clutching the phone to her ear. '*What?*'

'I'm outside, in the street. Can you come down?'

'Hang on. You're outside the flat? On Bijlokevest?'

'Yes.'

Veerle sat in the bed with the phone clamped to her ear, and for a moment she could think of absolutely nothing to say.

'Veerle?' said Kris's voice in her ear. 'Can you come down?'

'No,' she blurted out, thinking of Anneke and Geert a few metres along the corridor. Anneke never slept very deeply these days, with the baby pressing on her bladder; she was always getting up in the night. If Veerle got up and went down the hall to let herself out, ten to one Anneke would hear her, and then there would be a scene. Then she said, 'Let me think.' She was already pushing back the duvet, swinging her bare feet over the edge of the bed. 'I'll call you back.' She touched the red icon to end the call, and stood up.

In the dim light from her bedside lamp she stood and listened. The flat was silent, but what did that mean? Simply that Anneke wasn't moving around right now.

Veerle dressed quickly, pulling on trousers and a T-shirt, and then she switched the lamp off again. She let her eyes adjust to the darkness, and then she went cautiously over to the window and peered out, doing her best to stay behind the curtain.

Is he really down there?

It was difficult to see the stretch of pavement immediately below the window without actually leaning out. She went as close to the glass as she dared and looked out, and there he was. His face was turned up to the window, sallow in the light from the streetlamp, the dark hair falling untidily across his brow.

The phone began to ring again, and Veerle jumped. She picked it up from the bed, pressed the red icon to silence it. Then she went and opened the window.

She leaned right out and looked down, and at the same moment Kris stopped what he was doing, which was examining his own phone with an expression of frustration, and looked up.

'Stop calling,' said Veerle in a low voice. 'You'll wake everyone up.'

Kris approached the wall below the window, and she said, 'What do you want?'

She had spoken more harshly than she had intended, and she saw the reaction in his face, a brief flash of anger, or frustration.

'I want to talk to you.'

'At *midnight*?'

'I came earlier and you weren't here.'

'I was at school.'

Kris stared up at her and she felt that familiar feeling, as though something were tugging at her, pulling her to him. She fought the feeling. Longing and anger were swirling around inside her like oil and vinegar, never really combining, always separating out into distinct and painfully intense emotions. She wanted to go down to him and throw herself into his arms. She wanted to slap his face.

'Come down,' he said again.

Veerle looked at him. She thought about the bedroom door, which creaked like a sow in labour whenever you opened it. She thought about the front door of the flat, which had a deadlock that opened with an audible clunk. The door itself was heavy, and unless you were careful it was inclined to swing shut with a bang.

'Veerle . . . please.'

'Shhhh.'

She glanced up and down the street. No one about other than herself and Kris. Veerle climbed out onto the windowsill, stood up very carefully, and stepped over onto the bracket holding the drainpipe to the wall. A couple of minutes later she stepped down onto the pavement next to Kris, brushing her hands on the front of her trousers. Then she straightened and looked at him.

'How long have you known about Hommel, Kris?'

Her voice was steady but her heart was thumping and she was trembling.

'Veerle, it's not like—'

'How long?'

'Two weeks,' said Kris reluctantly. 'Well, maybe three.'

'Three weeks,' said Veerle. She was so angry that she felt light-headed. She would have liked to shout Kris's words back in his face, but she fought to keep her voice down, conscious of the open window above. 'You've been in Ghent for *three weeks* and you didn't tell me?'

'Not in Ghent,' said Kris. 'I only came here on Friday night. Look, will you let me explain?'

'What is there to explain?' hissed Veerle savagely. 'I'm not stupid. You were in her bed when I banged on the door, weren't you?' She hunched her shoulders angrily, hugging herself. 'I don't know why I came down here. I don't know why you came here, either.' She glared at Kris. 'You didn't phone me for a whole week, and if I phoned you, you didn't answer. It's just sheer chance that I found Hommel. If I hadn't, I'd still be wondering what the hell had happened to you, and you' – Veerle was rigid with fury – 'you'd be with *her*.'

Kris had been listening to Veerle with a deepening frown on his face. 'Veerle, I *couldn't* call you.'

'Why not? Too busy . . .' Veerle couldn't bring herself to finish the sentence. She turned her back on him and put a hand to her face.

'Look,' said Kris's voice behind her, 'I'm here now. Will you at least let me explain?'

Veerle said nothing.

'Hommel called me a couple of weeks ago. OK, three weeks ago. And I swear to you that I had no idea beforehand that she was here. I thought she was . . . dead.'

He let out a long breath. 'I couldn't believe it was her at first, when she called. It was like talking to a ghost. She sounded odd too, really shaken up.'

'Really,' said Veerle flatly.

'She told me she was here in Ghent, living under a different name. She calls herself Hannah.'

'I know.'

'She came here to get away from Jappe, her *klootzak* of a stepfather. That's another story. Anyway, she's not registered here. She's living in the flat over Muziek City and that fat bastard Axel pays her a pittance in cash to help out in the shop.'

Veerle could tell from Kris's voice that he had moved closer to her. She turned sideways, not wanting to let him get close enough to touch her, and not wanting to meet his eyes.

'I can see why you're angry.'

'Can you?' snapped Veerle.

'Yes, I can. I was really angry with her too when she rang me. We thought that she was dead, like Vlinder; that whoever had killed the others had killed her too. It made the whole thing personal, and we risked our necks trying to get the guy to show himself.'

'While she was actually selling CDs in Muziek City.'

'She said she was sorry. She had no idea.'

'She's sorry? I'm sorry too, Kris. You know how many bones I broke when I fell off the castle tower?' Finally she shot him a glance, full of white-hot anger. 'And you could have *died*. Is she sorry about that too?'

'Of course she is.'

'And that's *all right*?'

Kris sighed. 'No. But she *is* sorry.'

'So why did she call you? She got lonely?'

'It wasn't like that.'

'So what *was* it like, Kris?'

'She's scared,' he said.

'Scared?' repeated Veerle sceptically.

'She thinks someone's stalking her. She's doesn't have anyone else to turn to, Veerle.'

'What about Axel?'

'What do you think? He's only interested in himself.'

'So she phoned you, and you came running?'

'Do you have to make this so difficult?' Kris snapped back at her. He ran a hand through his dark hair, scowling. 'The first time she called I told her to forget it. I was just as pissed off as you are.'

I doubt it, thought Veerle.

'But she called me again about a week ago and she sounded like she was in a state of total panic. In the end I said I'd come up for a few days. I finished work late on Friday and came up for the weekend. I'm going back tomorrow on the early train.'

'And why didn't you call me and tell me all this?'

'Hommel doesn't want people knowing she's here in Ghent—'

'Kris, I'm not *people.* I'm your girlfriend. I mean, I thought I was.'

'That's the whole point. What would you have said? *Sure, Kris, go and stay with your ex?*'

'Well, if you knew I wouldn't like it, why did you do it?'

'Because she's terrified.'

'This is going round in circles,' said Veerle. She put her head back and looked Kris right in the eye. 'Why does she think someone is stalking her?'

'She's been followed.'

'By whom?'

'She's never had a good look at him. It's not anyone she knows, but she thinks Jappe might have put someone on to her.'

'Her stepfather? He'd have to be a psycho to do that. Isn't it enough that she's left home?'

'Veerle, he *is* a psycho. If he were just a *klootzak* she wouldn't have left. She's told me things ... If her mother would support her she could report him to the authorities. Only she won't.'

Veerle was silent for a moment, remembering her own encounter with Mevrouw Coppens, the way she had seemed so cowed and unconfident, yet had reacted so violently to the suggestion that she report her daughter's disappearance to the police. She had taken a swing at Veerle with her bag, right there in the street.

Finally she said, 'What does she want you to do?'

'She wanted to see if the guy would follow her again. It's always in the old part of the city, around the Sint-Baafsplein. If she thinks he's following her, she tries to lose him before she goes back to Muziek City. She's afraid of what he might do if he finds out she's staying there.'

In spite of her antipathy to Hommel, Veerle felt a frisson at that. Hommel was unregistered; that meant that officially she didn't exist at all in Ghent. Who would notice if she vanished altogether, apart from Axel, who didn't look like the sort of guy who would care? She shivered.

'If he did follow her, I was going to speak to him.' Kris's voice was grim.

Veerle studied him for a moment. He was tall and broad-shouldered, and although he was lean he was hardened with working outdoors. Even without that scowl on his face he'd have looked like someone who wouldn't take any crap.

If I were Hommel, I'd ask him for help, she realized. It wasn't much comfort.

'And did he?' she asked Kris.

He shook his head. 'No. At least we don't think so.'

'So what now?'

'I have to go back to Overijse tomorrow. I've already taken one day off.'

'But you're going to come back, aren't you?'

'Veerle . . .'

'*Aren't you?*'

'Yes.' Kris sighed heavily.

'When?'

'Next weekend. Probably.'

'And you're going to stay with her, there, in that flat?'

'Well, what else am I going to do? Book into the Grand Hotel?' snapped Kris defensively.

'And I'm not supposed to object?' Veerle's voice was rising again; with an effort she lowered it. 'I'm not stupid, Kris. I know you were in her bed when I banged on the door.'

'Nothing happened.'

And I'm just supposed to accept that?

'Kris, when she saw me in the cathedral she ran away. I chased her halfway across Ghent. That doesn't look like she has nothing to hide from me, does it?'

'She panicked. And anyway, we both knew how you'd react—'

'"We"?' Veerle's hands curled into fists. 'That says it all, Kris.'

'Well, what about you?' said Kris roughly. 'Do you want to tell me anything about the guy who was with you?'

'You mean Bram? I hardly know him.' Even before the words were out of her mouth Veerle could feel her face growing hot with guilt. She felt as though the burning marks of Bram's kisses must be standing out on her skin. As silence yawned between her and Kris she felt a desperate urge to fill it with words, to babble out the absolute innocence of her association with Bram. Only that would make it worse. *And it wouldn't be true, would it?*

'Nothing going on?' said Kris ironically. He stared at her for a moment. 'Looks like we're even.'

Veerle could feel everything slipping away from her, as though she were high on a rock face, her fingers sliding off holds that were slick with her own perspiration, her own weight dragging her off the climb, hurling her into the abyss. There was a hot, choked feeling at the back of her throat. She looked at Kris, at his dark hair and his sharp, handsome features and the bold dark eyes that still beguiled her even though they were scowling with anger and mistrust, and she desperately wanted to stop this chasm opening between them.

'I thought we were together,' she said, struggling to keep her voice steady.

'So did I,' said Kris.

They stared at each other.

'You're shivering,' said Kris. 'You should go back in.' He glanced up at the window. 'Can you get back inside the same way?'

'Yes,' said Veerle hopelessly.

'I have to go. I have to be on the early train.'

He paused for a moment, and Veerle briefly thought that he was going to lean towards her, perhaps kiss her farewell. But if that was what he had intended, he thought better of it. He turned up the collar of his leather jacket against the cold night air, gave her one last look and walked away.

20

It took Veerle a long time to fall asleep again, and when she did, she slept badly, dreaming of fleeing through a gigantic maze composed of tightly clustered dark green leaves. She had no clear sense of what she was running away from, but as she tore along something came whistling over her shoulder and she knew that she was being shot at. The thing missed her by centimetres; it was a bamboo cane, the kind used for tying up raspberries, and the end had been sharpened to a wicked point.

She woke up with a start with the name *Joren Sterckx* running through her head, hot and red and noxious, like the taste of blood in the mouth. First she felt angry. She hated the way he could still invade her dreams, even though he never actually appeared in person; he was as elusive as whatever haunted the rooftops of Ghent. Then she felt the weight of the night's events settle on her as heavily as a suit of chain mail.

Kris has gone, she thought. He hadn't just walked away from their conversation last night; he had walked away from her for good. Somehow seeing that, the last cool backward glance, the turning away, was much worse than anything that had come before. When he had opened the door to her hammering and she had seen him with Hommel she had been furious; now anger was replaced by a terrible dragging misery.

She didn't want to get out of bed, but when she looked at the clock it was already a little later than usual. An argument with Geert was the last thing she needed. She got up and dressed and went through to the kitchen, although she didn't really feel like eating much.

Geert was sitting at the small table sipping a cup of coffee and looking through a sheaf of papers. There was no sign of Anneke.

'Morning,' said Veerle, hoping that Geert wouldn't talk to her. She went to the fridge and took out a carton of orange juice.

'Leave enough of that for Anneke,' said Geert, watching her pour herself a glass. He let her put the carton back in the fridge, and when she was leaning against the kitchen cabinets, sipping listlessly at it, he said, 'We didn't really speak yesterday.'

That was true. Veerle had hardly come out of her room since her altercation with Anneke. She said nothing, and let Geert go on.

'You were out a long time on Sunday night,' he said.

'I told you, I went to the climbing wall,' said Veerle carefully.

'You're not usually gone that long.'

'No.'

Veerle saw Geert looking at her over his reading glasses and realized that he was waiting for her to say something more. It passed fleetingly through her mind that he would probably be pleased to know that she had spent the evening with Bram (though not what they had been doing), partly because he was a local Ghent boy but mainly because he wasn't Kris. She couldn't bring herself to say it, though.

'The wall was really crowded. I had to wait for ages for all the decent routes,' she told him.

'Hmm.'

'I'm trying to get fit again. It takes time.'

'If you're going to be late back, you should call me or Anneke.' Geert took off his glasses and stared at her. 'Ghent is a city, Veerle, not a village with a couple of thousand inhabitants.'

The accusatory tone in his voice roused Veerle from her gloomy apathy. 'I know,' she told him curtly.

'Anneke says you don't close your shutters at night.'

Veerle stared at him. *Did he hear me and Kris?* She couldn't believe that he had. There was no way he would have heard that and not intervened. She was aware too of a faint annoyance with Anneke for her tale-telling.

'It gets stuffy,' she said.

'Nevertheless—'

At that moment both of them heard a scream, muffled by the intervening walls but unmistakably Anneke's voice.

'*Geeeeeeert!*'

Geert was on his feet in an instant, moving so swiftly that his sheaf of papers were swept off the table and drifted to the floor like falling leaves. Veerle followed him as far as the kitchen door but then she stood there, irresolute, the glass of juice still in her hand as he ran down the hall.

Anneke was screaming his name again. Veerle saw her father charge into the bathroom. The door swung shut behind him, and then she could hear their two voices without being able to make out the individual words, Anneke's high and panicky, Geert's deeper and more measured but still somehow urgent.

After a few minutes Geert put his head out and said, 'The baby's coming. Veerle, get Anneke's bag.'

Veerle knew the one he meant; it had been packed more than a month ago. She ran to the hall closet and hauled it out, then placed it by the front door. After a moment she remembered seeing Anneke's mobile phone lying on the kitchen work surface, and she went and fetched that and added it to the bag. Then she waited.

Eventually Anneke came out of the bathroom supported by Geert. She was still dressed in her nightclothes and had an expression of almost comical shock on her face, as though she had hardly expected her long wait to end like this. Geert looked calmer; he wasn't the one having pains, and anyway . . .

He's seen all this before, Veerle realized. *When I was born.*

'Go to school, Veerle,' Geert told her before they left. 'I'll phone you later.'

After they had gone Veerle looked at the clock and realized that she was already late for school; the first bell would have rung some time ago. For a moment she considered the possibility of not going in; Geert was not here to make sure she went, after all. But she couldn't do it. You had to have a certain grudging respect for someone who would spend a whole morning holding a vigil to make sure you were doing what they thought you ought to do. It felt a little too callous to bunk off while he was watching his second child being born. She packed her bag and set off.

She hadn't had anything for breakfast other than the orange juice, so she made a small diversion from her usual route to school and went into a newsagent's to buy a snack. Amongst the rows of chocolate bars and crisps she found a small cellophane-wrapped frangipane tart. While she was fishing her wallet out of the bottom of her school bag she put the tart down on top of the fan of newspapers spread out on the counter, and it was when she went to pick it up again that she saw the headline.

GHENT: LATEST VICTIM, 17

Simply those words, *latest victim*, sent a sudden thrill of unease through her. Her mind skipped back to the morning when she had gone into school and found everyone red-eyed and grim-faced. None of Daan's friends had wanted to believe that it was suicide; and Daan hadn't been the first, either – there was the unnamed guy who had fallen from the cathedral earlier in the year.

Doesn't it creep you out just a little bit when you're up here on your own? she had asked Bram on the rooftop, and he had said, *Not really. I've never seen anything.*

That was enough for Bram – that he personally had never seen anything untoward – but it wasn't enough to put Veerle's mind at rest. She didn't believe in demons, but she believed in evil. She felt like a member of an ancient tribe who has looked away from the bright reassurance of the campfire and seen the carnivorous things that prowl just beyond the perimeter of the light. Once you had seen those things, you couldn't *unsee* them. She could have envied Bram for still believing in safety.

Perhaps Veerle had been standing there for a little longer than was natural, staring at the newspaper headline, because the man behind the counter said, 'A bad business, that.'

Veerle glanced at him, wondering whether he was going to suggest she buy the merchandise rather than simply reading it. He seemed friendly enough, uneven teeth gleaming under his brown moustache as he grinned at her, but all the same, she said, 'Thanks,' and left the shop as hastily as she could.

She walked on down the street, unwrapping the frangipane as she went, and thinking about that headline.

Latest victim. So there had definitely been more than one victim. *It could be anything*, she reminded herself. *Some horrible disease, or a dangerous stretch of road.* It probably had nothing to do with Daan, or with anyone she knew of.

She bit into the frangipane, tasting sugar and almonds. The tart was a little dry, not the best she had ever tasted, but still it reminded her of the ones Claudine had sometimes bought.

You've got to stop being so paranoid, she told herself.

The trouble was, what had happened in the old castle had ripped away a veil from her eyes. The brutality, the savage and implacable urge to extinguish life that had pursued her through the burning building was no longer something only glimpsed in films or occasionally in the news. There was no magic that made those things happen only to other people, she knew that now. Whatever foul and stinking cauldron had cast forth *De Jager* – the Hunter – the man she knew as Joren

Sterckx – it could create others too. There was no safety anywhere; only the hope that chance would never make her cross
the path of one of them again.

Thinking about the fire made her think of Kris again –
about the terrible moment when she had found him on the
floor of the castle, with the red and yellow fletching of a
crossbow bolt sticking out of his shoulder. She had dragged
him outside and then gone back in, risking her neck to try to
distract the killer.

We nearly died together, she thought. *And now he's walked
away.*

Veerle looked up at the sky, grey with the pearlescent glow
of morning. By now she supposed Kris would be passing
through Brussels, or already on a bus or tram on the other
side, heavy-eyed with tiredness from the shortened night,
perhaps dozing against the dusty window with his arms
folded across his chest, or perhaps staring out through the
glass and sharing her own bitter thoughts. He would be back
in Ghent next weekend, or the one after that, but she
wouldn't see him.

She thought about that, and she thought about Geert and
Anneke too, because she couldn't *not* think about that; it was
strange to think of having a tiny sibling when you had always
been an only child. She was pleased for her father in a
detached sort of way, but conscious too that she was the
cuckoo in the nest, the interloper in the nursery quite
literally. If she had not been occupying the second bedroom
of the flat, holding them off with her baleful presence, blue
rabbits and ducks would have been springing up all over the
walls.

It was all too much; it was so much that the impact was numbing. She felt that she could have wandered right past the school, continued into the streets beyond, carried on walking for ever. She went inside, though; there was nothing else to do.

21

Bram was as good as his word. When Veerle came out of school and switched on her phone, she found two missed calls, both listed as *Bram De Wulf*.

Veerle didn't call him back. She switched the phone off, feeling slightly guilty, as though she were purposely ignoring someone (which she supposed she was), then thought of Geert and Anneke and switched it on again.

When she got back to the flat it was silent and a little cold. There was no sign of Geert and she didn't expect to see Anneke. Veerle went into the kitchen and opened the fridge. There was still some orange juice; she didn't think Anneke would want that any more so she helped herself to what was left. Then she cut herself a chunk of Pas de Rouge cheese. After that she fetched her laptop and sat down with it at the kitchen table, thinking that she would hear Geert if he came in.

That headline, LATEST VICTIM, 17, was still on her mind. It wasn't the *only* thing on her mind – it was simply a single persistent note in the deafening requiem that was running through her brain – but it was the only thing she could do anything about right now. She powered up the laptop, went onto the net and searched for the regional newspaper whose headline it was. She found the article pretty easily under the paper's blue-and-white logo, and began to read.

After half a minute she sat back in her chair, letting out a long breath like a sigh.

OK, she told herself. *You* were *being paranoid. You have to stop doing this; you have to stop seeing* verdomde *serial killers everywhere.*

The seventeen-year-old was a girl called Marie De Smet and she was dead all right, but she hadn't fallen, or been pushed from anything. She had burned to death in a catastrophic fire on an elegant street close to the old Sint-Michielskerk. However, the tone of the article managed to imply that Marie was collateral damage: the fire had also consumed a local politician and a woman aged twenty-eight who were thought to have been in an upper storey of the building. Their deaths had evidently been reported in a previous edition – Monday's, Veerle supposed. She had spent most of that evening in her room, keeping out of Anneke's way, so she hadn't seen the news, but now she came to think of it, hadn't those two women on the tram on Sunday evening been talking about something like this? *The whole street was taped off*, one of them had said, and the other had replied, *They still don't know exactly who was in there.*

Veerle clicked through the previous articles, skim-reading them. The politician's death was evidently the hot piece of news, since he didn't live in that part of Ghent at all. The newspaper managed to imply a great deal by pointing out that the politician, who was fifty-three, had an expensive villa in a smart suburb and an equally expensive wife, aged fifty-one; it was *mysterious* therefore that he should have died in a two-bedroom apartment on Onderbergen, alongside an unrelated young woman of twenty-eight, in the small hours of the morning. There were suspicions of arson, and a call for witnesses.

Marie De Smet, who was nondescript looking and not famous and had not been closeted in an apartment with an age-inappropriate companion, was definitely the also-ran in news terms, though the editorial worked the 'tragic teen' angle as much as it could.

Veerle sighed. *A horrible way to die.* She should know; she'd heard the roar of flames all too close, and the shattering of windows blown out by the fire the night the castle had burned. She stared at the grainy photograph of Marie De Smet with terrible pity.

After a while she shut down the laptop and closed it. Thinking about someone's death like that, even the death of a complete stranger, was horrible and depressing. It was pointless too. There was no connection between what had happened to that poor girl and what had happened to Daan De Moor.

Veerle rose and went to open the window. The silence in the flat was oppressive, the atmosphere as stuffy as a mausoleum. She felt the need for some fresh air on her face, and the sounds of normal life going on: cars passing, people walking along the street, the wind moving through the slender trees that dotted Bijlokevest.

Maybe I'm going slightly crazy, she thought. *All the people who live here, all the tens of thousands of people, they don't see murder on every street corner. They tell stories about demons but it's just for fun, just something to scare kids with.*

Veerle looked down at the pavement below the window, at the empty space that had been occupied by Kris the night before. Less than eighteen hours separated them. If she climbed down and stood there she would be occupying the space he had occupied; she wondered if she would feel it, as though his ghost had passed through her. If she could rewind to that moment when they had stood face to face on the pavement in the dark, she would find something different to say, something to divert the conversation so that it would not end with him giving her that last long cool stare and then walking away.

She drew her head in and went to sit on the bed. After a while she lay down, and in spite of the thoughts that were going round and round her head like rats in a trap she must eventually have fallen asleep, because when she awoke it was nearly dark outside and her mobile phone was ringing. It was Geert, calling to tell her that she had a baby brother.

22

Geert came home late in the evening to eat and sleep. His eyes had a heavy, slumberous look and he was starting to need a shave.

He said, 'His name is Adam.'

Geert went into the kitchen and began to make himself something to eat – an open sandwich with cheese. Veerle followed him, feeling self-conscious. She felt that she should be offering to make her father something, since he looked all in, but even after a period of months the flat was still more his and Anneke's than hers. She would have felt strange taking over.

'Is Anneke OK?' she asked, feeling that she should say something.

Geert nodded. 'She's good.'

After a while Veerle left him to it and went to bed. When she got up the next day he had already gone.

It occurred to Veerle once again that she could quite easily have stayed at home all day without anyone knowing, but the silence and coolness in the flat drove her out. The temperature had dropped a few degrees and someone needed to adjust the heating, but Veerle had no idea how to do it and there was nobody else there. The cold deserted flat had never felt more like the empty packaging for someone else's life.

As she was walking to school under an oppressive ceiling of dark grey clouds, her mobile phone rang. Veerle looked at the screen and saw that it was Bram calling. She hesitated, her finger poised over the touch screen, and then she took the call.

'Veerle?' said Bram's voice in her ear.

'Mmm-hmm?'

'You want to go climbing this evening?'

Veerle went on walking, with the phone pressed to her ear. 'Where? Indoors or outdoors?'

'Outdoors.'

Veerle glanced up at the building she was passing, a high, white-fronted apartment block with ornate iron balconies.

The cliffs of Ghent, she thought.

'Veerle?'

'Yes,' she said. 'Where do you want to meet?'

'Good,' said Bram. 'How about Sint-Veerleplein, by the Gravensteen?'

'Hmm, well, I'm not going to forget that.'

She heard him give a little grunt of amusement.

'Just before seven?'

'Fine,' said Veerle. 'Bram . . .'

'Yeah?'

Don't take this the wrong way. I just want to be friends. Don't try to kiss me again.

'Nothing,' she said eventually. 'See you later.'

It was not difficult to get away that evening. Geert elected to work late, because he wanted to spend the middle of the day with Anneke and the baby in hospital. Veerle left him a note: *Gone to the climbing wall.* It was not entirely untrue, she reasoned.

She dressed warmly for the autumn evening: a dark soft shell jacket, comfortable trousers for climbing, her battered Converse. She pulled her dark hair into a sloppy knot at the back of her head, since it was unwise to be blinded at a critical moment by it hanging in her face. No rings or bracelet or necklace – nothing that could get caught on anything. The overall effect was practical rather than alluring.

It's not a date, she reminded herself. All the same, she added some blue and silver earrings. Under no possible circumstances could she imagine her *ears* getting caught in anything. She slid her phone and wallet into her pockets and set off on foot. It was possible to take the tram part of the way but she preferred to walk. The cool crisp air, the rhythm of her feet on the pavement, helped to clear her mind.

The route took her along the Coupure for a while and she remembered the night she had climbed out of her bedroom window and gone strolling, and met the older woman who had spoken to her so strangely. She had laughed in an odd, false way, and said, 'I saw them.' So mysterious, and yet there was a perfectly rational explanation. The figures she had glimpsed moving about up there were people doing what she and Bram were planning to spend the evening doing: enjoying the upper reaches of the city.

Daring, she thought. *Unusual. Illegal, probably. But nothing sinister about it.*

Except . . .

Except a couple of them had taken the short way down.

Stop obsessing about it, Veerle said to herself. *So two people had falls from buildings. Ghent's a huge place. There are thousands and thousands of people living here. Two out of all those people, dying in similar ways, that's not that much of a coincidence. Or maybe they are connected, and Daan De Moor's death was a copycat thing.*

She chewed her lip, looking up at the deepening sky.

What, are you going to get too jumpy to go up on the rooftops again? Snap out of it.

She crossed the canal at the bridge where she had lost Hommel that time. There were more people about here. Lights, voices, the chill of the evening air: those things were real. Demons . . . *no.*

When she saw Bram she wasn't sure how to react, but as she went up to him he just grinned and kissed her on the cheek. It was difficult to be unnerved by Bram; he was so good-humoured.

'Are we going up *de ladder* again?' she asked.

He shook his head. 'I thought we'd go to this other place.'

They set off through the darkening streets. At first Veerle hung back a little, not wanting to get too close to Bram in case he tried to put an arm around her. After a while, however, he took her hand, and she didn't object.

The *other place* proved to be the roof of a three-storey building with a shop on the ground floor. From the street it looked impossible, and far too public, but Bram took her down a narrow alleyway to the back where there was a fire escape running nearly all the way up to the roof. By standing on the metal railings that surrounded the stairs and steadying yourself on the drainpipe which ran down from the roof, it was quite easy to ascend the last part, as long as you kept your nerve.

They stood side by side on a flat section of roof and gazed out over the city of Ghent. The sun was setting and the illuminations had not yet come on, so the three towers were dark against a flaming sky, as though the other side of the city were burning.

'That's amazing,' said Veerle, and meant it. When she saw the city like this, its upper horizon, she felt more at home than she ever could at ground level. Up here there was no one asking difficult questions, no one speculating about you, no one hassling you. Nor did this landscape belong to the people who teemed in the streets below, the people of Ghent, to whose ranks she did not belong. It was empty, untrodden territory, waiting to be explored, waiting for them to claim it.

'How long do we have?' she asked, looking at Bram. When it became fully dark she did not think it would be possible to climb down the way they had come. The back of the building was unlit and she did not fancy hanging off the parapet feeling for an invisible rail with her feet.

'As long as we like,' said Bram. 'There's a building I know with a service ladder that goes almost to ground level. We could climb down that blindfolded.'

Veerle nodded. She didn't have to ask which way they were going. Only one route was possible; on the other side was a sheer wall.

They began to pick their way along the rooftop, moving west towards the sunset. After a few minutes they climbed down onto another flat roof, skirting a large expanse of shallow rainwater, made bright flame by the reflection of the evening sky, as though it were not water but blazing petrol. Once they disturbed a flock of pigeons roosting on a parapet, and the birds took flight, the sound of their panicked wings like the riffling of the pages of a book.

For a few metres they had to walk down the valley created by two pointed roofs. Up ahead Veerle could see the stepped façade of the building they were crossing. Clearly they were approaching the edge of the cliff. She moved towards it with caution, not wanting to be visible to anyone at street level who might take it into their head to look up.

When she did risk a peep over the corbie steps she could see the dark waters of the canal below. She sat on the sloping tiles and waited for Bram, who was some metres behind her.

When he slid into position beside her he was holding out a can of iced tea.

Veerle stared at him. 'Where did you get this?' She took the can; it was very cold.

'I left it up here earlier, behind those chimney pots. I've got other stuff too. You want some crisps?'

Veerle shook her head. She had a dampening instant of déjà vu, remembering the house with the pool that she and Kris had visited soon after they had met; how he had produced a little flask of bessenjenever. She had sat opposite him in that opulent black-and-red kitchen, sipping it and watching him work on some broken kitchen gadget. You couldn't drink bessenjenever up here, she realized; it would be far too dangerous to negotiate these rooftop mountain ranges with alcohol slipping insidiously through your bloodstream.

She didn't want to think about Kris, much less start comparing him to Bram, so instead she turned to Bram and said,

'How long have you been doing this? Coming up here, I mean?'

Bram shrugged. 'A year. Eighteen months maybe.'

'Do you see the others?'

'Sometimes. But I told you, it's not organized like your Koekoeken thing. We don't come up here and have pow-wows or anything.'

Veerle gave a snort of laughter at that in spite of herself.

For a minute or two they gazed at the sunset. Then Veerle said casually, 'Have you ever had any trouble with anyone up here?'

'Trouble?'

'Anyone . . . I don't know, getting funny about their own patch of roof or something?'

'Marnix caught a woman sunbathing nude on her roof once and she threw a flip-flop at him.'

Veerle began to laugh again. Bram grinned, pleased that he had amused her.

Leave it there, said Veerle to herself. But she just couldn't.

After a few moments she said, 'You know that guy from school I told you about, Daan – the one who fell off a rooftop near the cathedral? He was probably doing what we're doing, right?'

'I guess,' said Bram. He did not seem particularly keen to further the discussion, but Veerle was really curious. She was faintly conscious of wanting to find some evidence that Daan and the other guy, the one who had supposedly fallen from Sint-Baafs, had no connection with each other or with what she and Bram were doing, so that she could dismiss them from her mind. She still had a vague uneasy feeling about those falls, like a nail sticking up out of a polished floorboard, a nail you just had to hammer down.

'There was another one,' she persisted. 'Someone who fell from the top of Sint-Baafs.'

Bram had been looking away, towards the sunset, but now the gaze of his blue eyes was fixed on her.

'You mean Luc.' He sounded resigned.

'I didn't know his name,' said Veerle. 'Luc. Did you know him?'

Bram nodded. 'What did you hear?' he asked her. 'Were they saying Luc jumped? Because there was no way . . .'

Veerle nodded, her expression carefully grave. 'That's what they were saying about Daan at school,' she told Bram. 'That he wouldn't do that.'

'Well, I didn't know this guy Daan, but I did know Luc, and he wouldn't have done it.'

'It's kind of odd, though,' persisted Veerle. 'Two people falling from buildings like that.'

Bram was silent for a few seconds. Then he said, 'Is that why you asked if I ever had any trouble with anyone up here? You think there's something funny going on?'

'I don't know what I think,' said Veerle. 'It's just . . . odd.'

'Veerle . . .' Bram hesitated. 'The stuff that happened before . . .'

'I know,' said Veerle heavily. 'It doesn't mean anything bad is happening here.' She shot him a glance. 'You think I'm being paranoid?' She dared him to say yes.

'No,' he said finally. 'But I think you're safe here.'

'Maybe.'

'Definitely. You're with me, aren't you?'

Bram grinned and Veerle found herself smiling back. *He's probably right*, she thought. *And I probably am being paranoid. He knows this place a thousand times better than I do. It's his territory. If there were anything strange going on, he'd be more likely to know it than I would.*

She relaxed back against the sloping roof tiles and turned her head to gaze at the sunset. In spite of the flaming sky, there was an autumn nip in the evening air; she was glad of her warm jacket.

'Do you come up here in the winter?' she asked Bram.

'Sometimes. Not as often.' He shrugged. 'It's more difficult when it's wet or icy. But seeing it in the snow . . . that's pretty amazing.'

'I bet it's really like being in the mountains.'

'Just as cold too.'

Veerle looked at him, her head on one side. 'What about the castle, the Gravensteen?'

'What about it?'

'Are you going to try to do it before it gets really cold? If you slept out there in December, you'd probably freeze to death.'

'That depends.'

'On what?'

'It'd be kind of boring doing it on my own.'

Veerle looked down at her own feet in their Converse trainers propped up comfortably on the tiles opposite, study-ing them with apparent fascination, as though the heels had suddenly sprouted fluttering wings.

'And if someone did it with you?'

'Then I'd go. I'd go tomorrow.'

Bram had turned towards her, resting his shoulder against the slope of the roof; Veerle could see that out of the corner of her eye. He was a little closer too.

'So what would be the plan?' she asked. She didn't turn to meet his gaze – not yet.

'The Gravensteen closes at six. If we get into November it shuts earlier but we wouldn't want to do that because we'd freeze. We can take sleeping bags, OK – if we can fit them in a backpack – but not much else. They're not going to let us wander in carrying a tent or anything.'

'OK.'

'We pick a moment to go in when it's fairly busy. At this time of year it won't be packed but there are still groups of tourists now and again. We wait till one goes in and follow them. We don't want to go in on our own, because then there's more chance the people on the ticket desk will remember us.'

'Makes sense,' said Veerle.

'We go and do the tour, and we take our time about it, only we stay away from the bits with staff in them, like the shop in the cellar. We keep out of places like that so we don't give anyone an opportunity to notice us. We do the whole tour and then we go back to the beginning and hide.'

'Where?'

'Ah,' said Bram, and now Veerle could tell from the closeness of his voice that he was centimetres away from her, studying her profile at close range. '*That* you find out if you come with me.'

Veerle turned her head and looked him in the eye. Her gaze

was so direct that he paused in his gradual movement towards her.

'OK,' she said.

They stared at each other, Veerle's hazel eyes gazing into Bram's vividly blue ones. Veerle's heart was thumping but she kept her chin up and her gaze level, challenging him.

Don't make me say it, she thought. She liked Bram – well, she more than *liked* him. The memory of those kisses was so vivid that she almost wavered in her resolve, almost leaned towards him herself and pressed her lips to his. But the thought of Kris was a dragging ache inside her.

After a moment Bram sat back, but he didn't look annoyed; his gaze was simply quizzical.

'You'll come, then?'

'Yes.'

'How are you going to square it with your dad?'

Veerle grinned. '*That* you find out if you come with me.'

23

It was fully dark when they decided to return to street level. The rooftops had become a patchwork composed of the sallow artificial light of streetlamps below and the jagged black shadows thrown by gables and chimney stacks. In the distance the three towers of Ghent's great churches were gilded by the illuminations.

You can see why that legend started, about the demons, Veerle said to herself. It was easy to imagine something stepping out from those inky patches of shadow, showing horns against the golden glow, or scuttling all too deftly along the ridge of a roof. *What would I do if I saw that?* The thought made her skin prickle. She was not entirely sorry when they reached the edge of the building, even though it meant the end of an adventure.

Bram was right about the service ladder. It was sturdy and well-maintained and it ran from the rooftop most of the way to the yard below, ending perhaps two metres above the ground. It would have been difficult to climb up it, Veerle judged, because you would struggle to reach the bottom rung, but climbing *down* would be no problem because you could hang from the ladder by your hands and drop the last bit. She stood at the top and stared down into the yard below. The yard itself was unlit but there was an entrance large enough for a car to drive in, and the light of the lamps outside in the street poured through it like a sluggish river, tinting the stones and bricks that strange night-time colour that is neither properly yellow nor orange nor grey.

'Shall I go first?' Bram asked, nodding at the ladder.

Veerle shrugged. 'OK.'

She squatted by the top of the ladder and watched as Bram swung himself out onto it. He grinned at her cheerfully, and then he began to descend, with a series of metallic ringing sounds as his feet hit the rungs.

Veerle peered over the edge of the roof as Bram dropped below her line of vision. It was reassuring to see his blond head as he moved down the wall. She was conscious of a faint wish that she had gone first after all; she felt somehow exposed up here on her own, with her back to the darkened landscape of roofs and chimneys. It reminded her of that game she had played when she was a kid, 1, 2, 3, Piano, where someone had to stand with their face to the wall while the others crept up on them. Impulsively she put out a hand and tapped lightly on the top of the ladder.

'One – two – three – piano,' she whispered, making herself look forward towards the wall at the other side of the yard. Then she turned as swiftly as she could and swept the rooftops behind her with her gaze.

Nothing.

Of course there was nothing; they hadn't seen a soul up here the whole time. The evening air had a distinct chill to it; that was why the hairs on the back of her neck were standing up.

Veerle shivered. She peered over the edge of the parapet again. Bram was still descending with unhurried care.

'Hurry up,' she muttered under her breath. She wondered whether they had time to go somewhere for a coffee afterwards. Light and warmth were beginning to feel appealing.

Absent-mindedly she let her fingers play on the metal strut of the ladder. The words shivered out almost unconsciously under her breath.

'One – two – three – piano.'

She didn't bother to look behind her this time. Her gaze flickered down to the yard below, lit by that wide stream of yellowish light – flickered, and snagged.

Veerle drew in breath sharply, held it. Her eyes widened.

Someone was standing down there in the yard, just at the edge of the light.

Veerle's fingers curled around the ladder and tightened. She leaned forward, unwilling to believe the evidence of her eyes. Surely there hadn't been anyone down there before?

She blinked, willing the dark shape to be nothing more than a trick of the light, a shadow cast by some piece of lumber.

No. It was a person. She saw the hem of a long dark coat move as he half turned. The head was cowled in a hood that completely obscured the upper part of the face.

Probably a drunk who'd wandered into the yard looking for a place to piss, or some random druggie. Still, the sight of him standing there silently, as though waiting, was somehow sinister.

Veerle put her head right over the parapet. 'Bram,' she said in the loudest whisper she could manage.

Not loud enough; Bram didn't even look up. He just continued down the ladder, concentrating on moving his hands and feet carefully down the metal rungs.

Veerle looked past him, and the hooded figure had stepped out boldly into the yellowish light, as though setting his feet resolutely on an open road.

Her heart rate speeded up a gear. This wasn't just vaguely sinister; there was something very ominous about it indeed: the sheltered yard with its deep shadows, the jaundiced river of light spilling from the street beyond, and that dark figure standing there, the head muffled but the attention un-mistakably focused on the descending figure of Bram.

She abandoned caution. 'Bram!' she called. 'Bram!'

Now he had heard her; gazing down, she saw him glance up, and below him, out of the corner of her eye, she saw a sudden swift movement. The figure in the dark coat was striding forward, breaking into a run, making directly for the spot where Bram would land if he jumped the last section to the ground.

Bram was still looking up, at her, and not down, at the approaching figure. In desperation, Veerle pointed. She saw his blond head turn, saw him glance downwards.

How close was he to the bottom of the ladder? How close was the bottom of the ladder to the ground anyway? Veerle couldn't tell, but from here it looked as though Bram was almost within reach of someone standing underneath it.

'Bram!' she yelled, apprehension spilling over, and at that moment she saw the moving figure below reaching inside the dark coat that flapped around him. Dread accelerated into a terrifying certainty that made her heart race and her throat close as though there were a fist around it. She saw the murderous intent before she glimpsed the thin gleaming object that came sliding out from some place within the dark fabric, like a snake extending its fangs.

Bram saw that intent too. For one agonizing second he hesitated between fight and flight, then self-preservation got the upper hand and he lunged back up the ladder with a savage curse.

Veerle was still staring down. She was gripping the top of the ladder so tightly that it cut into her hands. She could see the top of Bram's head again as he concentrated on climbing back up, but she could see little of the man below them in the yard because he was almost directly underneath the ladder.

The breath seemed to be stagnating in her throat. She was praying that what Bram had told her earlier on, about it being difficult to climb up the ladder because it started a couple of metres above the ground, was true. If not, the owner of that deadly glittering thing would be up on the roof about a minute after Bram was. The very thought made her stomach lurch sickeningly.

What would they do? Could she and Bram defend the top of the ladder – even if it meant pushing another human being off it into the chasm that yawned below? If not, how far could they flee across the rooftops before they ran out of space?

Veerle couldn't move from her post at the top of the ladder. She had to see Bram climbing up; she had to listen for the sound of a second set of feet on the lower rungs, echoing the desperate tattoo of his shoes on the metal. In the tangled sounds of his hands and feet on the rungs she couldn't tell, but as he neared the top of the ladder she was able to look past him and see the cowled figure standing at the bottom, motionless.

Bram was breathing hard. Veerle sat back, releasing her grip on the top of the ladder, to let him climb onto the roof. The moment he was safely back on the parapet, the pair of them stuck their heads over the side to see what was happening below.

'Shit,' said Bram almost inconsequentially. He rubbed his mouth with the back of his hand. 'What's his problem?'

They stared down. The dark-clad figure was still standing there underneath the ladder, as though considering his next move. The slender gleaming thing Veerle had seen in his hand had gone, vanished back into the lining of the coat, no doubt. Veerle could see the edge of the hood, but nothing beneath it; he had his back to the light.

She scanned the yard with her gaze, wondering whether there was anything there – a bin perhaps, or a discarded pallet – that he might climb onto to reach the bottom of the ladder. But he showed no sign of wanting to do so.

'Bram,' said Veerle in a low voice, 'he had a knife.'

'Shit.'

'Did you see it?'

Bram was shaking his head. 'I saw him running at me. I could tell he wasn't playing about, but . . . are you sure?'

'Yeah.'

'I can't see one now.'

'He had one, Bram.'

'Crazy bastard.'

Neither of them liked to take their gaze off that silent figure.

'Bram – is there another way down?' whispered Veerle.

'Yeah. Not as easy as this one, but if we're careful . . .' Bram frowned. 'What's he doing now?'

They watched, but could make little sense of what they were seeing. The hand that had wielded the blade delved into another pocket and brought out something they could not see. The arm moved once, twice, with the motion of someone sowing seeds. Back into the pocket, and the hand removed something too small to be seen from here, but which made the tiniest metallic clink as it touched the ground.

A moment later the man had turned and was moving upstream in the river of amber light, heading for the opening into the street. Veerle watched him go and saw that there was a hitch in his step, slight but noticeable, as though he were a finely calibrated machine in need of oiling. He reached the place where the yard gave onto the street, turned right and vanished from sight.

Veerle heard Bram let out a long breath. He relaxed, sprawling back on the roof and running both hands through his blond mop.

Veerle didn't relax. She watched the gap between buildings for signs that the man was returning. Nothing. Seconds spooled lazily past and that wide river of yellow light was blank and empty.

After a few moments she felt Bram's hand on her shoulder and realized how tense she was; he might as well have been trying to rub some life into a marble statue.

'That was' – Bram struggled to find the right word – 'weird.'

Veerle glanced at him. 'It was close, Bram.' She hugged

herself. 'If you'd . . .'

She didn't finish. She had been about to say, *If you'd been nearer the bottom he might have had you.* The idea was appalling. Veerle had seen the dark figure running, the uplifted hand with the blade in it, and for one moment she had relived with sickening clarity the moments when she herself had fled from a brutal assailant with a knife. Her heart rate, her breathing had accelerated; she had almost *felt* the dusty floorboards of the old castle reverberating under her feet as she ran for her life. She put a hand over her face, feeling the warmth of her own breath against her skin, trying to take comfort from it, as though reassuring herself that she was still alive.

'Hey,' said Bram after a moment. 'Are you OK? You look freaked out.'

Veerle made herself nod.

'It was just some nut,' Bram told her. 'I mean, what was that stuff with sowing seeds? Bizarre. Probably totally out of it.'

'I don't think so,' Veerle managed to say. She had seen the savage intent in the way the cowled figure had launched himself at Bram. She didn't think he was a confused and shambling druggie. She thought he knew exactly what he was doing – what he *wanted* to do.

She said, 'I thought you'd never had any trouble up here, apart from the woman who threw a flip-flop at your friend.'

She felt Bram shrug. 'I haven't. Well, nothing serious. Mostly just threats.'

'*Threats?*' Veerle looked at him.

Bram's expression was unconcerned. 'We're not supposed

to be up here, right? I try to stay out of sight, but now and again someone sees me. Sometimes it gives them a fright and that pisses them off. Or else you get some busybody threatening to call the police because you're trespassing.' He grinned. 'Like I'm going to pinch their chimney pots or something.'

Veerle tried to grin back but the attempt felt unnatural. She said, 'Bram, the guy we just saw – he really *did* have a knife.'

Bram was silent for a moment, and when he spoke he neither contradicted Veerle nor agreed with her. He said, 'Look, we won't run into him again. We'll go down the other way. He's gone anyway, but just to be certain.'

Veerle could hear it in his voice – the desire to play down what had happened, to smooth things over. She had heard the staccato rattle of his feet on the metal ladder; she knew that the sudden assault had panicked him too. The fear in her own voice as she screamed down to him had infected him. Now he was beginning to think that he had let it be too obvious.

And he didn't see the knife.

Bram had only seen the man running at him.

He asked me if I was sure.

Bram hadn't accused her of seeing things, but he'd asked her whether she was sure about the knife. She had to see it through his eyes; he knew what had happened to her the previous summer. Anyone who'd been chased by a killer with a knife big and sharp enough to slice right down to the bone was going to be looking over their shoulder for a very long time. They'd be jumpier than someone who'd never been through anything like that. Maybe they'd be seeing knifemen everywhere.

Is it possible I imagined it? That I mistook what I saw?

Veerle bit her lip.

No.

She knew what she'd seen. What it *meant*, that was a different thing altogether. Perhaps Bram was right, and the figure she had seen in the yard below was simply some random druggie. But somehow, Veerle didn't think so.

She thought about it all the way across the shadowy rooftops, to the other way down that Bram knew. He was right about that: compared to the service ladder it was a pain. Part of the route involved crossing a flat roof in full view of lighted windows on the other side of the road, and the final climb down to the pavement was exposed; they spent a long time waiting for the street to be empty of pedestrians.

Bram seemed perfectly relaxed now, squatting on the rooftop and eyeing the street below. Once he reached out casually and tucked a strand of dark hair behind Veerle's ear for her, his fingertips lingering on the soft skin of her face. She could feel that he would kiss her if she turned her face to his; she could feel that only half his attention was on the people moving up and down the street. What she *couldn't* detect was any sign that he was unnerved or anxious.

Can he really shake off what just happened that easily? she wondered. His nonchalance made her doubt herself again.

When they were finally back at street level, walking back towards Bijlokevest, Bram said, 'So you'll definitely come?'

'To the Gravensteen?' Veerle felt a cold, shifting excitement in the pit of her stomach, a tightening in her throat. This was the tipping point, the moment at which she could still change her mind, still say no.

Bram was nodding, *Yes*, and there was only a single second

before she had to reply one way or another; a single second in which the reasons to call the trip off were fighting for supremacy in her mind: the need to deceive Geert, the fact that Bram wanted things to move faster than she did, the dread churned up by the inexplicable assault she had witnessed.

In the end, though, her lips opened and out came the inevitable. In spite of everything, in spite of the scars and the heartache and the fear, Veerle never backed off from a challenge.

'Yes,' she said. 'I'll come.'

24

Veerle went to the school office. There were two school secretaries, one of them fairly young, thin, untidy and harassed-looking, the other approaching retirement age, imposingly robust and forbiddingly stern. She had been hoping for the younger one, who would probably be too overburdened and disorganized to ask questions, but when she saw that it was the older one she decided to go ahead anyway. Time was too short to wait for another day. She leaned against the door with her shoulder to push it open, and stepped into the office.

The secretary saw her coming in, must have seen her, or at least heard the door slapping back into place, but still it was perhaps half a minute before she looked up from her avid contemplation of the morning's post.

'Yes?'

'The class trip to the Rijksmuseum,' began Veerle. 'In Amsterdam . . .'

'I know where the Rijksmuseum is.'

Veerle didn't rise to the bait.

'I can't go.'

There was a short silence during which Veerle was aware of

a pair of steely grey eyes gazing at her over the top of the secretary's half-moon glasses. Then the woman was reaching for
a folder on the shelf beside her.

'The trip is the week after next.'

'I know.'

Veerle watched the secretary leafing through the pages
clipped into the folder.

'De Keyser, yes?'

'Mmm-hmm.'

'You've paid. Or at least, your parents have paid.' The
woman shook her head. 'You can't have the money back. If
you'd cancelled a month ago . . .'

'OK,' said Veerle, doing her best to look regretful. 'I'll . . .
tell my parents.'

For a moment the secretary said nothing and Veerle
wondered whether the conversation was over, whether she
could simply turn and leave the office. She was about to say,
'Thanks,' and do just that when the woman said, 'I could
speak to the directeur.'

'Uh?' Veerle was momentarily confused. *She's going to
report me?* A hot sensation of guilt swept over her; she hadn't
lied in any way, she hadn't in fact given any explanation at all
for her sudden cancellation, but all the same, she had the
uncomfortable feeling that the secretary knew she was up to
something. She'd probably seen it all before, after all.

The woman was looking at her impatiently. 'He might be
prepared to refund part of the money – if you have a pressing reason for cancelling.'

'A pressing reason?'

'Why can't you go?' That steely gaze was on her again.

I was hoping you wouldn't ask that.

'Um . . . it's personal.'

'Well, obviously.'

After a few long moments Veerle realized that she was going to have to drop something into the silence.

'My . . . stepmother just had a baby.' Veerle didn't want to say *my father's girlfriend*. She was relying on presenting the whole thing as family business. *Girlfriend*, that sounded too temporary. *Stepmother* didn't sound particularly cosy either, but it sounded better than *girlfriend*.

'I see.'

'And my dad has to go away. On business.'

'And he doesn't want to leave her alone.'

'No.'

'Well,' said the secretary, 'I don't think we can really claim that these are unforeseen circumstances, can we?' She raised her eyebrows.

Veerle said nothing.

'I'll speak to the directeur anyway, though,' continued the secretary.

'Thank you.' Veerle was already backing away from the woman's desk.

'It's a shame,' said the secretary sharply. 'It *is* an educational trip, after all. I'm sure the directeur will say—'

But what the directeur would say was something Veerle was not destined to hear. The telephone on the secretary's desk began to trill. While she was occupied in answering it, Veerle made her escape.

Striding down the corridor, she put a hand to her breast pocket where her mobile was, touching it as though it were a talisman. As soon as she had the opportunity she'd text Bram and tell him that their plan was on.

That smouldering guilt about lying to the school secretary was giving way to the fizz of exhilaration, a feeling that was all the sharper because it was stained with apprehension. For more than thirty-six hours she'd been thinking about the thing she was going to do, and all that time the strange and appalling attack on Bram by that unknown person had been on her mind. Was there more to it than just some random act of madness? As the hours slid past, the idea seemed less and less probable.

Just a druggie. Just some klootzak *looking for a fight.*

Nobody could have known where she and Bram were. It had to be chance that he had spotted Bram coming down from the rooftop, whoever he was. There was nothing to say that he had attacked them *because* they had been on the roof. Maybe it was an attempt at a good old-fashioned mugging.

At any rate, she wasn't going to let some paranoid fear stop her visiting the Gravensteen with Bram. Just the thought of it made her heart race. She imagined herself soaring up to the rooftops on great plumed wings, Geert and Anneke and the painful memory of her mother's death, and yes, Kris, all of them dwindling below her as she flew higher and higher, until they were specks lost in the distance and the landscape of Upper Ghent, the roofs and corbie steps and chimneys that were its mountain ranges, stretched away before her.

There were risks, of course; risks to be negotiated as though she were picking her away along a knife-edge mountain ridge, where any false step would lead to disaster. The school secretary or indeed the directeur might take it into their head to telephone Geert about the cancelled trip. Someone she knew might spot her in Ghent when Geert and Anneke thought she was in Amsterdam. She and Bram might be caught and thrown out of the Gravensteen. Bram would almost certainly try to kiss her again . . .

Veerle didn't care about any of it. She was going to do this.

25

In the end, disaster nearly *did* befall the planned expedition, because Geert nearly did go away on business, and he talked quite seriously about Veerle skipping the trip to the Rijksmuseum to stay with Anneke.

Anneke came home from the hospital and Veerle had her first glimpse of her half-brother, a tiny wizened-looking face so muffled up in cap and blankets and the padding of his brand-new car seat that he looked like a small pinkish cameo lying on an overstuffed cushion. She waited to see whether she would feel a sudden rush of sisterly affection. Mostly she felt curiosity. She had lived through her entire childhood without a sibling, and now, just as she was checking out, here was her half-brother checking in. And then there was the fact that they had so very nearly not been in each other's lives at all.

I wasn't supposed to be here, in Ghent, in Geert's house.

Perhaps Anneke sensed that Veerle's feelings towards Adam, while friendly, were more curious than enthusiastic. At any rate, she flatly refused to be left with Veerle for company.

Veerle listened to Anneke shouting at Geert through the

closed living-room door. Anneke was worn down by hormones and lack of sleep, the bedrock of her feelings breaking through the thin topsoil of convention. She didn't bother to pretend that she was concerned about Veerle missing an educational opportunity, or that she regretted asking Geert to stay at home. She shouted at him that he *had* to stay, that she wasn't being left with Veerle, who shouldn't have been here anyway, who was in *Adam's* room, and that, *Verdomme*, she had been looking forward to a couple of days with Geert and Adam without Veerle hanging around.

Veerle listened to this not because she liked eavesdropping but because she wanted to know whether Geert was going to cancel her school trip or not. She found that she did not care very much what Anneke said or thought about her, so long as she could get away. She wanted to stand at the top of the Gravensteen at midnight, with the chill night breeze stinging her face, and see the contours of the city laid out before her, a kingdom that belonged to her and a few others.

When Geert said, 'All right, Anneke,' his gruff voice weary and resigned, she could have cheered.

The Amsterdam trip was on a Thursday and Friday. All the previous week Veerle waited for Geert to say that the school secretary had telephoned, or perhaps the directeur himself, to discuss the fact that Veerle was missing an important cultural milestone in the syllabus. He never did. Nor did he offer to accompany Veerle to the school in the mornings, not even on the day when Veerle was supposedly departing for Holland. In truth, Geert was looking haggard and preoccupied. He still reminded Veerle a little of a bear, but no longer a bluff, slow-moving droll kind of bear; now he looked like a bear that has had a ring inserted into the tender part of its nose and been made to dance to the point of exhaustion. Broken nights, and days spent trying to catch up with work he had missed were taking their toll on her father.

Veerle packed a small rucksack and walked to school by herself. She stood at an upstairs front window and watched her classmates milling around the bus that was to take them to Amsterdam. Suki stood a little apart from the rest, leaning against the side of the bus with a bored expression and chewing gum. Once she glanced up at the school building, but if she spotted Veerle looking down she gave no sign of it.

After the bus had gone Veerle went to spend the rest of the day in quiet study along with two other students who had been unable to take the trip.

Tonight, she kept thinking. It was all she could do to stay in her seat, calmly leafing through her textbooks and making notes. She kept glancing at her watch, marking off the hours, the half-hours.

Twelve o'clock. In twelve hours I shall be locked inside the Gravensteen. Her heart raced at the thought of it. *Or if we mess up, maybe we'll both be at the police station trying to explain ourselves.* She didn't think that was going to happen – she *hoped* it wasn't going to happen – but she wished it was six p.m. already. She wanted to be safely tucked away in whatever hideout Bram had in mind for them, listening to the staff locking the doors, the sound of iron keys jangling and heavy antiquated tumblers falling into place, footsteps retreating down stone stairs and fading into the distance.

When the final bell rang she was out of her chair with indecent haste, sweeping her books and pens up into her arms. She dumped everything in her locker and then she *ran* out of school, taking the stairs two at a time, the rucksack thumping on her back.

She'd arranged to meet Bram at Sint-Veerleplein. When she got there she couldn't see him at first; it wasn't until he came right up to her that she recognized him. He had put on a peaked cap that shaded the upper part of his face.

Smart, thought Veerle. *Why didn't I think of that?*

By comparison, she felt naked and exposed.

Better hope no one gets suspicious, because I'll be the one they remember.

'Ready?' Bram asked her. He seemed different somehow; Veerle realized that it was because he was not smiling at her as he normally did. There was a grim tension in his manner. He was just as keyed up as she was.

Bram nodded towards the front gate of the castle. 'We're just in time. There's a tour group about to go in.'

He was right: when they got to the gate it was almost completely blocked by a group of perhaps twenty-five elderly Germans, who were listening impassively to something their tour guide was explaining to them. Veerle and Bram pushed their way carefully through the crowd and went into the glass-fronted ticket office. Bram had barely scooped up his change and the tickets from the desk when the tourists began to crowd into the office behind them.

Veerle saw the heads of both the ticket sellers turn towards the press of elderly tourists. One of them stood up and began to advise them that if they were in a tour group they should wait outside; their tour guide would buy the tickets. When this advice got no response he switched from Flemish to

English. Meanwhile the tour guide herself was calling out something ineffectual from the back of the crush. Elderly men and women milled about in the enclosed space, their shoulders rubbing the glass, the air crackling with their voices.

Veerle and Bram walked out of the other door into the castle precinct.

'Perfect,' said Bram under his breath.

Veerle said nothing. She was too busy looking around. Bram had been right when he told her that nobody broke into the Gravensteen. From the outside it presented an impregnable mass of towering walls and turrets. Here, inside, there were open spaces and even grass, but the defences of the castle were constructed on such an enormous scale that she felt like a mouse running along a skirting board. To their left was a mighty wall studded with lookout points, as though anyone might have been able to cross the moat and assail the walls. To their right the imposing grey bulk of the keep loomed above them, its crenulated corner turrets like bunched knuckles thrusting brutally into the autumn sky. Veerle gazed up at it, her hand shielding her eyes. She was impressed, and not entirely pleasantly. She thought that spending the night up there would be like spending it on the exposed face of a mountain. Like ascending a mountain, it required commitment; it was very clear that once the main gate was locked for the night, there was no getting out until it was unlocked the following morning, no matter what happened. They would be sealed inside as effectively as if the gate were the steel door of a bank vault, with a timer set to open it in sixteen hours' time.

Assuming we don't get caught before they close up, she reminded herself.

Bram took her hand and began to pull her towards a doorway at the bottom of the keep. Veerle glanced back and saw that elderly German tourists were starting to spill out of the glass-fronted ticket office, like a swarm of wasps crawling from their nest. Then she and Bram passed through the doorway and the Gravensteen swallowed them up.

26

'Here,' said Bram in a low voice, coming to a halt.

'Here?' Veerle looked around, feeling slightly puzzled. 'But there's nothing here.'

They were in an empty room whose only feature was a large stone fireplace about a metre from where they were standing.

'I know,' said Bram. He glanced about casually. Then he said, 'I'm going to put my arms round you, OK?'

'What for?'

'So I can say this right in your ear,' said Bram, pulling her into an embrace.

'Say what?'

'Look, round the next corner is the weapons room. There's nobody keeping watch in *here* because there's nothing to keep watch over, but there might be someone in there, and we don't want them hearing every word we say, OK?'

Veerle tried to nod, and found that at these close quarters it was impossible to do so without nuzzling up to Bram like a friendly pony. 'OK,' she said hastily.

'You see this chimney?' Bram was saying into her ear. 'There's one like it in the weapons room. Looks nearly the same, but with one big difference. This one has been blocked off, and that one hasn't.'

'So?'

'So that's where we're hiding.'

Bram must have felt Veerle pulling back because his arms tightened around her. 'Hey, don't go running in to look. Like I said, there might be someone in there. We'll go in there in a minute and we can just wander past like we're admiring the architecture or something. We'd better not spend too long staring up the chimney. If there is a guard, it could make them suspicious.'

He let her go.

Veerle made herself stroll calmly round the corner, as though she had nothing particularly pressing to do.

The chimney? she was thinking. *We're hiding up the chimney? That's a crazy idea.* She imagined herself wedged in some narrow soot-encrusted gully, elbows and knees scraped raw by the walls and her nostrils full of the choking scent of old burnings. *I hope it's a big chimney.*

The weapons room was quite large and there were a number of glass cases in it, making it impossible to get a clear view of the entire room at once. For a moment Veerle thought that she and Bram *were* alone, but then she heard the sound of shoes scuffing the polished wooden floor and realized that there was someone else in there with them. She resisted the temptation to go and examine the fireplace immediately. Instead she wandered over to one of the display cases and pretended to examine the objects inside. There were enormous ornate swords, the type you had to hold with two hands at once, and what she thought were pikes.

'You could do a lot of damage with one of these,' she said to Bram, who was at her elbow.

'Wait till you see the torture chamber, then.'

'Charming.'

Veerle rounded the end of the display case, and now she saw that the other person who was in the room with them was indeed one of the castle staff: a rather stout middle-aged man with a name badge prominently pinned to his lapel. She saw him give her an incurious glance before turning on his heel and strolling away to the other end of the room.

She leaned close to Bram. 'What if *he's* here all afternoon? How are we going to get up the chimney without him seeing?'

'He won't be,' said Bram confidently.

Veerle was keeping an eye on the man, in case he came within earshot. 'How do you know?' she said.

'I've been in here before. They move about. It's not manned all the time.'

'What if he doesn't move?'

'He'll have to. They do a walk-through just before it closes, to make sure everyone is out. If he's here he'll have to go back to the start and shut the door. We just have to make sure we're ahead of him, and out of sight before he comes back through this room.'

Veerle stared straight ahead, as though fascinated by the contents of the glass case. She could see her own reflection in the glass, chewing her lip doubtfully.

'What if we don't manage it?'

Bram shrugged. 'Then we have to come back another day.'

'I can't.'

'Well, then, I guess we *have* to manage it.'

'Hmm,' said Veerle to her reflection.

'You didn't tell me how you managed to get away *this* time,' Bram reminded her in a low voice.

'School trip to the Rijksmuseum,' said Veerle. 'Dad thinks I'm on it but I cancelled the place.' She looked at Bram. 'He thinks I'm in Amsterdam right now. I'll probably have to phone him from the chimney and tell him I'm standing in front of that painting – you know, *The Night Watch*.'

'Have you actually seen it?'

Veerle shook her head. 'I looked at it on the Rijksmuseum website, just in case.'

She saw the expression on Bram's face at this revelation and turned away, biting her lip in case she laughed out loud.

Don't draw attention to yourself, she berated herself.

Footsteps on the wooden boards: the man with the badge was approaching. Veerle looked right through the glass case and saw him strolling along with his hands behind his back. She put her head down.

When he had passed, she and Bram drifted down the room towards the fireplace. It was massive, the chimneypiece a huge gable of grey stone supported by two thick pillars. The hearth was a combination of flagstones and reddish bricks. It was enormous, so big that she and Bram could have stood inside it. Veerle dared not linger there, but she risked ducking under the heavy stone gable and peering up the chimney.

The view was unnerving. All she could see was blackness. It was impossible to say how far up the chimney went; she supposed it must be blocked somewhere since there was no light coming down from above. Nor could she tell how wide it was. She pushed away thoughts of sticking fast in some dark narrow space, as though the ancient castle had swallowed her whole and she had stuck in its gullet.

When Veerle ducked her head to come out again she was restless with anticipation. She wanted to go up to the man with the badge and put her hands in the middle of his back and push him out of the room. Instead she made herself wander a little further along the line of display cases, as though the brief foray into the hearth had yielded nothing of interest.

After a couple of minutes Bram evidently judged that they had spent enough time strolling about looking nonchalant. He took Veerle's hand and led her to a doorway leading to a flight of stone stairs. Veerle followed him up, neither of them saying anything. She was conscious of the man still pacing the room below. She was not sure how well their voices would travel in a building like this, where everything was solid stone, with no soft furnishings to deaden sound.

Why would he listen in anyway? she asked herself. *You haven't done anything wrong yet.*

After a steep climb they reached a doorway leading out onto the top of the keep. Even on the way up the stairs Veerle could hear the whisper of the wind outside, but when they stepped onto the battlements it was more like a howl. The wind plucked at their clothing and battered at their ears. Veerle pulled her jacket tight around her body.

'We're going to freeze up here,' she said to Bram.

'What?' he shouted.

Veerle flapped her hand at him to say, *Don't worry, not important.*

She went and stood by Bram and stared out over the

battlements at the city of Ghent. From here they could see the three towers: Sint-Baafs, Sint-Niklaas and the Belfort.

'It's kind of strange,' said Bram in Veerle's ear, leaning close so that she could hear him over the wind. 'Anyone who stood here for the last six hundred years could have seen those towers. It's only the stuff in between that's changed.'

Veerle supposed he was right. When you craned over a bit and looked down at the streets below you could see cars and vans creeping about the busy streets, or the occasional tram swaying along the track that ran past the castle. There were traffic lights and illuminated shop-window displays, and the streetlamps were on too. Sometimes between the buffeting gusts of wind you could hear sounds floating up from below as well: car horns, tram bells, fragments of music. You could see and hear all that, and then, when you looked up you could see those three ancient stone towers, landmarks of Ghent for centuries. The twenty-first-century life that swarmed around them at ground level might as well have been waves breaking over the base of a lighthouse for all the impression it made.

Six hundred years, thought Veerle. She found herself thinking about that story Bram had told her, about Joos Vijdt, the rich man who had commissioned the painting of *The Adoration of the Mystic Lamb* that hung in Sint-Baafs cathedral.

Supposing the story was true and he really didn't die? she mused. *He'd have been roaming Ghent for nearly six hundred years himself by now. A traveller from a time when people believed in demons.* Veerle shivered in the chill wind. *It's weird to think how much of the city he would still recognize after all those years.*

After a while she and Bram wandered round to the north-east side of the battlements and gazed out there too. Veerle thought that the house Bram called *de ladder* and the rooftop where she had sat with him, watching the sun set behind the Gravensteen, must be visible from here, but she couldn't pick out either of them. She was becoming really chilled, and it was a relief when they crossed the rooftop and went back inside.

27

After a while they came to a room containing a guillotine standing on a blond wooden floor under the glare of modern spotlights. The blade was raised as though ready to sweep down with vertebra-cleaving force. Veerle went and stood by the guillotine and stared at it. The once-bright metal was spotted with brown, which logic identified as rust. There was a coarse-looking sacking bag waiting to catch severed heads. She couldn't resist peering into that too, although it was obviously empty.

The wooden framework of the guillotine was very clean and polished. There was nothing to suggest that it wasn't in perfect working order, although Veerle assumed that the castle staff must have immobilized it in some way. There were notices warning visitors not to touch the machine, but inevitably there would be a few people who couldn't resist trying to lie down on it and put their neck through that hole for a photograph. She looked at the blade again and thought, *Not me.*

They wandered on into a room full of torture instruments: a wax figure in manacles, a rack with a dummy stretched out on it, a scold's bridle, a wooden bed. The bed was the worst,

Veerle thought, because it looked so innocent. It was obvious what all the other instruments were for: the weights, the screws, the blades. The bed just looked like a bed, and it was impossible to stop your imagination running riot about whatever might be done to someone lying on it.

Are we going to have to come back through here in the dark? she wondered uneasily. She looked at her watch. It was past five.

'We should get going,' said Bram quietly.

As they left the torture exhibition, another of the castle staff came strolling in. Veerle kept her face turned towards Bram, avoiding the man's eye. No point in giving him a good look at her. Ever since they had entered the castle she had been conscious of a growing feeling of nervous tension; it had begun with little electric prickles in the pit of her stomach, but by now she was so keyed up that she was almost thrumming like a dynamo; she felt as though her eyes must be glowing and every hair on her body standing on end. The man *must* notice something if he saw her face. She kept her eyes averted, trying not to chew her lip.

They hurried through the rest of the tour. When they got to the door downstairs, they waited, watching to see whether any of the staff were pacing the grounds. Someone was disappearing round the side of the castle wall, but otherwise there was nobody in sight.

'OK,' said Bram under his breath. They made for the entrance door again, moving quickly so that the pack on Veerle's back thumped against her uncomfortably. It was all luck now. If they were seen going in or if the guard was still in the weapons room, there was barely time to complete the tour and enter a third time, not to mention the fact that it would instantly arouse suspicion.

They met nobody. They entered the keep and climbed the stairs to the spot where Bram had embraced Veerle and whispered the plan into her ear. There they stopped, and listened.

Silence. They waited for a couple of minutes, and there was still nothing. No footsteps, no clearing of the throat, no creaking of the floorboards. If the guard was in the weapons room he was standing as still and silent as the waxworks in the torture exhibition. At last they risked peeping round the corner. The room was empty.

Veerle felt an intense rush of nerves, as though she were on the apex of a rollercoaster ride, poised for the downswoop.

Bram was already starting across the room; he had to tug her arm to get her to move. 'Come on.'

She followed him, skirting the glass cases with their sinister cargo of ornate and embossed weaponry, moving inexorably towards the grey bulk of the chimneypiece as though it were some great mouth sucking them in. All the time Veerle was listening for the footsteps on the wooden floor, the sound of a door closing – anything that would tell them that they were not alone. Her hearing was strained to the point of hypersensitivity. Her own and Bram's footsteps sounded so loud that they must surely be audible to anyone within the keep. Her breathing was the creaking of a titanic bellows.

They reached the fireplace and Bram took something out of his pocket. A compact head torch, a tiny LED attached to an elasticated headband. The light was small but dazzling, and when they stood on the hearth looking up the chimney Veerle had her first proper glimpse of their hiding place.

I can climb this, she realized immediately. *But it's going to be hard staying up there.*

The chimney was constructed of grey stones fitted together like bricks. At the bottom it was as wide as the hearth itself, but it very quickly tapered to a much smaller aperture leading upwards into the dark. The stones and the crevices between them would provide plenty of holds, but she and Bram would have to brace themselves against the sides of the chimney to stay up there, and that was going to be a huge strain on arms and legs. The rucksack too was going to be a pain, but she couldn't see anywhere to stow it. There was no time to think about any of that now.

'You first,' said Bram under his breath. He stood back to give her room to climb, keeping the light directed onto the stone wall.

Veerle stepped up to the wall, ran her fingertips over it, searching for holds. The first few moves were going to be the most difficult; the hearth was too wide for her to attempt any bracing move. She found a stone that had a slight lip on the upper surface that she could grasp with her fingers, and tried to step up onto the wall, but as she shifted her weight onto her foot she felt it slipping off.

Verdomme.

She stepped down again.

Don't panic. Focus.

That was easier said than done when every nerve and fibre in her body seemed to be straining for the sound of someone approaching.

You've climbed more difficult things than this.

Veerle stepped onto the wall again, and this time she didn't slip. She went carefully up the stones until she was right inside the chimney. In the enclosed space she was able to brace herself against the sides but the rucksack was a nuisance; it was impossible to rest her back against the side of the chimney without something digging in.

Bram was already following her up, and she was on the point of whispering to him that he should wait a few seconds while she wriggled out of the straps and balanced the bag on her lap instead, when he froze.

They both heard it. Close by, a door had closed.

Verdomme verdomme verdomme!

Veerle wasn't sure whether it was the door round the corner by the other fireplace, or the one that led to the staircase to the roof. In either case they probably only had seconds before whoever had come into the room was within sight of the fireplace. Veerle looked down into Bram's blue eyes and saw that they were wide with alarm. He glanced downwards and she saw the beam of the LED sweep across the red bricks of the hearth.

She wanted to say, *Don't do that – whoever it is will see the light,* but she didn't dare speak. *Climb, climb,* she willed him. She was sick with fear that he would lose his grip and fall back into the fireplace.

Where is the guard? she thought, and then they both heard him. Firm, decisive footsteps pacing the polished wooden floor. If he were not already close enough to see Bram's legs in the fireplace, then he must be within the next few seconds.

Veerle heard Bram draw in a breath, tensing himself for a

lunge upwards, and her stomach seemed to roll sickeningly.

Surely he must hear that?

Bram moved smoothly upwards without falling, but Veerle heard the fabric of his sleeve whispering against the stones and her whole body seemed to clench with the agonizing certainty that he had been heard.

There was no time for Bram to make himself comfortable. He wedged himself in the chimney a little below Veerle, with one long leg braced against the opposite wall, a position that must have been excruciating to maintain for more than a few seconds. Both of them held their breath.

To Veerle's horror the footsteps were coming closer, resounding crisply on the boards.

Did he see Bram? she wondered feverishly.

The unhurried pace suggested he hadn't, but then, they were trapped in the chimney, weren't they? He could take all the time he liked; they weren't going anywhere.

The effort of remaining motionless inside the chimney, braced against the stones, was so great that she could feel herself trembling, her muscles screaming with the strain.

The footsteps were so close now that Veerle guessed the man was almost level with the fireplace. She glanced down past Bram, grimacing with the growing pain in her limbs, expecting at any moment to see a cold angry face appear beneath them, looking up as he spoke urgently into a walkie-talkie. She was aware of Bram trembling too as his muscles cramped.

He's going to look up the chimney. Any minute he's going to . . .

The footsteps passed the fireplace without a pause. Now

Veerle could hear them retreating up the room. A pause . . . a change of pace indicated that the man had reached a corner and turned. If he were completing a circuit of the room, he would have to pace down the other side before leaving.

Please, please don't let me fall; Veerle offered up a silent prayer. She had the heel of one hand pressed against the stones, the fingertips of the other curled around a tiny hold. Discomfort was rapidly turning to pain, the pressure on each point of contact excruciating, but she dared not try to move.

Still those footsteps were pacing the room with agonizing languor. Veerle heard a tiny exhalation from Bram, who must have been suffering twice as badly as she was. She shot him a glance, praying that he was not about to lose his grip and fall into the fireplace.

There was a kind of echoing click, and suddenly it was darker; the lights had gone out in the weapons room. A moment later both of them heard a door close.

They waited a few seconds more to be sure that the guard had really gone, that he really was on the other side of the door, on his way out. Then Bram dropped from his perch in the chimney, staggering as his feet touched the bricks below and his cramped legs took his weight.

Veerle climbed down after him, concentrating grimly in the low light. Neither of them fancied striding out into the middle of the room. It felt too exposed, with the guard barely gone. Instead they pulled off their rucksacks, slid into a sitting position side by side with their backs to the wall, and let their cramped limbs relax. They looked at each other, and in spite of the strain and the nerves Veerle found herself grinning at Bram. She felt a sudden surge of warmth towards him, as though a barrier had gone down; force of circumstance had overwhelmed it, like a deluge overtopping flood defences.

It's insane to be here, doing this – trying to get the knots out of our muscles after hiding up a chimney together and hoping like hell we don't get caught and arrested. Veerle looked into those very blue eyes, straight into them, not looking away, and she could see her own exhilaration reflected there. *But he really gets it. He really does.*

Something passed unspoken between them, something that neither of them wanted to put into words. When Bram leaned in to kiss her, Veerle didn't back away. She didn't give him that look again, the *keep off until I've made my mind up* look. When his lips touched hers she didn't pull back. She put her arms around his neck and kissed him back, and at that moment there was no doubt in her mind at all. Her heart was racing, she was filled with an eager joy that blotted out everything else. There was nothing else she wanted to think about anyway; no part of the past or the future that wouldn't spoil the moment, intruding like the tendrils of a weed pushing into the cracks between stones. She and Bram could have been the only two people on the planet; in a way they *were* because hardly anyone in the world understood her restless need to get away from her life. *Bram*, she thought. Her head was full of his name.

The sound of a heavy door closing somewhere nearby recalled her to herself. She stiffened, her head turning, and Bram said, 'It was the door downstairs. That's it. They've closed up.'

'Are you sure?'

He nodded. They scrambled out of the fireplace, taking the rucksacks with them. For perhaps half a minute they stood in silence and listened, but it was clear that the building really was deserted and closed. With the lights out the room was very gloomy; as night began to fall it would be pitch dark, with only Bram's little LED lamp to carve a tunnel through the blackness. They were really alone.

'We did it,' said Veerle in wonderment.

28

Bram and Veerle waited for nightfall before venturing to the top of the keep. They shared the limited rations they had been able to fit into their rucksacks along with bedding: a bar of Côte d'Or chocolate, a couple of apples, a chunk of Bellie cheese that Veerle had swiped from the fridge.

'You really want to sleep out on the roof?' she asked.

Bram shrugged. 'That was the idea . . . but I had the idea in the summer. I guess we could camp under the walkway, out of the wind.'

'We'll freeze to death.'

'We can huddle together.' He raised an eyebrow suggestively.

'We'll *still* freeze to death.'

'Let's sleep inside, then. There's that bed in the torture exhibition if you want one.'

Veerle shuddered. 'No thanks.'

'It's getting dark.' Bram nodded towards the window. The panes were small and made of thick, slightly tinted glass, so that whatever light there was entered the room in meagre rations. 'When it's too dark for anyone to spot us, we can go up.'

Veerle put the last piece of chocolate into her mouth. 'OK.'
When there was no more light seeping feebly through the thick windowpanes they picked up their bags and went upstairs, moving cautiously by the light of Bram's head torch. Neither of them said much as they ascended the stone steps. The silence within the massive stone walls of the keep had a kind of grim density to it, pressing in on them like fog, and the sound of their feet on the stone rang out eerily, echoing off the rugged walls as though other footsteps were following them up. Bram went first, lighting the way, and as Veerle followed him she cast the occasional glance behind her into the blackness of the stairwell, reassuring herself that they really were alone. As the dim circle of light from the LED moved upwards, the blackness below seemed to seep up after them like a spreading stain. Veerle kept close to Bram. Her heart was thudding and the excitement she felt was not entirely pleasurable.

The door at the top of the stairs was closed but it was fastened with simple bolts. Even before Bram had opened it, Veerle could tell that the wind had dropped. There was no longer that bitter howling sound from outside, and when the door opened the pair of them stepped out into a cold but clear and still night. Instinctively Veerle looked up for the stars, but there were none to see. The city lights gave the sky a strange opaque tint somewhere between grey and yellow, and the castle itself was lit up from below by powerful spotlights, so that it flamed like a birthday cake in the dark, obliterating the tiny points of light that were the constellations. Even the moon, which was nearly full, was faded and discoloured like a tarnished coin.

Bram switched off the head torch. They put the bags down by the door and walked along the battlements together, moving slowly as their eyes adjusted to the dark. The illuminations below provided quite a lot of light, but still there were deep inky wells of shadow.

After a while they stopped walking and stood side by side on one of the corner turrets, gazing out at the lights of Ghent and listening to the faint sounds of city life drifting up from below.

No one can see us, Veerle thought. She loved the feeling that the upper reaches of the city belonged to her and Bram alone. Nothing about her life down at ground level gave her a sense of belonging at all; school would be out for her for ever next summer, and she knew that Anneke would like to eject Veerle from the flat and her life with Geert as soon as was decently possible. Up here, though, she belonged, and she could imagine herself and Bram exploring the brick ridges and ranges together for as long as there were new places and new routes to discover. She could imagine *planning* things up here, in a way she never did in her life down there. They could try that other castle, the one that had been built by Geeraard the Devil, if they could only find some way of getting in, or they could try to follow the canal. She wanted to ask Bram a thousand questions, including *What was the longest stretch of rooftop you could traverse without coming down to ground level?* In her imagination they moved all over Ghent, never descending into the pit of the streets.

'Are you sure nobody down there can see us?' she asked him. The streets below were well lit and she herself could pick out individual people passing to and fro along them.

'Not unless we want them to.'

'No one would believe we were up here.'

'Maybe they will,' said Bram. 'I told Marnix what we were planning. He said he'd come later on when things are quiet, and see if we'd done it.'

'He can't get in, though,' Veerle pointed out.

'No, he'll go up onto one of the rooftops over there.' Bram pointed. 'I told him to wait until after midnight when there's nobody around, and I'll signal him with the torch.'

'And what then?'

'Then he won't be able to tell me it's impossible any more.'

They looked at each other, laughing.

'He's not there now, then,' said Veerle.

'No,' said Bram. 'Nobody's watching us now.'

He drew her in closer to him and bent his head to kiss her.

29

In the end they went inside for a while; it was simply too cold on the roof. They explored the staircases and rooms of the keep, moving cautiously by the light of Bram's head torch. It was strange to have so much room to move about, so many spaces to explore, and yet to find the outer doors so immovably secured. It made Veerle think of those large and complicated habitats for pet rodents, which gave the creature the impression of space and movement when in actual fact it was fully enclosed with no way out. She and Bram were sealed inside like wasps in a jam jar. She wondered whether it would be possible to get out if they had to, if some emergency overrode the need for secrecy. Whom would she even call?

As midnight approached they went back up. Veerle was beginning to feel tired. *Does Bram really want to sleep out up here?* she wondered as they went out of the doorway onto the roof. The night was very clear and dry, but the temperature had dropped even further. She was beginning to think about the morning, about how they were going to manage it. *We'll have to hide in the chimney again.* She shivered, rubbing her arms. *That's going to be nasty, if we're already stiff from sleeping out.* It occurred to her too that she was going to have the rest of the day to get through; the Amsterdam trip didn't end until late the next night. *Maybe we can spend it together . . .*

She was mulling this over when they reached the point overlooking the spot where Marnix was going to appear. Bram put a hand in his shirt pocket and produced a pair of compact binoculars.

'He won't be there just yet,' he said, peering through them. He adjusted something, then shook his head. 'Nope.'

He handed the binoculars to Veerle. 'Want to look?'

Veerle took them and raised them to her eyes. For a moment she couldn't see anything at all other than a swimmy greyish blur.

'There's a thing on top for adjusting them,' Bram told her.

Veerle touched the little dial with her fingertip, and slowly the view came into focus. She realized that she was looking at the darkened upper floor of a building, its shutters closed against the night.

Nothing to see there.

She lowered the glasses for an instant, trying to work out where she should aim them. Then she looked again, her gaze sweeping slowly across the rooftop. She wondered where Marnix was going to come from. In this part of the city there were a great many buildings of varying ages and styles jammed close together. The rooftops formed an irregular landscape of blocks and gables and chimney stacks, like something a toddler might build out of wooden bricks. Marnix might climb down that low wall to the left, or come clambering over the tiled roof to the right. Veerle studied the rooftop for perhaps half a minute. Then she thought, *Why am I looking for Marnix anyway?*

She swung round and focused the binoculars on the tower of Sint-Baafs cathedral instead, glowing golden from its floodlights. After that she picked out the Belfort, and then the Sint-Niklaaskerk. Finally she turned back to the rooftops nearby, stroking the little dial to readjust the focus, and there was Marnix.

'I see him,' she told Bram.

'Where? He's early.'

'By that . . .' She touched the dial again, very gently. 'The chimney stack on the right, the fat one with the four pots on top. At least' – she frowned – 'he was there just now.'

Beside her, Bram shrugged. 'I can't see him.'

Veerle scanned the area around the chimney, and now she detected a flicker of movement to the side of it. 'Yes, he's definitely there.' She handed the binoculars to Bram. 'I don't know why he's lurking back there, though.'

'Let me see.' Bram looked through the binoculars. 'No,' he said eventually. 'There's Marnix, coming down that gully between those two roofs. Over to the left.'

'I don't see how he can be,' said Veerle. 'Not unless he had wings. I just saw him over on the right.'

'Just a shadow, maybe,' suggested Bram.

'It moved.'

Veerle reached over and took the binoculars out of his hands again. She trained them on the rooftops below. Almost immediately she saw Marnix where Bram had said he was, moving carefully towards them along a v-shaped gully.

Odd.

She shifted her gaze to the right, to the spot where she had seen someone move.

It couldn't be Marnix – not unless he can teleport himself. Her brows drew together as she concentrated. *Maybe I did imagine it.*

A chill feeling of unease was seeping into her consciousness. She switched her gaze back to Marnix, who was approaching steadily but slowly, picking his way carefully in the limited light from the surrounding buildings.

'Bram? Was Marnix bringing anyone else?'

'Don't think so.'

Veerle swung the binoculars round, self-consciously aware that she was trying to pick up that movement by the chimney stack again, as though whoever it was could tell she was watching and could only be glimpsed if she moved quickly. And indeed, there it was again, a flicker of movement, something dark billowing or swinging. A coat tail? *A wing?* she thought briefly, her stomach lurching, and rooftop demons cavorted across the red backdrop of her imagination, horned and grinning.

She suppressed the thought instantly. *Come on, that's impossible. You're letting that stupid legend get to you. If anyone's on the rooftops it's real people, like Marnix. Like me and Bram.* Her fingers were clamped very tightly to the binoculars. *So who is this?* she wondered. *Just some random person?*

That was possible. It could be someone else checking out the Gravensteen the way she and Bram had done, gauging their chances of ever surveying the night-time city from its grim heights. All the same, there was something she didn't like about the way whoever it was lurked in the shadows, never clearly glimpsed. There was something furtive about it, something suggestive of malevolence. Her mind skipped back to the night she had seen that unidentifiable figure racing towards the bottom of the ladder, running at Bram with his arm upraised, in it a glittering blade. She swallowed, fear souring her mouth like bad medicine.

No, she told herself. *Maybe whoever it is just heard Marnix coming.*

That made sense. If she had been alone up there and a stranger came climbing over the next roof, she would have waited to see who it was before showing herself. All the same, her eye was continually drawn back to that shadowy corner by the chimney stack, and that sense of creeping unease was still there, like the sound of a slowly dripping tap. Her mouth was very dry; she ran her tongue around her lips.

'There's definitely someone else up there, not just Marnix,' she said to Bram.

She didn't give him the glasses; she had to watch now, she had to see who was lurking there, and what they were up to; she felt almost superstitious about it, as though she would be leaving Marnix vulnerable if she took her eyes off him.

Marnix had reached the end of the gully; she saw him stand there for a moment, the pale speck that was his face turned towards the great bulk of the castle. Bram had switched on the head torch and she wondered whether Marnix could see it, a single bright dot on the dark crown of the keep, like a single diamond on a roughly worked diadem. If he could, he gave no sign of it. He was hesitating, and she wondered whether he had heard something – a stealthy movement perhaps.

Veerle began to feel unaccountably anxious; there had been nothing threatening so far, and yet . . .

'Bram,' she said, 'do you have Marnix's number?'

'Yeah. Why?'

'I don't know. I just thought – maybe if we needed to call him . . .'

Bram patted his pocket. 'OK, I thought I had my phone, but I guess I left it in my rucksack.' He glanced towards the spot where Marnix was now descending carefully to the flat roof below. 'If he doesn't see us, I can go and get it.'

Veerle's gaze was still fixed on the tiny figure below them, as it made its way down a short section of wall and began to move across the flat roof towards the parapet. A brief sweep of the rooftop around him showed no sign of life, and yet still Veerle felt acutely anxious. She wondered where Bram had left his rucksack; she was tempted to look around for it but didn't want to take her gaze off Marnix.

He was walking across the roof towards the parapet, and from here it was like watching a beetle crawling across a brick. Veerle was very doubtful that Marnix would be able to see Bram's light, and calling to him would be completely useless from here; it would be like shouting across the Grand Canyon.

'Maybe you should get the phone,' she started to say, and at that moment a second figure burst from the well of shadows by the chimney stack and raced diagonally across the roof, aiming directly for Marnix.

For a second Veerle was too stunned to react. Shock was blooming inside her, white and silent like the explosion of an atomic bomb preserved in an old film.

Then she saw it; she understood. She knew instantly what it meant, the deadliness of the speed and the trajectory, the tiny figure of Marnix standing so close to the parapet with his face turned to them, the yawning gulf in front of him.

'Oh God,' she said in a soft voice, and the words slithered out of her mouth like bitter pips spat into a cupped hand. Then she was holding onto the rough stones of the wall and yelling at the top of her voice.

'Marnix! *Marnix!* Oh God, Bram, get the phone! Get the phone! The *verdomde* phone!'

Bram was at her shoulder and he had seen it too; even without the glasses he could see what was going to happen. He was shouting too, baying at Marnix at the top of his voice. Abruptly he pushed past Veerle, going for the rucksack, wherever it was. He jogged Veerle as he passed her and the binoculars jarred painfully around her eye sockets, but she barely noticed. She was screaming at the top of her voice, screaming so hard that her throat was burning, so beside herself that if the wall had been thinner or lower she might have been in danger of plummeting off it. There were tears in her eyes.

'Marnix! *Marnix!*'

It seemed to take an age for the second figure to reach Marnix, an age in which Veerle screamed his name, screamed and raged and clawed at the stone wall, struck at it uselessly with the binoculars, and maybe at the last instant Marnix *did* hear something across the gulf that separated them, because she saw him react. His head turned and he saw Death bearing down on him. He was forewarned, but too late. The assault was short and brutal.

Veerle clung to the wall and the scream died in her throat. She knew that Marnix was dead, or dying. At this distance the whole terrible scene was silent. If Marnix had cried out, she hadn't heard it.

Veerle lifted the glasses to her eyes again. Her throat was dry with screaming, her mouth full of the dull bitter taste of ashes. Where there had been two figures visible on the rooftop, now there was only one standing there, and something horribly inert huddled at his feet.

One of the lenses was cracked now, and she had lost focus. Her hands were trembling so much that it was difficult to turn the tiny dial or hold the binoculars still. All she could make out was the dark shape of a man, swathed in some black thing that might be a loose coat or cloak, the head cowled. At this distance she couldn't tell how old or young he was. With no other person near him for comparison she couldn't even tell if he were of average height and build or tall and broad. He was simply a black shape, a silhouette against the dimly lit surface of the roof. No way to know who he was.

All the same, Veerle could feel a terrible conviction rising within her, hot and toxic as radioactive fallout.

It's him. The one who tried to attack Bram.

It flashed across her mental screen then, the moment that dark and hooded figure had raced towards Bram, brandishing a blade that glittered in the amber light. She had the horrifying sense of disaster narrowly averted, of the great white shark cruising past, centimetres below the naked foot that is drawn up into the boat in heart-thumping panic. Her thoughts were a tangled mass of shock and fear and desperate groping for comprehension.

Bram – he tried to—

Then the figure on the rooftop raised its head, and although she could not see the face, which was still shadowed, she had the sense of eyes turned her way. He was scanning the ramparts of the Gravensteen, looking for *her*.

Something seemed to break inside Veerle. She turned away from the wall, the binoculars sliding from her grasp and landing on the walkway with a terminal-sounding *crack*. She staggered back, her hand pressed to her mouth as though to hold back the cry of horror and disgust that was welling up inside her. Bram was coming back – he was running towards her, and he was shouting something, but Veerle couldn't take it in. All she could think was, *He wants me. He wants me.*

Terror roared up all around her, like the flames of a self-immolation. She had seen Death in this form before, Death that lunged and swooped and carved the air with claws of cold steel; she saw it pressing at the fabric of reality, snarling, striving to get at her. It had clothed itself in the flesh of De Jager, the Hunter, to pursue her through the ancient castle; now it had wrapped itself anew in the molecules of another killer. It meant to have her.

Veerle turned and ran. Heedless of the drop at the edge of the walkway, she fled, the boards thundering under her feet. Her chest was tight; panic was enveloping her like poison gas. She blundered into the wall at the corner, righted herself and stumbled on again, one thought blaring through the tangled chaos of her brain: *Get away, get away.*

She reached the next corner, and here was a door. Veerle almost flung herself through it, and instantly she was plunged into blackness.

The stairs. She still had the presence of mind to slow down, to feel for the wall and the metal rail, although the hand that gripped it was shaking uncontrollably. Veerle forced herself to hold on, to keep to the outside, where the steps were widest. Still, she was going down them blindly and far too fast, the frantic rasping of her breathing echoing off the rough stone walls, her free hand flailing the air.

Bram had started down the stairs after her and was calling for her to stop, to tell him what had happened, but it was no use. All Veerle could think about was putting as much space as possible between herself and what she had seen from the roof, to burrow down into the stony depths of the castle like an animal going to earth. She stumbled down the last of the stairs, and then she was in an open space, but it was still too dark to see anything, so she put out her hands a second before she ran into something with bruising force. Her fingers touched wood, polished wood, and for one confusing moment she thought she had run into a table, but no – *the guillotine.* Veerle's head snapped back and she glanced upwards, seeing nothing in the blackness but imagining the tarnished blade suspended above her, shivering with the impact of her body against the wooden frame. She staggered back, turned, and then she was moving again, fumbling with her hands for the wall, uttering tiny sobs of shock and terror.

Someone was behind her; she could hear footsteps on the polished boards. Now the panic that was threatening to engulf her intensified until it was like a klaxon screaming in her ears. A pale light swept over her and she glimpsed an opening in the wall ahead of her. Someone was calling her name but Veerle didn't falter. She went straight for the doorway, disoriented now but still running, looking for the way down, the way to the courtyard and the front gate. If it was locked she would bang on the gate, she would scream at the top of her voice until someone came. If it was the police, then all the better because if they locked her up at least she would be safe. She blundered round a corner, and now she was in a room with windows. The windows were small and the panes tiny but the floodlights outside lit them up as though the perimeter of the room were lined with braziers full of glowing coals.

Where am I? Veerle stood for a moment in the near-dark, her eyes wide, her heart thumping, her chest tight as though she were trying to breathe in a rarefied atmosphere. *How do I get out?* She put out her hands again, feeling for something, anything, that would tell her where she was. Her fingers closed over something familiar and yet horribly unfamiliar. *Hands. Two hands.* But they were not warm, living hands; they were unmoving, hard and brittle, with a curious rough texture, and when Veerle gripped them she heard a faint metallic clinking sound.

The realization was like a punch in the chest, forcing the wind out of her. *The dummy in the torture room. I'm in the torture room.* She didn't need to be able to see to know what was in the darkness with her: the row of thumbscrews, the implacable iron face of the scold's bridle, the heavy executioner's blade. *That bed.*

Veerle realized that she had no idea how to get out. She could not even remember whether the room had two doors or only one. There were footsteps approaching, she could hear him coming, and she had nowhere to go. She was trapped, at bay in a room crammed with the rusting instruments of slow and agonizing death.

She sank to her knees on the floor, hugging herself, curling into a ball to try to make herself as small as possible, as though she were seven years old again, a terrified child who had just looked down from a height and seen something too horrific to conceive.

Don't let him get me. Please God, don't let him get me.

30

'Veerle?'

The voice was close to her. Veerle lifted her head and saw light, an intense point of dazzling white light. She squeezed her eyes tight shut, blocking it out, hugging herself. When he put a hand on her arm she jumped as though she had been stung.

'Veerle? It's me, Bram.'

'Bram?'

Veerle opened her eyes and saw that Bram had taken the blindingly bright head torch off and was holding it in his hand instead. His face was rather alarmingly underlit but he was still unmistakably himself. Bram: amiable and friendly, now not looking as laid-back as he normally did. His expression was distinctly tense and he was studying her with concern.

'Veerle, what happened?'

Bram touched her shoulder, and then she couldn't help herself – she flung herself into his arms and clung to him. She was still gasping with shock and fright, and for a while she could say nothing at all.

Bram held her calmly and after a while he asked her again. 'What happened up there?'

'Marnix—' choked out Veerle, and stopped.

'What about Marnix?' Bram held her away from him and shook her very gently. 'Veerle, what about Marnix?'

'He's dead,' Veerle blurted out.

There was a long silence.

'No,' said Bram at last. 'There must be some mistake.'

'It's not a mistake,' said Veerle. 'He killed him, Bram. He killed Marnix. And I was shouting and shouting and – and Marnix didn't hear me. And then he looked round and it was too late.'

'Maybe . . .' began Bram, and then he fell silent. Veerle knew what he had been about to say: *Maybe he isn't dead*. But she knew he was. She had seen no hesitation in the attack. It had been brutal.

'Veerle, are you *sure* that what you saw . . . I mean—'

'Yes, Bram,' snapped Veerle, much more violently than she had intended. 'I'm sure.'

'But . . .' Whatever Bram was going to say, he thought better of it. He felt for his phone, and thumbed in Marnix's number. He didn't have to tell Veerle there was no reply; she could see it from his expression.

After a while he said, 'What are we going to do?'

'We can't get out, can we?' said Veerle dully.

Bram shook his head.

'So we can't even go and check . . .'

'No.'

After a while Bram said, 'We could call the police.'

'We'd have to think what to say,' said Veerle slowly. 'What if they ask where we're calling from?'

'We don't have to tell them.'

'They'll have the phone number of whichever of us calls. Once they find out we're telling the truth, they'll try to track us down. It's murder.'

'We don't have to say we saw it from here.'

'Where else could we have seen it from?' asked Veerle. She was beginning to see the whole thing all too clearly. 'There's nowhere else high enough, unless we were on the rooftops with him when it happened. And even if we thought up some excuse, said we'd heard something from the street or whatever, we're stuck in here until at least ten a.m. tomorrow. Supposing they take it seriously and say they want to come and interview us?' *Then*, she thought, *I'll be busted. Dad will go mad, and we'll probably be prosecuted or something. And I don't think it will do any good. Marnix is dead – I know it. And if he isn't – well then I'm seeing things, like everyone always thinks I am.*

Bram put his head in his hands, and for a while all Veerle could see of him was the top of his head, his fingers laced through the strands of blond hair. He said nothing, and there was nothing she wanted to say, either. She kept thinking about what she had seen: the dark figure racing across the rooftop, Marnix standing facing the drop, looking for her and Bram, unconscious of Death speeding towards him. It made her feel sick. She felt even sicker when she thought about the moment she had seen the killer turn towards the castle, where she was standing looking down at him.

Was he looking for me? she wondered. It seemed impossible. Nobody knew she was in the Gravensteen apart from Bram, not even Geert, her own father. *Well*, she conceded, *Marnix knew . . .* She shivered.

'Bram? Can we get out of here?'

She hated sitting here on the floor surrounded by the instruments of pain and mutilation. In daylight it might be a cheap thrill to come in and look at these things. It all seemed remote, something that happened centuries ago, to people whose lives you couldn't imagine. In the dark, with the knowledge of what she had just seen, Veerle hated being near them. Cruelty and savagery were still alive. She had *seen* them.

They went back to the weapons room, taking care to bolt the rooftop doors closed. Veerle could not imagine wanting to admire the view from there ever again, even if they were shut in for days. As they passed the section of wall where she had been standing when she saw the attack on Marnix, she averted her eyes, although Bram looked over the wall, searching for any sign of movement on the rooftop opposite.

'Nothing,' he told her. He didn't say, *You imagined it.* All the same, Veerle thought she sensed him relax a little.

When they got to the weapons room Bram began to unpack his rucksack, pulling out his sleeping bag. There was a rough energy to his movements, as though he were taking something out on it. Veerle watched him for a moment, and then she began to do the same. It was hard to imagine sleeping, but she had no desire to explore the castle any further, and the hours until they could escape from the castle stretched out ahead of them with the grim monotony of a desert.

They laid out the bags near the fireplace, in case they needed to hide quickly. Veerle took the torch from Bram and ducked into the fireplace for a moment, shining the light up the chimney. *This is stupid, you know*, she told herself.

We can't get out, so nobody else can possibly have got in. All the same, she didn't feel safe until she had done it.

Bram watched her. He said, 'Veerle, is there any way you could be . . . mistaken?'

Veerle didn't say anything for a moment. She was remembering the night on the rooftop when she had asked, *You think I'm being paranoid?* and Bram had hesitated before he said, *No . . . but I think you're safe here.*

She couldn't blame Bram for not wanting to believe it. She didn't want to believe it herself, the thing she had witnessed. Bram had only seen someone running at Marnix; then he'd gone for the phone. Veerle had seen, but she wanted to *unsee*. It was useless seeing when you could do nothing to change what happened.

Bram reached out and grasped her by the upper arm. His face was set. *He doesn't look like himself*, thought Veerle. All his amiability was gone. He looked blank and bewildered.

'Veerle, what did you see? I know you said this person hurt Marnix, but what *exactly* happened? Did you see his face?'

Veerle shook her head. 'He had some sort of black thing on, a cloak maybe. Or a loose coat. His head was muffled up. I couldn't see his face at all. He ran at Marnix. You saw him. It looked like they were fighting.'

'Fighting?'

'Well, he attacked Marnix and Marnix was trying to defend himself. And then – then Marnix kind of slumped down.' Her voice began to waver. *Oh no. Don't let me cry.* 'He fell down and he didn't move any more,' she finished, struggling to stop her voice breaking. Then she looked at Bram, shot him a pleading look, wanting him to stop asking her questions because she was afraid she was going to break down, and she saw her own distress mirrored in his face. Was it for Marnix, she wondered, or was it because he thought she, Veerle, was breaking down?

He looked at her for a long time without speaking, and then he said, 'I know you couldn't see his face, but was there anything else about him, anything at all . . . ?'

'No,' Veerle said, shaking her head. 'I didn't see his face. I couldn't even tell how tall he was or anything, not from this far.'

'So there was nothing,' said Bram. 'Nothing that we could tell the police.' There was a note of something in his voice – relief? Pleading? Veerle looked at him and saw that he was waiting for her to say that it didn't matter what she'd seen, there was no way she could identify the man anyway – that they would be bringing the storm down on themselves for nothing.

'No,' she agreed reluctantly. Suddenly she felt terribly tired, as though she had been carrying something for a long time and had only just begun to feel its weight. She wanted to lie down and close her eyes and not think about what had happened to Marnix and whether or not they should call the police. 'Maybe we should sleep on it,' she suggested, and she was relieved when Bram didn't want to discuss it any further.

It was uncomfortable lying on the hard wooden floor, even with the padding of the sleeping bag. They lay close together, close enough that Veerle could feel the warmth of Bram's breath on her cheek, but he didn't try to kiss her. Although he was lying motionless beside her, eyes closed, not speaking, she knew that he was not asleep. She could feel the tension in his body, in the arm curled around her, the way the hand was tensed into a fist.

He's thinking that maybe, just maybe, his friend has just died. In all the previous year, when she and Kris had been together, trying to see the pattern in the disappearances of so many people – Vlinder, the girl in the lake; the English girl, Clare; the Dutch guy, Horzel – Veerle had never lost anyone she personally knew, not unless you included Hommel, and she hadn't exactly been a friend. Still, she remembered how shocked she had been at the news of each death. Vlinder, the girl whose body had been found frozen face down in the water – that one had struck her as particularly awful. There was a callousness in the way Vlinder had been left there, as though the killer were a fly-tipper offloading a pile of rubbish. And now she'd just told Bram that his friend, someone he knew, had been disposed of with that same casual brutality. Veerle could hardly imagine what that would feel like.

She worked an arm free from the confines of the sleeping bag and put her own hand over Bram's, trying to smooth the tension from the clenched fingers with her own. They lay there like that for a long time, and a little while after she felt him begin to relax, Veerle fell asleep.

31

And dreamed of Kris. They were in the old castle, miraculously resurrected from the flames that had consumed it, a fact that Veerle unquestioningly accepted in the dream. They were standing in the middle of the upstairs landing, where once they had picnicked on a blanket on the worn floorboards. Dust motes were dancing in the bright sunlight that streamed in through the large windows. The light picked out every detail with flat photographic sharpness: the banister rail, polished to a smooth sheen by years of hands sliding along it; the battered panelling topped by faded wallpaper whose pattern had nearly vanished in places; the loose board with a single nail sticking up, glinting in the sunshine. Veerle looked around at all this and then looked up at Kris, at his familiar face, his dark hair and eyes.

Kris had his arms around her, and then he was kissing her, and it was strange because although the interior of the castle itself now seemed somehow insubstantial, like a holographic projection or a reflection on the glossy surface of a lake, the feeling of Kris's lips on hers was real; it was warm and alive. It was an intense point of exquisite sensation, like a single splash of crimson on an enormous monochrome canvas.

Veerle awoke with a start, the transition from sleep to wakefulness so swift that she was disorientated. The wooden floor was uncomfortably hard under her hip and shoulder, and her upper body was chilled because she had pushed her arm out of the sleeping bag. For a moment she thought she was in the old castle, lying on the dusty boards.

Kris, she thought confusedly. Then she began to pick out details of the room in the dim light that came from the tiny windowpanes: the reflective surfaces of the glass cases, the rough stones of the walls. Bram's sleeping form beside her.

I'm in the Gravensteen. Not the other place, the old castle.

Veerle could almost *feel* Kris's kiss; her lips were tingling with it. It had felt so real. She sat up, and in the dim light she stared down at Bram.

Was he kissing me when I was asleep?

She had kissed him gladly the night before; she studied his handsome face, his blond hair bleached almost white by the sun, and thought that she would gladly kiss him again. But she hoped he had *not* kissed her in her sleep because that would be kind of . . . *weird.*

Veerle stared at him for a while, but it was soon obvious that Bram really *was* asleep. He hadn't been kissing anyone unless it was in his own dreams. She didn't wake him. She sat hugging her knees and shivering a little, watching him sleep.

Why can't it just be perfect? she asked herself. The dream of kissing Kris had stirred up all kinds of unwelcome feelings, as though someone had thrust a stick into a limpid pool and churned it up until the water was thick with brown and evil-looking sediment. She bit her lip.

Why am I dreaming about Kris? I don't want to see him

ever again. I want to be with Bram. I want to be happy.

That possibility seemed to be slipping away, though, running through her fingers like water even as she grasped at it. The events of the previous night were crowding into her mind, and although they seemed to have the quality of a nightmare, and she would dearly have loved to believe that she had dreamed the whole thing, the reality was sinking in with an appalling finality.

Bram's friend Marnix is dead. He's really dead.

Veerle rubbed her face with her hands, as though trying to rub sleep out of her eyes, trying to dismiss an unpleasant dream.

I saw someone stab him.

Someone. Veerle saw Bram stirring in his sleep and she knew that he was going to wake up soon, and then they would be faced with that same question again: what, if anything, were they going to do about what they had seen? They could, she supposed, go up to the rooftop where they had seen it happening, if Bram knew a way. She thought that Bram would probably want to do that. He'd asked her whether she was sure about what she had seen, whether it could be a mistake. If she were Bram, if it were her own friend who had died, she would want to know.

And then?

That was the problem. Veerle had not seen the killer's face, couldn't even swear to his height or breadth. What could she possibly tell the police, other than the obvious fact that someone had killed Marnix, there on the rooftop? And if she did that, it wouldn't be long before they knew who she was: the girl who had seen Joren Sterckx, long after he was dead.

Then they won't believe a word I say. We'll probably have a hard time persuading them even to look on the roof for the body.

Veerle gazed unseeingly at the nearest glass cabinet with its payload of ancient weaponry.

The girl who saw Joren Sterckx. Was that label going to follow her everywhere, making her an unreliable witness for the rest of her life? The trouble was, she couldn't even account for it herself. She had seen the impossible.

Veerle sighed. These massive stone walls, Bram asleep on the floor beside her, the growl of hunger in her empty stomach: those things were real. Whoever she had seen that evening at the castle was dead, gone, burned to a crisp. His identity had ceased to matter.

It didn't help, though; it never helped. Once you had seen outside the bubble of safety that enclosed everyday life, once you *knew* what was prowling around out there, that lust to kill, that brutality, you couldn't *unsee* it. The death of one killer wouldn't end it. Even now, while she sat here in the cool silence, hugging herself, another monster was at work. At this exact moment the light might be dying from another victim's eyes. Once you accepted that, she thought, the idea of demons on the rooftops seemed almost possible.

When Bram awoke Veerle was already rolling up her sleeping bag, ready to stuff into her rucksack.

'What time is it?'

'Seven.' Veerle shook unruly strands of dark hair out of her eyes. 'What time do you think they'll open up?'

'Not before nine. I've come down and watched them a couple of times.'

'When can we leave?'

'It's best to wait until the first visitors have been through,' said Bram.

'And what then?' Veerle stopped what she was doing and looked at him. She wanted to hear what he was going to say. *Don't make me decide on my own*, she thought.

'I want to go there,' said Bram. He didn't have to say where.

'OK.' More than anything, Veerle didn't want to go up onto the rooftops, to see what the killer had made of Marnix. The idea made her queasy. But she couldn't leave Bram to do it alone. She said, 'Bram, if – I mean, if I wasn't mistaken about what I saw . . . ?'

'Then we call the police,' said Bram.

'From one of our phones?'

'That depends.' Bram raised his eyes to hers. 'I'm not leaving him up there, if he's . . .'

'No.'

'But if there's nothing we can tell them, nothing useful – we'll have to find some way of reporting it without getting involved.'

'OK.'

Veerle looked down at the rucksack, as though absorbed in the problem of how to cram the whole of the sleeping bag into it. She thought, *We're going to end up not going to the police again, just like last time.* Then she thought, *What choice do we have?*

32

At eight thirty Veerle phoned the school office from her
mobile and told them she was ill. It was not difficult to sound
convincing; the effect of the events of the previous night was
like a hangover. She felt tired and faintly sick.

Escaping from the castle proved more straightforward
than getting into it. She and Bram clambered into the
chimney again and listened as the castle staff passed through
the room, switching on lights. Nobody lingered in the room,
and shortly after ten the first visitor came through: a middle-
aged man with a Ghent guide book in his hand.

'I thought I was the first one in here,' he said to Bram, looking surprised.

'I guess we were early,' said Bram politely.

The man watched him and Veerle hitch their rucksacks
onto their shoulders and head for the door. 'I was there when
the ticket office opened,' he said to their retreating backs.

Veerle shot Bram a glance but she didn't say anything. They
kept their heads down and made for the exit.

Bram had reckoned that the trickiest bit would be passing
the ticket office without anyone recognizing them, but in fact
it was crammed with schoolchildren when they passed, and

the staff were far too busy to notice a couple of stray visitors wandering towards the gate. A minute later and they were out on the street, crossing Sint-Veerleplein in the morning sunshine.

Veerle felt a little unsteady. At first she thought it was simply relief, the sheer release of tension once they had left the Gravensteen without a hand descending on either of their shoulders. Then she realized that she was starving. She had not eaten for over twelve hours and she had been up and about for three. She wondered what she looked like; hollow-eyed and dishevelled, probably, after spending the night sleeping on the floor.

I bet I don't look like I've spent the night in a hotel in Amsterdam, she thought. She would have to do something about that before she went home to Geert and Anneke.

'Bram? Can we get something to eat?'

As she spoke, Bram looked at her, and for a moment she could have sworn he wasn't even seeing her; there was a glazed look in his eyes, as though he were looking *through* her into some grimly absorbing mental tableau. Then a change passed across his face, subtle as a shudder, and he was really looking at her, and smiling sadly.

'Sure.' He touched her shoulder. 'I'm starving too.'

They went into a little tobacconist's shop whose windows were crowded with packets of food and other goods. They bought cans of iced tea and sweet rolls wrapped in cello-phane. Veerle tore open the wrapping and attacked the roll gratefully. Bram put his into his backpack, in spite of what he had said about being starving. There was a suppressed tension about the way he moved; he was dying to get onto the rooftop, hoping perhaps that Veerle had been mistaken after all, or knowing that she hadn't been and wanting to get it over and done with. Already he was drifting across the street, turning to look for traffic, stepping over the tramlines.

Veerle drifted with him. She said, 'Bram?' She wanted to tell him to slow down, to eat something, to prepare himself for what they were going to do, if that were possible.

Bram said, 'You don't have to come with me.'

His tone was not unfriendly but Veerle was piqued all the same.

'Of course I'm coming with you.' She hefted the backpack up on her shoulder. 'How are we going to get up there? *De ladder*?'

Bram shook his head. 'We can't get near enough from there. There's a street between the blocks.'

Then how? Veerle wanted to say, but Bram didn't look in the mood for conversation. She had never seen him look as grim as this, even last night when she had told him what she had seen. Instead she paced along beside him, doing her best to prepare herself for whatever lay ahead.

All the same, she was shocked when she found out what Bram had planned. He led Veerle down a backstreet, checking that there was no one in sight. The street was mostly lined with scruffy garage doors and windows with the security shutters rolled down. Bram walked down it at a brisk pace, scanning the façades, until he found what he wanted: a run-down-looking front door, the red paint faded almost to pink. Next to it was a dusty window, streaked with dirt, and above that a faded and hopeless TE KOOP sign.

Bram had his backpack off his shoulders and was stripping

off his jacket and the sweatshirt he had on underneath. Veerle watched in perplexity as he wrapped the sweatshirt carefully around his hand. She had some inkling of what he intended to do, but she still gasped when he stood a step forward and punched the window in.

Glittering shards rained down on the cobblestones. Bram kicked out the glass fangs that jutted up from the bottom of the windowframe. He picked up his backpack and threw it inside. Then he unwound the sweatshirt from his hand and threw that in too. As he was putting his jacket back on he glanced at Veerle, who was watching him open-mouthed.

'Are you coming?'

Veerle glanced up and down the street. Incredibly, nobody seemed to have heard a thing, or if they had, they weren't investigating. She took off her own backpack and, ducking a little to avoid the jagged edges at the top of the window, followed Bram through it.

Even once she was safely inside the building she didn't like to speak, not with the broken window at her back. She waited until they were climbing the scuffed wooden stairs before she said anything.

'Did you have to do that?'

'Yeah.'

'How did Marnix get up there?'

'I don't know. He had some route of his own. I've never done this block.'

Veerle grimaced to herself at that, wondering whether there would even be a way out onto the roof. She was praying that there would be; in Bram's current mood he seemed quite likely to break into a second property if this one was useless, and their luck wouldn't hold for ever.

This time it did, though. They zigzagged up dusty staircases and passed rooms with bare boards and nothing inside them except the musty smell of dereliction, and on the top floor they found a window that looked out onto a small square of ribbed metal roofing. Bram seized the latch boldly. The window opened without much difficulty; it was a little stiff but not locked. Bram climbed out without hesitation, leaving his backpack on the floor.

Veerle stood for a moment on the inside, listening for sounds from below – anything that would suggest that the break-in had been noticed. Silence. She put her bag next to Bram's and climbed out after him. She was trying very hard not to think too carefully about what they were doing.

Just do it, just get on with it. You're committed now, anyway.

She followed Bram, who was moving cautiously across the metal roof. This was unknown territory; presumably there were ways across it, since Marnix and the other person, the one she was doing her best not to think about it, had moved about up here. All the same, a false move up here could be literally fatal. Trying to follow Marnix across this rooftop terrain was as hazardous as trying to follow a mountaineer across an ice face. Any given point of the surface underneath could be the weak one, the rotted beam or the missing bolt, the place where a foot could go right through or, worse, a whole person. The sloping surfaces that gleamed dully in the morning sunshine could be the chutes that launched you screaming into space.

Veerle was used to heights, she was hardened to them from the climbing she did, but still she found her heart thumping and she could hear the sighing of her own breathing. She could see where she and Bram had to go, and she didn't like the look of it. The flat roof where they had last seen Marnix standing was on the west side of the block, overlooking the Gravensteen; the house they had broken into was on the east side. There was an unbroken series of rooftops from where they stood to where they needed to be, but in the centre of the block, like the caldera of a dead volcano, was a wide open space, a pit, a drop of several storeys into a scruffy-looking yard.

Veerle's gaze traced out the route they would have to take. Most of it was pretty easy, she judged – all of it in fact, except the traverse that would take her and Bram from east to west. From here, she could see no way of doing that without going along the side of a sloping roof, picking their way along a gutter that could be anything from a reassuring metre wide to a single foot's width.

Don't think about it. Just do it.

She followed Bram as he climbed from the ribbed metal section onto the neighbouring roof. The roof ridge had a convenient flat section wide enough to be a path if you kept your nerve. Veerle thanked heaven that it had not rained in the night. If that flat section had been slick with wet she might not have dared attempt it. As it was, the surface was dry and she was able to walk along it easily in her Converse trainers. The enormity of the open sky wheeled above her head, sending tiny prickles of cold apprehension through her, light and icy as falling snowflakes. She forced herself to keep her eyes firmly on the roof. It was a relief to get to the other end.

After that they had to scale a small tiled roof and slide carefully down the other side. There was no danger of falling off there because it abutted the wall of another, higher building, but Veerle could see very clearly that her fears had been well founded: there was no other way to go west than to walk along the gutter of the next roof, right next to the drop.

Bram turned to look at her. 'You can wait here if you want.'

'No,' said Veerle, but the word was leaden in her mouth. She found herself swallowing.

They examined the gutter. It wasn't so very bad, Veerle thought; the gutter itself was set into a parapet that was wide enough to walk along without difficulty. If it had been ten centimetres above the ground she could have run along it without thinking twice. But now . . .

She looked into the drop, and then wished she hadn't. If you fell from there, there would be nothing to break your fall until you landed in that disreputable-looking yard far below.

Don't look down, you idiot. She should have learned that by now.

Bram had started along the parapet, moving cautiously but with determination. There was a rigidity to the way he held his head which suggested that he too was willing himself not to look down. He held his arms a little way from his body, for balance, and Veerle saw that the hands were curled into fists.

She waited for him to reach the other end. How far was it? Only three or four metres, she judged. Not really so very far. All the same . . .

Veerle stepped onto the parapet. Instantly the empty space seemed to swoop at her, to press on her from all sides.

It was hungry, it wanted to suck her into itself, pull her over the edge.

She stopped, her breathing shivering in and out of her mouth.

Come on, she said to herself. *You've done other stuff just as bad as this. You'd think nothing of this on the climbing wall.*

On the wall, though, she always had a rope. The only thing that would spool out after her if she fell off here would be her own scream, and it would follow her the whole way, right down to the ground.

Three metres, she said to herself. *Maybe four.*

Veerle was conscious of Bram standing at the other end of the parapet, his face and blond hair a light patch at the periphery of her vision. She dared not look directly at him. It was useless to let her gaze snag on anything other than the way ahead, and even more useless to give anyone else pleading glances. The only person who could make her cross safely was herself.

She stepped forward and felt the side of her foot flex inside her trainer, as though she was about to go over on it. The rush of adrenalin was instant and fierce, a streak of silver lightning through her body. Veerle shifted her weight slightly, stabilizing herself. The fear thrumming through her was so strong that she was afraid she would actually be sick.

She tried to make herself focus. *Calm down, calm down*, she said to herself, trying to make the words louder in her head than the screaming of her nerves. She took another step.

Bram said nothing, afraid to distract her. The only sounds that came to her ears were the distant murmur of traffic, the cry of a bird, her own ragged breathing.

Don't think about it. That was the only way to tackle it. The more she thought about what would happen if she stumbled, if she fell, if she actually fainted from fright, the more likely it would be to happen. *Don't think – don't think . . .*

Veerle put one foot in front of another, and then she took another step, and then another. She imagined her vision narrowing down to a slim intense beam like a laser, everything outside it unseen: the sloping tiles, the drop to her left, Bram on the other side.

How far have I come now? A metre and a half, two metres?

Turning round to look was impossible. Reversing her steps was impossible. Veerle kept moving forward.

Suddenly it was impossible to unsee Bram. They were so close that she could almost have reached out and touched him. Veerle made herself cover the last metre slowly and carefully; it would have been too easy to lunge forward now, wanting to get the whole thing over and done with, and slip . . .

Then she was stepping onto the roof at the other end, into the safety of a deep gully between two neighbouring roofs, with nowhere to fall, and Bram was putting his arms around her, pulling her into an embrace.

Veerle felt an irresistible urge to move further down the valley between the two roofs, to put some space between herself and that appalling drop. The relief of having crossed it safely was so strong that she felt light-headed. She was almost afraid that at the very last she really would pass out and slide over the edge. She pulled Bram into the gully with her.

They sat down side by side, backs to one of the sloping roofs, feet pressed against the other, and caught their breath.

'Bram?'

'Yes?'

'I don't think I can go back that way. I don't care if we have to break into someone's attic or climb down the chimney or something. I just don't want to do that again.'

'OK,' agreed Bram. His voice sounded strained, out of breath. Veerle guessed that he had hated making the crossing as much as she had. He was silent for a few moments. Then he said, 'We should keep moving. If we stay here . . .'

His voice trailed off, but Veerle knew what he meant. If they stayed there, they would simply lose more of their nerve; they would have too long to contemplate what lay ahead.

They got to their feet and went to find Marnix's body.

33

It was not difficult to find the flat stretch of rooftop they were looking for with the looming bulk of the Gravensteen to orient them. The traverse along the gutter was the worst of the route; the rest was relatively easy. They slid along the ridge of a tiled roof, riding it like the scaled back of a dragon, climbed down a peeling section of whitewashed wall and found themselves in a cramped and filthy corner behind a stout chimney stack with four pots on top of it.

Veerle knew that chimney stack. The last time she had seen it, she had been staring down from the top of the Gravensteen, straining to catch a glimpse of movement behind it. It had been night, and what light there was had been the sickly amber of streetlamps and the castle illuminations, interleaved with jagged patches of black shadow. Now everything was defined clearly by the bright morning light. All the same, she had no difficulty recognizing the chimney stack: those four pots were distinctive. Marnix's killer had stood exactly where she and Bram were standing.

The thought appalled Veerle. Mere hours separated her and Bram from a monster. He had occupied the same space they were occupying – breathed the same air. Suddenly she didn't want to be in that confined space. She stepped over the corner of an adjoining roof and out into the open.

She saw Marnix almost immediately. What had been a person – Bram's friend – was now a lump, a shapeless black patch like a sack of refuse, huddled on the gritty rooftop near the parapet.

Veerle was conscious of Bram at her shoulder, his breathing an audible series of shudders. As if by mutual consent they began to walk slowly towards that huddled shape, each wanting to know but not really wanting to see, moving forward but delaying the evil moment.

Marnix was lying on his back, his legs drawn up slightly and twisted to the side. He was wearing dark trousers, the kind you'd have worn for climbing or hillwalking in cold weather, and a soft shell jacket in a colour that was nearly but not quite black. Under the jacket was a light-coloured T-shirt with a Rorschach stain of dark reddish brown on the upper part of it. There was more of that red-brown on the pale exposed skin and the surface of the roof.

Veerle saw that Marnix had very dark hair; it was thick and rather dry so that it stuck up in places like the thick fur of an animal. He was unshaven, and the dark stubble stood out against the skin, which was so pallid that it had an almost grey tinge in the cold morning sunlight. His mouth was open and so were his eyes. Veerle saw that they were blue-grey. There was a strange fixed look to that dead gaze that made her think of the opaqueness of glass tumbled by the sea.

Under Marnix's jaw there was a bloody and mangled rent.

Veerle wanted to turn her head and look away, but she couldn't. She just stood there, taking it in: the twisted body, frozen in place by Death; the open eyes; the gash under the jaw.

Bram made an incomprehensible noise beside her, a harsh sound in his throat as though he were choking on what he was seeing. Veerle reached out blindly for his hand, gripping it with her fingers; it was lifeless in hers, as though Bram were unaware that she was even there.

After a moment he said, 'I thought – I was hoping . . .'

'I know,' said Veerle, her own voice unnatural in her ears. Bram had hoped that perhaps she had been mistaken, that there would be nothing to find up here. Perhaps he had even been talking himself into thinking that she, Veerle, was deluded – seeing murder where there was none. She was, after all, the ultimate unreliable witness – the girl who had seen a dead man trying to drag the living back into Death with him. But Veerle had known what she had seen from the top of the Gravensteen: it wasn't a practical joke or a half-hearted scuffle. It was the brutal extinguishing of life.

The body still held her gaze with some grim magnetism.

'What's that?' she said suddenly.

'What?' said Bram. He sounded groggy, punch drunk.

'That white stuff.' Veerle let go of Bram's hand and pointed.

There was a line of it – or at least, there had been to begin with, before the white powder, whatever it was, had become soaked in the red-brown stain on Marnix's T-shirt. A wavering blurry line, running across Marnix's chest like a knife slash. Where there was no blood it showed clearly; where it crossed the drenched T-shirt it was visible only as a texture.

Salt, thought Veerle. Then she thought, *Salt, like that line of it we saw on the roof, the first time Bram took me up there. Salt, like they found on Daan De Moor's body.* She could make no immediate sense of it, but she understood that there was some meaning here, something she wasn't grasping.

Bram said, 'And what's that?'

Neither of them liked to get too close to the body, with those twisted limbs and those wide open eyes. Instead they leaned over, trying to see.

'It looks like a nail,' said Veerle eventually. 'An old one. It's all black.'

Bram moved forward, brushing her as he did so, and she reached out to try to grab his arm, to tell him not to touch the body; that was a job for the police. Too late: Bram was already squatting on the roof, but the thing he picked up was not the iron nail, it was something else, something that lay within an arm's length of Marnix's dead hand.

Bram picked it up carefully, making sure not to leave tracks on the dusty roof surface with his fingers. Then he showed it to Veerle.

'Marnix's mobile phone.' He slid it into his pocket.

'Shouldn't we leave it here?'

Bram shook his head. 'We need it.'

'What for?'

Bram looked at her, and his expression was so fierce that Veerle was taken aback. 'I'm not leaving him here. How often does anyone come up here? Practically never. We have to call the police.'

'I *know*, Bram.'

'We use my phone or your phone, the police are going to have the number in two seconds flat. There are probably a few public call boxes left in Ghent, but the only ones I can think of are at the station, which is full of people. You want someone standing next to you listening to every word?'

'No,' said Veerle. She didn't want to argue with Bram. This was grief wearing anger like mourning dress. There was nothing she could say to make it better.

After a moment Bram said abruptly, 'We should go.'

'Bram,' said Veerle reluctantly, 'I meant what I said. I don't want to go back the same way.'

'We'll try the way we saw Marnix coming,' said Bram.

They backed away from the body. Veerle looked at the flat roof surface, at the sweeps and gouges in the accumulated dust and grime. She didn't think either she or Bram had left an identifiable footprint in any of that muck, but who could say for certain? It was a relief when they got to the far corner of the flat section, and were able to climb into the valley between two roofs from which they had seen Marnix appear the night before. Here the surfaces were smooth, rain washing most debris into a central gutter.

They followed the gully to its end and found themselves on another flat section of roof. Perhaps it had originally been intended for a roof garden, although the only signs of occupancy were the droppings of birds. There was a small structure like a hut with a door in it, and the door was ajar. When they looked inside, the sunlight behind them showed steps leading down into the dimness below.

Bram looked at Veerle and raised a finger to his lips. She knew what he was thinking: there could be anyone in there. She was past caring, though; all she knew was that she was not going to walk along that parapet again, the one with the drop. No way.

They descended the stairs and realized that they were in an apartment block. *How did Marnix get in here?* Veerle wondered. She supposed they would never know.

They moved cautiously, making as little noise as possible, but all it would take was for someone to open their door and challenge them, and they would be in trouble. Especially when the police found out what was on the roof . . .

In the event, though, they got to the ground floor without incident. The front door had a simple pin tumbler lock, opened from the inside by turning a little knob. There was no need for a key. A minute later they were back on the street, walking away from the door without looking back.

Their bags and Bram's sweat top were still inside the other building, the one they had broken into, so they went round the block to see whether it was safe to go in and retrieve them. Incredibly, the broken window seemed to have gone unnoticed. Veerle kept watch while Bram retrieved their belongings. Nobody came down the street while she waited. She saw one person pass the end of it, but they didn't look her way. Then Bram was back, and they were hurrying away, putting as much space as they could between themselves and the empty house.

They walked for a long time, until the Gravensteen was no longer visible behind the buildings that surrounded them and the nature of the streets had changed – they were no longer passing groups of tourists and little boutiques; instead the streets were quiet and cool and they could glimpse the green surface of a canal.

Bram stopped and took Marnix's mobile phone out of his pocket. He and Veerle looked at each other.

Do it, telegraphed Veerle with her eyes.

Bram turned away, the phone to his ear, concentrating on the call. He spoke rapidly and urgently, and Veerle was surprised how quickly he had finished.

'They wanted me to stay on the line,' he told Veerle grimly. 'They must be joking.'

Already he was prising off the back of the phone, levering out the battery with his fingernails. He took out the SIM card too, and put both of them in his pocket.

They walked on for a while, each lost in their own thoughts.

Salt, Veerle was thinking, remembering the stuff that had been sprinkled over the body. But *had* it been salt? There was no way to be sure. It could have been sugar, or some kind of cleaning product, anything white and powdery. It made no sense at all. Why scatter something like that on someone you had just killed? Even if it had been something poisonous or corrosive, it couldn't hurt Marnix now. It couldn't make him any *more* dead.

And the nail? She wondered whether that was simply incidental, a piece of random debris. But she couldn't think where it had come from. It wasn't as though Marnix had been climbing something studded with them.

They came to a building site, temporarily deserted, and Bram ducked under fluttering tape to pick up a large chunk of stone. He put Marnix's mobile phone on the ground and struck it several times, smashing it until it was nothing but a heap of plastic shards. He swept them into his hand and pocketed them. Later, they came to a drain and he dropped the pieces down through the grille into the obscurity beyond.

The battery went into a rubbish bin on another street, and the SIM card into a drain somewhere else. Marnix's phone had ceased to exist.

They walked on, but any sense of purpose had evaporated now that the call had been made.

We got away with it, thought Veerle, but the knowledge gave her no pleasure. She kept thinking about that stiff and silent figure on the rooftop. The dark hair, thick as fur. The skin that was bloodless and almost grey. Those open eyes. Veerle thought she would never forget those.

She wished she could go home and climb into bed and pull the covers over her head, but of course that was impossible. The school trip to Amsterdam was not due to return until the middle of the evening. The rest of the day stretched out ahead of her, featureless and dismal.

They walked on.

34

Death looked for the blonde girl, the one he had seen that time outside the cathedral. Since then, he had seen her again in the streets of the old city, and he had known her immediately: the fine-featured, angular face, the arched eyebrows, the smooth light hair. The slender, small-breasted body, clad soberly in black. He knew her, and he knew that she must die. While she lived there could be no rest for him.

He would have killed her already but she was too quick for him. He was stronger than she was, and driven by a conviction that was so aberrant and all-consuming that it was like the rising of a huge and blazing sun in the discoloured sky of an alien planet. She must die. They must *all* die.

The girl, however, was very fleet and as skittish as a young deer, bolting at the slightest thing, the most trivial cause for alarm. She flew like an insect before the storm of his obsession, always just ahead of it.

He had seen her for the second time on a street west of the canal, not far from the Sint-Michielskerk. Knowing her at once, he had followed her as discreetly as he could, cloaking his intentions in stealth, but there had been few other people on the streets at the time, no crowds in which to lose himself.

He had followed her for perhaps a kilometre, his hand thrust deep into the pocket of his coat, fingering the knife, while she became more and more disturbed, quickening her pace, turning to glance back at him with a white and anxious face. Finally she had abruptly turned a corner, and then she must have taken to her heels and run from him full tilt down the narrow street, because when he reached the corner there was no sign of her. He had walked up the street a little way, and there was a puddle of dirty water which had collected in a dip in the square grey cobbles, and all around it the dry cobble-stones had been splashed with dark and wet, a ragged radius like arterial spray. He saw it in his mind's eye: her boot hitting the puddle and the filthy water spraying across the cobbles. She had run. She knew he was coming for her, coming to end her, and she had run.

Why? he had asked himself as he stood there scanning the empty street. She was as unreasoning as the animal that flees from the hunter. She had had more than her time, she must know that. And she could not run for ever.

His withered lips tightened. Sooner or later he would catch her, and then the thin edge of the blade he had in his pocket would pass like a caress across that pale throat and let the life out of it in a drenching red rain.

Since that day, he had seen her twice more in the streets of Ghent. Death was closing in on her; he was narrowing down the possible number of places in which she could have gone to earth. He thought now that her appearance on the west side of the canal was a fluke; wherever she went back to was on the east side, somewhere in the old city. She knew that he was looking for her and was taking pains to avoid him, that was clear. Once he had seen her wandering along Voldersstraat, and although he had stayed well back, mingling with the strolling shoppers, his dark hood pulled down low over his face, she had become uneasy. She had begun to walk more briskly and then she had gone into a shop. He had waited for a long time, hanging around at the corner of the street, but she had not re-emerged. The other time she had turned and seemed to notice him, but she had not run. She had very deliberately crossed the road and walked back the way she had come, but with the width of the street between him and her, and when she was level with him she had darted a glance at him, at once fearful and challenging, showing him that she knew who he was.

She could have met Death there and then, known him intimately, bloodily, but the street was crowded. Inevitably someone would intervene, someone would call the police. The chances of getting away would be close to zero. He would have taken a single step towards the achievement of his goal, but unless he had his liberty to pursue and exterminate the others, that single step would be worse than useless. He could not risk that; in spite of the almost overwhelming need to act now, it was unthinkable that anything should prevent him from completing what he had come to see as a holy quest.

The Demons of Ghent themselves shall not stop me.

So instead he had simply lifted his head far enough that she could see his yellowed teeth bared in a savage parody of a smile under the dark hood, and then he had dropped his head again and walked on, listening for the sound of pattering feet as her nerve broke and she ran. He was confident now that he would see her again, and that he would find her hiding place. To run into her three times, that was more than chance. She was not visiting Ghent; she was living here. She was living east of the canal, in the old city. Sooner or later, Death would find her hiding place. He would follow her home, and when they were there, when he was closeted with her in her private space, he would watch the life run out of her in pulsing crimson waves.

35

On the Saturday Veerle arranged to meet Bram again.

He's going to think we're together, she thought uneasily. Then: *Perhaps we are.* Before she looked down from the Gravensteen and saw that terrible assault upon Marnix, she had kissed Bram willingly; there had been no doubts in her mind at all. But now, looking back past that horrific time as though peering through a window filmed with filth, she wondered whether she had simply been caught up in the thrill of the moment. Or was the nagging doubt she now felt a product of the horror they had experienced together, a taint in the atmosphere between them?

She had to see Bram, though. The death of Marnix was with her every second of the day and night. It was a toxic reaction inflaming her whole body; it was the hot angry buzz of insects swarming inside a hollow tree. She wanted to talk about it, to try to work out the meaning of the things she and Bram had seen: the salt – if it *was* salt – on the body, the iron nail. Whether the salt had anything to do with the salt they had seen on the rooftops, sprinkled as neatly as a boundary fence. Whether it had anything to do with Daan De Moor. Even if Bram didn't want to *talk* about it, at least she would be with someone who had seen the same things. She would have to be on her guard when she was with Geert and Anneke, afraid that she would betray herself by some inadvertent remark. Afraid that the horror she felt would somehow seep into her expression and attract her father's attention. All the time she was with him and Anneke she kept her face carefully neutral, but the memory of what she had seen was like some angry demon screeching into her ear.

Bram, she thought. *I'll feel better if I can talk to him.*

Veerle arranged to meet him at Sint-Baafsplein. She had some vague idea of going into the cathedral again, of letting the confused tangle of feelings inside her diffuse into the vast empty stillness of its ancient interior.

When she got to the square, however, it did not look as though going into the cathedral would be peaceful at all. Before Veerle had got halfway across she could hear the altercation.

A group of tourists were milling about outside the main door but nobody was going in or out, and Veerle could hear someone shouting. She stood where she was for a moment, looking towards the cathedral door. There were two people standing in front of it, and a third standing in front of them with his back to Veerle. The two blocking the doorway had a certain grim immovability in their stance. As Veerle watched, one of them shifted his position slightly and the bleak autumn sunshine glinted off a security pass pinned to the breast of his jacket. *Cathedral guides . . . or security*, she guessed.

Of the man with his back to her she could see little other than that he was above average height and rather stooped.

The rest of him was hidden beneath a long dark coat and a woolly hat under which he could have had golden curls or dreadlocks or smooth bald skin. Veerle saw him move forward, towards the men blocking the doorway, and now one of them actually planted a hand in the centre of his chest and pushed him back. Arms were waved; faint angry voices drifted across the square like smoke from a distant bonfire.

'Not again,' grumbled a voice close at Veerle's elbow. She looked round and saw a short stout woman of perhaps seventy, muffled against the chill air in a grey padded jacket. No answer seemed to be required; the old woman was talking to herself as much as to Veerle, and she wasn't even looking her way. 'Always another idiot causing trouble. They should move that painting, or lock it up.'

Now she did give Veerle a brief glance, loaded with disapproval.

'The painting of the Mystic Lamb?' said Veerle, feeling that she was being called upon to say something in reply, but the woman was already sweeping on.

'There was that one they caught with a hammer under his coat. They knew him too. He'd tried something similar before.'

'Why would someone do that?'

The woman eyed Veerle with something close to suspicion. 'You're not from here, are you?'

Am I from Ghent now? wondered Veerle briefly, thinking of Geert and the flat on Bijlokevest.

'No,' she said.

The woman gave a little grunt under her breath. 'Well, if

you're wanting to see the cathedral, you'd better come back later.' With that, she waddled off.

Veerle looked at the crowd of people round the door and decided that she didn't care if she went inside or not after all. She was beginning to think that no amount of contemplative silence was going to help.

She tried sitting on one of the benches in the square to wait for Bram, but even through the fabric of her jeans she could feel the cold of the slats. She got up again and walked about until she saw him coming towards her across the cobbles, his hair white gold in the autumn sunshine.

As he came up to her he opened his arms and Veerle went into them. There was nothing else she could do.

'I haven't slept,' he said into her hair as she gazed up over his shoulder at the cold and limitless blue of the sky.

'Me neither,' said Veerle.

'I keep thinking about it. I told him to go up there, to look for us,' said Bram in her ear. He meant the block opposite the Gravensteen. 'If I hadn't done that—'

'You couldn't have known,' said Veerle. Even before the words were out of her mouth she felt a small guilty pang. *Perhaps we could have known. Perhaps there was a message in the salt we saw on the rooftop the time before, if we had only been able to read it.*

'Look,' she said, 'let's go and talk about this somewhere else.' Then, on impulse: 'Do you want to walk down to *de ladder*?'

'No,' said Bram immediately. 'Not up there.'

'We could get a coffee,' suggested Veerle, although she didn't feel remotely like drinking anything.

Bram was silent for a moment. Then he said, 'You could come back to my digs.'

The suggestion caught Veerle off guard. Before she had had time to think about it, she said, 'I can't.'

'OK,' said Bram after a pause. He pulled back to look down into Veerle's face, his blue eyes serious, but he didn't try to persuade her. 'We'll go and get a coffee, then.'

He slipped an arm around her shoulders and they set off across the square, leaving the cathedral behind them. Veerle didn't look back.

Walking down the street with Bram she had that feeling she'd had before, as though she were looking at herself from the outside. A girl of eighteen, with a home and family in Ghent. A fortunate girl with a good-looking boyfriend. A girl in her last year at high school, studying for the exams that would take her to university. Except that none of it felt real. The flat didn't feel like home, and Anneke didn't feel like family; sometimes Geert didn't, either. She liked Bram, she *wanted* to like Bram even more, maybe even love him, but Kris was always between them; Kris, who was at that moment very probably in the flat over Muziek City with Hommel. And as for school – when had she last given any serious thought to her coursework? She'd be lucky to scrape through the year even without the unofficial days off.

Not my life, she thought. *It feels like someone else's.*

She wasn't surprised that Bram had baulked at her suggestion that they go to *de ladder*. She had seen the expression that passed across his face when she suggested it, and heard the vehemence in his voice. Veerle thought that Bram was losing his nerve, that he was deciding that the cliffs and mountaintops of Ghent were best abandoned. And perhaps, she thought, they were. She had a very bad feeling about the whole thing.

Luc and Daan . . . she hadn't known either of them personally. Maybe they *had* both thrown themselves off the rooftops. She couldn't definitively know whether there had been malice at work. But she had *seen* what happened to Marnix. She had seen murder, and it hadn't looked like a random attack, either. It had been *meant*. Planned.

And then . . . there was the night she and Bram had been about to descend from the rooftops and that guy whose face neither of them had seen had rushed at Bram, arm upraised. There had been something in that clenched fist, something glittering, and she could think of nothing that it could be that was not deadly. The incident had been unnerving enough at the time, when Bram had thought it was just some random nut. Now Veerle was wondering whether it could have been the same person she had seen running at Marnix. There was no way to know. Whether it was or it wasn't, though, the rooftops were looking like a very dangerous place to be.

There are demons up there, all right, she thought, and shivered.

All the same, she missed being able to escape up to the rooftops, where the city felt as though it *did* belong to her, and she to it. She gazed up at them as she and Bram strolled along.

I hate you, she said silently to whoever lurked there. *I hate you for what you did to Marnix, and I hate you for making something fabulous into something foul and horrible.*

It came back to her again then, relentlessly – the sight of

Marnix lying there on the rooftop in the morning sunlight, his eyes staring sightlessly at the sky, his T-shirt stuck to his pallid skin with red wetness. And the salt.

Salt.

Bram stopped walking when he felt Veerle check her stride. 'What is it?'

It looked like he was sowing seeds, Veerle thought. She remembered the way Bram's assailant had cast out his arm once, twice. The tiny metallic tinkle of something landing on the concrete afterwards. *He wasn't sowing seeds. He was sowing salt. And he dropped something, something metal just like that iron nail we found. I was right. It was him. It was the man who murdered Marnix.*

'Veerle? What's the matter?'

If he'd been a bit quicker – if Bram had been at the bottom of the ladder when he attacked him—

'Veerle?' At last the anxiety in Bram's voice intruded into her consciousness.

Veerle turned a pale, round-eyed face to him. 'Oh, Bram . . .'

36

Death came to the priest, and not kindly. It had taken him a long time to find the man; he had never expected to find him hidden in the bosom of the church. The temerity of it astounded him.

For a long time Death had stalked the streets of Ghent, his grim visage cowled, rarely speaking to anyone but gazing sidelong into the faces of his fellow citizens with well-concealed hunger. His search was so very nearly done. He had not yet succeeded in running the blonde girl to ground, but he knew that it would happen soon – very soon. Still, there were the others, a mere handful of them now, but infuriatingly elusive. He longed to scythe them down.

He had found the politician in a newspaper, folded neatly and discarded or forgotten on a public bench, and had known him at once: the complacent bearded face with its high forehead, arched eyebrows and rather full lips. The printed face had crumpled as his hands gripped the paper, the knuckles whitening.

After that he realized the value of scanning the pages of newsprint whenever he was able.

The priest had been photographed amongst a group of

other people at a charitable event, and it was the setting that had given him away, the way he alone had glanced towards the camera at the moment the shutter clicked. The one face in the crowd that was turned to the observer; how could he not have known him?

Other than that, the priest might have been hard to recognize; his face was a nondescript one, with small eyes, a blunt but not excessively prominent nose and the beginnings of a double chin. A face you might see on any street in Flanders; a face you might have seen there at any time during, say, the last five hundred years. A face you would walk past without noticing.

Death had found him, though; Death finds *everyone* in the end. He found the church too, without much trouble. It was not a grand church like the cathedral, but that was a point in his favour. It was very difficult for him to enter the hallowed precinct of the cathedral, but there was no such bar to entering the smaller church. It was not hard to find the priest's dwelling place, and not particularly hard to get inside it. If you know that everything you touch will be smoking black ash by the time the sun rises, a few splinters of wood or shards of broken glass are nothing to be concerned about.

Death entered the priest's house on the ground floor, by the door whose lock he had broken easily. He stood, grim and silent, just inside the door, which would not now fully close; it hung awry, like a limb on a broken joint. The cold of the night seeped in around his bulk like a poison gas. If there was a window open anywhere in the house, if the priest liked a little fresh air while he slept, the through draught would suck the chill into the heart of the building, as though it were one gigantic lung inhaling deeply.

Death listened, his dark eyes glittering, and he heard no sound of movement, nothing to suggest that the priest had heard him entering. Above him, in the upper reaches of the house, he could hear the murmur of voices. From their cadence he recognized the radio, turned up for ears that were hard of hearing. This was good; with the voices filling the room upstairs, the priest would have heard nothing from down here.

Death was not thankful, though. He accepted that this good fortune was *meant*.

There were lights on in the house; the priest kept late hours. The man who was Death stretched out a sinewy hand and turned them out as he progressed through the house and mounted the stairs, so that darkness followed him like the sweep of a black cloak.

He paused on the upstairs landing, his nostrils flaring. Once that light too was extinguished, he identified the priest's location easily by the thin rectangle of yellow light that surrounded the closed door as though it were the door of a furnace and fire burned on the other side of it, as indeed it soon would.

He strode to the closed door and opened it.

Inside was a study with a large desk and a bookcase, although not as many books as you might have expected; the priest was practical rather than theological or political. There was a fireplace, but it had been sealed; instead there was a heavy radiator fixed to the wall. On the mantelpiece above the redundant fireplace was the radio. Behind the desk was the priest, starting back in his chair with an expression of outrage and terror on his jowly face.

'*Goeien oovent*, Gerard,' said the man who was Death, speaking in the Ghent dialect, his tone low and ominous. He came right into the room, his shoulders filling the doorframe, and closed the door behind him.

'My name's not Gerard,' said the priest. 'Who are you? How did you get in?' He pushed his chair back from the desk, intending to get up, but he dared not come out from behind it; one look at the intruder convinced him that it was best to keep the broad expanse of polished wood between them. His chubby hands clutched at the desktop, at the front of his own shirt, fluttering like fat pigeons in panic.

'You know who I am,' Death told him, pushing back the hood to let the priest see his grim and withered features.

The priest's face was a frozen mask of fear and anger, in which only the eyes were alive. Death saw their gaze flicker over to the telephone on the corner of the desk. He moved closer, letting the priest understand that to lunge for the receiver would be useless. Time had run out. Time was the one thing they all wanted more of, the people he destroyed, and for the priest there was almost none left.

Death moved closer, and now he opened his coat and let the priest see what he had brought with him, the gleaming triangular blade nestled close to his body.

'It's time, Gerard,' he said, and his voice was gravel and smoke, a pronouncement of coming execution.

'I don't have any money here,' babbled the priest.

'I don't want money,' Death told him.

'What *do* you want?' The priest's voice was high and

panicked now; the prospect of meeting his Maker did not delight him as you might have expected it to. But then the dark cloth he wore was simply a hiding place, a camouflage.

Death slid the knife smoothly out of the inside of his coat. The blade flashed golden in the lamplight. His knuckles were white around the handle.

There was a sound like steam escaping – the priest drawing in a thin and painful breath through a throat constricted with terror.

'Peace,' Death told him. 'I want peace.'

Afterwards he switched off the radio programme that the priest would never hear, and with crimson fingers he closed the eyes that would never see again, printing his marks upon their lids. Once again he listened – listened for the sounds that would mean that someone had heard him visiting bloody justice upon the priest – but there was nothing beyond the sound of his own ragged breathing. He went about then, preparing to sear away all traces of his work, opening internal doors, heaping up those things that would easily kindle – papers, books. The priest had very few possessions to interest him. Only one thing caught his eye: a little wooden statuette of the Virgin and Child, centuries old, the features blunted and faded by the passage of years, a fellow traveller from past to future. Rather than consign her to the flames, he put her inside his coat and carried her away with him into the dark.

The last thing he did before he pulled the outside door closed behind him was to toss the light back into the darkened house, as though he were releasing a bird into the air. As fire unfolded its wings and flew blazing down the hallway, he vanished silently into the night.

A little later, from his vantage point in the church tower (the key lifted neatly from the priest's cheerless kitchen) he watched the fire brigade arrive, too late to do anything but prevent the surrounding houses from going up. The orange glare of the inferno underlit his craggy features as he gazed down, dyeing them the colour of flames. If anyone had glanced up at him, they might have thought a gloating demon lurked there, relishing the grim incense of burning wood and charred flesh.

He was satisfied that no evidence of his presence could have survived the conflagration: not one hair, not one fingerprint; nothing but the marks of the blade on the priest's vertebrae – and perhaps not even those.

37

For days, and even weeks, Veerle waited for the visit or phone call that would tell her that someone had linked Bram to the death of Marnix, and her too, by association with Bram. The discovery of the body was mentioned in the local papers with an appeal for information; that was the moment when she expected someone to come forward and say that they had seen her and Bram breaking into the empty house, or that they had watched through the security peephole in the front door of their flat as she and Bram had hurried downstairs afterwards. But there was nothing: no visit, no call.

Soon the story was buried by a worse one: she found herself walking to school past newspaper stands with headlines screaming about the local priest whose charred remains had been found in the smoking pit of his home, and who had probably been dead before the fire started, cut down by persons unknown for reasons unfathomable. People were talking about crime waves, about the unacceptable level of violence that modern life had imported to the ancient city.

Marnix became a statistic.

At school Veerle heard Suki tell some of the others that the guy who had been found dead on the roof of a building near the Gravensteen was called Marvin, and that he had been covered with the marks of savage claws. She put her head down and didn't contradict the girl on either point.

As autumn slipped into winter Geert gave up escorting her to school, but still she went, and stayed. She tried to work, to catch up on all the things she had missed, but sometimes it was like trying to gather sand through open fingers. Sitting in a maths lesson she would think of Marnix, of the dead grey eyes staring up at the sky, and it wasn't just that she was distracted, it was that suddenly the lesson didn't seem to *matter*. Here was an equation she would never solve: Marnix was dead, and nobody had paid for it.

Veerle puzzled about the salt and the nail. She tried running internet searches and came up with a lot of stuff about iodine in salt. When she tried adding the word 'ritual' the search turned up some dubious-looking forums with comments about warding off ghosts and fairies.

I'm missing something, she thought, tapping the edge of the keyboard impatiently with her fingernails. Finally, though, she concluded that it didn't really matter. The critical thing was that the salt and the nail proved that whoever had killed Marnix had also tried to attack Bram that night. That was all it proved. Without a face or a voice it didn't help. They already knew there was a killer in the city, and the police did too. She wondered whether they had made any more of the salt and the nail than she had, but there was no way to know; if they had, they weren't sharing it with the press.

She saw Bram often. It didn't seem to matter that Veerle hadn't made up her mind about him; he had made his mind up about *her*, and he seemed to have enough determination for both of them. He invited her to the climbing wall, to the burger bar in the city centre, to the cinema. The one thing he didn't suggest was another trip to the rooftops of Ghent via *de ladder* or any other route.

Once Veerle suggested it, and pressed him into agreeing, but the expedition was a failure. The magic had fled with the end of autumn. It was chilly and dark, the roof tiles unpleasantly slick with damp moss and lichen, and every shadow a black pit concealing a nameless threat. It was no fun being on the rooftops when you were shivering with cold and looking over your shoulder all the time. Peering down over a set of corbie steps at the well-lit street below, Veerle found she was wishing herself *down*, not *up*: the street was full of warmth and light and voices; the rooftop felt like a graveyard. She and Bram climbed down and went to a café instead.

Bram didn't talk about Marnix; in fact you would have thought that he had forgotten about Marnix so completely that he might never have existed. Veerle knew better, though; she suspected that Bram was pushing the memory away on purpose, like someone trying to hide some noisome thing in open water, thrusting it down under the scummy surface with a stick. He didn't want to be reminded of what they had seen that night in the Gravensteen and on the rooftop the following morning; he didn't want to keep torturing himself by wondering whether he and Veerle had contributed to the death by asking Marnix to be at that spot. Veerle understood that; she had enough *what-ifs* of her own to last a lifetime.

All the same, it felt strange to do ordinary things together. It felt uncomfortably like acceptance: of her life in Ghent, her life without Claudine, her life without Kris. She would be sitting in the darkened cinema with Bram's arm round her and their faces lit an eerie blue by the screen, or sitting at a table by the window of a café waiting for him to come back with drinks, and she would have a sudden and desolate sense of dislocation which would coalesce into the question, *What am I doing here?*

There *were* good things here. The city was beautiful, she had to admit that, and although there was not much love lost between her and Anneke, Geert was all right; they got on together in a cautious sort of way. Adam, her little brother, was kind of endearing too. And Bram – Bram was amiable and kind and very good-looking. It was natural to swim up from the black depths of the water towards the surface, to push your way up like a green shoot towards the light. She couldn't help herself, and yet it still made her feel like a traitor. She felt as though she had taken all her memories of her mother, Claudine, and of Kris, the nine-year-old Kris of her childhood and the later Kris, the Kris she loved, and put them into a keepsake box, and closed the lid and locked it. Time would pass and nothing new would be added to those memories. They would be a for ever unfinished story; they would be like flowers pressed between the pages of a book, preserved for ever but growing slowly more brittle and faded.

It was the ordinariness of it all, that was the thing. Being up on the rooftops, in that deserted landscape of weathered brick and stone and dusty glass, of geometric shapes and long shadows – that had been different. It had been outside life, neither past nor present; it wasn't her home in Vlaams-Brabant but it wasn't really Ghent either, not the Ghent that everyone else knew, the ones who swarmed down there in the streets. Up there the world had been a blank canvas, an unfinished map whose details she could ink in herself. She had not been called upon to accept anything up there, nor forget anything.

But, she thought, *that was before.*

So she and Bram stayed off the rooftops, and went instead to the kind of places ordinary people went to. Bram started talking about introducing her to some of his friends or, more alarmingly, picking her up from the flat, which would mean him meeting Geert and Anneke.

Meanwhile Veerle would catch Geert watching her across the kitchen table with a complacent look on his face, and she knew what he was thinking: *She's settling down. She's getting over it.* He asked her whom she was meeting all these times when she went out, and when she told him, *A friend – yes, all right, a male friend,* he wanted to know where this male friend was from, and when he found out that Bram was local, he was from Ghent, that complacent look came over his face again. It wouldn't be long before he was asking her to bring Bram back to the flat himself, so they could meet.

Sometimes Veerle felt like screaming. At other times she was almost grateful for the ordinariness of it all, the dull procession of days that seemed to be slowly accumulating like layers of varnish.

Weeks went past like that, and then it all fell apart.

38

Veerle was blindsided. She had spent hours, days, fighting shock and sadness and guilt over Marnix. She'd tried to deal with the leaden dragging feeling she had every time she thought about Kris, and she'd spent the rest of the time worrying about where things were going with Bram and whether it was possible to be fair to herself and him. The one thing she hadn't thought about, the thing that had slipped so far to the back of her mind that it was lost in the distance, was the conversation she had had with the school secretary.

I could speak to the directeur, the woman had said, and later: *He might be prepared to refund part of the money – if you have a pressing reason for cancelling.*

But then they had agreed that the reason Veerle had given for cancelling her place on the school trip – that she had to stay with Anneke and her newborn baby – was hardly an unforeseen circumstance. Veerle had assumed that that was the end of it, or at any rate she had hoped it was, and then circumstances had brought other more urgent considerations to the front of her mind and she had forgotten all about it. Now it appeared that the thing she had overlooked had turned to bite her, like a snake on a path.

She had no idea that anything was wrong until she got home from school, and then the sky fell on her head.

Veerle had walked home as usual, stopping by the Coupure bridge to read a text message from Bram. There was no particular hurry to get home. It was a clear day in early December; it had been very cold in the morning, but by late afternoon it had mellowed and bright winter sunshine was gilding the buildings that lined the canal. Veerle took her time, walking as far as she could along the bank before she turned off towards Bijlokevest. She was thinking about her homework – there always seemed to be mountains of it, and she still had so much catching up to do – and about Bram's suggestion that they meet at the climbing wall at seven-thirty.

She reached the apartment block and let herself in via the street door. There was nobody about in the hallway or on the staircase. Veerle was humming to herself under her breath as she got to the door of the flat and slid her key into the lock.

As the door swung open she was aware of a sudden burst of activity inside the flat. She looked down the hallway, and there was Anneke with Adam in her arms, hurrying into the bedroom she shared with Geert. Anneke gave Veerle a swift glance as she went, a short flat stare that gave nothing away. There was an abruptness about her disappearance into the bedroom that struck Veerle as slightly odd – not that she had expected Anneke to greet her with joy. Then Geert came out of the kitchen, and that was a surprise because normally he didn't get home until a couple of hours after she did. One look at his grim expression told Veerle that she was in trouble.

Still she couldn't think what she had done. Had she

somehow offended Anneke, who was as touchy as a lapdog? She closed the door and put her school bag down on the rug.

'Go into the kitchen please, Veerle,' said Geert, and there was such an ominous tone in his voice that she obeyed without saying a word. She felt an obstinate little flare of resentment at Anneke, although she knew it was entirely unreasonable. Anneke had known this was coming. She hadn't shown any emotion, either scorn or satisfaction, but all the same, Veerle suspected she would get some grim enjoyment out of the storm that was clearly about to break over Veerle's head. When Geert closed the kitchen door Veerle thought, *At least she won't be able to hear every word.* Her heart was beating very fast; whatever she had done, it was apparently serious. She didn't think she had ever seen Geert look like this, even when he had found out that she was cutting school. His blunt features were rigid with the effort of suppressing some strong emotion; rigid as iron – or no, she thought, like glass, because through that ghastly rigor she could perceive something toxic boiling up like the smoking contents of an alchemist's flask.

Geert didn't tell her to sit down, and he remained standing himself. He said, 'I dropped in at the bank this morning and printed off a statement. There was a credit on it from the school, paid in a couple of days ago.' He paused for a moment, seeing from Veerle's face that she was beginning to understand. Then he went on. 'I wasn't expecting a payment from them, and it was an odd amount, so when I got to the office I telephoned the school.'

Verdomme. Veerle knew what was coming now, but she didn't dare say anything, didn't dare take her eyes off Geert's angry face, didn't dare move a muscle in case the lightning of parental anger should strike her.

'The secretary was very helpful,' said Geert. 'She was apologetic, in fact. She told me the reason for the odd amount was that the directeur had only agreed to refund half the money for the school trip to Amsterdam.' His gaze was searing; Veerle flinched under it. 'The school trip that you were unable to attend at the last minute, because you were at home looking after Anneke and her new baby.'

A muscle worked in the side of Geert's face. He said, 'The directeur felt we could have foreseen that, she said, otherwise they would have returned the whole lot.'

Geert stopped speaking and there was dead silence in the kitchen. Veerle looked at his face, and what she saw there made her feel sick. All at once she couldn't hold his gaze. She looked away and then she looked at the floor, at the homely beige tiles under her feet. She was completely unable to say a word. There was nothing she could say, nothing that could explain what she had done in a way that Geert would want to hear.

'Veerle,' said Geert at last, when it was plain that she was not going to speak, 'please tell me that this is some kind of mistake.'

'I can't.'

'What did you say?'

Veerle put her head up. 'I can't,' she repeated, more loudly.

'So you really didn't go? To Amsterdam?'

'No,' said Veerle.

'Well, where *did* you go? What were you doing?'

'The first . . .' Veerle began to speak, but her mouth was so dry that her words trailed off in a croak. She swallowed, running her tongue around her mouth, and tried again. 'The first day I went to school.'

'To school? And will the school be able to confirm this?'

Veerle nodded dumbly.

'That was the first day. What about the rest of it?'

'I . . .' Veerle fell silent.

'Veerle? I asked you, what about the rest of the time?'

The idea of telling Geert the truth flickered briefly in Veerle's mind and then guttered like a match burning out. She *couldn't* tell her father where she had been that night. Supposing he did something like marching her down to the Gravensteen and insisting she confess what she had done, maybe demanding to check that she hadn't done any damage? Veerle didn't have the benefit of years of living with her father, but she knew him well enough to think that there was a real risk of this. She recalled the way he had stood outside the school for hours, making sure she stayed inside, where he thought she ought to be. If it became known that she had been in the castle that night, there was a risk that someone would put two and two together and ask her if she had seen anything, because that was the night that boy had been stabbed to death on the roof of the building opposite – a boy whom she and Bram *knew*.

All this passed through Veerle's head with lightning swiftness. It was *impossible* to tell Geert the truth, so instead she said nothing at all, although she could see that he was not going to be satisfied with silence.

He took a step closer, and now he was standing over her, with a truly thunderous expression.

'Veerle, you were out all night *and* the following day. I *insist* you tell me where you were, and what you were doing.'

Veerle fixed her eyes on the buttons at his throat, biting her lip. It occurred to her that she could lie, that there were plenty of things she could tell Geert that would be less dangerous than the truth, and less inflammatory than silence. She could tell him that she had gone back to the village, for example; that she had missed it so badly that she'd had to go, but she hadn't wanted to hurt his feelings by telling him.

I could say that, she thought. *He'd understand that.*

The trouble was, it wasn't true. Veerle had never had the slightest problem lying to Claudine, because sometimes it was like withholding the painful truth from a child too young to understand. Geert was a different matter. Geert was as straight as the parallel lines that meet only at infinity. She didn't think Geert would *ever* lie, and she didn't think he'd forgive her if he caught her out in a lie. She kept her eyes fixed on those buttons, not daring to look at her father's face.

'Veerle, I'm waiting.'

Still she said nothing. There was nothing *to* say.

'Look at me when I'm talking to you,' ordered her father.

Veerle put her head back, shaking back a strand of dark hair, and made herself look Geert in the eye. Anger was emanating from him like radiation from an exposed radioactive core. It was all she could do to keep looking at him; she wished she could look anywhere else – at the floor or the ceiling or the closed door.

'Where were you?' demanded Geert, and Veerle said nothing.

Unexpectedly she could feel a pricking in her eyes, the

beginning of tears. She squeezed her hands more tightly into fists, willing herself not to do it. She could feel herself beginning to tremble.

Abruptly and shockingly, Geert broke first. He put one of his big hands over his eyes as though he wanted to blot out the very sight of her, and turned aside with a muffled curse.

Veerle continued to look straight ahead. A hot tear ran out of the corner of her right eye and slid down her cheek. She ignored it. She was aware of her father moving restlessly about the little room, as though he would have liked to escape from this situation as much as she longed to.

After a few moments he stopped pacing. The kitchen was small, but he had contrived to put as much space as possible between the two of them.

'Please tell me you weren't with the Verstraeten boy,' he said.

'Kris,' said Veerle under her breath.

'What did you say?'

'His name is Kris,' said Veerle, more loudly than she had intended.

'And were you with him?'

Veerle looked at her father mutinously, and now the tears were running down her face and she couldn't stop them. 'No,' she said.

'Because if I thought—'

'No,' shouted Veerle. 'I wasn't with him, OK? I wasn't with him.'

'So who were you with?'

Veerle pressed her fingers to her mouth, trying very hard to repress the treacherous sobs that were trying to break out of her. She shook her head. *I'm not saying anything.*

Geert raised a finger warningly, as though he were at a witch trial, as though he were about to say, *That's her – that's the one I saw.*

'It *was* the Verstraeten boy, wasn't it? He's behind this.'

'*No,*' screamed Veerle.

'Then who?' Geert bellowed back at her.

Silence.

'Who were you with, Veerle?'

He took a step towards her, and for one moment Veerle actually thought he might strike her. But all he did was point towards the kitchen door.

'Go to your room.'

She had her hand on the door handle when he said, 'Wait.'

Veerle didn't want to wait; she was dying to bolt for the sanctuary of the room she slept in, the room that should have been Adam's. She didn't dare antagonize Geert any further, though, so she stopped and waited to hear what he had to say.

'From tomorrow,' said Geert in a voice that was thick with suppressed fury, 'I will take you to school every morning, as I did before. I will wait until you are indoors. After school you will come directly home. You will not take part in any after-school activities, nor will you go to the climbing wall or anywhere else. At the weekend you will stay here in the flat unless you are accompanied by me. Do you understand?'

Veerle nodded.

'And another thing. If I have any cause to think that you are meeting anyone – *anyone* – unsuitable, I will be confiscating your mobile phone and your laptop.'

This time Veerle couldn't help it; a gasp escaped her.

Geert stared at her flatly. 'I'll give you once last chance. Where were you, and who were you with?'

Veerle shook her head. While she said nothing, there was still the possibility that she had done something relatively harmless, like staying with a friend back in the village.

Geert continued to look at her for a few seconds, and then he said, 'Go to your room.'

Veerle opened the door, wondering whether Anneke had heard them shouting from the other end of the flat, and what Geert would say to her about it. She would have liked to say *Sorry* to her father; she *was* sorry – she hated to upset him like this. It was no use, though. She couldn't tell him what he wanted to know. She slipped out of the kitchen and went to her room.

39

Night fell, and Death came out of his hiding place again, as though the dying of the light had created a vacuum that drew him out. The climb up to the roof kindled the familiar searing pain, as if a fuse had been lit and was burning slowly through him. His sinews were wires heated white hot; the marrow of his bones was glowing charcoal. But Death is rarely unaccompanied by pain; he accepted it, embraced it even. The passing years had branded it into him; soon there would be an end to it. He moved determinedly and felt the pain ebb, the grip of its fiery claws on his ancient flesh weakening.

The door to the rooftop was ajar. Once there had been a chain across it. The chain now lay in two pieces on the bare boards. He pushed the door open and stepped outside, onto the flat roof.

The air was very cold but utterly still, as flat as dead lungs. The sky overhead was black but there was enough yellow light to see; it bled up into the sky, turning the hem of the black a sickly grey. After dark, Ghent was gilded by floodlights. The cathedral of Sint-Baaf became a golden Gothic reliquary.

Death stood upon the parapet and looked down upon the old city, his eyes dark and fathomless under their papery lids. How long had it been his home? The years were so many that he had lost count. It was beautiful, that was true. He asked himself whether he loved it; whether he had ever loved it enough to think that he could spend eternity here. At any rate it was better after dark, when the streets emptied of their bustling population and their roaring, spluttering vehicles, all of them moving about to a daily pattern like tiny parts in some complex automaton. He gazed down for a while at the now empty street, and then he turned away, his heavy features cold.

It was hard going, moving about over the rooftops. The upper landscape of Ghent was haphazard. Like a geode, all its most elegant and regular structures were on the inside; the outer crust was rough and ugly. He toiled his way along valleys lined with weathered tiles, and trekked across deserts of metal sheeting. There were places where he had to traverse routes as exposed as paths cut into the side of a mountain. He kept his eyes open too for the other hazard that sometimes lurked in these heights: the dark figures scrambling away into the shadows. They assumed cunning forms, but he knew what they were.

Demons. They would hamper him if they could. He did not fear them. Some of them he had already cast down from the heights to the streets far below, rupturing their assumed shapes on the cobblestones, painting the ground red. Some of them he had cut, with the sharp steel he always carried with him. Always, always, when he killed one of the demons he sealed the death with salt and iron, making sure that they could not come back.

His goal tonight was on the outermost extremity of the area that could be reached from his own eyrie without descending to street level. After that, there was a gulf between blocks, impassable as a canyon.

He was aiming for a little window, a skylight set into the slope of a roof. He had gazed through the window at the occupant of the room below several times before, his eyes unblinking and baleful. He had known her the first time, would have known her even if he had not seen her sleeping face on the pillow, a sliver of moonlight silvering the hair spread out around her head like a halo. He had seen the viola – had recognized the instrument immediately.

She had never woken, had never felt the dark and venomous radiance of his presence above her, infecting her with the truth of her own approaching death. He thought that this was a sign that his goal would soon be achieved. He did not expect forgiveness, no, but he thought that his long march through Purgatory might be drawing to an end. The fact that the demons were weakening, that he was able to snuff out their physical forms, simply confirmed it.

The girl with the viola would be almost the last; after that there was only the blonde girl, the one who kept eluding him. *Eva.*

He could have taken the girl with the viola before; it would be easy enough to do, and he craved it very badly. But carrying it out was not the difficulty. The danger was the proximity to his own place. If he were thorough, there would be nothing left at the site to connect him to the girl's death, but still there was the risk that someone would stand in the blackened remains of the room, look upwards and think of the rooftops. There were only so many nesting places under the eaves of the buildings, and if they found his, he would never complete his work.

Now that he was so close to the end, he thought he could risk it. He did not need so very much more time. When the night's work was over he would dedicate what remained to searching the city for the blonde girl.

He was confident that he would find her. And when he did, because she was the last, there would be no need to employ stealth. Half a minute in the open street was all he needed to let the steel bite into flesh and free them both.

Death approached the skylight and peered through his own silvered reflection into its depths, like a witch gazing into a scrying glass. There was the sleeping form of the girl; there was the viola. His glittering eyes picked out other things too – small details of her existence: a book, the spine cracked, on the bedside table. A metal stand with sheet music on it. A china mug full of pencils. Soon, all of it would be gone.

He slid the tool out of his pocket and began to work on the window. He took his time. Speed was not important. What was important was not waking the girl before he had gained access, and not leaving visible damage on the windowframe, in case it survived the inferno to come. So he worked slowly, and sometimes he paused for a moment to peer down into the room and check that she had not stirred. The girl slept on, fearless, unsuspecting and beautiful.

She looked like an angel already.

40

Good as his word, Geert walked Veerle to school every morning as he had threatened. He was generally a taciturn person: not unfriendly but simply not given to torrents of small talk. Now, however, there was a grim quality to his silence; the air between them was thick with the insinuating ghosts of words unspoken.

Tell me, said Geert's severe face and heavy tread.

I can't, replied Veerle's hunched shoulders and downcast eyes. She folded her arms across her chest as she walked, as though shivering under the frosty blast of his disapproval.

The first morning, Veerle thought that her father would leave her on the pavement outside the school as he had before, but to her embarrassment he came right inside, into the foyer. Veerle thought she saw a few heads turn, saw a few people pause and cast curious glances her way. This wasn't nursery school; if one of your parents was with you, something was up. It was a relief when Geert finally turned to go; she had started to fear that he might actually accompany her to the classroom.

'Straight home after school,' her father said before he walked away. 'Or Anneke will call me.'

Veerle said nothing at all. She looked at her father's retreating back for a few moments and then she turned away.

At registration she wondered whether it was her imagination that the teacher put some small emphasis on her name when he called it; that he looked at her for a little longer than one might have expected. Had Geert asked the school to keep an extra close eye on her, to inform him if she disappeared again? The thought was depressing: the teaching staff here, Anneke at home. She might just as well have been under surveillance.

And so it went on. Every morning Geert delivered her to the school; every evening when Veerle arrived back at the flat Anneke was waiting with one eye on the phone. Once Veerle was ten minutes late because the teacher had kept the class in after the bell had rung, and when she got home Anneke was holding the telephone receiver, the smoothness of her expression belying the malice in her eyes.

Veerle wondered how long it would go on. Could Geert keep this up indefinitely, the house arrest and accompanying her right into school, the ominous silence, the constant policing of her whereabouts? The trouble was, she rather thought he could. Since she was not going to tell him where she had been during the missing night and day, they had reached an impasse. There was a break between them as profound as a geographical fault-line, with occasional magmatic pyrotechnics and the long weary attrition of rock grinding against rock.

She did her best to concentrate at school, but sometimes it was difficult: thoughts of Geert's stony face and Anneke's swift cool glance before the storm broke and the guilty memory of the night in the Gravensteen that she could never,

never tell them about would keep intruding into her conscious mind. Veerle would find herself being dragged down into a spiral of grim reiteration – *I have to end this; I can't tell them but I have to end this* – the thoughts running faster and faster, sucking her down into themselves like a hungry whirlpool – and then a voice would pierce her consciousness or the girl next to her would give her a surreptitious dig with her elbow and she would realize that the teacher had spoken to her, that she was expected to reply. It was useless, like coming into a conversation halfway through, and she could feel the gaps in her knowledge from the days she had missed, like blank patches on a map she could no longer read well enough to follow. Veerle wasn't stupid; she could see the looks she was getting from each successive teacher in turn, and she knew well enough which way *that* particular road led: it was the easy downhill path that led from *Trouble* to the place sign-posted *Deeper Trouble*.

And then there was the question of Bram.

Being grounded by Geert meant not seeing Bram, not unless he came to the flat, and now wasn't the right time to introduce the two of them, that was plain. Especially not when she considered that the information Geert had been trying to prise out of her was also in Bram's keeping, as though she and Bram had shared it like the two halves of a lovers' token. No; Bram had to stay away for the time being. That wasn't the thing that was really bothering her. That was the question of how she felt about not seeing Bram.

Not seeing Kris, not being with him any more, that had been like having some soft tender part of herself roughly hacked out.

Maybe, she thought, *I just can't feel like that again. Something's just . . . gone.*

Sometimes they spoke on the phone, but nearly always when Veerle was at school. Veerle thought that if Geert overheard her chatting to Bram while he was in his current mood, there was a definite danger that he would decide that Bram was unsuitable, and that would be sufficient grounds to confiscate her phone.

The school term ended, and the Christmas holidays passed dismally, with Veerle closeted in the flat with Anneke and the baby most of the time. She suspected that Anneke was finding the curfew on Veerle as irksome as she was herself, but she didn't try to remedy the situation by asking Geert to relax it. Instead she became more and more waspish. Nothing that Veerle did – or didn't do – was right. It was a relief when the new term began in January.

The first two days back passed without incident. On the third day Veerle switched on her mobile phone when the lunch bell rang and found that she had eight missed calls.

Eight? she thought, looking down at the tiny screen with a furrowed brow. That was over-enthusiastic even for Bram, and she felt the faint stirrings of disquiet. Before she had time to press LIST and see whether all of them were from him, the phone went off in her hand, a sharp trill that actually made her jump. She fumbled with the phone, almost dropped it, then thumbed the ANSWER CALL button.

As she pressed the phone to her ear she started to say, 'Hi, Bram,' but it wasn't Bram on the other end.

'Veerle?' said the voice. 'It's me, Kris. Don't hang up.'

41

Death continued to stalk the ancient streets of Ghent, crossing and recrossing the same paths, and at last his feverish zeal was rewarded. He found the blonde girl again, and she was alone and unaware of his presence.

He had hoped to track her to wherever she habitually hid herself, which he believed was within close walking distance of Voldersstraat, but she had eluded him for so long that he suspected she was aware of his hunt, was deliberately evasive, taking varying routes as she went about the city, and always, always, checking behind her.

Nobody can hide for ever, though. Now he had found her, the blonde one, and he was determined to finish it. She was the last; once his blade had carved the life out of her, he could turn it on himself. It would not take long; he was skilled at taking life now. A brief agony and then peace – peace for ever.

The long waiting had made him hungry for the deed. He trailed her at a distance of perhaps one hundred metres, his collar turned up to hide the lower part of his face, his strong hands thrust into his deep pockets where they could caress the things that hid there, the hungry sharp things.

He went stealthily, turning slightly to slip knife-like between other pedestrians where the pavement was crowded, not wanting a collision or anything that might draw attention to him. As ever, he felt the familiar pain as he moved, the smouldering of old fires in his joints that cooled and faded as he went along, as his body kindled to the task in hand and his will asserted itself over corporeal considerations. He thought of the blonde girl, of ending her, ending his own long search, and he felt a kind of savage joy that seemed to strip the years from him. *The last one.*

She was perhaps seventy metres away now, a thin black-clad figure topped with that striking and unmistakable pale hair, sleek and luminous as white gold. There was a little backpack on her back and she had something in her hand – a mobile phone, probably. There was a sense of purpose he hadn't seen in her before, and she seemed to have relaxed her guard somewhat; in the last two blocks she hadn't looked behind her once.

Do you not feel Death approaching? he wondered, watching the crown of bright hair threading its way through the assortment of other bobbing heads, dark, fair, bald, muffled in winter hats. *Do you not feel me coming for you?*

It baffled him, the human ability to live alongside Death, to know that it was coming for you, inevitably; that there was no escape for anyone. Such a short span, even for the longer-lived: perhaps seventy or eighty years. Perhaps that was the reason they tried to deny it, because otherwise what would life be except a short painful scream into the endless dark? The blonde girl was denying him, he thought; she *must* have felt his proximity, felt the imminence of her own end like the beating of great dark wings in the air about her, felt the feather-light touch of wingtips on the skin of her face.

Sixty metres; fifty.

The streets were crowded, and she was showing no signs of deviating from her route along the busiest of them. He began to feel real anger; anger and frustration. To be thwarted at this critical moment by the mindless crowds of pedestrians pressing in on them! He wished he could cut them all down, scythe them down like a strange bloody crop.

With an effort he controlled himself. *The girl – focus on the girl. On Eva.* He simply needed her to turn down some street that was quieter than the others, one where he could be confident that no passer-by could intervene when he struck. If they stopped him before she was dead, it was all for nothing.

Up ahead was a De Lijn tram stop, and he saw that the girl was crossing the street diagonally, making straight for it. She was swinging the little backpack off her shoulders, and then she was feeling through the front pockets, looking for something: probably her wallet. Sure enough, she drew something out of the bag just as she reached the tram-stop sign with its yellow-and-white De Lijn logo.

Of course. He had not lived this long in Ghent without learning its routes and rhythms intimately. From here the trams ran south towards Gent-Sint-Pieters railway station. The backpack, the sense of purpose, all suggested one thing. She was planning to leave Ghent.

He could have howled with fury. When he spotted her, he had felt so strongly that this was the time. Success had been so close that he could almost smell it on the air, like the coppery tang of blood. His lungs, inflating and deflating like bellows, awaited the smooth passage of the knife between their cage of ribs, releasing him. All he had needed was a few brief moments in some secluded place.

But she was going to board the tram, and then she would be at the teeming railway station, and then she would be on a busy train. Even if he could follow her without being seen, how could he unsheathe the blade in such places without some foolhardy passer-by hanging on his arm while others called the police?

He came to a halt, watching her approach the tram stop. It was very busy; unusually busy, in fact. Probably the next tram was overdue.

He thought about that; about forty tonnes of metal and glass approaching rapidly through the streets, ready to carry the girl away with it. And then suddenly he knew what to do.

He joined the waiting crowd with ease. Nobody gave him a second glance; today it was cold enough to see your breath, even in the middle of the day, and nearly everyone was just as muffled up as he was: collars were turned up, scarves stretched over noses, hats pulled down over ears.

The girl was standing on the very edge of the pavement now, gazing up the tramlines, eager to be climbing aboard, to get away. There were other travellers on either side of her: a stout older woman with a shopping bag on one side; on the other a tall, broad-shouldered man in a long black coat of some thick woollen material. All of them had their backs turned to him. He was able to move closer without difficulty, so close that he could have stretched out a hand and touched that gleaming pale hair.

It was distinctive, that hair; it was one of the things that had first alerted him to her. He wasn't the only one to notice it, he saw; the tall man in the black coat was looking down at her, and now he was saying something to her, and she was muttering something in return, not meeting his eye, making a play of leaning out over the edge of the pavement again, looking for the tram.

Here it came at last, he saw: gliding down the street towards them, the harsh metallic voice of the bell blaring out, a great metal monster like a battering ram. Heavy enough to crush anything in its path, even at braking speed. The girl was close to the end of the queue; the tram would not have stopped braking until the driver's end was well past the place where she stood. He edged closer, taking care not to attract attention to himself by shoving anyone else. He took his hands out of his pockets.

She was so close to him now that he could not help himself: her name slipped out of his mouth, as subtle as smoke, and there was one appalling moment when she half turned and he thought that she would see him, and know. But she did not pick him out from the tightly packed bodies in their uniform drab cocoons of winter coats. She turned to the front again, because here came the tram, and the attention of everyone on the pavement was focused forwards.

In the second before the tram swept past, he said her name again, and this time when she glanced over her shoulder, momentarily distracted, he placed both hands firmly in the centre of her back, and with one brutal shove thrust her forward into its path.

42

Hommel had been relieved to leave the flat that morning. For some weeks she had been free of the sensation of being followed when she went about the city; she judged that her strategy of varying her route home, of avoiding the streets where she thought she had been tailed before, of going in and out at odd and unpredictable hours, had been successful. Whether her follower had given up or whether the trail had simply gone cold, she couldn't say.

In spite of the absence of any further incident, however, Hommel found being in Ghent a strain. Sometimes she would be alone in the darkened grotto that was the music shop, and someone would pass the front window; she would see a dark shape flitting past and she would think, *I'm alone here. It doesn't matter that it's broad daylight out there; if something happens to me, who's going to stop it?* Or she would awake in the middle of the night on her mattress in the comfortless flat, listening to the creaks and groans of the old building and wondering whether she could pick out anything else amongst them: a furtive tread on the stairs, a rustle on the landing outside the door.

So she had decided to take a few days off. Kris couldn't

come to her in the week – he had to work – but she could go to him.

Just a couple of days, she thought. Three days, two days. One, even. Just to spend a little time feeling *safe*, not looking over her shoulder every time she went out. So she went to Axel, and after a little negotiation she agreed to work a whole week without pay in exchange for three days off. Axel was getting the best of the bargain but she had no leverage: if he threw her out she would be homeless as well as jobless. *The pay is rubbish anyway*, Hommel reminded herself. *You're only losing a percentage of nothing.*

The moment she walked out of Muziek City with her backpack on her shoulders – not much in it, just a couple of clean T-shirts and a few other bits and pieces – she knew she had done the right thing. She felt light, free, as though the bright wintry sunshine had burned off some oppressive dark fog that had been hanging over her. As she threaded her way through the shoppers on Voldersstraat the only thing that was on her mind was her destination. Normally she would have slowed her pace from time to time and glanced swiftly behind her, but now there seemed no need; in less than an hour she would be out of Ghent anyway.

The tram stop was unusually crowded but that wasn't a problem; even if she had to wait for the next one she had enough time. Hommel took her place on the pavement and glanced up the street, looking for the tram. It was a cold day, in spite of the sunshine; she could see a trace of her breath hanging on the air. People were beginning to push forward towards the kerb, in readiness to board the next tram: to her right, a robust-looking, grim-faced old woman who was clearly determined not to let anyone ahead of her, and to her left a tall man in a dark coat. Out of the corner of her eye she saw the man glance down at her, but she didn't react, didn't look back at him. Then he spoke to her.

'Cold, isn't it?'

She looked up fleetingly and saw that he was no more than a few years older than she was, with a pleasant, open-looking face and a shock of light brown hair. He was looking at her in a way that she recognized; there was more to it than simple politeness. The interest would have been flattering except for the all-pervading knowledge that she was not officially a resident of Ghent at all; for all she knew, she was a missing person back in Vlaams-Brabant. So she didn't return the stranger's smile; she just muttered, 'Yes,' in the most neutral tone she could manage, and concentrated on looking out for the tram, a little more self-consciously than she had before.

Here it came at last, sliding down the street towards her, its metallic bell as strident as a clash of swords. She was close to the back of the line; it would have to pass right by her before it came to a full stop. She waited.

It was at that moment that she heard someone say a single word. A name.

'*Eva.*'

It wasn't *her* name, which was Els, although she hardly ever called herself that, preferring her nickname of Hommel. It wasn't even the fake name she had given Axel, which was Hannah, and it wasn't a voice she recognized, either. She knew no one with that hoarse, guttural way of speaking. All the same, there was a certain insistent urgency to the tone in which the name was pronounced that caught her attention, that made her feel that it was somehow intended for *her*.

She half turned, but there was a crush of people behind her, and since whoever had spoken had fallen silent after that one emphatic word, she had no way of knowing who it had been, nor to whom it was addressed. Here came the tram, only a few metres away now; she turned her attention back to the front. It was braking now, you could hear it, but it was still moving quite quickly; she took care to hang back a little from the edge of the pavement.

In the very last moments before it swept past her, she heard that harsh voice again, only this time it was louder and there was no mistaking the sense of purpose in it.

'*Eva.*'

Hommel didn't mean to turn round; it could have nothing to do with her, after all. Still, she couldn't quite help herself; instinctively she reacted, glancing over her shoulder and away from the approaching tram with its hurtling blunt head of tinted glass and steel.

At that moment she felt a savage shove from behind, which propelled her forward with sudden and shocking violence. It happened so quickly that she was unable to prevent herself lurching forward. There was just time for her to think, *The tram – I'm going to go under the tram!* as a surge of terror rose up in her like the upsweep of a tsunami. Then she felt an agonizing pain in her left arm, as though it were being pulled right out of the shoulder socket, and she was jerked forcibly back onto the pavement. The side of the tram shot by so close to her right cheek that she felt it passing like a cold and savage breath, and at the same moment her hand hit the side of the carriage with a shattering force that sent a jarring pain right up the arm.

Panic broke over her like a wave, and for a moment she could not breathe. She could hardly believe she was still alive, that she was not at that very moment being dragged along the grey Ghentish cobblestones in bloody tatters.

'Fuck, what the hell are you doing?' said someone, and Hommel blinked once, stupidly, and found that she was in the grip of the man with the long black coat, the one who had spoken to her about the cold. His hand was still grasping her upper arm, so tightly that it hurt, and he was staring down at her, his face white and shocked. 'You trying to kill yourself?'

Hommel looked at him and her mouth opened, but what came out were not words; it was not even a sob or a scream but a kind of animal wailing sound, the keening of a hurt thing. She twisted in his grasp, trying to wrench herself free, but he wasn't letting go.

Some people were starting to push past them to get onto the tram, but others had stopped to stare at the blonde girl writhing in the tall man's grip.

Finally Hommel found her tongue, and the words burst out of her, as raw and shocking as blood coughed up from damaged lungs.

'He pushed me!' Her pale eyes were round and panicked. 'He pushed me!'

Now more people were stopping, and others were beginning to push from the back of the queue, impatient to move forward.

'What? The hell I did!'

The shock on the man's face was dissolving into

indignation and a kind of horrified fear; he could tell people were listening just as Hommel could. Now he wasn't just holding onto her, he was shaking her, and the pain in her outraged shoulder joint intensified. Tears sprang to her eyes, blurring the watching faces.

'I didn't push you. I saved you!'

His face was close to hers now, distorted with emotion that turned pleasant features into a caricature by Brueghel.

'Crazy bitch!'

'What the fuck is going on?' This was the tram driver, who had departed from custom and come out onto the pavement, pushing his way through the clustering passengers. The driver had the same look as the man who was holding Hommel's arm: a toxic mixture of fear and anger. He had peered over the edge of reality into an alternative universe where he had just run down a young blonde woman who had thrown herself into his path; he could practically *see* the crimson blood leaking out from under the tram, *smell* its coppery odour. He would have had to move the tram, in case there was any chance that a spark of life remained in the body, and he really, *really*, wouldn't have wanted to look at what was under it; the mere thought made him sick and sweaty, and since he was an older man, close to retirement, and not given to weeping in the street, he became angry instead.

'What the fuck did you think you were doing?' he shouted into Hommel's face. 'You want to kill yourself?'

Hommel looked from one furious face to the other, and then she darted a glance around and saw other faces, expressions deliberately neutral, eyes gleaming with avid interest as though through smooth masks. The feeling of panic was so strong now that she felt as though she might implode. Everything she had ever done since she arrived in Ghent was aimed at making herself as inconspicuous as possible, at trying to live her life under the radar. Now she felt trapped by the searing gaze of all those eyes, as though she were poised in the centre of a web of security lasers. All she wanted to do was bolt, to put as much space between herself and them as she possibly could, but she couldn't move; the man in the black coat was still gripping her upper arm tightly enough to cause pain.

'No,' she blurted out. 'He pushed me.'

'Who pushed you? *Him?*' The tram driver spoke so roughly that she knew immediately that he didn't believe her.

Hommel was about to protest, but then it came to her in a sudden rush. She had felt *two* hands in the curve of her back, *two* hands shoving her forward, in almost the same moment as the man in the black coat had grabbed her arm with jarring force. It was not possible that he had pushed her.

'No,' she said in horrified amazement, then: 'No. Not him. Someone . . .' She was going to say, *Someone else*, but the words died on her lips because she was turning her head this way and that, looking for the person whose two hands she had felt shoving her towards the tram, towards a bloody death only averted by the quick reflexes of the man beside her.

It was useless, of course, with all these people milling about. The sound of raised voices had attracted the attention of passers-by who hadn't even been queuing for the tram in the first place, and they were slowing down, adding to the crush on the pavement. If you added to that the people getting *off* the tram and the ones still trying to push past to get *onto* it, it was impossible to pick out any one person who might have done it. All the faces looked alike to Hommel anyway: the raw cold weather made people red-faced and haggard-looking.

It was him, she thought, *the one who followed me,* but she couldn't see anyone she even half recognized in the crowd.

'Too right,' the man who held her arm was saying bitterly. 'It wasn't me. The stupid bitch tried to jump in front of the tram and I stopped her. I didn't push her. I saved her life.'

'I'm sorry,' Hommel managed to say, but the words were inadequate, as though she had shouted them into a howling wind. Now that he was exonerated, the man who had pulled her back from the path of the tram was working himself up into a righteous anger at having been accused. She tried to pull away again, but he simply tightened his grip. Pretty soon he would be shaking her again.

'I don't know,' the tram driver was saying. 'I'll have to call this in to the company.'

Hommel saw herself quite clearly then, as though she were hovering some three or four metres above her own head; she saw herself in the grip of the man in the black coat, and hemmed in by the tram driver; she saw the ring of interested spectators around her, and beyond that other people, passers-by drawn in by the promise of a scene, and if you moved even further out there were people coming down the street who hadn't even seen the commotion yet, but who would inevitably be attracted to it, as though they were iron filings and she the magnet. Pretty soon officialdom would come pushing its way through the crush of interested onlookers, and then she would *never* get away.

Panic lent strength. Hommel twisted in the man's grip and aimed a kick at his legs. Her boot connected with his shin, not hard enough to knock him over, but enough to make him lose his balance. His grip on her arm slackened for a second and she wrenched herself free.

The tram driver saw what she was doing and made a grab at her, but she was too quick for him. She ducked away, shoving at the nearest bystanders with her open hands to make them let her through. Most of them were too startled to react, but someone quicker than the rest caught her by the little pack on her shoulders. Hommel twisted savagely, pulling her arms out of the straps. She felt a moment of resistance and then one of them actually burst and she was free. She abandoned the pack – her ID card, wallet and phone were in her jacket pocket anyway – pushed past a couple more people, and as soon as she saw her way clear before her she broke into a run.

The shock of what had happened and the wild beating of her heart made her feel sick and tremulous, but the sheer driving need to put as much space as possible between herself and the scene of the incident drove her on. Hommel ran down the street as though the gates of Hades itself had opened and every horned and leathery-winged creature in it were bounding after her, shrieking and cackling. Behind her there were shouts, and for a few moments the slap of feet on the cobbles, but either her pursuers were not determined enough or she was simply too fast for them. She pelted down the centre of the street, ignoring a sudden squeal of brakes and the blare of a horn. An intersection was coming up; instinctively she bolted right into the side road, without slackening her pace.

The glass shop fronts and the lights and the strolling pedestrians were sliding past her in a blur, as though she were swimming upstream. She could hear her own breathing and it was indistinguishable from sobbing. All thought of her original destination had evaporated; Hommel ran for home, for the music shop, like a terrified animal going to earth.

She was only a couple of blocks from Muziek City when it came to her that she was doing precisely what she had always avoided doing: running straight back to the flat without taking a single detour or bothering to check behind her. If the person who had stood behind her at the tram stop and thrust her into the path of the tram with both hands were following her now, she would lead him straight back to her hideout. The realization struck her like a slap in the face and she stumbled to a stop, her chest heaving and her hair hanging over her eyes in damp tangled strands. Her gaze slid from side to side, eyeing the shop fronts as though pursuers might be lurking anywhere.

Verdomme. Where now?

It was no use standing still; if anyone had followed her this far, her hesitation might alert him to her mistake. She had to keep going.

Hommel took off again but she had lost impetus. The first rush of adrenalin had gone out like a tide, leaving her battered and exhausted. She became aware of the ache in her shoulder, and the agonizing throbbing in the hand that had struck the side of the tram. She tried to flex her fingers, and the resulting explosion of pain was nauseating; she stumbled, gasping, barely able to think coherently.

Keep going. Stay away from the shop.

Hommel staggered onwards, and when she was so worn out that she could no longer manage anything faster than a walking pace she limped on anyway, cradling the injured hand. She had no specific destination in mind, no motive other than to keep moving, but at some point she must have doubled back on herself, because now she found herself emerging from a side street onto Cataloniëstraat, and in front of her was the great grey bulk of the Sint-Niklaaskerk.

Hommel looked up at the old church with dull eyes. The architecture of the Sint-Niklaaskerk had a mathematical precision, a clarity of line that was both chilly and reassuring. *Over seven hundred years have I stood here*, said those cold lines. *Another seven hundred shall I stand*. It drew her in like a great bird lifting a wing to let a fledgling nestle into its side. Hommel crossed the road with a ragged weary tread and entered the ancient building.

43

Veerle held the phone to her ear, and for several long moments she said nothing at all.

'Veerle?'

I should hang up, she thought. Whatever Kris wanted to say to her, he had waited too long to say it. She took the phone from her ear and looked at the tiny screen, her thumb hovering over the END CALL button. Kris's voice was still coming out of it, faint and tinny, saying her name.

In the end she couldn't do it. Veerle was in the corridor, with other students pushing past her, so she couldn't speak, either – at least she couldn't say any of the things she might have said to Kris with anyone else within earshot. She put the phone back to her ear and shouldered open the door of an empty classroom.

'Yes,' she said flatly.

'Don't hang up.'

'I'm not going to.' She waited.

'Veerle, I'm sorry—'

'Sorry?' Veerle felt a lump in her throat, and swallowed. She was tingling with hot indignation. 'For ringing me at school or for dumping me like that?'

She heard a brief noise of frustration over the line. 'I didn't dump you. I—'

'True,' said Veerle. 'You didn't even do that. You just moved in with Hommel and didn't tell me, remember?' She let out a shuddering breath. 'So why are you ringing me now? Did she drop you?'

'*Veerle!* Just listen.'

'No, Kris.'

She was about to end the call but his next words snagged her attention.

'Look, someone's just tried to kill her.'

Veerle took her thumb away from the red button. It passed fleetingly through her head that perhaps this was some new story of Hommel's, some attention-seeking ploy.

'What do you mean?' she asked cautiously.

Kris spoke rapidly, trying to get it all out before Veerle decided to hang up. 'Someone tried to push her under a tram. She was on her way to the station – she was going to get out of Ghent for a few days.' He didn't say where. 'And while she was waiting at the tram stop someone came up behind her and tried to shove her under the tram.'

Veerle tried to absorb this. 'Is she—?'

'She's hurt. It was hard to get any sense out of her but I think maybe her hand is broken – or her arm.'

'So – wait – you're not with her?'

'No. I'm in Overijse.'

'So where is she?'

'In some church in the middle of the city. Sint-Niklaas.'

'Well, why are you . . . ?' Veerle thought quickly. 'Are you coming to Ghent?'

'Yes, but it's going to take me at least three hours. I've got to get to Brussel-Zuid first and then take a train.

And . . . someone needs to go to the church *now*.'

'And this is why you're ringing me?' said Veerle slowly.

'Veerle, I know it's not fair to ask you. I just don't know what else to do.'

'Kris . . .' Veerle put a hand to her head. 'What makes you think I can get away that easily? I'm at school. I can't just bunk off.'

I'm already under a curfew. Dad will go ballistic if he finds out I've gone off again during school hours. She didn't say that. That was about her and Bram, and she wasn't about to share it with Kris.

'Please, Veerle. There isn't anyone else I can ask. She rang me about ten minutes ago and she was hysterical. I tried to get her to call the police but she wouldn't. She was crying with the pain.'

Kris went on talking, trying to persuade her, but Veerle already knew she would have to go. Not for Kris. Not even really for Hommel, but because she knew how she would feel about herself if she didn't go, knowing that Hommel was hurt. Knowing how it felt – the pain, the shock of realizing that someone had tried to end your life, just like that, without a second thought, without pity.

Of course she would go. There was a terrible, self-destructive inevitability about it, like having to jump from the top floor of a burning building: it was something you had to do, you couldn't *avoid* doing it, but it would almost certainly end in disaster, with your life pumping out of your shattered body in crimson spurts while people stood around you with wide eyes, their hands over their mouths.

I might just manage it, she thought with a shifting sense of unease. She glanced at her wristwatch. *It's a little past one now. If he can get here in three hours . . .*

Veerle calculated. *I'd be late home, but probably not enough to cause a really big scene. Anneke will report me to Dad, of course she will, but if I'm back not too much later than normal – and if the school don't notice I've gone and ring him before then . . .*

Still there was a cold empty feeling in the pit of her stomach. *If Dad finds out about this I'm worse than dead.*

'Look,' she said at last, 'I'll do it, but it will take me a little while, OK? Did she say exactly where she was? Inside the church or somewhere outside it?'

Veerle listened carefully. Once she knew exactly where to find Hommel, she ended the call. She didn't want to listen to Kris's thanks. If he tried to say something about caring for her she thought she would start screaming. She cut him off with a curt statement that she would call back later, and rang off.

She slipped the phone back into her pocket. She waited for a moment inside the deserted classroom, thinking.

I registered this morning. There's a chance no one will notice I'm not here, as long as I can get away without anyone seeing. She considered. *I could tell them I'm going – say I feel sick and have to go home.* That was just as risky, though. Geert was bound to have alerted the school – she was pretty sure of that from the way the teacher double-checked her presence at registration. If they rang him to say she'd gone home sick, then after the two minutes it would take him to call Anneke and see whether she'd come home he'd *know* she'd bunked off. *Nothing for it. I'll have to go without saying anything and pray nobody notices.*

She left the classroom and headed downstairs, making for the main door. Luck seemed to be with her; she didn't run into a single teacher, and the only other students from her class that she passed had their backs to her, studying a notice board. In a couple of minutes she was out on the street, drawing the chill January air into her lungs and feeling her bag bounce against her back as she hurried to put as much space as possible between herself and the school. Even after she had turned a corner she felt uneasy.

Please God, she thought, *don't let them notice I've gone.*

44

When Veerle reached the Sint-Niklaaskerk it was beginning to rain. The skies had darkened ominously during her hasty journey from the school to the old church, and she could feel the first droplets on her face like icy tears.

She crossed Cataloniëstraat, headed for the church door and slipped inside. There was one middle-aged man whom she took to be a church warden standing in the aisle with his hands clasped behind his back, contemplating the towering Baroque altar with its mitred saint and flaunting angels. Other than that, the church appeared to be deserted.

Where had Kris said Hommel was?

At the back.

Veerle made her way down the side aisle, past a silent rank of white marble saints, their graven eyes staring blindly as she passed them. The church warden (if that was what he was) turned his head as she went by. She gave him a quick strained smile and then walked on purposefully, hoping that he would understand that she did not need answers to questions, or assistance, or interference of any kind.

She found Hommel right behind the altar, sitting on the black-and-white tiles with her back to the wall and her legs sprawled out in front of her. Veerle judged that the church warden was unaware of her presence, that she had slipped in here unseen: if he had seen her, he would certainly have reacted; he would not be standing in the aisle complacently admiring the church fittings.

Veerle was shocked at the sight of her. Hommel looked terrible, so drawn that her skin appeared almost grey, her eyes red-rimmed, her normally sleek pale hair hanging in damp clumps over her angular face. She was cradling her injured hand protectively against her body; Veerle could see blood on the knuckles. If the church warden, or anyone else, stumbled on her, Veerle doubted that she would get a sympathetic reception: they would think Hommel was a drug addict, or that she had been in a fight. At the sound of footsteps on the tiles Hommel looked up. The moment she saw Veerle she began to cry.

Shock gave way to pity. Veerle had wondered whether she was a fool to come, to risk a titanic row to help out her ex-boyfriend and his attention-seeking other girl. But Hommel looked so pitiful that Veerle was moved in spite of everything.

She went over and squatted down on the tiles next to Hommel.

As she did so, Veerle was acutely aware of the church warden; if he decided to investigate they would both be in trouble. She saw that the situation was not going to be easily resolved; it would take more than a pep talk and a visit to a pharmacy for sticking plaster. It would most likely take more than the couple of hours that she had free before Anneke expected her at the flat too – even assuming the school didn't notice her absence.

There was a horrible inevitability to the whole thing. Veerle didn't seem to be able to avoid trouble; it stalked her as relentlessly as the person who had pursued Hommel. Still, she knew she was going to see the situation through, trouble or not.

The strange thing was, she looked at Hommel and found herself thinking of Claudine – or not *thinking* exactly, but *feeling*. They were nothing like each other in appearance, her mother and Hommel, and yet when Veerle looked at Hommel's bowed head and beaten expression she experienced emotions that were painfully familiar: a wave of protectiveness mixed with a dragging sense of responsibility. For a moment she was so overwhelmed with conflicting feelings that she was unable to say anything to Hommel at all. It was the other girl who broke the silence between them.

'I'm sorry,' choked out Hommel, looking at Veerle's grave face and interpreting its grim solemnity as a reproach.

Veerle sighed. 'It's OK.' She held out her hand. 'Let me look at those fingers.'

She could tell immediately from the stiff wincing manner in which Hommel unfolded her arm that the damage was pretty bad. There weren't any actual bones protruding anywhere, thank God, but the hand was turning black and puffy with bruising; just the sight of it sent a cold tingling feeling through the base of Veerle's spine.

'Shit,' she said.

On the other side of the altar she heard the church warden clear his throat and wondered whether he had heard her utter the expletive.

'Look,' she said to Hommel, 'we can't stay here. We have to go.'

322

'Where?'

'I don't know,' Veerle told her truthfully. She cocked her head to one side, silently indicating the listener on the other side of the altar. 'But we have to go. We'll go to a café and then . . . we'll think of something. OK?'

She helped Hommel to her feet. Veerle continued to hold onto Hommel as they began to walk down the side aisle; there didn't seem to be anything wrong with Hommel's legs but her face was so shocked and drawn that Veerle didn't trust her not to collapse there on the black-and-white tiled floor. As they made their way towards the door the church warden stepped out in front of them, his face grim, but when Veerle met his eyes with a flat challenging stare he elected to say nothing; he simply stood there watching, waiting for them to leave.

Outside, it was raining steadily, and the cobbles were slick and shiny. Veerle debated briefly where they should go, then led Hommel towards a burger bar a little way up the street. Brightly lit and anonymous, it was as safe as anywhere. She thought that if she could coax Hommel up the stairs, out of sight of anyone passing by in the street, they could stay there as long as they liked, quite unnoticed, while they waited for Kris.

He'd better come soon, she thought. Now that she had actually seen Hommel, she knew she couldn't just walk off and leave her. She'd have to stay until Kris arrived. Briefly she considered calling Anneke, making some excuse. She rejected the idea; if Kris managed to get there quickly, if no one at the school noticed she had gone, she could make it home without being very late and nobody need know she had bunked off at all. If it was just a matter of being a few minutes late maybe Anneke wouldn't even call Geert. No; there was no point in stirring up trouble if she could avoid it.

But if he's really late, if he gets held up . . .

Well, then she was going to be in trouble so very deep that it would make her eardrums hurt. Geert wasn't bluffing about confiscating her laptop and her mobile phone, she was quite sure of that, and she'd be under a tighter curfew than ever. There'd be no getting away for anything ever again, emergency or not.

She helped Hommel up the stairs and into a seat away from the plate-glass windows, and then she went downstairs again to buy hot drinks. The burger bar didn't have hot chocolate, it only had coffee, so she bought two and loaded Hommel's with sugar. She carried them upstairs, slid into the seat opposite Hommel and pushed the sweetened coffee towards her.

'Thanks,' said Hommel listlessly, putting out her good hand to take it.

Veerle felt in her pocket. She usually carried a few painkillers, the sort you could buy over the counter, a residue of the time when they were the only thing that could douse the fire in her battered limbs.

'Here,' she said, sliding the little strip of tablets towards Hommel.

She picked up her own coffee, eyeing Hommel as she did so. That hand was going to be a problem, she judged. Briefly she considered asking Hommel whether she was registered with a doctor in Ghent, but then she didn't bother. She already knew the answer to that. Still, it would soon be Kris's problem, she supposed.

'So what happened?' she said eventually, after Hommel had washed two of the tablets down with coffee. 'Kris said someone tried to push you under a tram.'

Hommel looked up, into Veerle's eyes, and now her lips were trembling, as though she might burst into tears again at any moment. She nodded. 'Yes.'

'It couldn't have been an accident? Someone shoving to get to the front of the queue?'

'No,' said Hommel. 'I felt two hands – in my back. Pushing. It wasn't an accident.'

'Shit.' Veerle stared. 'So did you see him, the person who did it?'

Hommel shook her head. 'No, I . . .' She put her good hand up to her face and Veerle saw that it was shaking. 'I wasn't thinking. Normally I look out for him when I'm walking through the city – you know, the one who's been following me. But I was going to the station, to get out of Ghent. I was thinking about that, and I didn't look.' She put her fingers to her lips, biting at them. 'It must have been him, though. Who else could it be?'

'I suppose some random . . .' Veerle's voice trailed off.

Some random act of madness. She'd thought for a while that this was what the attack on Bram had been, the night they had tried to climb down the service ladder into the yard. If it had stopped there, with that one isolated incident, then perhaps she might have believed that. But she thought that Bram's assailant was also the person who had cut down Marnix, had butchered him on a rooftop and left him bizarrely scattered with salt, dyed red with his own blood. And there was the fact that dead Daan De Moor had been found with salt around him. Veerle was rapidly disbelieving the whole idea of randomness.

All the same, there was nothing to connect what had happened on the rooftop with what had happened to Hommel. *There are reasons why someone might be following Hommel*, Veerle reminded herself. *Well, one reason, and it's called Jappe. That fat poisonous* klootzak.

'Look,' she said, 'I know you don't want to go to the police . . .'

She saw Hommel start at that word, police, and sighed inwardly.

'But look, supposing we did – just *supposing* – is there anything at all that would help identify the guy? Hommel? You could describe him, right?'

Hommel was shaking her head. 'Not his face – I haven't seen it clearly. He's clean shaven, I think. He has a wide mouth or maybe there are just lines here.' She touched the corner of her mouth with a fingertip. 'I think he's taller than me. He wears some kind of dark coat with a hood. That's all, really.' Hommel shrugged hopelessly. 'I've never seen him really close up.'

'A hood?'

No, thought Veerle. *Get a grip. He doesn't want his face to be seen so he wears a hood. The guy who went for Bram, he probably didn't want his seen, either, so he wore one too. It doesn't mean anything.*

Aloud, she said, 'Could it possibly be your stepdad?'

'No,' said Hommel emphatically, no tears now. 'He's got the wrong build. Too tall. Jappe's fatter too.' Her gaze slid away from Veerle's and her lip curled in disgust.

Veerle sighed. 'What about when he pushed you? Did you notice any of the other people at the tram stop before it happened, anyone you recognized?'

'No.' Hommel shook her head. 'There was this guy next to me, a guy with light brown hair and a long black coat on. He was the only one I noticed because he spoke to me. He said something about it being cold.'

'A black coat? Maybe—?' started Veerle, but Hommel was already shaking her head.

'It wasn't him. He was the one who pulled me back.'

'Are you sure?'

'Yeah, I'm sure,' said Hommel grimly. 'I thought it was him at first. He had my arm and he was calling me a crazy bitch because he thought I'd tried to jump, and I was going mad because I thought he had tried to push me – in fact I *said* he'd tried to push me.'

'So how do you know he didn't?'

'Because I felt two hands in the middle of my back. He couldn't have done that *and* grabbed my arm. It wasn't him.'

'So whoever did push you was right behind you?' said Veerle. 'But you didn't see him?'

'No.' Hommel's voice was taut with frustration. 'I think the tram was late and there was a crush at the tram stop. I couldn't pick anyone out. And after it happened things just went mad. The guy who pulled me back was shouting at me, and the tram driver got out and started shouting as well. Some people were trying to get off the tram and others were trying to get on, and there were people standing there staring and getting in the way of the others. It was chaos. I couldn't work out who'd done it. I just shook them off and ran.'

'Hommel,' said Veerle levelly, 'just think back. Is there anything else, anything at all, that you can remember from before it happened? Did you see anyone odd in the street before you got to the tram stop, anything like that?'

Veerle saw Hommel close her eyes for a moment, considering, trying to throw her mind back to the moments before it had happened, when she had been standing on the kerb, staring up the street towards the approaching tram, the man beside her making his remark about the weather, the crowd behind her clustering close . . .

Hommel's pale eyes opened. 'He said something.' She sounded amazed, as though the memory had taken her by surprise. She stared at Veerle. 'He said . . . *Eva*.'

'Eva?'

Hommel was nodding. 'He said it twice. The first time I glanced back because the way he said it was kind of odd, like it had some sort of meaning. I didn't see anything and I couldn't work out who'd said it so I just thought, *Oh well*, and started looking for the tram again. And then he said it again – just that word. *Eva*. And then I felt this massive shove.'

There was a silence for a few moments as they contemplated this: the two syllables spoken behind the turned back, the sudden murderous thrust.

'Are you sure he was speaking to you?' asked Veerle quietly.

'No,' Hommel told her truthfully. 'But I *felt* that he was. There was something . . .' She struggled to find the right words. 'The way he said it, it sounded as though he was trying to get my attention. Like it was meant for *me*. I can't explain it.'

'And it was definitely *Eva* he said? It couldn't have been part of something else? *Even* or *evenzo*?'

Hommel shook her head. 'It was *Eva*. I'm sure of it.'

'It doesn't make sense. Why would he call you that?'

'I don't know. I don't know anyone called Eva.'

'Well, what did he sound like? Old, young? Did he have an accent?'

'He sounded – odd. Like there was something wrong with his voice. It was rough. Hoarse. Like – like he'd been smoking forty a day for years and years or something.'

'Well, that's something,' said Veerle cautiously. She wasn't optimistic, though. She was imagining herself telling the police that the person who had tried to push her unregistered friend under a tram was definitely, or at least probably, a smoker. It would be bad enough when they realized that she was the Girl Who Saw A Dead Killer; when she told them there was another one on the loose and the best description she had was *Smoker*, she'd lose what little credibility she had left. And this was even assuming Hommel agreed to talk to the police in the first place.

Eva, she thought. That made absolutely no sense at all.

'Look,' she said, 'are you sure you don't know anyone called Eva? A distant cousin, or a friend of a friend?'

'Yes, I'm sure,' said Hommel. She sighed. 'It didn't sound like he was – I don't know, *mentioning* the name or some-thing. It sounded like he was calling me that.'

'Maybe he mistook you for someone,' suggested Veerle.

'Maybe,' said Hommel, but her voice was bleak. 'But if it's the same guy who's been following me, he's seen me quite a few times.' She looked down into her coffee cup.

Silence stretched out between them. After a minute Veerle said, 'I'm going to call Kris and tell him where we are.'

And pray he's going to be here more quickly than he thinks, she added silently.

Kris answered her call on the second ring.

'It's me,' said Veerle. 'Where are you?'

'On the metro.'

Verdomme. Not even at Brussel-Zuid yet?

'I've got Hommel,' she said. 'It's her hand that's injured.' She glanced over at the other girl. 'It's busted pretty badly. You'll have to take her to a doctor.'

She heard Kris sigh. 'Where are you?' he asked.

'In a burger bar. You can see it from the Sint-Niklaaskerk.'

'I know the one.'

Of course you do, thought Veerle. *You spend the weekends here with Hommel.* Any residual warmth she might have felt drained away.

'Hurry up,' she told Kris. 'I'm going to be in trouble anyway. I don't want to make it any worse.'

Veerle hung up without waiting for a reply, feeling obscurely restless. She put the phone down on the table with a precise little *click*, pushed back her hair, took a mouthful of coffee and glanced at Hommel.

Hommel had a strange look on her face, a blend of expectancy and hesitation, as though there were something she wanted to say but was unsure how to express, or perhaps wondered whether she should express.

Veerle looked away, gazing through the rain-streaked window, and it was then that Hommel spoke.

'Veerle . . . you know, I'm not with Kris.'

Veerle's head jerked up and she stared at Hommel, her face blank with astonishment. 'What?'

'Kris and I . . . we're not together.' Hommel spoke quietly, seeming to shrink under Veerle's gaze.

Eventually Veerle found her tongue. 'You've finished with him?'

Hommel put her head down, pushing the fingers of her uninjured hand into her draggled hair. She said: 'It was finished a long time ago. Before you.'

Veerle looked at the crown of Hommel's head, at the slender fingers threaded through the hair. She wished Hommel would look up; she hadn't finished studying her – she wanted to look into those large grey eyes and see that Hommel was speaking the truth. She suspected that Hommel was simply trying to make peace in some misguided way, reasoning that it didn't matter much anyway since she, Veerle, was presumably now with Bram. Hommel had seen him, after all, the day they had come to the flat over Muziek City.

'Why are you telling me this?' she said gruffly.

'Because . . . it's true.'

Veerle felt a constricting sensation in her chest, a tightening of the painful knot that seemed to be there whenever she thought about Kris. She leaned towards Hommel across the plastic table-top. 'But he's been living with you at the weekends,' she said, making a titanic effort to keep her voice level.

Now Hommel did look up. 'Kris is a good person, Veerle. There wasn't anyone else I could go to when all this started, when that guy started stalking me. That's why I asked him. I knew he'd come. It doesn't mean we're . . . He's helping me as a *friend*.'

Veerle couldn't help herself; she had to keep probing. 'A friend who stays over?'

'I know how it looks, but . . . what else can he do? He can't afford to stay in a hotel every weekend.'

Well, what else am I going to do? Book into the Grand Hotel? Veerle remembered Kris saying that, the night they had argued in the street beneath her bedroom window. Hommel's words were consistent with what Kris had said, that was true. All the same . . .

'Look, why are you telling me this now?' she asked.

'Because you've been kind,' said Hommel simply. 'You didn't have to help me.'

She looked down again; Veerle found herself looking at the top of her blonde head once more.

Maybe, thought Veerle. *Maybe it's all true and Kris really does just stay at the flat as a friend, sleeping on the other side of the room in his sleeping bag.* She chewed her lip, thinking. *Or am I being a complete idiot to even think of believing that?*

There seemed no point in questioning Hommel any further. Either she was telling the truth or she wasn't; Veerle might as well have flipped a coin. So she said nothing, simply put out her own hands and covered Hommel's good hand with them, and she and Hommel sat in silence, waiting for Kris to arrive.

45

Kris arrived at 4.45 p.m.

Veerle had spent most of the preceding hour sitting in front of another empty coffee cup, watching the slow progress of the minute hand around the dial of her wristwatch and trying not to panic.

Three hours, he said. He has to be here soon.

If she had left school promptly at the end of the last lesson, and walked back to the flat on Bijlokevest at a brisk pace, she would have been home for half an hour by now. Anneke would have called Geert, Veerle was absolutely certain of that. If the school had phoned the flat to report her disappearance, Anneke might have called him two or three hours ago.

At 4.15 she had wondered briefly whether she could just go home, leaving Hommel in the burger bar to wait for Kris. But she had looked across the table at the other girl and known she couldn't do that. Hommel was leaning against a pillar next to the table, with her eyes closed and a taut expression of pain on her angular features.

When Veerle said, 'Hommel?' in a tentative voice, Hommel hadn't reacted at all. It wasn't clear whether she was asleep or simply sealed into a capsule of her own pain.

Veerle had a view of the top of the stairs from where she sat. Periodically she glanced up from her gloomy perusal of the passing minutes, hoping to see Kris appearing.

Come on, come on, she thought. The feeling of bright panic was sliding into a queasy and fatalistic dread. There was trouble ahead, looming large on the horizon, and it was solidifying into a hideous certainty with every moment that passed.

Sometimes she looked out of the window, through the distorting streaks of rain, her gaze flickering over the rooftops opposite. She was beginning to feel very tired now – tired of fretting about the row ahead, tired of thinking. Nothing seemed to make sense. There was no pattern to any of the things that had happened, other than the vague impression of some ill-perceived and brutal malice, recurring like the sweep of a great pendulum.

The brutal assault on Marnix. The attempted attack on Bram. Daan De Moor, and that other guy, the one Bram knew – Luc. And now this attack on Hommel. She was certain that the person who had killed Marnix was also the person who had tried to attack Bram, maybe even Daan De Moor, but as for the others, Luc and now Hommel . . .

Maybe this is just city life, Veerle thought wearily. There was always some murder in the news, some of them truly horrible. There was that girl Marie De Smet, burned to death in the fire that had also claimed the politician and his girlfriend. And then there was that priest whose house had been torched with him inside; they still weren't one hundred per cent sure whether he had been dead or dying when the flames took him.

The thought of it, so much violence and blood lust and cruelty, made Veerle feel sick to her soul. She looked at the rain running down the window, turning the city lights into streaks, and she wondered how the people out there lived with it, these horrors happening practically under their very noses. Maybe they thought it only ever happened to *other* people.

I know different, she thought. Absently she pushed back her sleeve, rubbing at the fading scar on her forearm. The knowledge set her apart from other people – it turned her into a Cassandra, a prophet of doom whom nobody else believed. *The girl who saw a dead man.* It sounded like a bad joke.

Veerle looked at her watch again, and then she looked up and there was Kris at the top of the stairs, looking around for her.

She had been so determined not to react to seeing him, so determined to drown any residual feeling she had for him in the foaming mill race of her anger. And now it was only that anger that enabled her to show him a cool, unmoved exterior. As he came towards her she stood up, and her heart was thudding guiltily, as though she had been caught doing something she shouldn't.

Kris was wearing jeans and the black leather jacket he had worn for most of their night-time excursions with the Koekoeken; because he had walked bare-headed through the rain his dark hair was plastered to his forehead. Drops of water ran down his face like tears. His expression was sombre but not unfriendly.

He came up close, much closer than she expected. His gaze flickered briefly over Hommel, who was still leaning against the pillar with her eyes shut. Then he was looking at Veerle, his dark eyes serious. When he spoke, it was in a low voice and Veerle realized that he was trying not to rouse Hommel.

'Veerle, thank you for doing this.'

'That's—' Veerle began to say, *That's OK*, but she stopped abruptly. It wasn't OK, not really. She was still annoyed at Kris for presuming on their past to persuade her to do this. She was annoyed at herself for being persuaded, and for the effect he still had on her. And there was trouble on an unimaginable scale waiting for her at home. *OK?* No.

She couldn't hold his gaze. Warmth had come into her face; she was afraid that the colour had come into it and that he would see it. She glanced away, towards the watercolour blur of the window.

'I'm sorry for asking,' Kris was saying.

Veerle shook her head. 'You'd better get her to a doctor, Kris,' she said gruffly. 'That hand is a mess. I'm pretty sure it's broken.'

Kris glanced past her. 'Shit. Where?'

'I don't know. There are hospitals in the city – one of them must have an emergency room. I have to go, Kris.'

Actually, now that he was here, she would have liked to ask him a million questions herself, nibbling at the edges of the wider situation in an attempt to get closer to the one issue that was really on her mind: had Hommel been telling the truth about him or not? But she could feel the coming trouble like the building pressure before a storm. It was dragging her into itself, nagging her to get moving before things became significantly worse. To get home at five o'clock would be bad; by six Geert might be home and that would be truly catastrophic.

'Now?' said Kris, taken aback.

'Yes, now.' Veerle looked him in the eye then, forcing herself to keep her expression neutral. 'I told you I couldn't get away that easily. I'm going to be in serious trouble anyway. I can't make it *worse*. I have to go.'

She glanced at Hommel, but the other girl hadn't moved.

'I'm sorry, Kris,' she said, and hoisting her school bag onto her shoulder she began to push past him.

'Veerle, wait a minute—' Kris caught her arm. 'Look, can I phone you later?'

Veerle sighed. 'Kris, you could have called me at any time over the last three months.'

She pulled her arm free. Catching a movement out of the corner of her eye, she looked at Hommel again and saw that she was stirring. Kris followed her gaze, and when he turned back to Veerle she was halfway to the stairs.

Veerle didn't look back. She hurried down, her school bag bouncing on her shoulders. A turn of the staircase, and she was out of sight anyway. She reached the ground floor and ran for the door, the brightly lit counter a golden blur to her right.

It was almost dark now and the lights of shops and restaurants were reflected in slick wet pavements. Veerle saw a cluster of pedestrians at the tram stop by the church, people heading home at the end of the working day. In an hour Geert would be home too. She began to run for the flat, weaving in and out of the evening strollers, swerving to avoid a bicycle.

She had turned two corners and the burger bar was far behind her before she automatically brushed at her eyes and realized that she was crying, and swore under her breath. Veerle hated crying.

46

Veerle stood in Bijlokevest, a little way up from the flat, looking at the building's façade and the balcony and her own window. The rain had stopped but it was cold; her breath was visible on the air like some strange ectoplasm. Everything seemed very clear and sharp: the memory of tears prickling at her eyes, the dull gleam of fallen rain on the pavement, the weight of her school bag on her shoulders. She felt as though she were saying goodbye to something, taking a long last look before she left, memorizing everything. Maybe this was how people felt before they went into prison, she thought; as though you could capture that last moment of freedom, bottle it and take it with you.

It was no use standing here for ever; every passing second was making her later. Veerle began to walk towards the flat. She kept scanning the street ahead as she went, looking for any sign that Geert was home already or that either he or Anneke was looking down from the flat. Nothing. Trouble was lurking inside, like a scorpion under a stone. That, at any rate, was one small piece of good fortune to set against the avalanche of woe that she suspected was even now sliding towards her with unstoppable force. She let herself into the block and began to mount the stairs with all the enthusiasm of a condemned aristocrat climbing the scaffold towards the grim silhouette of the guillotine.

Even when she was standing outside the closed door of the flat she hesitated, wanting to savour one last moment of uncertainty before the reality of trouble solidified into a fact. Then she took out her key and opened the door.

She wasn't particularly surprised to see Anneke standing in the hallway, with the telephone receiver in her hand. There was no sign of Geert.

Veerle came right into the flat and closed the door behind her. Then she stood there in the middle of the hallway waiting to see what Anneke would say. She kept her expression deliberately neutral; at this stage of the game there was nothing to do except take whatever was coming and flinch as little as possible.

She was aware of the gaze of Anneke's grey eyes but she stared past the woman, blank-faced, like a soldier preparing to deliver name, rank and serial number.

There was a small *click* as Anneke put the telephone down on its cradle. She had not said a word since Veerle entered, no *Goodbye* or *I'll call you back*, or even, *Here she is*. It crossed Veerle's mind that perhaps Anneke had been waiting for her to arrive, that she had simply posed with the phone in her hand, having made the call long since but wanting Veerle to know that she had done so.

The silence stretched out for so long that eventually Veerle said, 'I know. I'm very late.'

She swung her school bag off her shoulders and put it on the floor.

'Have you called Dad?' she asked, keeping her voice as even as possible. She felt slightly sick. Her pulse was racing but she struggled to maintain her composure.

'No,' said Anneke quietly. She still had her hand on the receiver; now she tapped it gently with her fingers, as though considering.

'Well, go on, then,' said Veerle heavily. 'Or are you going to wait till he gets home?'

Anneke looked at her with an expression that was almost thoughtful. 'Actually,' she said, after a pause, 'I'm not at all sure that I'm going to tell him about this.'

'Anneke,' said Veerle levelly, 'I'm late.'

'I know.'

Veerle bit her lip. *What does she want? Does she want me to beg her to call Dad and tell him?*

'Don't you want to know where I was?'

'I know where you *weren't*,' Anneke told her. 'The school rang me this afternoon.'

Great. Veerle wanted to sink to the floor and put her head in her hands. She made herself meet Anneke's eyes.

'Look, Anneke, a friend had an emergency. I can't tell you anything more than that . . . but it was a one-off.'

'I hope so,' said Anneke. She let go of the phone and clasped her hands in front of her, against the blue fabric of the rather prim dress she wore. A little colour had risen to her thin features. After a moment she said: 'Geert is going to be late back. He has a meeting. So I think we should take this opportunity to talk.'

'OK,' said Veerle warily. She could not imagine what she and Anneke had to talk about – nothing good, anyway – but if that was what she had to go through to avoid being reported to Geert, well . . .

She followed Anneke into the kitchen, and sat at the tiny table.

'Do you want a coffee or something?' Anneke asked her.

'No,' said Veerle.

Anneke leaned against the kitchen cupboards and looked at her.

'You don't like me much, do you, Veerle?' She smiled wryly at Veerle's startled expression. 'Well, that's OK, because I don't like you all that much, either.' She shook her head. 'It's nothing personal. When I met Geert I knew he had a daughter from a previous marriage, but I didn't think she'd ever be living with us. That room you're in, it was supposed to be Adam's. The money we're spending keeping you while we wait for that house to sell, that was supposed to be spent on baby things, or saving for when he's older.' Anneke looked away from Veerle, gazing at the corner of the ceiling, considering. Then she looked back at her. 'In fact, you know, it *is* personal. You keep upsetting Geert. This was supposed to be the time when he thought about me and Adam, not worried himself sick because you keep bunking off school all the time.'

Veerle had been listening to Anneke with wary equanimity – Anneke wasn't telling her anything she hadn't already heard being shouted through the bedroom wall, after all. Now, however, she felt a sudden and terrible longing for her mother, so sharp that it was like an actual physical pain. Her sorrow for Claudine was always there in the background, a dull dragging ache that followed her wherever she went, but now she felt the absence as though she had had a hole blown through her, as though the grief were a shrieking hurricane wrenching chunks of her away with savage force.

Veerle looked at Anneke, at her thin face with its small cold eyes, the skin slightly rough and reddened as though she lived in a perpetually chilly environment. Anneke must love Geert; certainly she must love Adam. Still, if there was anything soft inside her, it was as completely sealed inside that cold carapace as the pulpy insides of an insect are encased in chitin. Veerle could not imagine communicating to Anneke how she felt, why she had started running away from school in the first place: the blind need to get away from a life that felt wrong, from the kindly interest and curious questions that threatened to make it all real. She had run away from the requirement of ever saying, *My mother is dead; I live in Ghent now.*

She could not tell Anneke any of this. They had no common currency; there were no words that she could hand over in exchange for understanding. Instead she looked down at her own hands, studying the familiar lines, the scar on the back of the left one, a remnant of her fall from the castle the previous summer. There seemed to be little that she had carried from the past into the present other than her own self; even Kris, whom she had known since they were both children, had virtually gone.

Anneke was silent for a few moments too, but hers was a speaking silence: it radiated disapproval like the glow of an isotope. At last she said, 'I'm not going to tell Geert you bunked off school again today because frankly he doesn't need the worry. And I'm not going to ask you where you went, because either you won't tell me or you'll lie.'

Veerle's head jerked up at that and she stared mutinously at Anneke. Her temper was rising, but she wanted to know what Anneke was going to say, where this was leading, so she bit it back.

'This is what I'm going to do,' Anneke went on. 'I'm going to pretend the school never rang me, and that you came home exactly when you were supposed to. If you bunk off again, it's up to you to make sure that Geert doesn't find out. If the school ring *me* again and say you've done it, I'll keep quiet about it. You know when he gets home. As long as you're back here before then, I don't care what you do with your time. Go to school and study for your diploma or bunk off and hang around with that ruffian who called at the flat before Christmas – it's up to you.'

Anneke unclasped her hands; now she stood with them held tensely at her sides as though she thought she might have to fend off an attack from Veerle.

'And here's what you have to do,' she told Veerle. 'At the end of the school year, you leave. You're eighteen now; nobody can make you stay on, even if you fail the year. If you've got any sense at all you'll work for the diploma and then you can go to university somewhere. But if you fail, you go anyway. Understood?'

Anneke's chest was heaving; her thin face was flushed. She was waiting for Veerle to reply, but Veerle was simply staring, trying to digest what Anneke had said to her.

She's telling me to go to hell, she thought. *Go away to study, or go away and work in some crumby unskilled job, just as long as I go away.*

'Veerle?' There was a nervous tremor to Anneke's voice, as though delivering the ultimatum had excited her. Her grey eyes had a slightly feverish sparkle.

Is she enjoying this? thought Veerle.

She nodded. 'Yeah, I understand.'

'Hopefully it'll be university,' said Anneke, though her tone implied that she thought this unlikely. 'If not . . .'

'I go anyway,' finished Veerle heavily.

'I want to make sure we both understand this,' Anneke told her. 'It's quite possible that Geert will feel he should offer to support you while you re-take the year. If we both work on him, he'll agree to let you move out.'

Veerle wasn't entirely convinced of that; an image flashed through her mind – of Geert standing outside the school for hours, stolidly enduring the elements, ensuring that she was really inside, where he thought she ought to be. There was a steadfastness in Geert; she didn't believe he'd throw her overboard as readily as Anneke seemed to think. The memory was a fish-hook in a tender part of her, a painful and insistent tugging that could not be ignored. Now that Veerle found herself on the outside, with the cold iron of closed gates at her back, she began to wish that she had built something different with her father: trust, understanding.

Too late, she thought. There was no way ahead of her that led back to that. If she didn't agree to move out at the end of the year, Anneke would certainly tell Geert that she had played truant again.

She gazed at Anneke, deliberately keeping her own expression neutral. Probably Anneke would think she was indifferent, or defiant. Veerle told herself that she did not care what Anneke thought, but her inner voice lacked conviction. Anneke had moved between her and Geert with the finality of a chess piece sliding into the checkmate position. She had won.

'OK,' said Veerle evenly. 'I agree.'

47

The weekend passed slowly. Veerle wondered what had happened to Hommel – whether Kris had managed to get her injured hand treated without too many of the inevitable questions. Had he persuaded her to speak to the police? She was not optimistic about that. Even if he had, it was hard to see what would come of it other than aggravation for Hommel.

She also spent a lot of time thinking about what Hommel had said to her about Kris.

Kris and I . . . we're not together.

It was finished a long time ago. Before you.

Kris is a good person. He's helping me as a friend.

The thing was, she *wanted* to believe it. And that was the very thing that made her distrust Hommel's words.

Veerle wondered what she would say if one of her friends came to her with a similar story – *I didn't hear from my boyfriend for ages, then I went to his ex-girlfriend's place and he was there; he'd spent the night. He says nothing went on. Should I believe him?*

If another girl had said that to her, Veerle's immediate re-action would have been, *It stinks to high heaven, don't believe it.*

Veerle lay on the bed in her narrow little room, staring at the ceiling. She held her mobile phone in her hand, turning it over and over in her fingers. She might as well have been playing with a stone: the phone remained obstinately silent.

You could have called me at any time over the last three months.

It seemed that Kris had taken her words to mean that it was too late now. But was it? Veerle remembered the time before, the night Kris had turned up under her window in the small hours, his upturned face sallow in the lamplight. She had climbed down to him, full of bitter emotion, wanting to hear what he had to say. That time, it had ended with him turning and walking away.

And if he came back now? She wondered whether there was anything either of them could say that would lead to a different outcome. She wished at least that they could try. But the phone remained silent all through Saturday, and when at last it burst into trilling life on Saturday evening, Veerle looked at the screen and saw that the caller was Bram.

She hesitated for a moment, then pressed the green button to accept the call.

'Hi, Bram.'

'Hi. How's it going? Any sign of your dad backing off yet?'

'Nope.'

'He's kept this up for a long time,' said Bram.

'Well . . .' Veerle sighed. 'He's pretty angry.'

'This is crap. At this rate you won't get out until you're an OAP.'

The exaggeration gave Veerle a sudden impulse to laugh

in spite of her woe. 'Will you wait for me?' she asked mischievously.

'Sure.' She heard the grin in Bram's voice.

'Bram,' said Veerle, her mood tilting back to sombre, 'I did get out yesterday. Only – it wasn't good. Something's happened.' She hesitated. She didn't want to talk to Bram about seeing Kris, but she'd thought about this: Bram had to know what had happened to Hommel.

There was no sense in what was happening in the city – no pattern that she could see. Someone falling from a rooftop. Someone else purposely cut down on another rooftop. A stalker who had tried murder in a crowded street. Did these things even mean anything in a city where someone had torched a priest's house with the priest inside? Sometimes Veerle thought that she could feel Ghent shrinking around her, tightening into a maze of Gothic towers and narrow cobbled streets and heavy stone walls, a grim labyrinth inhabited by one or many minotaurs.

But she had to warn Bram – although against what, she had no idea.

'Look,' she said carefully, 'you remember Hommel, the girl who works in Muziek City?' She waited for Bram's assent. 'I had a call yesterday when I was at school. Someone had tried to kill her. They tried to push her under a tram.'

'*What?!*'

'I'm not joking. You know someone was following her? Well, it seems like they caught up with her.'

'What happened?' asked Bram, horrified.

'Whoever it was stood behind her at the tram stop, and when the tram came – he just shoved her. She'd be dead if someone standing next to her hadn't grabbed her just before she fell.'

'Shit.'

'Yeah. She hurt herself, though. She hit her hand on the side of the tram and it's probably broken.'

'Did she call the police?'

'No.' Veerle took a deep breath. 'She called Kris. And Kris called me.'

For a moment there was silence on the other end of the line.

'OK,' said Bram slowly.

Veerle's heart sank. She could almost *hear* him thinking, *You can't ever get out to meet up, but Kris calls and somehow you manage it.*

'He didn't have anyone else to call,' she told Bram hurriedly. 'He doesn't know anyone else in Ghent and he couldn't get up here himself for hours. She'd just crawled off into the Sint-Niklaaskerk on her own. So I bunked off school again and went to find her. I took her over the road to that burger place, and waited for three hours while Kris came up from Overijse. As soon as he got there, I went. Dad doesn't know I bunked off, not yet anyway. Anneke covered for me.'

'That was nice of her.'

'Not really.' Veerle sighed. 'The point is, the guy who's been following Hommel, well, at first she seemed to think it was something to do with her stepfather, Jappe. But apparently it wasn't him.'

'Well, who else could it be?'

'I suppose it could be anyone. A stalker, or some psycho who gets their kicks trying to push strangers into traffic. But here's the thing. He's always wearing some kind of dark coat with a hood, so you can't really see his face properly.'

'Well, I'd do that if I was going to go around pushing people under trams.'

'Bram, doesn't it remind you of anything?' asked Veerle. 'The guy who attacked Marnix, he was dressed like that. And the guy who was down in the yard that time you were climbing down the ladder. Maybe it's the same guy.'

'Maybe,' said Bram doubtfully. 'But look, Veerle, half the criminals in Flanders probably have a hood or a scarf or – I don't know – a balaclava on. And anyway, it's January. Everyone has a hood or a woolly hat or something.'

'I know,' said Veerle resignedly.

'If there was some other way to identify him . . .'

The hoarse voice, thought Veerle, but she didn't say it aloud. Being a heavy smoker didn't narrow it down much.

'Look,' she said eventually, 'I'm just saying – take care. Especially if you go – you know – up there.'

'I'm not going up on the rooftops at the moment anyway,' said Bram. 'Look, are you sure you can't get away, just once?'

'Bram . . .'

'Come on, there must be some way.'

Climb out of the window again.

'I probably can,' said Veerle cautiously. 'But it has to be the right time. I can't risk Anneke catching me out again, Bram. She covered for me this time because she wanted something. She made me agree to leave when I've finished the school year – even if I fail it.'

'Wow,' said Bram. 'She really is a piece of work.'

'Yeah, well, I don't want to give her anything else she can hold over me. Look, just give me some time. I'll work something out.'

After she'd ended the call Veerle stood for a long time by the window, staring down at the darkened street below, her mobile phone still clasped in her hand. She could hear Geert and Anneke moving about the flat, and once she heard a little shriek from Adam. She had a very strong sense of the three of them carrying on their lives without her, as they would be doing in some months' time.

I could tell Dad the truth.

Veerle examined that idea for the hundredth time. The trouble was, she knew where that would lead. He'd discouraged her from seeing Kris after she moved to Ghent; now he'd probably ban her from seeing Bram. On the whole it was probably better to wait, keep her nose clean and hope Geert's anger wore down with time. If she managed to persuade him that she was staying out of trouble and concentrating on her school work, he might decide to forgive and forget. Then Anneke's scheming might go for nothing. She could hardly threaten to tell Geert next August that Veerle had bunked off school for a single afternoon in January.

Perhaps she really is doing it for him, thought Veerle. *You never know, she might soften up a bit and stop being such a cow if she thinks I'm not causing him aggravation any more.* But somehow she didn't believe that.

She wished she could have gone out with Bram, right now, this instant, in spite of the chill winter dark. They could get away from everyone – maybe even go up to the rooftops again, to move about unseen by the pedestrians below, their faces gilded by the streetlights as they peeped over parapets at the streets laid out before them.

But, thought Veerle, *we may never do that again. Not after Marnix.*

She kept the phone with her all evening, and when she fell asleep that night it was sitting on her bedside table, but it didn't ring again.

48

Afterwards, Veerle tried to trace the moment when it started, the event that was the seed of all the subsequent events, the spark that followed the long fuse to the powder keg. If she had confided in Geert – if she had given Bram a different answer – if she had suggested a different meeting place . . . the possibilities for averting the final outcome were endless, when you considered them. They ran back through past events and past decisions like a pathogenic disease moving from vector to vector, spreading its net ever wider, contaminating everything. All of them were interdependent; you could have plucked any one of them out of the air and said, *That was it, that was the moment when it started.*

It need not have been the moment when she decided to go into the cathedral to shelter from the rain; it might have been the moment when Anneke's oldest friend, now living two hundred and seventy kilometres away in the Dutch city of Zwolle, decided to stop procrastinating and send Anneke an email, inviting her and Geert and Adam to visit for the weekend, so she and Anneke could catch up and she could admire the baby. She didn't think of inviting Veerle, of whom she was only dimly aware, and Anneke didn't suggest it, thus making another decision whose outcome contributed to future events, as a tributary flows into a river. Anneke was taken with the idea of visiting Zwolle. It meant a weekend of showing off her partner and her new baby, and forgetting about the not-quite-stepdaughter whose presence was such an irritant, who had loomed like an albatross over her first Christmas with Adam. When Geert suggested mildly that they might ask if Veerle was invited, Anneke squashed the idea; the visit was over a weekend anyway, so the girl could hardly bunk off school.

Geert told Veerle solemnly that he was expecting her to behave responsibly, and to continue to observe the curfew he had imposed on her.

'Do I need to telephone you every hour?' he asked her.

'No,' said Veerle, looking him in the eye. She meant it too, observing the curfew. She didn't want to aggravate Geert any further.

All the same, a whole weekend alone in the flat that didn't feel like home was a grim prospect, one that didn't get any more attractive the closer it loomed. And then there was Bram . . .

I'll work something out, she'd said when he pressed to see her. And here was an opportunity, the working out practically done for her. Geert and Anneke would both be away, and there'd be no school to bunk off, nothing anyone could really complain about.

Dad can't object if I go out for an hour. Supposing I went to the bakery or something?

Still she hesitated, thinking that Geert might well object; a curfew was a curfew, and going out even for an hour to meet someone he didn't know certainly counted as breaking it.

Maybe Bram could come here for a couple of hours, Veerle thought. Geert hadn't expressly forbidden her to invite anyone over.

She slept on that idea, and on the Thursday she called Bram. She was expecting him to accept her suggestion; instead he took her aback.

'Let's spend the whole weekend together.'

Veerle had been wandering around the bedroom with her mobile phone to her ear, glancing idly out of the window at the grey street outside, but when he said that, she stopped pacing.

'The whole weekend?'

'You could come here, to my place,' said Bram's voice in her ear.

'You mean . . . stay over?'

'Well, yes.' Bram sounded almost amused, as though he was surprised she had to ask the question.

'Bram,' began Veerle slowly, 'Dad's told me to stay here. If he catches me going off again—'

'What's he going to do? You're not a little kid. If he says he rang and you didn't pick up, tell him you had your headphones on and didn't hear the phone. Or tell him you ran out of something and had to go out to the shops. Come on, when are you going to get another chance to get out again? Once your dad's back home you'll be back under his thumb.'

Bram must have read the hesitation in Veerle's silence because he started to try to persuade her.

'We'll have a great time. We can go to the wall again if you want – or, I don't know, the cinema, the pizza place – any-where. Whatever you like. And you can . . .'

'Stay over,' finished Veerle flatly.

'Why not?' A warmth came into Bram's voice. 'You know I love you, Veerle.'

The way he said it, so easily, took the wind right out of her sails. She couldn't say anything at all. Memory skipped back, lightly and treacherously, to the first time she had heard Kris say that, the day she had met him in the café and told him about her mother, about Claudine's terrible anxiety and the problems it was causing. They had had a bare half-hour, and then they had parted on the pavement, and as they embraced he had murmured those words into her hair. *I love you.* She had carried them away with her, like something precious.

Now Bram was silent; he was waiting for her to say the words back to him, and she wished she could do it as easily as he had, she really did.

As the moments stretched out excruciatingly, Veerle said haltingly, 'Bram, it's— I'm not . . .' She put up a hand and pushed back the strands of dark hair that fell over her brow. 'I'm not sure I'm ready.'

In the silence that followed she began to pace again, biting her lip. At last Bram said, 'Just come. I'm not going to push you into anything.'

'I know,' said Veerle. She believed him too. The problem was not that she didn't trust him; it was that she didn't trust herself. Her life had become an empty room, populated by ghosts: her mother, Kris, the father Geert might have been if Claudine hadn't pushed him away and Anneke claimed him. Bram cared about her, and she cared about him, only perhaps not in the right way, or not enough, or not enough yet. But once they were alone at his place, if he started kissing her again the way he had before, slowly and passionately, kind of softly but hard at the same time . . .

'Please, Veerle.'

'Bram – can I think about it?' She didn't give him time to interrupt; she went on, 'Let's arrange to meet anyway. Look, Dad was saying something about phoning me every hour to see whether I'm still here at the flat or not, and I'm not a hundred per cent sure he was joking. Let me see if I can really get away for longer than an hour or two, and just . . . let me think about it, OK?'

At the other end of the connection she heard Bram sigh. 'OK. I guess.'

'They're not going until late on Friday,' she told him. 'After Dad gets back from work. So Friday night might be difficult. How about Saturday lunch time? If Dad does try ringing I can say I had to go out to buy bread or something.'

'If he doesn't ring—?' began Bram.

'Then I'll think about staying.'

'OK. Where do you want to meet?'

'What about Sint-Baafsplein at twelve? And if it's raining I'll go into the cathedral and wait.'

On the Saturday, it *did* rain; it began to rain about the time that dawn was seeping slowly up the sky, and then it settled down into a drizzle that lasted all morning. Veerle looked out of the window at pavements that shone like sealskin, and endless grey broken only by the taut span of a bright red umbrella passing along the street below. Geert hadn't telephoned, except once to say that he and Anneke had arrived safely in Zwolle.

There was nothing, Veerle realized as she looked at the raindrops that slid like tears down the window, to stop her from staying with Bram all weekend, if she wanted to. But did she want to?

While she was getting ready to go out she was still thinking about it, as though thinking about it would make it any clearer. In fact it made things worse.

If it's right, shouldn't I just know? she thought.

All the same, she took a small backpack, and put a few more things in it than she would have needed if she were just popping out for an hour or two. Just before she let herself out of the flat she almost took the backpack off and left it, but in the end she took it with her.

She was going to be early; the incessant inner debate had made her restless and impatient, and the rain was so unpleasant that she hurried along, keen to get to her destination. When she got to Sint-Baafsplein there was still half an hour to kill.

The square was almost deserted; nobody wanted to be outdoors in the chill and wet, it seemed. As Veerle approached the cathedral a group of tourists came out, perhaps twelve of them, dressed in identical thin orange rain ponchos, and scuttled miserably across the cobblestones, heading for the shelter of a café. Veerle waited for the last of them to come out, and then she went in through the right-hand door.

The rain was so heavy that she could hear it inside the cathedral: a kind of relentless drumming sound, dreary as nagging. Perhaps it was the overcast weather outside that made the interior of the ancient church so cheerless; in spite of the electric lights the nave was dim and gloomy, and it was so *cold. Hardly better than being outside*, Veerle thought. The only advantage was being out of the rain, and she had brought quite a lot of *that* indoors with her; she looked down at the waterproof fabric of her jacket and it was covered with tiny droplets, sparkling like polished gemstones. She touched one with a finger and the tip came away wet.

Damp strands of hair were falling over her eyes. Veerle shook them back and glanced around. She seemed to be alone. On previous occasions when she had been inside Sint-Baafs there had been other visitors and a few cathedral guides, including the one who had admonished her for running inside the building the day she had chased Hommel outside. Evidently the weather had sent the few unseasonal tourists scurrying to the nearest coffee shop, and the guides, redundant, had retreated to some better-heated corner of the church. Veerle wandered towards the north aisle and looked at the ticket booth for the Ghent altarpiece. That was deserted too, unusually; there was a handwritten note stuck to the glass, reading: *Back soon.* The reinforced doors behind it were locked.

Veerle went back to the middle of the nave, where she had a view of the door. Her footsteps sounded very loud on the tiles; it gave her the uncomfortable sense of disturbing the calm of a funeral. All the same, she couldn't stand still; Bram was going to arrive in the next thirty minutes and she was aware that she had still not come to any firm decision. It was as bad as standing in the wings before a theatrical performance, knowing that you hadn't learned your lines; she supposed that she could wait and see how she felt when she saw Bram, but somehow she didn't want to wing it. She wanted to *know* what to do, how she felt. She found herself pacing restlessly, and if anyone else stirred within the dimly lit cathedral she didn't hear them over the thunder of her thoughts.

Minutes passed with agonizing slowness and nobody entered the cathedral. Veerle whistled under her breath, and tapped the toe of her boot on the tiled floor. Then, feeling self-conscious, she wandered over to look at a painting fixed to one of the gigantic grey stone pillars. A quick glance at the opposite pillar showed that the painting was one of a pair, one male figure and one female. This one was the female.

It was an odd-looking painting; Veerle couldn't have begun to date it. It showed a young woman framed within a wooden archway. In the half-hemisphere above her head were some much smaller figures who seemed vaguely familiar; they seemed to be fighting, or at any rate one was attacking the other, who was lying on the ground defending himself ineffectually. You could see how that was going to end. It was the figure of the woman that puzzled Veerle. She had the high forehead, the smooth features and the delicately arched eyebrows that went with very old paintings, the ones that were hundreds and hundreds of years old, but she was wearing a dress that was startlingly modern-looking: it was asymmetrical, leaving the left shoulder uncovered, and it ended halfway up the thighs, leaving the knees and calves completely bare.

Veerle took a step closer, her interest mildly piqued in spite of herself, and it was then that she heard a movement some way off, the scuff of shoes on the tiled floor. One of the cathedral guides returning, she supposed. She didn't look round; instead she continued to study the painting, thinking that the young woman seemed vaguely familiar – had she seen the painting reproduced somewhere before?

Thus it was that Veerle had her back to the other person and her attention fixed elsewhere; she didn't hear him come closer; she was not even aware of his proximity until he spoke.

His voice was deep and hoarse, the voice of someone who has drawn smoke deep into his lungs; a ruined voice. But it was not the voice itself that sent a terrible jolt of icy shock through Veerle's body; it was the single word he said.

'*Eva.*'

49

Cold horror enfolded Veerle, as though a great bat had settled upon her, wrapping its leathery wings about her, sinking its fangs deep into her shrinking flesh.

Eva. He said Eva.

The man who tried to kill Hommel is standing right behind me.

All those nights she had dreamed of running for her life, and now she couldn't move. She was frozen, paralysed with shock. Her eyes were still turned towards the strange painting of the girl; they felt like the only living things in a body that had turned to marble. She looked at the girl but did not see her. In her mind she was seeing the edge of the pavement and a crowd of people clustering close and a tram approaching, forty tonnes of metal and glass; she was hearing the single word *Eva* and feeling that terrible shove that would send her straight into its path. It did not matter that there was no tram here, that there was no open sky wheeling above her; that kind of malice could transform itself into a blade, a bludgeon. It could attack an innocent person in a darkened yard behind a line of shops, for no other reason than that they were there. It could cut a throat and leave the body to the elements on a city rooftop.

A ragged breath escaped her. She could hardly believe that she was still on her feet, that her consciousness had not imploded to somewhere deep inside herself, the shell of her body crumpling. She saw death coming, she saw it running her down, and still she couldn't move.

The voice came again, hoarse and rasping, as though the larynx were an engine with grit in its gears.

'It is Eva.'

Veerle stood there motionless in the nave, her rain-damp hair still clinging clammily to her face. She stared at the painting. At last realization forced its way into her consciousness through the seething terror, like flotsam thrown up by the boiling maelstrom of a tempestuous sea.

Eva. The painting is of Eva.

She couldn't make sense of it. Her mind struggled to grasp the meaning of it, as a climber's fingers skitter across a sheer rock face, searching for a hold. *Eva* – the damaged voice saying the name, here in the cathedral and out there on the street, seconds before Hommel had nearly been pushed under a tram. There was Eva here, in the painting, but out in the street there had been no painting; there had only been a skinny, nervous blonde girl, leaning out over the edge of the pavement to see the tram coming.

Eva. Hommel. Veerle couldn't make the connection; too much of her mind's processing power was concentrated on the terrible thought that he was standing right behind her and all of the rest of the ancient cathedral was empty; its emptiness was the vast sky in which they both wheeled, the hawk and the dove, before the killing plunge.

She couldn't help herself then; she had to turn round and

look at him. She had to know who he was, even if it was the very last thing she ever did. Slowly, Veerle turned.

He's old, she thought in shock. She registered that instantly, but there was no relief. Old, yes, but not feeble. She knew danger when she saw it, and it was radiating from him in waves, an instability as precarious as nitro-glycerine.

He was aged, but tall and broad-shouldered, the remains of a strong and muscular man. His features were large and heavy, the mouth wide with deeply lined corners, the whole effect that of a pitiless deity carved in stone. He was wearing some kind of dark coat with a hood, but he had pushed it back revealing a wide forehead and deep-set eyes overhung by craggy brows. The skin of his face was more wrinkled than that of any other living being she could recall seeing; it was a network of tiny fine lines, textured like linen. It was the eyes that held her gaze, though: they had a flat glitter, the gaze of a fanatic.

Veerle could believe that this man had tried to push Hommel into the path of the tram. She believed it immediately. He must have seen something in her face – the grim realization, a kind of subtle accusation; she saw him react minutely as she faced him, the wrinkles shivering and re-forming.

He said, 'Are you one of *them*?'

Veerle saw his right hand slide deep into the pocket of the dark coat. There was nothing casual in the gesture; the arm remained tense, as though he was on the point of drawing something out.

Her mouth was dry. *What does he want me to say?*

'No,' she said very firmly. 'I'm not one of them.'

Veerle wanted to turn and run for the door, for daylight and the presence of other people. But she dared not; she was afraid of what was in that pocket. She was afraid it would be buried between her shoulder blades before she made it to the doorway. She watched the old man with wide horrified eyes.

The right hand never moved, but now the left hand dipped into the other coat pocket and drew out a handful of something. The gesture the old man made, once, twice, was instantly and grimly familiar.

Sowing something. Not seeds. Salt.

The white grains pattered down onto the floor, pale and ominous as fallout.

Instinct did what conscious fear had failed to do and galvanized Veerle into life. She stepped back smartly, as though the white stuff were quicklime.

The old man saw her do it and his right hand jerked up out of his pocket. The knuckles were white around the hilt of a knife. Even in the dim light the long blade gleamed.

'Did you lie?' demanded the old man in his smoky voice.

'No,' said Veerle, the word escaping like a sob.

'Then come here.'

Veerle shook her head desperately. *No.*

'Come here or I shall know you have lied.'

Veerle saw the blade coming up in a glittering arc.

'Cross the line or I cross it.'

Dimly, through the panic that threatened to overwhelm her, Veerle found understanding, as though dredging up some barely recognizable and barnacled object from the depths of the sea.

It's a test. Whatever they *are, he wants me to prove I'm not one of them by crossing the salt.*

That would mean stepping closer to the old man and the evil thing he held in his right hand, not moving further away. The idea made her light-headed with horror. Still her gaze stole to the pointed end of the blade quivering eagerly on the air.

One chance. If I'm wrong . . .

Veerle stepped forward, taking care to let the scattered salt crunch under her feet, ostentatiously trampling it. She was so close to the old man now that she could *smell* him, a nauseating reek of unwashed body and greasy clothing.

The blade descended, but uselessly. The old man had believed her. The knife vanished back into the black coat. Now he was eyeing her with sly complicity.

'I won't be stopped,' he said to her in that strangely grating voice. 'They try, but I am stronger. I bar the way to them with salt and iron, and the ones I catch – I kill.'

'Who?' whispered Veerle. 'Who do you kill?'

'The demons,' said the old man, and the matter-of-fact way in which he said it was chilling.

Veerle wanted to step back, wanted to turn and run, but she dared not, not while that blade was a fingertip's length away from the old man's grasp. She did not want to hold the gaze of those glittering eyes; instead she focused on that grim mouth, waiting for the words that dropped from it like toads.

She saw the old man turn away from her, towards the painting of Eva.

'It is a good copy, the face,' he said in that scratched and damaged voice. 'But it is not as good as the original.'

The altarpiece. That was what he meant, Veerle realized. The painting of Eva was a copy of one of the panels. Somehow the way the old man switched like that, from talk of killing to an inconsequential remark about an ancient painting, was more terrible than the knowledge that he had a knife in his pocket.

Veerle's eyes were the only things that moved in a face that had become a mask of deliberate neutrality; she was terrified of drawing that murderous insanity to herself.

The cathedral was still empty apart from her and the old man. Where was everyone – the guides, the tourists? Still the rain was beating that monotonous tattoo outside.

As the moments stretched out she fumbled for something to say, anything that would maintain the thinly stretched pretence that they were simply two strangers idly waiting out the downpour.

'I've seen the Lamb painting,' she offered at last. 'It's incredible.'

'Incredible,' he repeated in a voice loaded with grim significance. 'Yes, it is – incredible.'

'I have a friend from Ghent,' Veerle blurted out. 'He's told me the story. He's meeting me here in a minute.'

Immediately she winced inside. *Clumsy.* She might as well have said, *I just want to let you know I'm not really alone, whatever it might look like.*

'Really?' came the reply in that smoky voice. The wrinkled lips worked, but what obscure emotion they were expressing she could not tell. 'What did he tell you, your friend from Ghent?'

'He said – he said all the people in the painting are still alive, walking around Ghent.'

'Did he?' said the old man, and there was an ominous quality to his tone that made Veerle's stomach turn over, nauseatingly. 'Your friend is wrong.' Before Veerle could say anything he went on, 'There are only two of them now, as you say, "walking around Ghent".' He nodded towards the painting. 'One of them is Eva.'

And the other one?

Veerle didn't say that out loud; hardly even had time to think it. Her whole mind was filled with the barely controllable desire to put some space between herself and this terrifying ancient person who looked like a statue that has been pitted and corroded by centuries of weather. Her eyes turned towards the cathedral door, longingly. She dared not even look at her watch, but still she hoped that Bram might appear, reassuringly tall and broad-shouldered.

'I suppose,' said the old man, 'that you will say, why would anyone want to die, when they could live as long as the painting survives?'

'I don't know,' whispered Veerle.

'Then you are fortunate.' The old man took a step closer, and Veerle had to force herself not to recoil. How long did someone have to go without washing to smell like that? Or was he sick, rotting from the inside? 'Life can become a burden, from which the sufferer is gladly freed.'

Veerle could not help herself; she took a step back. She dared not take her eyes from the old man's seamed face, from the madness that seeped out of those eyes like the dark stain of an octopus.

Where is Bram?

The old man was waiting; she had to say something.

'That's . . . very sad.'

' "Sad"?' The ruined voice took on a sly quality. 'Such a small word. It is more than "sad". More than "terrible". It is something monstrous, to outlive yourself. I was there,' he went on in that cracked voice that made every word sound painful. 'I was at Gavere, when the soldiers came. So many years ago, but I cannot forget a single detail. The savagery of the troops, the screaming, the blood – all the blood, red, seeping into the earth. So very many died, but I did not. I did not,' he repeated grimly. 'And every day that I have lived since then has been a weight upon my shoulders.'

The war, thought Veerle. He would have been young then – a child perhaps. Even through the paralysing sense of menace the old man instilled in her, she had the feeling that she had been given some critical piece of information, as though someone had handed her the largest shard of pottery from a broken vase and invited her to guess what the entire design had been, from that one fragment. No time to think about it, though; suddenly Veerle heard footsteps hurrying towards them, ringing out on the chequered tiles, and the relief that swept over her was like a flash flood, obliterating all other thoughts.

Bram? Had he been inside all along? But no – she saw that it was one of the cathedral guides. He was tall and lean and smartly dressed, officious-looking even, and he had a face like thunder.

He was not looking at her, he was looking at the old man, and as he approached he spread his arms wide, as though shepherding some rogue animal away. He didn't seem intimidated by the old man at all, or perhaps it was simply the rage distorting his features that carried him along regardless.

'Out!' he shouted, really shouting, his angry voice expanding and filling the chill empty space of the cathedral, leaving no room for protest. 'Out now, or I call the police.'

The guide wasn't looking at Veerle at all, he didn't even seem to be aware that she was there, but all the same, his fury was so all-encompassing that she was afraid it included herself. He swept past her, though, with the blind objectiveness of a guided missile, and bundled the old man towards the doorway with what seemed like surprising roughness.

Astoundingly, the old man didn't resist. Veerle saw his face turn towards the painting of Eva one last time, and then he allowed himself to be hustled out of the door.

Veerle didn't move. The relief of seeing the old man disappear out into the rain-soaked square was so great that it was all she could do to stay on her feet. Suddenly her legs were trembling under her. She became aware of the wet strands of hair still clinging to her face, of her damp clothes, of the fact that she was shivering with cold. She touched numb fingers to lips that were like cool marble, staring at the doorway through which the old man had vanished.

A few moments later the cathedral guide came back, his face still congested with anger. He came up to Veerle and said, 'Were you speaking to that man?'

'He spoke to me,' said Veerle. She felt too drained to bridle at the guide's irritable tone.

'You don't know him?' the guide demanded.

'No.' On impulse, she said, 'Has he done something?'

'You could say that,' said the guide grimly. 'He's banned from the cathedral completely. A couple of years ago he went into the altarpiece and tried to break the glass with a hammer. It's a good thing it happened to be locked when he got in here. God knows what he would have done. *Verdomd maniak.* Every so often he tries it again.' He eyed Veerle narrowly. 'What did he say to you?'

'He – he said some of the people in the painting are still walking around Ghent.'

The guide snorted angrily. 'There. I told you. Crazy.' He looked at her again, this time more carefully. 'Have I seen you in here before?'

'I don't think so,' said Veerle. The suspicious tone in his voice had a reviving effect on her; she began to think that it was time to leave. She didn't think this was the guide who had tried to stop her running inside the cathedral the day she had chased Hommel, but if he had been there, if he had seen it happen, he might turn his annoyance on her. He might detain her, and that would be bad, because it was beginning to dawn on her that at this very moment the old man was walking away across the Sint-Baafsplein, walking away over the cobblestones to some unknown destination, bearing his baleful secrets within him as though they were locked up tight inside a deeds box.

Let him go, screamed some deep-rooted part of herself.

Her body had reacted instinctively to the old man's presence, to the miasma of *wrongness* that seeped out from him, the sense of malevolent energy barely suppressed, even the rank physical stink of him. She had reacted like an animal confronted by a predator, and even now, when the danger was seemingly past, she felt a strong compulsion to bolt for cover, to hide herself.

But . . .

If he disappeared into the maze of streets beyond the limits of the square, she might never find him again. She knew what he looked like now – she could give the police a description, assuming Hommel agreed to it, assuming they listened to her anyway and didn't dismiss her as a nut. If he'd been in trouble before, for trying to vandalize the altarpiece, they might know where to find him.

But what if they don't? Then he's free to go on killing – and killing . . .

The thought of confronting the old man again was horrific, impossible. Veerle knew of the things hidden inside that filthy coat – things that could carve the life out of you in an instant. But letting him get away – that felt as bad as standing on the top of the Gravensteen watching him kill someone Bram knew, and not being able to do a thing about it.

Can't confront him. Can't let him go. What do I do?

The urgency of the situation was like a slap in the face. *Think. Think!*

Already she was moving towards the door, and she could feel the pulse fluttering rapidly in her throat; she knew what she was considering doing – knew it was dangerous, knew she was probably going to do it anyway.

If I followed him – as long as he didn't see me – if I could just see where he goes – I won't confront him – if Bram is outside we could follow him together, I needn't go alone.

Framed in the doorway of the cathedral, she scanned the

square, looking for the old man's tall spare figure in its dark coat. The rain was still coming down, more lightly now, but still blurring the scene. For a moment she thought she had lost him – he had vanished already – but then she saw him stepping over the tram tracks at the left of the square. He had pulled the dark hood of the coat over his head to keep off the rain, but she knew him all the same.

Bram, where are you? she thought desperately as she stepped out into the rain. *Come on, come on! I can't wait.*

Even as she started to move diagonally across the square towards the old man, she risked a quick glance at her watch and saw that it was ten to twelve.

Too early.

Bram would still be streets away. If she waited, she'd lose the old man. Already he had a good head start on her; if she hadn't known where to look, she would have lost him by now.

Veerle set off over the cobblestones at a trot. Her heart was thudding, her mouth dry. Her skin seemed to prickle all over – the acupuncture of fear.

This is insane. But she couldn't think what else to do.

She felt for her mobile phone as she went, but there was no time to stop and call Bram, not now; in the time it took to scroll through the names, the old man would have disappeared. He was heading north-west, past the Belfort tower, moving surprisingly quickly for someone of his age, and there were any number of side streets he could turn down.

Veerle increased her own pace, glancing swiftly behind her before launching herself across the tramlines. The rain kissed her face coolly and lightly. When she reached the belfry she looked back once, towards the cathedral. There by the door she saw a tall figure with a bright shock of blond hair.

Bram?

Her head swivelled back to the street ahead of her and *Verdomme*, the old man was turning down Heilige-Geeststraat. For a split second she hesitated. Then she put her head down and ran after him.

50

Veerle followed the old man through the rain-slicked streets, keeping well back in case he should glance behind him, but not so far back that he could escape her. That was the extent of her thinking; she had no idea what she was going to do when she found out where he was going. Her heart was racing; she was almost dizzy with the insanity of what she was doing, and yet she did not turn back. She *couldn't* lose him.

One chance, she thought feverishly. *Only one chance to see where he goes.*

The cold and rain were keeping most people off the streets. It was easy to follow, but more difficult to follow unseen. That was bad; Veerle tried to tell herself that even if he spotted her behind him, he would do nothing in the open street, but she had seen enough to know that he was capable of anything. Her nerve almost failed her; the thought of being caught was as sickening as vertigo. The old man did not look back, however; safely cowled in his dark hood, he hurried on, taking a dogleg route through the wet streets.

Veerle kept up her pursuit, horribly conscious of Bram at the cathedral, at the widening distance between them. It could only be a little after twelve o'clock now – but how long would he wait? She wished she could phone him, but she dared not stop.

The old man cut left into another side street.

Where is he going? She was almost certain that this was a deliberately circuitous route, that it was a well-worn ruse to ensure that nobody could pin him to a particular location.

Veerle expected that he would lead her to some run-down apartment block, away from the old city centre with its brightly lit shop windows. It was a shock when the chase led her out of a narrow backstreet onto a wider one lined with smart-looking boutiques, and she saw the old man slow down, quite deliberately. He was perhaps forty metres ahead of her, sauntering along, when finally he stopped.

Instantly Veerle stopped too, and hastily made a pretence of looking in the nearest shop window, which was full of ugly and expensive knitwear in shades of green, white and blue. When she glanced casually up the street she could still see the old man, but only because she was looking for him. He had chosen his stopping place well; he was standing outside a shop – or perhaps it was a restaurant, she couldn't tell from where she stood – that had several potted trees on the pavement in front of it, and he had positioned himself close to one of them.

Afraid of being caught staring his way, she looked back at the hideous sweaters behind the plate-glass window, her breath coming fast, and when she glanced towards the potted trees again he had gone.

Frustration and disappointment assailed her like a pair of scolds.

How could I lose him? How could *I?*

Caution thrown entirely to the winds, she stepped back to the edge of the pavement, trying to see round the tree in its pot. There was nobody there.

Veerle could have screamed.

I only took my eyes off him for a few seconds.

She began to walk up the street.

Calm down, she said to herself. *Maybe he's gone into one of the shops.* She forced herself to go slowly, as though she were strolling along, innocently window-shopping, as though she had enough money in her pocket to spend sixty euros on a leather purse or a hundred and fifty on a dress. One of the shops she passed was a jeweller's with a large clock hanging over the door; the time was now twenty past twelve, she saw. She thought desperately of Bram, standing outside the cathedral in the rain, or perhaps pacing the dim interior, searching for her.

I'll call him . . . just let me see if the old man is here . . .

As she neared the two trees in their pots she saw that they stood outside a little restaurant; there was a kind of mat laid out on the pavement where tables and chairs might have stood if it had not been cold and wet outdoors. There was a sign on the door reading GESLOTEN and all the interior lights were off; if the old man had gone in there he would have had to have a key.

Veerle stood on the mat and did her best to peer into the darkened interior. There was no sign of life in there, not even a telltale rectangle thinly drawn in light that would mean a lit room on the other side of a closed internal door. She stepped away from the window and looked around.

There had not been time for the old man to cross the

road without her seeing him do it, she was sure of that.

Veerle looked at the next shop in the row, and that did not look promising. It was one of those expensive-looking places that sold the kind of elegant things that fashionable people wanted but nobody actually *needed*: new candlesticks deliberately made to look like old ones, heart-shaped decorations made of tin or wood, and bookends made of seated cherubs. Everything seemed to be in shades of cream and silver, and the shop was terrifically well-lit, so that the whole effect was rather dazzling, like looking into the nest of materialistic angels. Veerle could see every centimetre of the interior, and it was plain that a very old man with a miasma of body odour surrounding him like a force field would not be welcome in it for an instant; nor could he escape notice should he manage to gain entry.

So where is he?

For a moment she imagined him standing somewhere close by in the shadows, watching her silently, and the thought made her skin prickle unpleasantly.

No, she told herself firmly. *He's gone in somewhere. But where?*

He was not in the restaurant; he was not in this shop. Veerle took another half-dozen paces up the street and there was a door.

It didn't lead into either of the shops that flanked it; she could see that immediately from the shabby state of it. Veerle glanced around warily, saw nobody on the street, and pushed gently at the door. To her surprise, it swung inwards and she found herself looking at a scruffy corridor with daylight at the end of it – a service entrance, she supposed. Looking down it, she could see a small yard at the back of the building. The latch on the door was broken.

He must have gone down here.

That was odd; it didn't look like the entrance to flats. What she could see of the yard at the back was drearily neglected.

Maybe he did *know I was following him.*

In which case the entrance was either a dead end or a trap, she realized with a cold thrill of horror.

Veerle knew better than to step inside. Instead she went and stood in front of the deserted restaurant, and phoned Bram. She kept her eyes on the entrance all the time, as though its malevolent occupant might launch himself forth at any moment, like a conger eel lunging out of its hole.

The first time the call went straight through to voicemail she didn't even wait to hear the number being recited; she cancelled the call and tried again, thinking she must have called the wrong person.

The second time, the call went through to voicemail again. Veerle took the phone away from her ear and looked at it in sick dismay, as though her eyes might give her some other answer than the one her ears had given her.

No, Bram. Not now.

In her mind's eye she saw the whole thing playing out. Bram had reached Sint-Baafs as she was leaving the square; it had almost certainly been him she had seen as she glanced back from the Belfort tower – it wasn't as though the square was crowded with visitors on a filthy day like this – and seen that blond hair. He had looked around, and he hadn't seen Veerle anywhere in Sint-Baafsplein, so he had gone into the cathedral, thinking she must be inside. He had found the west end of the nave empty apart from the cathedral guide. Perhaps he had asked the man if he had seen a dark-haired girl hanging about in the church, but more likely he had gone to look for her himself, strolling up one of the aisles with his hands in his pockets, past the gated chapels and the still white faces of marble saints. He would have made a complete circuit of the interior before he realized she wasn't there; perhaps he'd even gone down into the crypt and searched there too. All of it would have taken time – twenty minutes, half an hour – before he gave up.

Why did he have to switch his phone off?

If Bram had been there in front of her she would have grabbed his shoulders and shaken him bodily.

Is it so annoying that he can't even speak to me, me not being there?

But she knew in her heart it wasn't that. He'd asked her to take a step closer to him, and now he would be assuming that she had decided not to. Worse, that she had not even come to tell him. She had apparently simply decided to stand him up.

He would be upset, and yes, possibly angry, and hadn't trusted himself to speak to her just yet. So he had switched off the phone and gone off somewhere to think, or perhaps just to forget the ignominy of waiting about for someone who clearly wasn't going to appear.

Verdomme. Veerle felt like screaming. *Turn the phone back on, Bram. Please. I'll apologize. I'll grovel. Just turn the phone on.*

She waited for another minute, but then she couldn't stand it any longer; she had to try again. She called Bram a third time, and again she got his voicemail. Veerle hung up without leaving a message.

Shit. What am I going to do?

She glanced towards the shabby door leading into the yard. The old man hadn't emerged so he must be inside there, either in the yard itself or in one of the buildings. Veerle instantly rejected the idea of going in there alone to look for him. That narrow corridor opening into the yard reminded her unpleasantly of a lobster pot: easy enough to get into, difficult to get out of in a hurry. Even the thought of it struck her with a cold dread.

If only Bram were here. They might have risked it together. Or if the old man came out, one of them could have followed him, and the other investigated the yard. On her own, however, there was absolutely nothing she could do. Nothing *safe* she could do. And Veerle had learned her lesson about going into a dead end on her own when there was something lurking in it.

I'm not going in there alone, she thought.

51

Forty-five minutes later she was still standing out in the street, shivering a little now with the cold and wet, and Bram still hadn't switched his phone back on.

He must be really, really mad at me, thought Veerle miserably.

The old man had not re-emerged and the scruffy door that led to the yard was still slightly ajar, as grimly alluring as a baited trap.

Veerle still had no intention of going in. She considered the options as raindrops slid down her cheeks like tears.

She could forget it for now, and come back later with Bram. The trouble with that was, they would have no idea whether the old man was in there. He was in there some-where *now,* and if she saw him leave she'd know he *wasn't* in there, but she didn't fancy going in blind later on, even if she had Bram with her. The old man had a brutal gleaming friend for a sidekick.

She could call someone else, and that really meant Kris. Veerle thought about that. That he would come, she had no doubt. This was Saturday, so he was almost certainly at the flat over Muziek City. She knew that Kris wouldn't turn down an opportunity to investigate, if it meant a chance of catching the person who had been tailing Hommel.

Yes, Kris would come over here like a shot. And then, when Bram finally snapped out of his anger or swallowed his pride and switched his phone back on, she would have to explain that she was very sorry she had stood him up, but she was here with her ex-boyfriend, the one she'd played truant for.

Veerle winced. *No.* She would wait, and perhaps Bram would switch his phone back on, or perhaps the old man would come out again.

There was a bistro on the other side of the street. Normally she wouldn't think of going in anywhere like that on her own; if she wanted coffee or a Coke there were loads of places that were far cheaper. At the moment, however, it seemed the best option. A peep into her wallet showed that she had fifteen euros in notes and a handful of change. Veerle crossed the road and went inside.

The place was empty apart from one member of staff, a woman of about thirty who was sitting on a bar stool reading *Het Nieuwsblad.* She did not look thrilled at the sight of this single rain-drenched customer, but she came over and languidly took Veerle's order of a hot chocolate.

Veerle settled herself at a table near the window, and kept her eyes fixed on the doorway opposite. The hot chocolate arrived. She tried calling Bram again but his phone was still off. Veerle left a brief message asking him to call her. She hated to do that – some things were best said in person – but there seemed no other option.

Time passed. The old man failed to reappear.

Where is he? thought Veerle, watching. She watched

obsessively, as though the old man might drift past like a wisp of smoke if she let her eyes stray elsewhere for an instant.

Perhaps there was some way into residential flats through there, run-down though it looked. Maybe there was another way out of that yard at the back, and he was long gone. Maybe he hadn't gone through the door at all.

He must have, she reminded herself. *There isn't anywhere else he could have gone.*

Eventually the woman came back with a small printed bill.

Pay up and go or order something else, said her unsmiling expression.

Veerle looked at the menu. There was hardly anything she could afford with the cash she had left. She ordered the very cheapest dish, a salad with goat's cheese and bacon. It was going to clean her out of money; when she'd finished the meal she'd have to pay up and leave. Veerle ordered the salad, and then on impulse she said to the woman, 'That door over there – do you ever see anyone go in or out of it?'

The woman's gaze flickered over Veerle with ill-concealed disdain. 'No,' she said shortly.

The way she spoke implied that she would not have told Veerle anything even if the doorway opposite had been the daily conduit of an entire circus troupe, complete with elephants, dancing horses and acrobats in spangled leotards. She picked up the menu and walked away, towards the back of the bistro.

The salad when it arrived was very good, but Veerle paid it little attention. She ate as slowly as she dared, keeping her mobile phone on the table next to her, hoping that Bram would switch on his mobile, pick up her message and phone her back.

Halfway through the meal she looked down at her plate, looked up again and across the road, and there was the old man. He was out on the pavement, and he was already walking away from the doorway between the shops, striding out, his dark coat pulled close around his throat.

For a moment Veerle stared at him in shock, and then she was on her feet, heart thudding. She grabbed her mobile phone from the table, her fork clattering unnoticed onto her plate.

Equally rapidly the woman who had served her was out of the back of the bistro and moving smoothly into the space between Veerle and the door.

'Oh no you don't.'

Veerle tried to see past her, to see where the old man was going, but the woman dodged to the side, blocking her view.

'You've a bill to pay.'

'I wasn't trying to—' Veerle broke off, speechless with frustration. She dragged her wallet out of her pocket, took out the fifteen euros and thrust them at the woman. 'I have to go!'

'This is two euros short. You had the hot chocolate.'

'Shit.' Veerle was beside herself. She upended the wallet, caught the handful of coins that fell out, and dumped the lot on the nearest table. 'There.'

Then she bolted for the door.

'Hey! Wait until I—'

But Veerle didn't hang around. She burst out into the street.

The old man had already vanished.

Veerle ran to the first intersection and gazed down every

street, but there was no sign of an old man in a dark coat.

After that, heart thumping, her breathing rasping in and out in short gasps, she walked back to the scuffed door through which he had undoubtedly emerged, and contemplated it in silence.

Well, she thought, *I know he's not in there now.*

She looked behind her once to make sure that nobody was watching her, and then she slipped inside.

52

The corridor leading to the yard behind the shops was not only narrow, it was unlit and it stank of urine. Veerle picked her way cautiously along it, hoping that the floor was not as filthy as it smelled. She could not imagine anyone from the shops on either side using this corridor; to go from here into the dazzling interior of the candlestick shop would be like tracking mud into an operating theatre. If there were flats through here, they must be squalid. She remembered the thick stench that had hung about the old man, and grimaced. It was a relief to step into the yard.

It was an odd, ill-favoured little space. Simply being inside it made Veerle deeply uneasy. The surrounding buildings stretched to four or five storeys at least, so that being in the yard felt like being at the bottom of a deep crevasse. There were a couple of rubbish bins whose contents some unfortunate soul probably had to haul through that stinking tunnel every week, and various bits of lumber: a couple of broken chairs, some rain-engorged cardboard cartons, and a splintered wooden pallet. A black metal fire escape zigzagged its way up one of the towering walls.

Veerle looked around, very cautiously. It did not seem

possible that anyone could spend several hours in the yard; ergo, the old man must have gone up and down the fire escape. She thought that she would climb up and try some of the doors, but first she would call Bram again, and, she decided heavily, if Bram still had his phone switched off, she would call Kris. She would feel better if someone knew where she was, or preferably if someone came down here and climbed the fire escape with her. Knowing that the old man had gone did nothing to reduce the atmosphere of dereliction and decay, of wrongness, in this place. It stank of menace, like the bone-littered entrance to a dragon's cave.

Bram's phone was still off. Veerle ended the call, thought for a moment, then called back and left a new message.

'Bram, it's me again. Look, I'm really, really sorry I stood you up. I know what you must be thinking, but I wouldn't have done it if I hadn't had to. Can you call me back as soon as you get this?' There was the briefest of pauses before she added, 'I . . . love you.'

Veerle hung up, and stood motionless for a few moments, the phone clasped in her hand, looking up towards the open sky. Then she called Kris. She made herself do it without thinking too hard about it – there was no other option, after all – and she was completely unprepared when the call went straight to his voicemail too.

Veerle thumbed the OFF button on the touch screen. Her heart was racing now. She felt a little sick.

This is ridiculous. This can't be.

She stared down at the phone.

Did I call Bram's number again by mistake?

She called again, taking meticulous care that it was

definitely *Kris Verstraeten* she phoned, and nobody else, but the call diverted straight to voicemail again.

Verdomme.

Veerle felt like hurling the phone across the yard to certain destruction on the wall, but she restrained herself. Instead, she left a message, forcing herself to speak calmly.

'Kris, it's Veerle. Something's happened. I was in the cathedral and there was this horrible old man. Look, he's the one who attacked Hommel. I *know* he is. He said the same thing – you know, *Eva.* He's got some kind of thing about the painting, the one in the cathedral.' Veerle rubbed her forehead with her fingers. *Am I insane, even thinking about doing this?* But she made herself finish the call. 'The cathedral guide threw him out and I didn't want to lose him so I followed him. I'm at . . .' She gave the street name. 'There's a doorway leading through into a back yard. It's next to a shop with all this home decoration stuff and opposite the bistro. The old man isn't here – I saw him go out a few minutes ago – so I'm going to go in and have a look around.' Veerle paused. 'I just wanted to let someone know where I was, in case I never come back, OK?' She spoke in a deliberately light tone, but she wasn't joking. She gave the street name again and then she hung up without ceremony.

So, she thought queasily, *I'm on my own.*

She tried hard not to think too carefully about that.

I'll go in and look around for a couple of minutes – five, max – and then I'm out of here. Long gone before the old man even thinks of coming back.

She went to the foot of the fire escape and looked up. Then she pocketed the phone and began to ascend the metal staircase, moving slowly and carefully to minimize the sound of her footsteps. It seemed sound enough but looked sadly neglected, the black paint flaking off in numerous places as though the staircase were shedding its skin, snake-like. There was nothing to indicate that anyone ever used it: no cigarette ends, no discarded food wrappers or till receipts, not so much as a muddy footprint. All the same, as Veerle moved higher and her view of the yard below encompassed every corner, she became more and more convinced that the old man must have used the fire escape. There was nowhere else he could have gone. There was a set of double doors leading into the back of the shop next to this one, but she could see the chains across it from here.

Veerle reached the first floor and the blank closed face of the fire exit. There was no handle to work at, no lock to pick. It looked secure, and indeed, when she touched it, it refused to budge a millimetre. She glanced down into the yard, checking that she was still alone, though she was committed now, anyway; if the old man or anyone else appeared below she had no escape route other than to continue upwards. The yard was deserted. She continued her climb.

As soon as the second-floor fire door came into view she could see that she had found what she was looking for. It had been pushed almost closed but there was the hint of a shadow running up the side of it like a broken seal.

There was a hard knot of grim excitement in Veerle's chest, the dark reflection of the exhilaration she had felt whenever she and Kris had explored a new house back in Vlaams-Brabant or Brussels. It felt as though a line had been drawn, and she was about to step over it. It was as brazen and deliberate as saying *Sometimes I hated my mother*. Or saying *I love you* when perhaps you didn't. It was a toxic rush, compulsive and suicidal as bad drugs.

Veerle touched the edge of the door, curling her fingers around it, proving to herself that, yes, it really was open. She listened too, holding her breath, straining her ears for the slightest sound that would tell her that someone was inside. Nothing. The air was still; the interior of the building exuded nothing but cold. She might as well have put her ear to a corpse's lips and hoped to feel warm breath on her cheek.

Veerle pulled the door open and looked inside. The fire escape looked into a passage and internal staircase. The interior of the building was dimly lit, the light apparently coming from the front windows. There were light fittings with naked bulbs at intervals along the corridor but none of them were on. The cold natural light that spilled from open doorways along the passage showed bare wooden floorboards and unadorned walls.

She stepped inside and pulled the door almost closed behind her. Then she began to explore, treading as silently as possible, all her senses on high alert.

The floor she was on, the second floor, was deserted – that was soon obvious. The rooms were large, with high ceilings decorated with elegant moulded plaster, and if the weather outside had not been so overcast they would have been pleasantly light. They were also very clearly uninhabited, and had been so for a long time. There not a stick of furniture in any of them, and the dust lay so thickly on the boards that her feet left visible tracks in it, as though she were wading dispiritedly through a layer of fall-out.

The fall-out of time, she thought. It got everyone in the end – everyone, that is, except Joos Vijdt and his fellows, if you believed the legend.

Veerle approached one of the front windows, moving sideways like a crab so that she could peer out and down without being seen from the street. There was nothing untoward to see, no black-clad and wrinkled old man coming up the road towards the building. She turned away.

It made sense to check the first floor too, although she didn't really think the old man lived there. She was beginning to think that if he lived in this building he was squatting illegally, and in that case he'd probably go further up, as far from the shop with its chic and haughty staff as possible. She went down stairs that were as thickly coated with dust as everything else, and found more deserted rooms, and a great stack of boxes piled up near the head of the staircase that led down to the ground floor.

Veerle opened one of them and was not surprised to find the fat and gleaming face of a ceramic cherub pouting up at her from a mass of packaging material, like the obese victim of a landslide.

Stock from the shop below.

She closed the box, thinking.

They've just left it all here, by the stairs, so they obviously don't think anyone is going to come through here and help themselves to anything.

The only tracks in the dust on the landing were her own, so she didn't think anyone ever came any further than this point either. Veerle glanced up at the ceiling.

So he goes up there.

She thought about going up.

Five minutes, max, that was what I said. I've probably had five minutes.

Stillness; nothing moving, no sound other than her own rapid breathing.

Five more minutes, then out, she said to herself.

She climbed the stairs again, carefully, still listening, still hearing nothing. She passed the deserted second floor and made her way up to the third. Now she *could* see marks in the dust on the treads, a myriad of them: either a whole crowd of people had gone up and down just once, or one person had done it a hundred times. It was easy to follow the trail now, although she still peered into each of the rooms, just for the sake of thoroughness. All empty. In one, a single torn curtain hung from a rail; otherwise, they might never have been inhabited.

The fourth floor was the same. Now the front rooms were a little lighter in spite of the gloom outside, because they were closer to the rooftops. In one of them there were scuff-marks leading to a spot just to the side of the window; someone had done what Veerle had done; he had positioned himself where he could see out with little risk of being seen himself. Still there was no sign of anyone actually *living* here.

Maybe he doesn't *live here. Maybe he just comes here to . . .* what? To spy on passers-by or the occupants of the building opposite? Veerle couldn't imagine it. The rooms were bleak and bare, and the higher she went, the colder they were, as though she were slowly ascending to a mountain peak crusted with snow.

Veerle thought that she must be nearly at the top now. One

final floor to go, and then nothing more except the roof itself. She stood at the bottom of the staircase looking up towards the fifth floor, and that dark dangerous excitement she had felt gave way to a sense of seething unease.

It's very dark up there.

The floor she was on wasn't exactly well-lit; the daylight seemed to seep in grudgingly through the dusty windows. It was light *enough* though, even if somewhat gloomy. But up there, on the fifth floor, there was no light at all.

Veerle looked up towards the head of the stairs and she could make out nothing except that darkness, a thick muffling darkness that seemed to expand and drift like fog the longer she looked at it.

Why?

There had to be some prosaic explanation. Perhaps someone had decided to close all the shutters on the top floor.

In spite of leaving them open on every other floor?

It didn't feel right. Veerle stood at the bottom of the stairs and hauled out her phone again to check for messages or missed calls. She knew she hadn't missed any calls, but she checked anyway. Nothing.

Shit. Bram, Kris, anyone, just switch your phone on.

She leaned over the banisters and gazed down at the floor below, listening. Nothing to see or hear. No sign of the old man returning.

Still, she thought about it before she made up her mind. It was horribly ominous, that blackness at the head of the stairs, and yet she could think of no alternative. She had not traced the old man to a regular address, somewhere they could knock politely on a neighbour's door and ask questions, or that they could pass on anonymously to the police. The old man was long gone; he might return but equally she might never run into him again. If there were any answers to be had, they were upstairs, cocooned in the smothering dark.

Veerle put her hand on the banister, feeling the wood cool under her hand, the grain slightly rough where the varnish was worn away. She held on as she climbed the stairs, as though to steady herself. If anyone had been standing below on the landing, they would have seen her ascend slowly, her face turned upwards, like a saint in a stained-glass window rising towards the heavens. The darkness swallowed her.

53

Veerle moved haltingly through the darkness, one hand clutching the banister, one stretched out in front of her, groping the air for obstacles she hoped not to find. She was praying that the boards beneath her feet were sound; there was nothing to suggest that they *weren't*, but it was unnerving not being able to see where she was treading. That was the *logical* fear, but worse were the irrational ones that clustered about her like phantasms. She imagined her questing fingers touching something in the blackness – a lipless mouth, a corroded eye socket – and it was all she could do to keep moving forward.

Get a grip, she told herself sternly. *It's just a bunch of rooms with the shutters down. The dark can't hurt you. It's the old man you've got to listen out for.*

That didn't help – the mere thought gave her a cold feeling in the pit of her stomach. A rapid pulse throbbed in her throat.

Veerle stood still for a moment, her right hand still resting on the banister, her eyes gazing into the darkness, straining to see the slightest chink of light, anything that would tell her whether to go on or turn back.

And she did. As her eyes adjusted to the blackness she could see the thinnest of lines sketched in the air in front of her: delicate as cobweb, and curiously insubstantial, seeming to flicker in and out of existence. So evanescent was it that she doubted the evidence of her eyes at first. But no – she was not imagining it. It really *was* there.

What am I seeing?

She began to move towards it, still advancing with great care, and now she saw that it was not simply a single line, it was part of an infinitesimally slender outline traced in the darkness with a faint and inconsistent light. A door – a door with light behind it, only not daylight; something very much weaker.

Veerle knew that she was on the outer limits of the *second* five minutes she had promised herself. It was time to go, time to cut her losses and leave the building, to thank heaven that she had got in and out of it without being caught.

Just one minute more, maybe two. Just time to try the door. If it's locked, I'll just go. If it opens, I'll take thirty seconds to look and then I'll go.

Veerle knew she was pushing her luck. This was not a good place to be. There were plenty of hiding places but only one way in and out. Every nerve and fibre in her body was screaming at her to *get out, right now*.

Still, for the sake of a single minute, not to know . . .

Thirty seconds was long enough to see whatever was behind the door. It might be long enough to photograph it with her phone, or to pick something up, some small item she could show to the police as proof.

Veerle glanced behind her, at the faint light coming from

the bottom of the stairs. Then she continued to inch her way towards the door. She let go of the banister and put both hands out in front of her, and at last they touched polished panels.

The floor was gritty under her feet here. In the darkness she could see nothing, but she thought she knew what it was. Salt, a thick border of it, barring the way to the door. She swallowed.

Running her fingers lightly down the cool wood, she found a metal doorknob, cold to the touch. She didn't open the door, though; not yet. Instead she moved as close to it as she possibly could, and laid her right ear against it.

Veerle was not sure what she expected to hear. If the old man shared this dim eyrie with some other person, they might be inside. But she didn't really think he shared it with anything but the phantasms of his obsession, and although she listened for several minutes, she could hear nothing at all from the room within. She turned the doorknob with some difficulty, as it was worn to a state of slippery smoothness and very stiff. Then she pushed the door open.

Candles. That was the first thing she saw, and that was the first thing she understood. The shutters were down in all the windows, as she had suspected, and the light that she had seen tracing the dim shape of the door in the darkness was the light of candles, perhaps a dozen of them. She saw how the flames flickered with the slight draught from the open door.

They were fat yellowish candles – church candles – and they had been placed very carefully in metal holders so that they could not fall over as they burned down, and set light to any of the other things in the room. They were not the only candles, Veerle now saw: there were many others, perhaps *hundreds* of them, all unlit. If all of them had been burning at once, the room would have been bright, and the air warm, heavy with the smell of hot wax.

Instead, with a dozen of them alight, it was bathed in a dullish amber glow that gave everything a faintly sepia tint. The air was tainted with the body odour of its recent occupant. The room had the atmosphere of a vigil for a corpse that has lain out for too long.

Veerle pressed her hand to her mouth. She looked around the room and saw objects that showed that someone *was* living here: a makeshift bed of grubby blankets heaped on the bare boards, a little cluster of tin plates with a spoon and a small pointed knife but no fork, a battered water bottle. Oddly, a small heap of what looked like scraps of iron scavenged at random – nails, a hinge, a crudely cut key. Standing behind this, as though offering a benediction, there was a little wooden statue of the Virgin and Child, the carved features softened by the candlelight. It looked old, an antique – a strange thing to have in what was obviously a squat. A moment later the statue was forgotten, because she had seen the other thing, the monstrous thing that dominated the entire room.

The back wall, the one that faced the blinded windows, was covered with *people*. In the candlelight dozens, perhaps hundreds, of faces stared back at Veerle: flat, monochrome, accusing. Paper effigies – some photographically sharp, some in halftone, blown up so that the faces were melting into a kaleidoscope of black dots, others sketched with crude skill, all of them gazing out into the room with the impassivity of a hanging jury.

Shock slithered through the pit of Veerle's stomach with the slimy insistence of a fat worm pushing its way through the black earth. She looked at those images pasted to the wall and the *wrongness* radiating from them was so strong that it was almost tangible; she could almost taste it in her mouth like the cold metallic tang of fear. She looked at them and she did not know them; and yet she knew them, the shape of them.

There was no consistency of scale or colour or detail to those faces, and yet together they made something that was instantly recognizable, that anyone in the city of Ghent would have known. The person who had made this thing – this diseased masterwork – had traced out the framework in which the human faces and figures appeared like intaglios in a set of panels. He had made his canvas a patchwork of lining paper, smoothly and evenly applied behind the human figures, but creased and bubbled at the edges as though it were wet muslin sticking to the wall. He had outlined arches and Gothic tracery and a distant skyline, trees and turrets. In the central foreground was a crude octagon, and above it was the only non-human figure.

Veerle approached the wall, her mouth dry, and took a closer look. The Lamb was a copy of the real one, Van Eyck's lamb. It had been cut out of a book – a large and expensive art book. The paper it was printed on was thick and glossy. Somewhere there was a thick heavy volume about the Ghent altarpiece with one of its pages cut out, or mutilated.

There was something disturbing about that minor act of

vandalism, but as Veerle began to examine the wall and its images in closer detail she began to suspect something very much worse. She began to think that all these people were *dead* people.

Run, she thought. *Get out of here.* But she had to see all of it, she had to *know*.

The seated male figure in the centre, above the Lamb . . . she knew him, or at least she knew the features: the high forehead, arched eyebrows and rather full lips framed by a beard. The body, the robes, had been sketched in, but the face was a large printed photograph. You'd have had to be blind to live in Ghent and *not* know who he was; his death by arson while in the flat of a younger woman who was not his wife had made all the headlines. Veerle thought that the picture of him had been cut from an election poster.

Marie De Smet had died in that fire. Was she recorded here somewhere too? Somehow Veerle thought not. She thought the politician's death was meant; Marie De Smet was collateral damage.

Most of the other faces she *didn't* recognize, but there was something suggestive about them, the way so many of them were obviously private family photographs reproduced in newsprint. There was usually only one reason for that: it meant that something had *happened* to the person; those sorts of photographs were usually accompanied by a legend reading something like ACCIDENT VICTIM or STABBED 23 TIMES.

In one of the clusters of figures she found another face she knew: a rather nondescript one, small-eyed, with a blunt nose and the beginnings of a double chin. It took her a little while to realize who it was: the priest who had died in a house fire, probably also arson.

Veerle had a very bad feeling about this. The person who had created this bizarre collage hadn't made it simply to *record* deaths; she thought he had played a more personal role in those deaths than that. Still, as she studied it, conscious of the moments slipping past her like fleeing vermin, she felt increasingly perplexed.

Some of these pictures are really old. He can't have done anything to these *people – can he?*

She wasn't sure but she thought that some of the hairstyles and the visible items of clothing – a hat, a collar, a scarf – dated back to the 1960s or even the 1950s.

Supposing one of these was taken in 1950 . . . supposing the old man is in his eighties . . .

It was difficult trying to do the simplest arithmetic in her head when her heart was thumping madly and every one of her senses was strained to the utmost, listening for the slightest creak or bump that would tell her that the old man was back in the building. All the same, she worked out that he would have been perhaps twenty back then.

So if he started early . . .

Then she noticed other pictures, and now she really was moving into the realms of impossibility because these had been taken when the oldest person alive would have been a child. No woman would have worn such a gigantic feathered hat in a later decade, no man those moustaches and old-fashioned spectacles.

How far back do these go? Veerle wondered queasily. Far further than any one person's lifespan, that was for certain.

Now that she was hunting for older images she could see that some of them were so old that they were artist's impressions rather than photographs. In half a dozen places there was no portrait at all, simply a crude oval of newsprint. Veerle supposed these must contain reports of deaths but she found the typeface impossible to read – it was ancient and crabbed, and almost every instance of the letter *s* was represented as a kind of *f*.

A small proportion of the faces had been cut from a repro-duction of the original painting, like the Lamb. What did that mean?

Veerle took a few paces back, away from the wall, wanting to see the thing in its entirety again. How many figures were there altogether? She seemed to recall that Bram had said one hundred and seventy. And all of them – except two – were represented by those dead faces, pasted onto the wall. She supposed that included the ones taken directly from a repro-duction of the altarpiece, since the models for that were long dead too.

The missing faces belonged to two of the larger figures. The tall empty space to the right of the centre was mirrored by a similar space on the left, filled by the figure of Adam. Veerle had no idea to whom the face belonged but the body had been sketched in, and it was clearly a naked male. If that was Adam, the opposite space, the empty one, belonged to Eva.

Two missing, and one of them is Eva.

Veerle remembered telling the old man what Bram had said, that all the people in the painting were still alive, walk-ing around Ghent.

Your friend is wrong, the old man had replied. *There are only two of them now, as you say, 'walking around Ghent'. One of them is Eva.*

This is insane.

Still Veerle had to keep looking. She knew that she should go, that she should get out of here *right now*. But the mural held her with a sick fascination; it was a view over the border of sanity, into the abyss.

She stared at the other unfilled space, which was on the very far left. She surmised that the panel in which it appeared had been on the back of the left-hand wing, which would originally have closed over the painting like a cupboard door.

Who was it? Veerle wasn't familiar enough with the altarpiece to make a guess, but after a moment she hit upon the idea of looking at the figure at the far right. She recognized it immediately because it was one of those taken directly from a reproduction of the original. The wife of the donor, Joos Vijdt. What was her name? Veerle thought it was Liesbeth or perhaps Lijsbeth.

No – Lysbette, that was it.

If that is Lysbette, then the other one – the space – must be for him. Joos Vijdt.

Veerle stared at the wall.

Lysbette.

Joos Vijdt.

Eva.

An idea was forming in her mind, an outline of something dimly perceived, as though she were leaning over the side of a boat and gazing down into deep clear water at the remains of a wreck: first you would see nothing but the shifting light on the surface of the water, then you would look *through* and see the shape of something dark down there; and as you stared and stared, suddenly it would leap out at you, the form of the ship that it had been. So Veerle looked with her mind, and the shape of something began to appear out of the darkness.

There are only two empty spaces.

Everyone else is dead.

Joos Vijdt and Eva are still missing because they are still alive. Walking around Ghent. That's what the old man said.

Veerle looked at the wall and she put her hands over her mouth, pressing her fingers against her lips as though she wanted to seal every possible sound within, every gasp, every scream.

Supposing, she thought, *he were Joos Vijdt.*

That was impossible, of course, in the literal sense, but the old man might *believe* he was. He might identify with the rich burgher of Ghent to the extent that their identities had merged in his own mind, that he no longer saw any distinction between them. The question of *why* was a more difficult point, but he had told her that he had witnessed a massacre. *The savagery of the troops, the screaming, the blood*, he had said. That had to be the Second World War.

He saw something when he was a child, something terrible. And he was the only one who survived. The guilt became too much to bear, so he decided he didn't want to be himself any more, whoever he was, Jan or Hendrick or Pieter. He decided to be Joos Vijdt.

Her gaze slid to the empty space where the image of Joos Vijdt should have been. Joos Vijdt, the rich man who, according to local legend, had commissioned a painting whose subjects would never die, except by violence. She remembered what Bram had told her, that first night they had visited the rooftops.

It's their punishment. They didn't want to die, so now they can't. They have to keep roaming the streets of Ghent. As long as even one of them is left alive, the souls of the other ones can't rest.

Veerle thought, *He thinks he can rest if they're all gone.*

Perhaps, she said to herself, *he sees it as a holy task. A duty.*

Of course, he wouldn't have had to deal with every single one of them himself. Some would have died in accidents, or in the wars that had burned their way across Flanders over the centuries since the painting was completed.

The ones who died within their normal life span, those are the ones that are reproductions of the figures in the painting. The really old newspaper reports, he hunted for those – maybe he searched through old papers until he found deaths that he decided were of people from the painting. The others, the later ones . . .

Death glided across the landscape of her mind. She saw the stinking, deadly vomitus that pattered through the letter box of an apartment building on Onderbergen, and the tiny flame that kindled it, filling the stairwell with searing, inescapable light. She saw the smoking remains of the priest's house, its occupant reduced to a bundle of blackened sticks barely distinguishable from the charred timbers that covered it. She saw a tram approaching with that metallic sound they always made, something between a scream and a whistle, the blonde-haired girl leaning out over the edge of the pavement, the sudden sharp thrust – but before it, that name, spoken aloud.

Eva. The old man thinks Hommel is Eva.

The whole idea was utterly insane, it was impossible – and yet Veerle was becoming more and more convinced. It was like staring at an optical illusion with something hidden in it – a face, a figure. Once you had seen it, you couldn't *unsee* it.

He thinks that when Hommel – Eva – is dead, he will be the only one left, and when he ends his own life there will be rest for all of them at last. Maybe he thinks the guilt will end.

Veerle stepped backwards, away from the wall. She was remembering the *other* part of the legend, the final piece.

And he thinks the only ones who can stop him are the demons.

Are you one of them? the old man had asked her, and now it made hideous sense. He had been asking her whether she was one of his adversaries. *The Demons of Ghent.*

Thank God she had said no – thank God she had taken the step he had demanded, crossing the line of salt, even though it had taken her under the shadow of that upraised blade. Because otherwise . . .

I won't be stopped, he had said to her. *They try, but I am stronger. I bar the way to them with salt and iron, and the ones I catch – I kill.*

Veerle swallowed, her throat dry.

Who did he kill? Who did he think these demons were?

Images raced through her head: Luc, plummeting from the belfry of Sint-Baafs. Daan De Moor, dead on the cobble-stones. Marnix, savaged within her own view.

Salt and iron.

Marnix lying dead. Salt dyed in his blood. A black iron nail standing out like a melanoma against the pale skin.

The demons are anyone he finds on the rooftops. Anyone he thinks is standing in his way. Oh God, how many people has he killed?

Suddenly she was dreadfully aware of the sound of her own feet on the floorboards, of the audible hiss and suck of her breath on the cold air.

Out out out, she was thinking, the impulse to flee suddenly so strong that she could feel the ghosts of movements as twitches in her muscles and sinews, the *yearning* of her limbs to carry her away from here as fast as they could. She could span the minutes, the obstacles that lay between her and the neutral safety of the street: the expanse of dusty floor studded with candles skewered onto their holders like baited traps; the stifling darkness of the fifth-floor landing; the flights of wooden stairs that zigzagged downwards and away, the treads creaking and groaning under her feet in a strange percussion; the door; the yard; freedom.

That would not be enough, though – for Veerle to be in the street, hurrying away, head down, unseen. No; that would not be the end of the story at all.

I have to tell Hommel. She's the one he wants – she's the one he's out there searching for, right now.

It made Veerle queasy to think of it.

Once, when all this started, it wasn't just about her. It was about one hundred and seventy people. But now it's about her – only her. Eva. Hommel. The one, the very last person, standing between him and everlasting rest.

She turned her back to the wall with its hundreds of eyes and crept towards the door.

He won't stop. He won't change his mind at the last minute, whatever she does, whatever she says. He wants to die but she has to die first.

There was a terrible cold buzzing inside her, as though a thousand insects were rising up in a black cloud.

He won't care what he does now, or who sees it. He could take her down in the middle of a crowded street, in a packed tram car, in a busy shop. He could spatter passers-by with her blood, he could make the gutter run red with it. Just so long as he has ten seconds to turn the knife on himself, to follow her into the dark.

Veerle reached the doorway on legs that felt as unsteady as stilts. She paused there, touching the doorframe, steeling herself for her passage along the darkened hallway. She would have to close the door behind her to conceal the evidence of her visit, and yet she was reluctant to shut out even the feeble amber light from the candles and enfold herself in the darkness.

Veerle paused, motionless, and in the silence she heard someone coming up the stairs.

54

No. Veerle's eyes widened. She drew in air sharply and released it, her breath, faintly visible on the cold air, dissolving into the dark. *NoNoNoNoNo –*

Then she was moving, because it didn't matter how horrifying it was to hear the stairs creaking under that furtive tread, it didn't matter how shrilly the rational part of her brain was screaming at her for entering this place, this trap, in the first place: standing still and waiting for him to reach the spot where she stood was no better than lying on the sacrificial altar and handing him the knife.

Veerle knew how this went: it was putting as much space as possible between yourself and the monster; it was knowing when to forget the heroics and run.

She was half a dozen paces from the door when she realized that she would give herself away immediately if she left it open. When she had come along this landing there had been nothing to see but the vaguest ghost of a doorway, an outline sketched faintly in the darkness by the muted light on the other side of it. Now there was an amber rectangle stamped into the blackness and she was outlined in it like a silhouette portrait in a frame – like a target.

Precious moments were slithering out of her grip but Veerle made herself turn round and go back anyway. She trod as softly as she could and she drew the door closed very gently, but still she gasped silently at the audible *click* as it shut. Her heart was thumping violently now, a savage tattoo that bawled *RunRunRun*. But he would hear her if she did that, his ears would detect the staccato rhythm of running feet on the boards. Veerle forced herself to move slowly and silently, schooling the lungs that wanted to scream and the limbs that wanted to sprint like a harsh taskmaster disciplining a terrified animal. There was a flat metallic taste in her mouth. She felt for the wall to her right, and when her hand connected with it she let her fingers skate along the surface, feeling for a doorframe.

Two floors below, a board creaked under the weight of passing feet, and she froze.

It was after she had resumed her stealthy progress along the landing that she heard a second creak and paused again, fighting down panic.

Are there two *people down there?*

No, no, she said to herself. *There can't be.*

She listened again. Silence.

The sound was identical, I'd swear to it. That wasn't one guy stepping on two different floorboards, it was two people stepping on the same one.

The implications of *that* were too appalling to consider. Two people sharing the same hideous delusion . . .

Veerle's fingertips touched vertical ridges. A doorframe. She felt for the doorknob, found it, tried to turn it. Nothing.

Locked. She was almost faint now, light-headed with

adrenalin, her limbs strangely loose, as if each joint were a mechanical hinge and the screws had been undone. She was afraid she would fall, and then she would be heard. *Stay calm. The next one might be unlocked. Just because you can't open this one doesn't mean the next one is locked too.*

Veerle kept moving down the landing until she was almost at the head of the stairs, and she was able to see more of her environment in the light that filtered up from the floor below. She could see now that there was one more door in the wall. After that she had run out of options: there was only the staircase down, and someone was coming up to meet her.

She grasped the doorknob and turned it, and was almost shocked when the door opened easily. Inside was only uninviting blackness, but there was no time to debate the matter, and no other choice. Veerle slipped into the dark and pulled the door to behind her.

The shutters must be down in this room too: the darkness was absolute. She thought the room was empty: the air was cold and the tiny sounds she tried so hard to stifle – the scuffle of her feet on the boards, her own breath shivering in and out – had a flat hollow quality to them that suggested echoing nothingness. The room also stank, an evil mixture of mildew and stale urine and some sweetish rotting thing that might be food waste.

Veerle pulled her sleeve down over her right hand and pressed it to her mouth and nose. Now her stomach was roiling and it wasn't just the smell; it was the sound of those footsteps ascending the stairs. Even with the sound muffled by the closed door she could tell that more than one person was coming up. It wasn't just some kind of reverberation she could hear; now she could pick out two distinctive sets of footsteps.

Suddenly her mouth was so full of saliva that she had to swallow.

Please, she prayed silently, *don't let me actually throw up.*

The only hope was that they – the old man and his unknown companion – would go right past the door of the room without suspecting her presence; once they had passed it and gone into the room at the end she could make a break for it and hope that she reached the bottom of the stairs and the yard before they did. With one person, there was always the faint possibility that she could talk her way out or shove her way out. With two, there was no chance.

Veerle pressed her ear to the door, the wood cool against her cheek.

Now she thought she could hear voices. She held her breath, straining to hear the words that would tell her they had realized they had an intruder, but they were speaking in such hushed tones that she could make nothing out, not even the gender of the speakers.

Veerle could not imagine what they could be saying to each other. What did people who shared such a monstrous secret say to each other at all? Imagination failed; it was like going up to the heavily fortified border of a strange country and peering in, trying to recognize some landmark in the unknown.

The footsteps were on the last flight of stairs now, ascending slowly and furtively. Veerle listened to that careful progress, to the creaks that were followed by watchful silence, and the horror welled up in her so that she bit down on the knuckles she had pressed to her mouth, grinding them painfully between her teeth to stop herself crying out.

Do they know I'm here?

Veerle couldn't think why else they were moving so cautiously, as though they were stalking a reclusive animal. She was terribly, mortally tempted to wrench the door open and confront them, to get it over with, to end the appalling suspense. She forced herself to remain still and silent.

Now they were on the landing. Veerle could feel the floor-boards vibrating under their feet.

All that separates us is a couple of metres of space and a door that isn't even locked.

The footsteps stopped. Silence.

A voice said, 'Veerle?'

55

For one terrible fleeting moment Veerle thought, *The old man, he knows it's me.*

Then she knew the voice.

A second later she was fumbling for the doorknob in the dark. Some instinct urged caution even though she knew who was out there. She opened the door a crack and saw the flash of a torch moving across peeling walls like a searchlight.

Veerle opened the door a little wider and said, 'Kris.'

'Veerle?'

He turned towards her, torch in hand, and the right side of his face was briefly lit up, showing one sharp cheekbone, a dark eye.

Veerle came right out of the room onto the landing. She did not waste time saying, *Thank God it's you not him.* She said, 'We have to go. Right now.'

There was a movement behind Kris, the scuff of shoes on the bare floorboards. Kris half turned and the torchlight moved across the person behind him. It gave Veerle a fleeting glimpse but it was enough.

'Oh *shit.*' Her voice was rising, amplified by horror.

No, she thought. *No. Of all the people – all the people in the world.*

'Why the fuck did you bring her?' she screamed.

She kept staring into the dark, staring at the place where the other person stood, even though she could barely see her, until her eyes felt as if they must bulge out of her head.

Hommel. He brought Hommel here.

She couldn't believe it – she didn't *want* to believe it.

Hommel. Here.

If the old man came back and found Veerle here, that would be very bad, she knew that. But if he came back and found Hommel here . . .

He'd do anything, literally anything, to kill her. He wouldn't care if he killed himself in the process, he wouldn't care if he killed half a dozen other people. He'd go for her, and he wouldn't be stopped.

She felt sick with horror thinking about it.

Every single minute she's here she's in danger – every single minute could be the minute when he comes back.

'*Why*, Kris?' she demanded again. 'What the hell were you thinking?'

'She wouldn't stay at the flat on her own,' snapped Kris, firing up at the accusatory tone in Veerle's voice. 'She was scared.'

'Don't talk about me like—' began Hommel behind him.

'Anyway,' finished Kris, 'you said the guy wasn't here, and he was old.'

Veerle stared at Kris.

Old, yes, but not harmless. Not harmless at all.

Panic was filling her, it was putting her on like a glove. All she could think about was the urgent need to get Hommel

417

down the stairs, out of the building, out into the street and as far away from here as possible.

'We have to go, Kris, we have to go *now*.'

She grabbed at his arm, trying to pull him along with her, back towards the head of the stairs.

'It's not safe here, not for any of us, but especially not for *her*.'

Kris was resisting; he was standing his ground, refusing to be harried into moving.

Veerle was almost weeping with frustration. 'Come *on*, we have to go!'

'Wait a moment.' Kris put out a hand, and now *he* was the one holding *her*, grasping her upper arm so that she couldn't escape.

'You left a message telling me you were here. You said there was some old guy and you thought he was the one who attacked Hommel. So I came here, and now you want me to just leave, just like that, without any explanation?'

'Kris – he *was* the one who attacked her. I know he was.'

'How?' said Kris bluntly.

'Because . . .' Veerle stopped trying to pull away. She tried to make herself stay calm, to explain enough to make Kris and Hommel leave with her. 'Because I've seen – he's squatting in one of the rooms up here and there's this thing on the wall – it shows the whole thing.'

'Up here?' repeated Kris grimly. 'Show me.'

'Kris, I told you, it's not safe, especially not for Hommel. Let's get out of here and then I'll explain everything. *Please*.'

'I want to see,' said Kris flatly.

'Oh . . .' Veerle didn't say it; she didn't hurl any more curses his way. A horrible resignation was settling over her. *Of course* Kris wasn't going to leave without seeing the room for himself, and the vast diagram of death that it contained. He wasn't going to turn his back and walk away now. She began to think that the best option, the inevitable one, was to show him the room and its contents as quickly as possible, so that she could convince him of the danger and they could leave.

'All right,' she said finally, although the word was leaden in her mouth, unpleasant as biting on metal. 'Give me the torch.'

When it was in her hand she said, 'And be quiet. If he comes back while we're here . . .' She didn't bother to finish. She turned away and began to retrace her steps, back along the landing to the closed door with its chamber of horrors within.

With the torch it was very much easier to negotiate the landing than it had been in the pitch dark. Veerle was relieved to see that all the boards appeared to be sound, and all the banisters whole; a foot through the floor or a fall down the stairwell would have been catastrophic. She was also surprised to see something she had not been aware of before – how could she have been, in the dark? The door to the room was not the only thing at the end of this passage; there was also a short flight of steps going up to a drab-looking door that almost certainly led up onto the roof. Veerle let the torch beam linger on it for a few moments. She couldn't see a padlock or chain or anything else to suggest that it was secured. A way out, if it came to it? She didn't think she and Bram had ever explored the rooftops of this particular block.

Veerle let the torch beam drift back to the door of the room – *that* room. She paused for a moment, listening. She could hear Hommel's shoes on the floorboards; she heard Kris exhale slowly like a sigh. There was not a sound from below.

Veerle opened the door. When they were all inside the room, she turned to the others and said simply, 'There.'

Kris went right up to the wall. He said, 'What is this?'

'It's the altarpiece,' said Hommel. She looked at Veerle. 'Isn't it?'

Veerle nodded. 'Yes.'

'What does it mean?' demanded Kris.

Veerle had her head on one side, listening, straining to pick up the slightest noise that would indicate that someone had entered the building by the fire escape storeys below. There was nothing. *So far.*

She said, 'I think he believes he's Joos Vijdt.'

'Joos who?'

'Look, this is a kind of copy of the altarpiece, right? *The Mystic Lamb* or whatever they call it. Joos Vijdt is the person who commissioned it.'

'Isn't it really old?' asked Kris.

'Nearly six hundred years,' said Veerle.

'Then—'

'I know it sounds insane. I spoke to the guy – in the cathedral. I was supposed to meet someone and I was standing looking at this painting and he came up behind me and said, *Eva.*'

Veerle saw Hommel give a start at that. She was afraid that the pair of them, Kris and Hommel, were going to start asking dozens of questions, that the explanations would keep them all here far longer than was safe. She spoke swiftly, trying not to give either of them time to interrupt.

'That's how I knew it must be him. Look, there's this legend about the altarpiece, though most people haven't heard it; only people whose families have lived in Ghent for ever. Supposedly all the people in the painting were real ones – I mean they had real-life models – and as long as the painting is in existence none of them can die, except by violence. I know it sounds nuts,' said Veerle, seeing that Kris was preparing to say something. 'I'm just telling you what I think this old man believes. According to the legend, if any of them do die, their souls can't rest while any of the others are still alive. And the demons that people say live up on the rooftops of Ghent – they are there to stop any of them dying, if they can, because it's their punishment. They wanted never to die so now they *can't* die.'

She paused to draw breath, and now Kris did interrupt.

'Veerle, what are you talking about? This is crazy.'

'Look,' said Veerle, 'he thinks that for everyone in the painting someone has to die.'

'And how many people is that?'

'A hundred and seventy.'

'And how many are already dead, supposedly?'

'A hundred and sixty-eight. The ones that are left are Joos Vijdt and Eva. The old man thinks he is Joos Vijdt and he thinks Hommel—'

'Is Eva,' finished Kris.

'Yes,' said Veerle grimly. 'And he thinks once she's – gone – he can rest too.' She couldn't look at Hommel's face. Instead she gazed at Kris desperately, pleadingly. 'Look, this is why we have to go. We can't be here when he gets back – we really can't. Especially not *her*. He's very dangerous.' She licked her lips nervously, looking past Kris at that wall with its myriad monochrome faces. 'I don't think he just counted those deaths. I think he *caused* some of them. And anyone who gets in his way – he thinks they're a demon and he kills them too.'

Silence.

Then Hommel said, 'Shit. I want to go. Right now.'

Thank God, thought Veerle.

'Wait,' said Kris. 'If we're going to the police with this, maybe we should take a couple of photos.' He slid a hand into his jacket, feeling for his phone.

'Let's just go,' said Veerle. She was shifting her weight from foot to foot, desperate to get away; a delay at the last moment was almost more than she could stand.

'It's going to take ten seconds. If we don't have anything to show them they'll think we're mad or messing them about. Six-hundred-year-old serial killers? Right.'

'I think we should go,' insisted Veerle.

'Ten seconds,' said Kris. He had the phone in his hand.

'I'm out of here,' said Hommel suddenly. She pushed between them and headed for the door, her footsteps hard and brittle on the bare wood. She didn't make it to the doorway.

They all heard it. It froze Hommel in her tracks; it froze Kris in the action of raising the phone to take a photograph.

Three floors below, someone had closed the fire door. A moment later they heard a series of heavy creaks as he began to ascend the stairs.

56

Time stretches when you are subjected to intense fear, but not enough. Not enough, say, to search an unknown room for something you can use as a weapon, or to barricade yourself inside it, put up all the shutters and scream for help from people below you in the street. Not enough to phone police who can't possibly get here in time.

All those options pass through Veerle's mind with lightning swiftness, like images on a filmstrip, and she rejects them. She thinks about the room at the other end of the landing, the darkness that stinks of filth and rot like an oubliette. The room is nearer to the head of the stairs than the one they are in, but if they can reach it before the old man does, and enter it unseen and unheard, they might escape notice.

She looks at the others, and although they both look shocked – Hommel looks as though she is about to faint – they have the sense not to make a sound. Veerle tilts her head at the doorway, and when she moves they follow her. On the landing, as Veerle is drawing the door closed behind them with infinite care, she can hear those footsteps labouring up the stairs. The old man is vigorous and he has a single-minded objective to drive him on, but he is still carrying the

423

weight of years. Veerle thinks they can get to the room at the end of the hall and shut themselves in long before he gets here. She thinks that she can risk switching the torch on for a moment, that it is worth it to get everyone into the room at the end as quickly and silently as possible. She is feeling for the button with her thumb when her mobile phone begins to ring.

The sound is brutally, shockingly loud, strident as a burglar alarm, advertising their presence to the person below. If Veerle was anxious before, now terror hits her like a tidal wave; it feels as though it will knock her off her feet. She struggles to get the phone out of her jacket pocket, but suddenly she is all fingers and thumbs, and still the wretched thing keeps ringing and ringing like a klaxon, blaring out *I'm here, come and get me.*

Bram, she thinks through a fog of panic. *Why did he have to ring back now?*

She doesn't even bother to check; she just stabs the red OFF icon. The phone is silenced abruptly but it is way beyond too late; all three of them can hear that the beat of the footsteps coming up the stairs has accelerated. Before, he was stumping up the stairs like a troll moving ponderously up a zigzagging mountain path; now he is *pounding* up them with a speed that would be wonderful in someone of his age if it were not powered by murderous intent.

Veerle looks down the corridor in the dark, and in her mind it telescopes to an impossible extent, until the room at the end is a hundred metres – two hundred metres – a kilometre away. They can't reach it before the old man reaches the last flight of stairs. If they manage to get inside it he will know where they are; they will be trapped. There are three of them and only one of him, but he has the knife and the murderous obsession that is the spark to the powder keg. If he attacks, they won't get away, all three, and who wants to be the sacrifice? No one.

Veerle has to make a decision. She snaps on the torch and chases its beam up the short flight of stairs to the door that leads to the roof. If it is unlocked it is a doorway out into a kind of landscape that she knows: a jagged vista of metal plains and brick outcrops, of steep slopes made of tiles, and smooth tarns made of glass. Veerle thinks she can vanish into a landscape like that; with her as their guide, Kris and Hommel can do it too – at least she is bargaining that they can.

She throws herself at the door, not really expecting it to open but hoping all the same, and it bursts outwards, spilling her onto a flat expanse of roof. She staggers and rights herself, dark hair flipping back and forth as her head turns, scanning the rooftop for escape.

It is nowhere near nightfall yet but the sky is overcast. The downpour has stopped, but still the heavens look angry. Thick dark clouds press down like fists; in the chinks between them the sky has a strange lurid tint. The flat roof is wet with fallen rain, and reflected in its surface those same clouds strain up to meet themselves, as though the space between is a narrowing gap that Veerle must run through or be crushed.

She looks left and sees walls; the building on that side is taller than this one. It is probably possible to climb those walls, but it will take time, and time is one thing she doesn't have. She looks to the right, searching for something easier, and sees a tiled ridge, the angle shallow enough to scale. No time to debate the matter; she hares across the rooftop, the reflected sky shivering into a mosaic under her feet.

She glances back, and Hommel is behind her but Kris has stopped to try to secure the door.

'*Kris!*' she screams, and when his head comes up she gestures frantically. *Hurry.*

Any minute now the old man is going to burst out of that doorway like a greyhound out of a trap. Kris is younger and stronger but the old man is single-minded and relentless and he has nothing to lose. He will not hesitate to cut down anyone who stands in his way.

'*Kris!*' she screams again, and now he is running towards her across the rooftop, and behind him the unsecured door is as ominous as the gaping mouth of a tomb.

Veerle begins to scale the tiled roof. It should be easy. The tiles are weathered and the slope is not particularly steep, but the need to escape, to *RunRunRun*, is too strong; she scrabbles uselessly in her haste and slides back. She looks over her shoulder, wide-eyed, like someone sliding down a muddy bank into the water where a crocodile waits, fanged jaws agape. Then she makes herself *think*, makes herself slow down a little, and now she manages it – she is able to lunge far enough up the slope to grasp the ridge of tiles at the apex of the roof and pull herself up. She turns and puts out a hand to Hommel, who is struggling even more than Veerle did; Veerle has boots with a profiled sole but Hommel's have shiny leather ones and she cannot get a purchase.

Hommel slithers down the other side of the roof, into a gully created by an adjoining wall. Veerle watches Kris racing towards her but her gaze keeps flickering towards that door-way, to the strip of blackness at the right-hand side of it where it stands open. To anyone *inside* the building that narrow strip will appear as a photographic negative of itself, light against the darkness. The old man can't help but notice it, but the question is: did he reach the top of the stairs in time to see where they went?

Her question is answered a split second later. The door opens, but it does not *burst* open as she thought it would; it opens slowly and the old man in the long dark coat steps out onto the roof.

Veerle stares at him from her perch on the roof ridge, even though she knows she should be ducking down the other side. She cannot help herself staring, even as prickles of cold apprehension sparkle up and down her spine.

The old man isn't running; he isn't raging. He looks unhurried, calm even.

Why?

The answer bobs up to the surface of her mind, repellent as a drowned thing.

Because he knows he doesn't have to.

Veerle glances around, and she cannot see the extent of the rooftop landscape on which she is perched like one of the very demons that supposedly haunt the city. It looks as though she and the others could keep running for ever, as long as they have the strength to climb and jump and slide. The old man doesn't think so, though; he thinks he has them trapped – he knows he has the advantage. He begins his unhurried progress across the wet roof, and because he does not run, like Veerle did, his reflection accompanies him so that he appears like a figure on a playing card, mirroring himself.

Kris reaches the tiled roof and launches himself up it. He is not a climber like Veerle but he has a longer reach, so he manages it without too much difficulty and slides down the other side. Veerle sees him glance to the right, to the place where the gully they are now standing in ends in thin air. Kris does not like heights. She hopes this is not going to be a problem. Veerle is not afraid of heights but she is very afraid of the old man; she feels terror unfurling inside her like tremendous dark wings.

She turns to the left instead and lopes along the gully to its other end, where it terminates in a short drop onto a metal roof. She wants to get out of the gully; it makes her feel trapped, and *trapped* is not a good thing to be, especially not when you do not know what the person pursuing you might hurl down after you. She jumps down onto the metal roof and hears it ring dully under her feet; at any other time she would have tried not to make a sound up here, but now she *hopes* someone below her will hear it; she hopes they will be outraged and call the police – that they will pick up the phone and do it this very instant. She isn't optimistic, though.

She glances left, and it is as though she has been punched in the chest; all the air seems to drain out of her. *He* is standing there on top of a wall, the dark coat clinging about him like the folded wings of a bat, the wrinkled face impassive. He knows another way across this stretch of rooftop, and he has shortened the distance between them and himself. A hand with the grainy texture of papyrus drifts towards a pocket, as though dreaming of what lies within.

Fear multiplies like a virus, spreading itself exponentially, colonizing every part of Veerle's consciousness. It makes her feverish with the need to keep moving; barely time to think about *where*. She cannot go left because *he* is there; she cannot go straight ahead because she sees that the roof there is made of glass. It cannot be trusted to take the weight of one person, let alone three. Instead she goes right, Kris and Hommel at her heels. Behind them the metal roof clangs ominously under a sudden descent.

At the other side of the roof they have to climb a wall but it seems their luck is in: it is less than two metres high and easily scaled. Veerle follows Kris up the wall, and while he is hauling Hommel up after him she looks down the other side and sees the remains of a roof garden below her. She jumps down into it. The garden was probably beautiful once; someone sat up here amongst the potted trees and ceramic planters full of bright flowers, enjoying the sunshine. Now it is neglected, probably has been for years: there are plants, all right, but they are all black and shrivelled like mummies, and the plastic sun lounger reclining under the oppressive sky is faded and speckled with mould. When Veerle moves across the open space something soft gives unpleasantly under her feet.

There is a door leading into the building and she tries it but it is very firmly locked. It doesn't budge a millimetre when she pushes against it with her shoulder, using all her weight. Kris might be able to kick it down but she isn't confident and there isn't time to waste on the impossible. Instead she heads for the far end of the garden with the others following her, and her eyes begin to widen because she can see very clearly that *we have a problem*.

It isn't a problem for Veerle – at least not for the old Veerle, the one who cheerfully scaled the fronts of buildings, as comfortable with the height as a bird. This might make the new, unimproved Veerle think twice, not that she really has a choice because there is only one way to go. But Kris is not going to like it, and she can't see Hommel going for it, either.

Directly ahead of them is a triangular wall, the side of a peaked roof. You can't go up it, or through it, and you can't go to the left of it because there is another chunk of wall, smooth, high and unscaleable, blocking the way. The only way to go is to the right, along a metal gutter that runs the length of the roof. It is wide enough to walk along – that is not the problem. The problem is the parapet, which is not much more than ankle height, and the drop to the street below.

Is this why he didn't bother hurrying? He knows he's trapped us here?

Veerle looks at the parapet, at how small it is, how low. She remembers how she felt the time she and Bram had to walk along that gutter to find Marnix's body – how paralysingly afraid she was, in spite of all her experience of climbing. She looks back at Kris and Hommel, at the blank non-comprehension on their faces; they think they have run out of options. She looks beyond them and sees the old man climbing down into the roof garden. His feet touch the spongy ground and he feels in his pocket, carefully, taking his time.

Veerle turns to Kris. 'We have to go along there.' She points at the metal gutter, at the pitiful protection of the parapet.

Kris looks, and when his face turns back to her it has that

strange unreadable look on it that she has seen once before, the time they had to climb down from Tante Bernadette's apartment in Brussels.

'No,' he says, and his voice sounds strange too.

Hommel begins to protest as well, but Veerle isn't really tuning in to her.

'You have to,' she says to Kris.

'I can take him,' says Kris, meaning the old man.

'It's too risky,' says Veerle. She glances the length of the garden; she sees what the old man draws out of his pocket, sees him unsheathe it. Light hits it, and suddenly the knife seems to be *made* of it, a pure triangle of white light. It only lasts a second and then the blade no longer looks ethereal; it looks horribly, brutally, real.

Veerle sees this, and suddenly the terrible fear that has been seething through her like a fever dream rolls back like a tide and calm descends on her. She knows that the old man is coming but she looks Kris in the eye.

She says, 'He will kill Hommel if he can. He won't care what it takes to get past you or me. And if he does, she's dead. You have to go along there. You have to go *now*.'

'What?' shrieks Hommel incredulously before Kris can reply. 'You're insane. I'm not going up there.'

Veerle doesn't look at her, doesn't even glance her way. She keeps looking at Kris, fixing him with her gaze.

'You have to,' she says again.

'You go first,' says Kris.

Veerle pauses for a moment. The idea has occurred to her; how could it *not* occur to her, when her deepest animal instincts are telling her to *run*, regardless of anything or anyone else? She could negotiate that gutter easily; that is not to say that she would *like* it, but she could do it; she has done things just as bad before. The gutter she negotiated that time with Bram was worse: it was narrower than this one.

But if she does that, she will be the only one who escapes. Kris and Hommel aren't going to *run* along that gutter like squirrels; they are going to creep along it, fear acting like a drag anchor. They may refuse to attempt it altogether. Veerle may reach the other end and turn round in time to see them cut down, one or both of them. She has to make them do it; she has to buy them time or the old man will overtake them and the terrible thing he is carrying will open up great rents in them and let the reflected light in.

'No, you have to go first,' Veerle tells Kris very firmly. 'You have to make sure *she* goes. You have to make her keep moving.'

'I . . .' Kris hesitates.

'I know,' says Veerle. 'Look, it's perfectly safe. If it were ten centimetres off the ground you wouldn't think twice. You can do it.'

She says this steadfastly, as though she believes it one hundred per cent.

'What about you?' demands Kris.

Veerle darts a glance sideways and sees that the old man has covered half the length of the garden. He moves more fluidly than you would ever expect from someone his age, but he does not make any attempt at speed. He doesn't have to, after all.

'I think I know how to hold him off,' says Veerle. She is amazed at the conviction in her own voice; what she really means is, *I have a desperate idea that might hold him up for half a minute.* 'I can follow you when you're over there. It won't take me as long – I'm used to climbing stuff.' She glares at Kris. 'Go on. Now, before it's too late.'

Hommel starts to protest again: she can't go up there, she *won't* go up there, it is insane even to try. Her voice rises, shrill as a bird's, and it catches the old man's attention. He pauses in his cat-like approach, and when he speaks he says one word, clearly and calmly.

'*Eva.*'

Hommel gives a start; now she *knows* what is coming. Finally she begins to move.

Veerle is close enough to pick up his tone; she hears a grim significance in it. She hits Kris on the shoulder.

'Go,' she says, and he does.

Veerle puts her back to Kris and Hommel. Now she keeps her gaze on the old man and the thing in his hand. It is Hommel he wants, but she has no illusions about her own safety. She hears scuffling behind her as Kris and Hommel climb up into the gutter. Hommel gives a wavering cry, a kind of wail, as she looks at the drop.

Don't look down, thinks Veerle almost absently: nearly all her attention is fixed on the old man, this strange, withered, terrible creature who survived a war and then lost himself in a painting.

She tries not to look at the knife. She says, 'Joos Vijdt.'

The old man stops in his tracks. He is perhaps three metres away from Veerle. He looks at her with fathomless eyes. Something moves like the dart of a fish in the murky depths of that gaze. Recognition. He knows her.

'Joos Vijdt,' she says again, challenging him.

'Yes,' says the old man in that smoky voice she heard in the cathedral.

So she is right; he *does* believe he is Joos Vijdt. Veerle's mouth is dry; there is an unpleasant silvery feeling at the back of her throat.

'What are you?' he says. 'You told me you were not one of them, but you stand in my way.'

'You must stop,' Veerle tells him as firmly as she can.

'No,' he says, shaking his head. The hood is back, showing a corona of grey hair surrounding his ancient features. 'It is time for Eva to die.'

'She's not Eva,' says Veerle. 'Her name is Els Lievens.' Her heart is thudding.

She curls her hands into fists, the nails digging into her palms so hard that her hands tremble. She makes herself continue, tries to show him that Hommel is human, a person. 'Her friends call her Hommel. She's *not* Eva.'

Veerle dares not look round but she is praying that Kris and Hommel have started along the side of the roof. She watches for any sign that the old man is going to move towards her; especially she watches for white lightning in the air between them, the sign that the blade is swooping towards her.

The old man says, 'You wish to stop me.'

There is a movement at his side, a brief flash of light. He holds his right arm loosely but the hand twitches and the blade draws tiny shapes on the air.

'I don't . . .' Veerle swallows. She can hardly get the words out. 'I don't want you to make a mistake. She's just a girl from Vlaams-Brabant. She's not the one you're looking for.'

The old man's mouth works, as though he is champing on something, as though he would like to bite her, tigerishly. He says, 'You are lying.'

'No.' Veerle shakes her head emphatically.

'Devil.'

He takes a step towards her, and Veerle automatically takes a step back.

She tries one last time, desperately.

'You know I'm not. I crossed the salt – in the cathedral.'

'Satan has strengthened you.'

Veerle's eyes widen; her face is a frozen mask of terror. No matter what she says, he won't believe her. Now it is a matter of *when* he will strike, whether Kris and Hommel have had enough of a head start, whether she can follow them in time.

Veerle backs up another step, and now she has wall at her back. She risks a glance behind her even though she is afraid that the old man will lunge at her when her head is turned. Kris is halfway along the front of the roof. Hommel must be on the other side of him but Veerle can't see her clearly from here, not in that one brief glance. What she does see is that Kris has frozen; he has his hands on the sloping roof and his head down. There is an ugly, stiff look to his posture, as though his whole body is wincing with fear, which she supposes it is.

Her head turns; she looks at the old man, willing him to keep his distance. She shouts, '*Move, Kris.*'

His reply is too faint to be clearly heard, nearly lost in the vast empty expanse of air that surrounds him on almost every side like a vast throat waiting to swallow him, but she knows what he is saying anyway.

'I can't.'

'You *have* to!' she screams.

In the second that her attention is focused on Kris the old man makes his move.

'Silence,' he tells her. He brings up his arm, and the light that flashes on the blade curves through the air like electricity arcing between two points.

Veerle puts out a hand defensively and the blade whispers past her palm, so lightly that she is not sure for a moment whether it has touched her at all.

Next to her is the mould-speckled carcass of a garden chair; she kicks it over so that it is between them. Then she looks at her left hand and there is a long slash across the palm; big drops of crimson blood are welling up all along it as though she is holding a necklace of cabochon rubies in her hand. The cut is so clean that for a few seconds she does not even feel any pain, in spite of what she sees with her eyes. Then it begins to sting intensely, the pain increasing with the sharpness of a musical note climbing the scale until it is a glass-shattering shriek.

It would be easy to collapse then, to fold herself around the wounded hand, but if she does that she is dead. Instead she uses her good hand to grab the nearest projectile, a chunk of masonry that has fallen out of the neglected wall and is nestling in a desiccated planter, and she throws it at him. As he ducks she begins to scramble up the wall to the gutter.

With adrenalin fizzing through her veins like a lit fuse,

Veerle might be able to ignore the pain from her left hand, but what she is not prepared for is the loss of strength. He has cut something important and now she struggles to get a good grip, relying too much on her right hand. He closes in again with the blade. Veerle kicks out savagely and it glances off her boot.

She lunges upwards and almost *falls* into the guttering on her stomach, her head over the tiny parapet. Veerle is better with heights than most people, but the shock of it, the way her shoulder hits the stonework, and *wham!* she is suddenly looking into the abyss, is too violent; for a second she thinks she is falling, that the pavement six storeys below is coming up to meet her, the façade of the apartment building with its vanishing perspective whizzing past underneath her like train tracks. She opens her mouth and a terrible strangled sound comes out. She shuts her eyes, opens them, wants to shut them again but daren't.

Death is coming up after her, climbing slowly but inexorably. Veerle realizes with horror that the traverse along the narrow gutter with its appalling drop to the street below is not going to stop him at all.

She forces herself onto her hands and knees. The gutter is just wide enough. She looks at Kris and he hasn't moved.

'Kris!' she screams at him.

He doesn't respond; there is no sign that he has even heard her. Veerle knows that look; she has seen it before, at the climbing wall when there is a group of novices. Kris is paralysed by the height. His limbs will be trembling and that will make it worse: the feeling that his body is betraying him, that it can't and won't keep still when his life depends on it, will boost the fear to stellar levels. The longer he stays there the harder it will be to make him move.

Veerle begins to crawl towards him. Some of her own nerve has gone; it fell away from her when she looked into that terrible emptiness, six storeys to the street. She does not want to stand up, so she goes along on her hands and knees, leaving spots of blood like garnets on the metal gutter. She shouts at Kris, screaming his name and then using terrible words, words as blunt as the blows of an axe – she doesn't care how terrible they are, as long as they goad him into moving. Veerle can see past him now, and Hommel has done what she is doing – she is crawling along the gutter; it is slow progress but it is better than standing there as Kris is doing, waiting for nemesis to overtake you.

'Get down, Kris!' she shrieks at him. 'Just crawl. *Move!*'

At last Kris seems to understand and he *does* move, although so stiffly and haltingly that you would think he is older than the man who is pursuing them. Veerle's relief is tempered by the fear that Kris will actually go over the parapet because his fear has made him clumsy. At last, however, he manages to get down and begins to creep slowly along the gutter.

Their progress along the rooftop is painfully slow but the expected assault from their pursuer never comes. When they get to the other end and Kris is climbing down, white-faced, onto the safety of a flat roof, Veerle risks a look behind her and the old man is standing at the other end of the gutter, watching them.

Briefly she thinks that perhaps after all he will not dare to follow them – the path is so narrow and the drop so intimidating – but her relief is short lived. He waits for Veerle to climb down after Kris and then he begins to walk along the guttering towards them, careless of the drop.

He knows this way, Veerle realizes, but there is more to it than that: he actually believes he is impregnable. He is taking a risk following them like this; they could try to push him back when he reaches the end of the gutter, or even push him off altogether, into that yawning space below. He has the knife, though, and anyone who tries to touch him with their bare hands risks having them cut to ribbons.

She sees Kris staring at her, his face a mask of shock, and she looks down at her own left hand, which she is holding with her uninjured right one, as though it might come apart if she let it go. Blood is oozing between her fingers; hot red pain splits it from side to side.

No, she thinks.

If there were anything up here that they could use as a weapon – a piece of wood, a length of metal piping, anything – they could try to push him back with that. But there is nothing to hand. The three of them turn their backs and flee across the rooftop.

57

Veerle runs out of space; if the rooftops were a map she'd have reached the edge of it. She had feared this. She doesn't know this part of Ghent's upper landscape, but from her conversations with Bram she knows that it is impossible to get right across the city without descending to street level; every block, no matter how extensive, is an island surrounded by the deep canyons that are the streets of Ghent. The problem here, however, is not a street bisecting the block but fire damage. The entire top floor of a building has burned out, leaving a blackened hole too deep and wide to pass. The fire itself is long gone: the charred beams and blackened bricks are cold and damp. All the same, the destructive power of the blaze still shows itself in the seared devastation it has left behind; it looks as though a bomb went off in the building. Somewhere in that wet black pit are the remains of a viola, burned almost to nothingness, but Veerle does not know this, cannot know this. All she knows is that she cannot get across this wreck.

There is no further to go, no way to burrow down into the buildings below their feet, no way to go back that does not involve going through that blade. There is only this flat broad expanse of rooftop with a low stone wall running around it – for ornamental purposes only, not to stop anyone falling off, because there should not be anyone up here.

The three of them look at each other and Veerle sees it in the others' faces too: they know. They are trapped.

Kris's face has lost that sickly tinge now that he is no longer teetering on the brink of a drop, but his expression is grim. In the strange livid light of that overcast sky his aquiline features look sharper than ever, almost sculpted. His dark eyes are fierce. He hates heights like a cat hates water but now that he feels his feet on solid ground he wants to fight. He is reckoning his chances against someone who is older and slower but armed, who can slice open an artery with one casual gesture.

Hommel does not look as though she wants to fight. There is a stillness about her, the stillness of death. She has vanished to some secret place deep inside herself. Perhaps it is the place where she used to go when her stepfather was tormenting her. If there is panic going on, there is no sign of it on the surface; it is like the struggles of someone drowning many fathoms underwater. Her angular face is smooth, beautiful even, but it is a beautiful façade. The great limpid eyes are no more expressive than tourmalines.

Veerle looks from Kris to Hommel, her face a mask of horror. *No. Please don't let this be happening.* She feels a terrible, crushing sense of responsibility. She made the call that brought them here. She led them across this unforgiving vista of bricks and metal and glass. *My fault,* she thinks, but she has no more solutions to offer them, no way out. She means to fight too, she won't give in without a struggle, but her hands are slippery with her own blood and the pain is gnawing raggedly at her consciousness, making it difficult to think clearly.

The old man climbs down onto the roof with them. He looks lopsided, a cyborg, the way his right arm terminates in that sharp triangular blade that twitches so restlessly. His seamed face is absolutely pitiless.

Instinctively the other three begin to spread out; he cannot attack them all at once. There is no time, though; the old man sees what they are trying to do and the rage that has been smouldering within him erupts like a pyroclastic flow. He lunges forward, runs at them full tilt.

No time to think – not one second left. Kris doesn't hesitate. He steps in front of Veerle. Veerle, her right hand still gripping her left one, crimson leaking between her fingers, turns her head, shocked, her mouth open, and looks at Hommel. For about a second she and Hommel stare into each other's eyes and Veerle sees a terrible knowledge there. Then the old man slams into Hommel like a human shark, a human avalanche. He doesn't even need to use the blade. The impetus of the collision carries them both onwards – one, two metres, and clean over the inadequate stone barrier that bounds the edge of the roof.

It all happens so quickly that Veerle cannot really believe her eyes. One moment Hommel is there, the next she has gone, sucked over the edge of the building and into empty space. She does not even give a cry. Veerle thinks perhaps the old man said a single word, *Eva*, but she is not sure. She does not trust her ears; she does not even trust her eyes. She cannot believe what she has just seen. She stares and stares at the stone wall, at the spot where Hommel vanished over the brink. Her wet knuckles are cold in the wintry air; the blood is cooling. She keeps staring at that same spot, as though time were a film that could be rewound, as though what has just happened could be unmade.

Kris makes a terrible sound, as though the blade that went over the brink with Hommel and the old man were buried in him instead of falling after its owner, end over end through the cold air. He drops to his knees and crawls to the edge of the roof. What he sees lying six storeys below on the damp pavement Veerle never knows. She does not look. She stands on the rooftop with blood on her hands, not moving. After a little while she begins to shiver.

Kris puts his arms on the stone wall and puts his head on his arms. Perhaps he cries. Neither he nor Veerle speak to each other. There is nothing they can say. Veerle knows about Kris now, she knows the truth about whom he loves, but she didn't want to know it like this. So she says nothing.

She waits. After a while she hears sirens in the street below. She looks up and watches the sky darkening, and waits for them to come up and find her.

58

Will I ever see Kris again?

That was not a question Veerle wanted to ask herself, not for a very long time.

The police came, and for a while there was a difficulty about getting her and Kris down from the roof because nobody wanted to walk along that narrow gutter with its useless parapet, particularly after seeing what had happened to Hommel and the old man.

After that there were a few questions, but not many because someone noticed that Veerle was bleeding. The cut was deeper than she had thought, requiring surgery. While the paramedic was assessing it, someone took Kris away, and that was the last she saw of him. Maybe they treated him for shock. Maybe they took him off for questioning right away. Nobody told Veerle anything.

Some of the tendons in the hand were cut so Veerle underwent a period of welcome unconsciousness while they were stitched up and the hand and forearm were plastered. The surgery went well, apparently: the doctors told her the hand would be as good as new when it had finished healing. Presumably they meant *as good as new* for someone who wanted to carry out ordinary tasks. They didn't tell her whether it would be any good for climbing. That was something else she didn't want to ask.

After that came the questions – clustering, probing, stinging, like a cloud of poisonous insects, sonorous with suspicion. Obviously the police were considering the possibility that Kris and Veerle had pushed Hommel and the old man off the building as some kind of thrill or dare, or that Hommel had been in on it too and the whole thing had gone wrong, leading to her accidental death. Veerle had no idea what Kris was saying. She just told the truth. The dead girl was a friend from Vlaams-Brabant who had been staying in Ghent. She had believed someone was following her; it had made her nervous – that was why she had got in touch with Kris. Yes, he was Veerle's ex-boyfriend. No, that didn't mean Veerle had a grudge against her. Veerle had gone to help her when someone attacked her. They'd tried to push her under a tram. No, she hadn't reported it to the police. Why . . . ?

At some point someone made the connection with the case last summer, at that castle just outside Brussels. The questions intensified. A body had been found there too. Like the one here in Ghent, there was no identification found. That body still hadn't been identified. The policeman doing the talking described an interesting scenario for Veerle, in which a couple of young people lured down-and-outs into isolated places and killed them for kicks. He invited her to comment on whether this seemed a realistic scenario or not. He speculated on how Hommel had come to be involved, how she had come to meet her death, whether it was intentional or not.

He kept calling Hommel *Mevrouw Lievens* – except once

when he suddenly used her first name, *Els*, perhaps hoping to startle Veerle into a reaction of some kind.

Veerle noticed that he never called the old man anything. No name was ever mentioned.

She stuck to her story. Hommel had heard someone call her *Eva* just before the attempt to shove her under the number 1 tram heading for Gent-Sint-Pieters railway station. She, Veerle, had heard someone say the same thing in the cathedral – yes, the Sint-Baafs cathedral, the same one the young man fell from last year – and she had been suspicious enough to follow him home. She had called Kris because she was afraid the old man was dangerous and she wanted someone to know where she was. She hadn't expected him to bring Hommel with him.

'The old man . . .' said the policeman a little wearily. 'Had you ever seen him before?'

Veerle shook her head. 'No.' She'd thought about that question before it was even asked, and there was no way she could say she'd seen him before without saying where and how. *I saw him from the top of the Gravensteen one night, murdering a friend of the friend I'd broken in with.* No.

Anyway, she hadn't been able to see his face that night, or the time he attacked Bram on the ladder. Saying she'd seen him would lead to a whole load more trouble and she couldn't prove anything anyway.

'Do you have any idea who he is?' the policeman was saying. 'Did he tell you his name?'

Veerle sighed. 'Not exactly.'

'Well, what, exactly?'

'He answered to Joos Vijdt.'

'Joost Vijdt?'

'Not Joost. Joos.'

Veerle could see from the blank expression on the police-man's face that the name meant nothing to him. She sighed.

'Joos Vijdt was the person who paid for the Ghent altarpiece.'

Now she had his attention, not that she wanted it; she wished she could go somewhere where there was nobody else at all, and just sleep. Forget.

Veerle told him her theory. She talked doggedly, seeing the incredulous expression on his face. City police deal with lots of things – drug dealers, rapes, knifings – but not killings carried out by someone who believes he is six hundred years old, inspired by an Early Flemish polyptych. It was easier to believe that Veerle was a fantasist as well as a delinquent who killed for kicks.

There was the fact of the wall in that fifth-floor room, though, with its uncanny resemblance to the painting that any resident of Ghent and nearly every visitor would have recognized. After Veerle had told the open-mouthed police-man that she had seen the politician who had died by arson in his mistress's flat and the priest whose body had been found in his burned-out house amongst the faces pasted carefully to the wall, someone was sent back to examine it again, more carefully. The little wooden statue of the Virgin and Child was recovered, and in due course someone had the idea of sending for the priest's cleaning lady, who was able to confirm that it had belonged to him.

Eventually it would be proven that the old man had handled the statue but Veerle hadn't, as was the case with everything in that fetid candle-lit chamber, and the knife that had been found on the pavement near his body. That was some way in the future, but all the same, the talons of justice that had been tightening so ominously about her began to relax. The cathedral guide who had spoken to Veerle was able to confirm that he had seen her with the old man in the church. He also confirmed that the old man had been banned from Sint-Baafs for trying to vandalize its most precious treasure, the Van Eycks' altarpiece. His obsession with it, and his violent unpredictability, were established.

Then there was the matter of the other, earlier deaths, some of which had occurred when Veerle was too young to grip the handle of a large knife, let alone wield it. The deaths before those, the ones that ran back into past time like the roots of some grotesque plant pushing their way down into deeper and darker soil – those ones the police discounted altogether. Nobody who is killing in the twenty-first century can also have been killing in the eighteenth – or the seventeenth.

After the tide had turned and they were beginning to see Veerle as an almost-victim rather than a potential killer, the direction of the questions changed too. *Why?* That was the thing they wanted to know.

She did her best to answer that.

'He said life had become a burden. He said he was at Gavere, and soldiers came and killed a load of people. I guessed it must have been during the war. He was talking about blood soaking into the ground and people screaming.'

'He was where? Gavere?'

Veerle nodded.

'OK, we can check that. Maybe someone there knows who he is.'

They didn't, though. Later on – they'd let Geert take her home by then – the police wanted to speak to her again.

'We've checked, and there was no massacre in Gavere during the Second World War, nothing like that at all. Nothing during the First World War, either. Are you sure it was Gavere he mentioned?'

'Yes, I'm sure.'

'It wasn't Vinkt? That's about twenty kilometres from Gavere. There was a massacre there in 1940. German troops killed over eighty people, including civilians. If our man was a boy then, he'd be in his eighties now, which fits, from the look of him.'

'It was definitely Gavere,' Veerle told him.

'Take a little time to think about it. I know the names aren't alike but maybe something else put Gavere in your head. Are you sure it wasn't Vinkt?'

'I'm sure.'

Veerle knew they didn't believe her. She couldn't explain it herself. It wasn't as though she knew every little village within a fifty-mile radius of Ghent; she couldn't suggest any other place with a similar name. But she knew the old man hadn't mentioned Vinkt.

59

Questions, questions. They hung over her in a cloud wherever she was. It wasn't just the police wanting to know whether she'd thought about it any more, whether it couldn't have been Vinkt the old man had mentioned and not Gavere. It was the school, wanting to know whether Veerle was going back or not: not just because of the coursework she was behind on, but also the regrettable fact that although the directeur had banned discussion on school premises of what she had been through, it was impossible to stamp it out completely. Speculation was rife; it might be more comfortable for Veerle elsewhere.

Bram was going to have questions too, she knew that, and she owed him some answers. At first she couldn't face going through it all again with anyone, not even kind, amiable Bram, but she knew she couldn't avoid talking to him for ever. She hoped he wasn't going to be upset or even angry with her for failing to wait for him that day at the cathedral. She didn't think that, however annoyed or disappointed he was, he could regret that as much as she did.

And then there was that other question, the one that had been answered. She had wanted to know that answer so badly, but now she couldn't let herself think about it at all. Someone had lost her life because of that answer; she couldn't get past that. And Hommel had *known*, that was the worst thing about it. It didn't matter whether Veerle was asleep or awake, whether she had her eyes tight shut or wide, wide open: she kept seeing it again, that moment just before Hommel had been swept away like driftwood on the tide, when they had stared into each other's eyes. A split-second later the old man had cannoned into her and they had gone over the edge, and Veerle had been staring into thin air, staring and staring, as though if she looked long enough the thing would be undone. Hommel *knew* that she had not been chosen; she had died knowing it.

It was useless for Veerle to tell herself that it had all happened too quickly, that Kris had not had time to make a conscious decision, that he would have shielded them both if he could have – that if he had known what was going to happen, he would have gone on the attack himself. All of it was undeniably true, but Veerle was discovering that however much Geert might insist upon it, Truth was a poor inadequate thing. It couldn't put Hommel back on the rooftop; it didn't even make Veerle feel better; it made *nothing* better.

So she tried not to think about Kris at all, or what the answer to the question meant. It couldn't mean *anything* now.

The only person who didn't have dozens of questions was Geert. That Anneke had plenty, Veerle had no doubt, all of them pent up and waiting to descend on her in a shrill rush, but Geert only asked her one.

He said, 'Are you all right?'

He was there when she woke up from the anaesthetic after they fixed her hand. He was sitting by the bed, and when Veerle saw him she was reminded of waking up in hospital after the fire at the old castle the summer before, and seeing him and Anneke at her bedside. Only now he was here on his own; Anneke wasn't with him.

It was not until much later that it occurred to her that Geert had done it on purpose, that he had made Anneke stay away, not just because Anneke would fill the air with her reproaches but because this was not between the three of them, it was between Geert and Veerle alone. At the time she was exhausted and numb, and the only emotion she could summon up was gratitude that he was there and that he didn't seem to be furious with her.

Geert sat with her for a long time, and that one question was almost the only thing he said. When he saw that Veerle was awake he leaned forward and covered her curled fingers with his own large hand. His touch was warm and reassuring.

Geert had a slightly baffled look on his face, as though he were a zoo keeper who had suddenly found himself in charge of an alien species. Perhaps he did not ask questions because he did not know where to start; perhaps he was afraid of upsetting Veerle. Instead he was just *there*, as sturdy as a milestone sunk into the earth, the one solid thing on her journey from a past she would gladly have forgotten into a daunting future.

Geert was also there at the police station, and he was there when she came home again. Anneke was at the flat too, of course; there was no avoiding her for ever. In the event she said very little to Veerle. The hailstorm of questions, the reproaches about the trials she was putting Geert through, never came.

Veerle began to see that her father had *told* Anneke to stay out of it. Veerle had no illusions. She had made a promise to Anneke, and she was going to have to keep it. She saw the way the older woman glanced from her to Geert, her eyes narrowing and her lips pursed, and she knew that Anneke was remembering that promise too. Besides, the cold hard truth was that Geert belonged to Anneke and Adam more than he belonged to Veerle.

Still, Geert had done this thing for her, and no doubt he was suffering for it when he was alone with Anneke. Veerle remembered the day Anneke had confronted her, the venom with which she had spoken, the cold urgency to extract Veerle's promise to leave. She thought Geert was suffering all right; Anneke had enough bile to keep haranguing him about this for years. He had stuck his neck out for the daughter whose disobedience he couldn't begin to understand.

They had one conversation about the future, and one only; Geert wasn't the sort to keep returning to a subject to worry at it.

Geert asked her, 'What do you want to do about the school? Do you want to change?'

Veerle looked at him steadfastly and said, 'No. I want to do the diploma there. I just want to get it out of the way.'

She didn't say what she thought, which was that she was not going to pass. That would mean opening a whole area of discussion that was pointless anyway since she had promised to leave. Instead she was silent for a while, and then she said, 'Dad, I'm sorry.'

Geert didn't ask her what she was sorry for; he didn't tell her not be sorry, either. At last he put out his arms, and Veerle went into them. Veerle leaned in to her father and heard the strong beat of his heart, and in spite of everything she was comforted for a little while.

60

There came a day when Geert knocked on the door of the bedroom that Veerle still didn't really consider her own – never *would* consider her own, now – and told her that Bram was here to see her.

Veerle didn't know whether she was ready to see Bram, but she owed it to him, so she said yes. She stood up, too full of nervous tension to stay seated. A few moments later Geert ushered him in, then left, closing the door noiselessly.

Veerle and Bram stared at each other. Bram looked a little self-conscious. For a moment there was silence.

'Hi,' he said awkwardly.

'Bram, I'm so sorry,' burst out Veerle. She felt like crying, except Veerle *hated* crying; she forced the tears back, biting her lip. She said, 'I went to the cathedral to meet you – I didn't stand you up.'

Bram came a little closer, but he didn't try to touch her. He stood an arm's length away and said, 'What happened?' When she didn't reply immediately he said, 'I've heard all this stuff – I don't know what's true and what isn't.'

'It's probably all true,' said Veerle, trying to smile at him, and found that she was crying after all. 'Hommel's dead,' she said, rubbing uselessly at her traitorous eyes. 'The guy who was following her – he did it. He's dead too.'

'But you—?'

'I'm OK,' Veerle told him, and then she couldn't control it any more. She began to sob, great heaving sobs that couldn't be disguised. She felt a wave of useless anger at herself, but she couldn't stop it. 'I'm OK,' she said, weeping.

After a moment Bram went up to her and put his arms around her.

Veerle leaned in to him. 'I'm so sorry,' she wept.

Bram's arms tightened around her, but he didn't say anything for a long time. Finally, when Veerle had cried herself out and was fumbling in her pocket for a tissue to blow her nose on, he said again, 'What happened?'

'I went to the cathedral like we arranged, only I was early. And it was dark in there, and there wasn't anybody around, just me. I was standing there waiting and looking at this painting of a woman when someone came up right behind me and said, *Eva*. Just that, the name. And the thing is, Hommel heard someone say that right before the guy tried to push her under the tram.'

'Shit,' said Bram. He held her away a little so that he could look into her face. 'No kidding? So it was him – the guy who tried to push her?'

Veerle nodded. 'Yes. He was old, really old. I didn't expect that. And he had this look – like there was something boiling up inside him, like a rage. He asked me if I was one of *them* and I didn't know what he meant, so I said no. Then he did something weird. He scattered a load of salt on the floor and made me walk over it, like a sort of test.' She looked at Bram. 'And Bram, when he scattered it—'

She made the motion with her arm, twice, and she saw that he understood.

'The guy who ran at me that night when I was coming down the ladder,' said Bram. 'But why salt? It's just ... it doesn't make sense.'

'He was talking about demons,' said Veerle. 'He said he barred their way with salt and iron. And then he started talking about the painting of the Mystic Lamb, the one there in the cathedral, and all the people in it, the ones who weren't supposed to die ...'

She told Bram about the old man's wartime story, the one the police still hadn't got to the bottom of, how he had said that sometimes life was a burden. How he had been thrown out of the cathedral, and Veerle had decided to follow him – now or never.

'I saw you,' she told him. 'I was on the other side of the square, by the Belfort tower, when you went into the cathedral. I wanted to call you but you wouldn't have heard me, and there wasn't time to phone you. I'd have lost the old man.' She put the heel of her hand to her forehead, rubbing as though she could expunge the memory from her brain. 'Maybe it would be better if I had. It *would* be better.'

Bram sighed, but he didn't interrupt; he waited for her to go on.

'I followed him to this building – it had a shop on the ground floor but pretty much all the other floors were empty. I kept trying to call you but I couldn't get through.'

'*Verdomme*,' said Bram. Veerle felt his body tense. 'I was angry because I thought you'd stood me up. I thought you'd decided – you know. And I didn't want to hear the excuses.'

Veerle heard the self-reproach in his voice but there was nothing she could say to it. She had spent so much time herself going over her own actions, the decisions she had made. If she had agreed to spend the weekend at Bram's as soon as he asked her, instead of arranging to meet at the cathedral; if she had phoned him *before* following the old man; if she had called the police instead of Kris. If. If. If. It was true that she wouldn't have called Kris if Bram had answered the phone, but once you started thinking like that the only thing that lay ahead was madness. You could keep going backwards through every decision that had ever been made, for ever. If Hommel had chosen anywhere other than Ghent to hide herself. If Veerle had never bunked off school, and had never run into Hommel at all. If Veerle had never got into trouble back in Vlaams-Brabant, so that her mother had never been out on the street that afternoon, distracted with worry, not noticing that the lorry was too close to the kerb . . . In a way you could argue that it all came back to that; that De Jager or Joren Sterckx or whoever he was had extended his evil influence as far as this, even if he hadn't intended it . . .

Bram was asking her to go on. He wanted to know what had happened after she tried and failed to reach him.

'I called Kris,' said Veerle reluctantly. 'It wasn't that I was angry with you for not replying. I just thought someone ought to know where I was. I didn't know he'd actually turn up, and I definitely didn't know he'd bring Hommel with him. I'd have told him not to, no matter what.' She sighed heavily. 'Anyway, the old guy came out and went off somewhere and I lost him, so I decided to go into the building and see if I could find anything. I reckoned it was safe enough; he'd probably be gone a while.'

'And did you?'

'Yes. He had this room on the fifth floor. A squat. And there was this thing on the wall – this terrible thing . . .'

She described the mural the unnamed old man had made, with its sea of silent paper faces, and two remaining spaces that would never be filled. When she told him about the Lamb in the centre, cut from some glossy book, she saw him start.

'He'd copied the *Ghent altarpiece*?'

Veerle nodded.

'With pictures of dead people? For God's sake – why?'

'He thought he was Joos Vijdt.'

She didn't have to explain whom she meant as she'd had to with the policeman; it was Bram who'd told her the story of Joos Vijdt in the first place, after all.

'That's insane.'

Veerle didn't disagree. 'He had it all worked out, like the legend you told me, the one only people who were born and bred in Ghent know about. He thought once all the people in the painting were dead he could rest, and apart from him only Eva was still alive. And Eva was Hommel.'

'So he *killed* her?'

'Not just her,' said Veerle. 'At least some of the people in the mural.'

'How many?' asked Bram in a horrified voice.

'I don't know. He'd pasted up newspaper reports from ages and ages ago, so far back that it couldn't possibly have been him.'

'What, you mean, from the 1950s or something?'

'A lot further back than that. Try the 1750s.'

Bram gaped at her. 'You have to be joking.'

She shook her head. 'No. I think he'd gone through old newspapers, looking for them. Anyway, while I was in the squat Kris turned up with Hommel. He said she was afraid to stay behind at Muziek City on her own. And then . . .' She took a deep breath. 'Then the old man came home.'

Veerle didn't tell Bram about the phone call, the one that had given their presence away. She'd looked, long afterwards, and yes, it had been Bram who had called. But she saw no reason to spread the reproach around; he couldn't have known, after all. So she said nothing about that.

She went on, 'It was my idea to go up on the roof, but anyway, there wasn't really anywhere else to go. We couldn't get down the stairs because he was coming up them, and if we'd gone into any of the other rooms we'd have been trapped. So I took a gamble that we'd be able to hide or find another way down from there.' Her voice wavered a little. 'I guess I was wrong about that.'

'And what . . . ? I mean, if you want to tell me—'

'What about Hommel? We came to the end of where we could go. There wasn't anywhere else – there was this burned-out building and we couldn't get past that. We were on this flat roof and he ran at us. It all happened really quickly – we didn't know what he was going to do. He ran right into Hommel and they went over the edge. It was just . . .' Veerle looked at Bram helplessly. 'It was all so fast. One moment she was there and the next . . .'

'Shit.'

Veerle could feel that hot stinging in her eyes again. She dropped her gaze from Bram's. 'I keep seeing it,' she said.

'Flashbacks.'

'I suppose so.'

Bram pulled her close again, and for a while Veerle just let him hold her, feeling the reassuring warmth of his body seeping into her.

At last Bram said, 'So did he think Marnix was one of the people in the painting, like Hommel?'

'I don't think so,' said Veerle. 'The thing with the salt was supposed to ward off demons. Those little bits of iron were supposed to do it too. He thought that's what the people on the rooftops were – the Demons of Ghent, trying to stop him going to his rest. I think he killed that boy from my school, Daan De Moor, because he ran into him on the rooftops, doing the same stuff we used to do. And that other guy, Luc. I don't think he jumped off the cathedral. I think he was pushed.'

'So if he'd been quicker that night we saw him – or if he'd run into us one night on the rooftops . . .'

'Yes,' said Veerle swiftly, not wanting to hear the rest.

'I'm glad he's dead,' said Bram. He spoke more bitterly than Veerle had ever heard him. She looked up at him, surprised; he didn't sound like the Bram she knew, calm and amiable.

'Don't be glad,' she said. 'He got what he wanted. He's got his rest.'

'I hope he's in hell.'

The way he spoke cut Veerle. She didn't like to hear that new harsh tone in Bram's voice, not for the old man's sake but for Bram's. She said, 'He was already, I think.'

She told him what the old man had told her about the massacre at Gavere, about the blood and the screaming and the guilt. She told him how the police had gone over the story again and again, asking her whether she couldn't have been mistaken, whether it couldn't have been the Vinkt massacre he was talking about.

'He was probably lying,' said Bram resentfully.

'I don't think so,' said Veerle. 'I think he thought he was telling the truth.'

'Well, if the police said there was no massacre at Gavere in the Second World War . . .'

'Maybe they were wrong. They aren't local historians, after all. The one who asked me about the old man's name hadn't heard of Joos Vijdt.' Veerle shrugged wearily. 'I tried Googling it myself and I didn't find anything about Gavere in the Second World War, but maybe I was looking in the wrong place. Maybe it happened *near* Gavere, or somewhere else altogether. He would have been a little kid then anyway, and it would have been so horrible, seeing something like that . . . maybe he got mixed up. But he *believed* it, Bram.'

It seemed important to Bram to know whether the old man was suffering from trauma or was simply a bare-faced liar seeking sympathy. It ended with Veerle dragging out her laptop, booting it up and running a new search for *Gavere + Second World War*. When that didn't yield anything much other than a photograph of a couple of graves, she tried *Gavere + massacre*.

When the results came up, Veerle clicked on one of the links. She was sitting at the desk, Bram leaning over her shoulder, his face illuminated by the screen. They read the first couple of lines of text simultaneously. Then they looked at each other.

'No,' said Bram. He shook his head. 'It's not possible.'

'I know,' said Veerle.

They looked at the screen again. *The Battle of Gavere: 23 July 1453. Thousands of citizens of Ghent killed by Burgundian troops.*

'Are you sure—?' began Bram.

'Don't ask me if he might have said Vinkt,' said Veerle. 'It wasn't Vinkt. It was Gavere.'

'But if he was claiming to be at the massacre at Gavere, that would make him—'

'Six hundred years old. Yes.'

'Which is not possible.'

'No,' agreed Veerle. 'It isn't.'

'Why didn't the police find this?' demanded Bram.

'Because they were looking in the twentieth century,' said Veerle. 'Not the fifteenth, because that would be . . .'

'Impossible.'

'Yes.'

'Nobody lives to be six hundred,' said Bram. 'Not even Joos Vijdt. It's just a Ghent legend.'

'I know.'

They talked about it a little longer, but there was only one thing they could agree on: it is completely impossible for anyone to live to be six hundred years old.

After a while Bram had to go. He asked if he could come back and see Veerle again, and she agreed. He kissed her before he left, but it was not one of those long, lingering kisses that he was so improbably good at; his lips simply grazed her cheek, almost experimentally.

After he had left the flat Veerle opened her window and watched him striding away down Bijlokevest. It was dark now and his shadow was very long in the light of the streetlamps. She did not call out to him, simply watched him walking away, and he did not look back.

The cold night air on the bare skin of her face and arms made her shiver. She shut the window, pulled the curtains closed, and after consideration she let the shutters down too.

She went to bed thinking of Bram, and dreamed of Kris.

ACKNOWLEDGEMENTS

Once again I would like to thank Camilla Wray of the Darley Anderson Agency for her support and enthusiasm. I would also like to thank Annie Eaton, Ruth Knowles and the team at Random House for helping *The Demons of Ghent* to claw their way to the light of day!

Particular thanks are due to those who helped with the research for this book: Tom Alaerts and Rebecca Benoot for their advice about Flemish culture; Adinda Demildt, André Demildt and Hedwige Cornel for arranging and conducting a tour of Ghent and sharing their local knowledge; Gaby Grabsch for providing transport and accommodation during my research trip; the staff at Sint-Baafs cathedral in Ghent for responding helpfully to my queries. Special thanks go to Ian Mundell for author assistance beyond the call of duty: he climbed the bell tower of Sint-Baafs to take photographs for me as I was unable to be there myself during the single annual week of opening.

And thank you, as always, to Gordon.

Read on for a taste of Helen Grant's
terrifying follow-up novel,

URBAN
LEGENDS

COMING SOON

'So all of a sudden the light goes out and she sees this dark shape coming towards her. He's getting nearer and nearer and she recognizes her boyfriend's face, only his hair is all standing on end, which freaks her out really badly. And there's something wrong because the body isn't like her boyfriend's – he's kind of heavy but this guy is thin and wiry. The next moment the head is just ripped from—'

'Oh come on,' interrupted one of the others. 'This is just a variation of *The Hook*. It's old.' He rolled his eyes sardonically, his face underlit by the flickering orange flames.

There were four of them in the darkened tunnel, huddled around the fire, which burned in a battered coffee tin. Light danced on damp black walls spotted with uneven growths that spread like disease across the crumbling bricks. In the spaces between the crackling of the fire and the echoes of their voices came the relentless dripping of water into water.

The one who had been telling the story slumped resentfully, the sullen glitter of his eyes obscured by overhanging clumps of hair.

'Fine. Someone else can tell one then.'

No one was bothered by the silence that ensued between them; they didn't have that kind of bond. If the story was bad, that was the storyteller's problem.

The fire and the falling water talked softly and persuasively in the background. After a while the girl spoke. She was the only female amongst them, small, light-boned and fox-faced, with hair dyed a vivid red and pulled into a knot at the back of her head. She deliberately avoided the role of peacemaker as she would have avoided pink or frills, but she was getting bored; she didn't want to sit here all night watching the storyteller sulk.

'Why don't *you* tell us another one, Thomas? Yours are always cool.'

She was looking at the big man opposite her, broad shouldered and hulking in his padded jacket and trapper hat. Thomas wasn't *likeable* exactly; there was a stillness about him, a suggestion of something suppressed, that gave her a faint sense of unease. Still, his stories were easily better than everyone else's. He'd earned his place amongst them. Next time she was in a group and he wasn't there, she might retell one of them, pretending it was her own.

Thomas sat in silence for a few moments and then he said, 'I'll tell you *The Angel Smile.*'

There was a small cracking sound followed by a tiny splash, as the original storyteller, whose turn it had been, sent a pebble skimming across the tunnel with bitter energy. Nobody reacted.

'Two people, one male and one female,' began Thomas.

A couple, thought the girl.

'Went to explore an abandoned sanatorium at night. It was a big place, and old. It was impressive in its day, but now it had been locked and disused for over forty years. Some of the windows were broken; others had been boarded up. The grounds were overgrown with nettles and weeds as tall as a man. Sometimes animals died in the undergrowth, and their bodies would lie there rotting until they crumbled into the mulch around the roots of the plants. If a human being died there, the same would happen to them; in so many acres they'd never be found.

'The two explorers parked their car a little off the road, where the darkness and the overhanging branches of the trees would hide it, and got out. By the cold light of the moon the pair of them examined the fence that surrounded the sanatorium's grounds. They had brought bolt cutters, but they didn't need them, because part of the chain-link fence was pulled away from the metal gate posts, leaving enough space for a person to climb through. That didn't strike them as suspicious, because they knew other people had been here before, exploring the grounds and the deserted buildings. So they slipped through the gap and began to make their way uphill to the sanatorium.

'The drive had originally been wide enough to let two vehicles pass each other, but after all these years it was almost completely overgrown. They had to wade through vegetation, tearing at it with their hands. The drive wound its way through trees so it was difficult to see very far ahead. When they came out from under the trees it was almost a shock to see the old sanatorium.

'It was much bigger than either of them had expected, even though they had seen photos of it online. There was one massive central building and two sweeping wings. In the dark, with only moonlight to see by, you couldn't tell how dilapidated it was, how the paintwork was peeling and the shutters hanging off their hinges. It looked impressively large and grand, and with not one single light burning inside, deeply forbidding.

'Why did they go in anyway? Perhaps neither wanted to lose face in front of the other. Perhaps they didn't want to have come all this way for nothing.

'The main entrance was a set of double doors with reinforced safety glass in the panels and a heavy duty chain and padlock fastened across them. They might have got through the chain with the bolt cutters but it would have taken a lot of time and effort, so they began to walk along the building, looking for an easier way in.

'Very soon they found a narrow door standing very slightly open, perhaps only a centimetre or two. The door was heavy and the hinges were rusty, but with two of them leaning on it with all their weight they were able to push it open far enough to get inside.

'The boy switched on his torch and played the beam up and down the walls. They were in a stairwell, the stairs zigzagging up into the darkness above them. The metal handrails were still in place, though battered and dented, but the steps themselves were covered in debris. It looked as though someone had tried to clear things out from the upper floors by simply flinging them down the stairs. There were files, collapsed cardboard boxes, a metal clipboard, the splintered remains of a wooden chair – all of it thick with dust.

'"I'm not sure about this," said the girl, and her words floated up the stairwell like air bubbles rising through murky water.

'"I'll go up to the first floor and look. You stay here," said the boy.

'The girl protested but she didn't make any attempt to go with him. She didn't want to stay there on her own, but on the other hand she didn't want to stray too far from the open door, the only bolthole to the open air. So she stood at the bottom of the stairs and watched the boy pick his way up the first flight, carefully skirting the heaps of rubbish. When he came to the bend in the stairs and started up the second flight, she could still see the light from the torch, slowly moving upwards.

'After a minute she heard him say something – she couldn't tell what – and then she heard footsteps and a kind of scuffling noise. After that, there was silence for a long time.

'The girl could still see a faint glow from the torch, but it wasn't moving any more. So she waited, but she was beginning to feel uneasy. She called the boy's name a few times, but there was no reply.

'She could have left the building and fetched help, but she didn't. Maybe she thought it would take too long, or maybe the boy was the one who had driven the car, and she didn't have a licence. So eventually she decided to go upstairs and see what had happened to him.

'She went slowly and carefully up the stairs, taking the same route the boy had done around the heaps of rubbish. Up the first flight, round the corner, and up the second flight to the first floor landing.

'As her gaze became level with the landing floor she saw the torch lying there at the end of a long gouge-mark in the dust, as though it had skidded across the tiles. The door to the first floor landing was off its hinges and she could see straight into the long dark tunnel of the corridor, but the boy was nowhere to be seen.

'She said his name again, and now her voice was high and wavering with fear. She knelt to pick up the torch. It felt slightly sticky but she couldn't tell why. After a moment she took several halting steps into the corridor, swinging the torch from side to side to rake the filthy walls with light.

'There were doorways on either side of the corridor but she didn't go inside any of them. She kept to the centre of the hall because she was afraid. That was her mistake. If she had looked into the first room on the left she might have seen who was in there, and if she had been very, very quick she might have got away. But she didn't look.

'The moment she passed that door, someone stepped out of the room behind her, and now she was cut off. He didn't bother to tread silently, so she heard his footsteps very clearly and turned around.

'Even in the dim light she knew immediately that it wasn't the boy she came with. This man was much taller and heavier, with broad shoulders and muscular arms – and he was holding a crossbow. She didn't dare run away.

'She said, "Where's -?" and named the boy, but she didn't really want to know the answer.

'The man came right up close, pointing the crossbow at her. He didn't tell her where the boy was. Instead, he said, "You have a choice. I kill you, or you take the Angel Smile."

'The girl didn't know what the Angel Smile was, but she didn't want him to shoot her with the crossbow, so she said, "The Angel Smile."

'The man put down the crossbow, but it was too late to run away. He was close enough to reach out and grab her arm. He was very strong. She couldn't pull away. He pulled out an enormous very sharp knife and cut her twice, here, at the corners of the mouth. Then he let her go.

'The girl dropped the torch and put her hands up to her face. She could feel the terrible cuts, and feel the blood pouring out of them, but she didn't dare scream. She didn't make a sound, even though she was almost dead with fright, because she was afraid the cut flesh would tear. That is the Angel Smile, you see, when the new mouth runs from ear to ear.

'She still thought the man would try to kill her, but he didn't. He just stood watching her.

'When she didn't scream, he said, "Do you want to see the boy?"

'The girl didn't say yes or no, because she didn't dare speak, but the man took her by the arm and dragged her towards the open doorway. He stooped and picked up the torch from the floor and shone it into the room beyond.

'There was the boy, propped against the wall, stone dead of course. There was something sticking out of his eye and in the light of the torch the girl could see that his whole jacket and shirt, from the collar to the hem, were drenched with dark blood. That was what she had felt on the handle of the torch.

'The killer waited for her to scream and give herself the Angel

Smile. But what neither of them knew was that the girl had a heart defect. She took one look at the dead boy and her overburdened heart gave out. She went limp in the killer's grasp and sagged to the floor. Very soon the blood stopped flowing. So she never had the Angel Smile at all.

'The killer dumped both the bodies deep in the undergrowth in the grounds of the sanatorium, and they were never found. He left the car where it was, knowing that it would soon be covered in vegetation. And indeed nobody has ever found that, either.

'But the killer was denied the satisfaction of creating the Angel Smile. So he still prowls around the deserted sanatorium and other lonely places at night with his crossbow and his knife, looking for a new victim to give the Angel Smile. Places,' said Thomas, 'like this.'

At the end of the story there was silence for a minute or two. Even the original storyteller, who had begun listening with such a poor grace, had become unpleasantly engrossed in the tale. The foxfaced girl cast uneasy glances around her at the deep shadows encroaching on all sides. She was thinking about leaving, about having to walk through the dark tunnel on her own, and wondering whether to ask one of the others to walk with her; she didn't want anyone to see that she was rattled but that black maw was looking increasingly uninviting.

Then the fourth person, the boy who hadn't spoken much until now, broke the silence, his tone deliberately challenging.

'So if the bodies were never found, and neither was the car, and the killer escaped, how did the story get out?'

There were a couple of seconds in which they all contemplated that, and then the original storyteller let out a short laugh.

'It's a made-up story, idiot.' He shook his head. 'And you've just wrecked it.'

The girl looked at Thomas, but he didn't say anything.

The group broke up pretty soon after that. The girl made a swift decision and said as casually as she could, 'Is anyone going my way?'

Only Thomas nodded. She looked at him and said, 'Don't tell me any more stories on the way, OK?'

Thomas inclined his big head. He said, 'One was enough.'

Together, they vanished into the dark.